DONE
DEAL

ALSO BY LES STANDIFORD

Spill

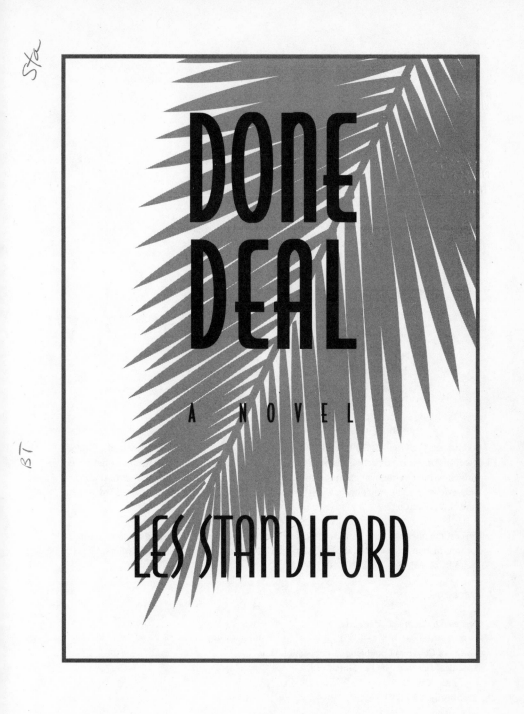

DONE DEAL

A NOVEL

LES STANDIFORD

HarperCollins*Publishers*

HarperCollins books may be purchased for educational, business, or sales promotional use. For information, please write: Special Markets Department, HarperCollins Publishers, Inc., 10 East 53rd Street, New York, NY 10022.

FIRST EDITION

Designed by George J. McKeon

Library of Congress Cataloging-in-Publication Data
Done deal : a novel / by Les Standiford.
        p.   cm.
   ISBN 0-06-017731-4
   I. Title.
PS3569.T331528D66   1993
813'.54—dc20   92-56204

93 94 95 96 97 ❖/HC 10 9 8 7 6 5 4 3 2 1

This is for Doug Fairbairn and Bart Swapp,
craftsmen without peer.
And, as always, for Kimberly, JR, Hannah,
and Alexander.

Deal and I would like to extend heartfelt thanks to Robert D. Orshan, Esq., Nat Sobel, Georgia Newman, Rhoda Kurzweil, and Jim Hall for their invaluable advice, assistance, and encouragement throughout the process.

. . . thirty miles of dusty road, there is no other life.
    —Gary Snyder, "Why Log Truck Drivers Rise Earlier
    Than Students of Zen"

Author's Note

Though I love South Florida just as it really and truly is, this is a work of fiction and I have taken occasional liberties with the landscape and place names involved. May they please the innocent and the guilty alike.

Prologue: Little Havana

Manolo Reyes glanced at his watch, a digital model with *Drakkar* printed across its face, then looked out the office window, across the deserted service bays of the station. The afternoon thunderheads had passed over, but the sun was dying, sinking into the Everglades a few miles west.

It was time to go home, but he hesitated, watching a scrawny street cat worry something flattened on the pavement.

There were no longer any gasoline pumps out there. Sinclair had pulled out of Little Havana a decade or more ago, certain the neighborhood was a lost cause. That was okay by Manolo. He'd come over from Cuba twenty years ago in a sailboat stolen from a tourist hotel. Bankrolled by two cousins who'd been running a restaurant in the States since Castro seized power, he'd been able to buy the property, keep up the payments on what he made repairing automobiles in the converted gas station.

He had found a doting wife, Angela. It was she who'd given him the watch, along with a bottle of the cologne it was named for, on last Father's Day. He had two sons, Carlos and Manolo Jr., sixth and seventh graders speaking perfect English, doing well in the Shenandoah Middle School. He'd been able to buy a modest bungalow a few miles west in the suburbs.

Indeed he had achieved a good life, and he mumbled a vague prayer of thanks as he stood up from his desk. Outside, the cat pricked its ears up and dashed across the street into the shadows. Manolo stared back down at the papers in front of him and shrugged. So what if he'd never get rich.

"Raymundo," he called, closing the ledger book he'd been doing his figures on. Raymond was his new helper, a dark-skinned Dominican of indeterminate age. He'd come in off the street a few days before in response to a sign Manolo had placed in the window. He couldn't pay much and his helpers rarely stayed around long.

Raymond stuck his head in from the garage that adjoined the office. His doleful eyes, yellowed, spidered with tiny veins, questioned Manolo silently. He hadn't spoken a dozen words in the week he'd worked, but he knew how to change a tire and pull a battery, had shown up every morning, did everything asked of him without complaint.

Manolo hadn't bothered Raymundo for a phone number, or even an address. He suspected the man slept under an overpass somewhere. He paid him in cash each evening and hoped he'd reappear the next day. Often, when he looked at Raymundo, Manolo thought sadly of how his own life might have turned out.

"Go ahead, close the gate. We're through for today," Manolo said. Raymond nodded and slunk out across the bays toward the heavy chain-link fence that surrounded the property. Even topped with razor wire, it couldn't dispel the thieves. Hardly a week went by that someone didn't come in to help themselves to a carburetor, a wheel or tire, a car radio. Manolo had kept a dog for a while, but someone tossed it poisoned meat seasoned with clock springs one night and he'd lacked the heart to get a replacement.

"Let them take a little," Manolo told Angela. "It costs too much to stop them." So he rarely kept customers' cars overnight, and when he did, he locked them behind the heavy metal doors of the garage where they'd be safe. Let the night people pick the bones of the wrecks in the yard.

Manolo locked his ledger book away, straightened the desktop, and stepped outside, suppressing a shudder despite the summer heat. He could still envision himself clambering over the wire in the darkness, a man who'd do anything to survive.

As he came out under the canopy, Manolo stopped short, frowning. The gates were still open and Raymundo had disappeared. A faded sedan, some kind of bargelike Oldsmobile or Buick from the 1970s, sat idling beneath the canopy, its windows darkened to an impenetrable slate, blue smoke wafting from under the engine compartment. It was as if the driver were waiting for an attendant to scurry out and fill the tank from one of the nonexistent pumps.

A ghost car, Manolo found himself thinking. He shook his head and moved around the snout of the big car. They could bring this beast back tomorrow.

As he passed in front of the grill, he could hear the throb of music from heavy speakers inside the car and incongruously, the muffled barking of dogs. The engine gave a sudden roar, and Manolo dance-stepped backward. He approached the driver's side, angry now. Kids. Always messing around.

He was still a step away when the door opened and a massive black man got up from behind the wheel. The man wore a suit, a very expensive suit, not right for the car he was driving, Manolo was thinking. The man smiled at Manolo and said something. With the door open, the music was thunderous, drowning out the man's words.

"What?" Manolo said, shaking his head.

As he bent closer, the big man snatched him by his collar. Manolo had opened his mouth to protest when the base of the man's palm slammed against his temple. Manolo's legs went limp and he felt himself being slung into the front seat of the sedan, the big man sliding in after him, squeezing him up against someone else. Manolo's head lolled back and he saw a Latin man with an acne-scarred face staring impassively down at him. The man shook his head and turned away.

Manolo fought to keep his eyes open, but he was dizzy and thought he might vomit. The big man rammed the sedan in gear and backed it, tires squalling, into one of the empty bays in the garage.

The Latin jumped out and pulled down the heavy doors while the big man dragged Manolo out of the car and propped him against the open door of the sedan. The music echoed off the concrete walls and the vapors from the engine were thick now. Manolo felt his stomach heave. The black man held him upright by his hair while he vomited.

When he finished, he felt a little better. Tears leaked from his eyes, but at least he could see again. The Latin with the pock-marked face approached the car, reaching into the pocket of his sports coat for something. The black man still held him by his hair. Two other Latins stood in a corner by a work bench, holding Raymond's face down in a welter of tools and grease. Again, Manolo heard the muffled barking above the music, which seemed to rock the car with its beat.

"There is no much money," Manolo gasped. "Take it. Leave us alone."

The black man laughed. "Shit, man, we're not robbers." He bent to yell into Manolo's ear. "We came to negotiate." Manolo's ear rang. "Show him, Alejandro," the black man was saying. "This man's in a hurry."

The Latin with the scarred face cut a sharp glance at the big man, then took a thick document out of his coat. He spread it out on the hood of the sedan, was flipping through the pages.

The big man jerked Manolo's head up. "Man made you an offer. Made you plenty of very good offers. You keep turning him down."

So that was what it had come to, Manolo thought. The fresh-faced Anglo woman from a Kendall office with her offer. Then another Anglo in a suit, from an agency in Coral Gables. And finally some oily men from an unnamed agency who'd called again and again, pressuring him.

"Buy some other corner," he'd told them. "For cheaper." But they'd needed *his* corner too, they said. Too bad, said Manolo. Too bad. This was his land.

"I don't sell," he said. His lips felt puffy, twice their normal size.

"Um-hmm," the big man said. "That's the problem, isn't it."

The man jerked him along toward the back of the sedan, kicked the rear quarter panel so hard that a metal "Le Sabre" tag clattered to the floor. He pressed Manolo's head against the top of the trunk. The barking was unmistakable now, savage, mixed with slobbering growls and moans, as if whatever was in there was feeding on itself.

The man banged Manolo's head against the trunk a few times. "Man says today's the last day. Say he's through fucking around with you. You want to be reasonable or no?"

Manolo squeezed his eyes shut against the pain. He felt tears leaking out as he shook his head.

The big man jerked him upright and nodded to the two who were holding Raymond. They dragged Raymond forward.

Raymond stared at Manolo, his eyes with the same questioning glance. Maybe just a bit wider. One more ration of misery in an already miserable life. What are you going to do about it, *jefe*? What in the names of the saints are you going to do?

The big man snapped open the lid of the trunk. Manolo caught a glimpse of fur, teeth. Something . . . no, *two* somethings colliding in a frenzy, frantic for the light. On chains, jaws snapping, spit flying, an awful smell of shit and animal stink . . .

. . . and then Raymond was flung inside and the lid slammed down. Snarls. Rap Steady. Raymond's screams. The man with the ruined face leaned in to turn the music higher.

The car bucked and heaved until Manolo felt his stomach give way once more. When the big man jerked his head up again, the growls had subsided beneath the steady beat of the music.

"Now," the black man said, dragging Manolo through a puddle that ran from under the car. He slapped the papers down on the hood. "You sign the mother fucker or go to work in the trunk."

A tremor coursed the metal of the hood, then another. Manolo nodded. Still weeping, he took the pen.

Leon Straight was tucking the papers into his pocket, was about to go check on what Alejandro was doing in the office, when he heard one of Alejandro's helpers shouting.

"*Cuidado,*" the guy was saying. Whatever that meant, he didn't sound happy. Leon turned.

It was Reyes, the guy who owned the place—or had, that is—swinging a big pry bar, what you might use to strip a tire off a rim or jack an alternator snug against the belt while you tightened the nuts.

In this case, Reyes was using it for body work. He had roundhoused the thing toward—Leon had to stop and think—Kiki, Tati, some fucked-up name like that. Anyway, Kiki or Tati was reaching for his pistol with one hand, was raising his other for protection. He shouldn't have bothered. The heavy bar cracked through his forearm like it was a twig, glanced off his collar bone, thudded into his neck, just below his ear. The guy went down without a sound, his arm flapping.

Alejandro's other helper stared out from behind the wheel of the old Buick, his mouth opening and closing like he was some kind of fish couldn't get enough air or gill juice, however that worked. Alejandro was away in the office, leaving what had to be left.

Which meant that Leon, as fucking usual, would have to deal with the matter.

The force of his swing had pulled Reyes clear past the fallen Kiki or Tati, what did it matter because he was a dead little shithead now, his eyes open and staring off into nowhere. The things you don't expect to come up in the real estate business, Leon thought.

Meantime, here comes Reyes toward him, running, or trying to, as if you could run across all the grease and crud caked since the beginning of time on the floor of the service bays. He had the sharp end of the crowbar pointing at Leon like it was some kind of a spear, which made Leon shake his head, it was so pathetic.

Leon sidestepped, feeling some of the crud cake up on the side of his new Bally's—$129.95, marked down—pissed him off, and flung the owner past him, into the wall that separated the service bays from the office. There were a couple of fifty-five-gallon barrels had been stored in that spot. The big pry bar plunged into one of them and lodged fast, oil spraying out around the hole the thing had made in the metal.

Leon looked down at his slacks. Del Georgios. Nice camel-colored wool, doubled pleated, hung on him nice and soft, felt like a girl breathing up and down his legs, not to mention they seemed to take twenty pounds off his gut. Magic slacks. Same tailor as Alejandro. Two hundred scoots. Now they were two-toned. Beige and crankcase oil.

Alejandro had made it to the doorway of the office, stood there staring. The other lame had his head poked over the top of the car, pretending he'd be on the case any second.

The owner was spread overtop of the other barrel, groggy, maybe his head had banged the pump that stuck out of the top. Leon knew what it was inside there. Kerosene. You brought your can in, the man filled you up, you walked five miles back home through the piney woods and your old man slapped you upside the head for thanks, then lit the lantern so he could sit there and drink and stare at his boot tops till it got time to pass out. Mmmm-hmmm, Leon knew about kerosene.

Reyes stirred, then came lunging at him with a screwdriver he'd found—all the dangerous items lying around a gas station, Leon thought. He caught the guy's hand, grimaced when he felt the grease and grit, squeezed and shook, the screwdriver clattered to the floor behind the barrels. Never see that again, no sir.

Leon slammed Reyes back over the kerosene barrel, pulled up the pump handle, scooted the guy underneath it, shoved down, caught him there, the handle levered down tight, just under his chin. Kerosene gushing out of the spout in the other direction.

"*Fock,* man!" That was Alejandro, dancing out of the way, worthless bastard worried about his own Del Georgios, fuck him.

Leon held Reyes down for a long time, at least ten gallons' worth, the guy staring up at him bug-eyed and pissed, his face going through a whole range of colors like some speeded up movie of the sun going down. Leon didn't flinch. What did he expect, come at Leon with a pry bar. Could have been Leon instead of Kaki-wah-te over there with his head dumping out there in the oil slick. It is a tough life, my friend.

Finally, Reyes stopped kicking. Leon glanced up at Alejandro, shaking his head. "You fucking want something done right," he said to Alejandro, "you fucking got to do it yourself."

Some time later, Leon sat alone in his own car, a black BMW leased to a nonexistent exporter of optical instruments, waiting to be sure things were settled. He'd retrieved his cassette tape from the Buick, which Alejandro and his pal had on its way to the bottom of a canal in the Everglades somewhere.

Alejandro wouldn't miss the tape. He'd bitched about the music the whole afternoon. He'd be wheeling the Buick out the Trail, tuned in to some AM station that played Cuban doo-wop or whatever it was, everybody talking so fast it put your teeth on edge just thinking about it.

Leon popped his tape on in the Beamer, at a more reasonable volume now, maybe the music would make him forget about his clothes. *Dope* clothes, the very best. And look what happened. Alejandro going on home, still looking like he just got dressed, Leon looking like he worked at the garage across the way. Nothing fair about it, so forget it, listen to the music.

Luther and the Crew, he thought, moving idly to the rap. They talked some bad shit, but Leon wasn't convinced. He'd been at a party one night, some enormous house on an otherwise white folks' golf course, caught a look at the group members close up. Tell those boys *his* stories, Leon thought, they'd be singing soprano.

He heard a muffled *whump* from the direction of the station and turned down the music in time to hear another. Probably gasoline cans in the garage. Lot of shit that'll burn on you in a garage.

The flames were casting a glow into the office section now. From where Leon sat, across the deserted street, it looked as if Manolo Reyes was leaning back in his swivel chair, staring at the ceiling, running it all over in his mind.

"Mmmm-hmmm," Leon said, being Reyes. "How come that mother fucker I hired off the street had to choke on me, steal my money, set my place on fire? Why is that, Lord?"

"Why, cause it please me to do so," Leon said, taking the part of the Lord.

Leon shook his head at Reyes's stupid question and reached for the ignition.

A window in the office popped, showering the concrete outside with glass. Reyes's body pitched forward suddenly, landing face down on the desk in front of him. The chair he'd been propped in was on fire now.

Leon tapped his coat pocket to be sure he had the papers Reyes had signed, everything dated months before. Smoke was curling out under the station canopy now, time to go on home.

"You *were* a dumb sonofabitch," Leon said, as he sent his window up. The office was burning brightly now. Reyes down, just a few to go. Too bad. He'd taken a liking to real estate. Just when the deal gets done, the man have you moving on to something else. He could write a book. Maybe would someday. And wouldn't *that* be something? He laughed, cranking up the music, and dropped the Beamer into gear.

"You look like Gatsby, all alone out here." It was Janice, come to hand him a drink.

"I could use his money," Deal said. He'd been standing away from the party at the stern of the *Mandalay Queen*, staring eastward out to sea. The tail end of a perfect south Florida sunset, the water gone steely blue, so calm it was hard to tell where the horizon left off and the mirrored sky took over. A lone pelican up there, now, lumbering through the last of the light toward shore.

"Could we buy this boat, then?"

Deal smiled, still watching the pelican saw its way along. *The Queen* was a hundred-foot wooden yacht, built in Seattle in the 1920s for a lumber titan. It was laden with teak and brass and was worth several times more than the apartment house Deal was building. To their host, it was just a minor business expense, a kind of floating office. But it *was* a wonderful boat, and for a moment, Deal had forgotten he would have to be up at six.

It was cool on the water, especially for a June evening, and except for the trio of musicians stationed near the entrance to the stateroom, he'd had the afterdeck to himself. Quiet Cole Porterish music, cocktail chatter like a distant rain shower for background, the glow of one Myers and Coke inside him, and a view of paradise laid out before him. This was why Florida had been invented, he was thinking, trying to jump-start his party mood.

There was a blinking green marker buoy a half mile off to port, marking the way through the shallow waters of the bay. Beyond it, to the east, a group of strange-looking shadows shimmered, looking almost like houses floating above the water. Which is very nearly what they were.

"Stiltsville," he said, taking the drink. He gestured toward the horizon. "I worked out there one summer. Did you know that?"

She followed his gaze. "No," she said thoughtfully, "I don't think you ever said."

"With Flivey Penfield," he said.

"Oh," she said. She was still staring out that way. When she squinted, a fine network of lines gathered near her lips, her eyes, but you'd have to be standing close to see it. Take one step back, she'd look like burnished gold in the last, reflected light. She wore a black party dress that looped around her neck, left her back exposed. He could see the slightest crescent of white where the fabric dipped to cup her breast.

"So you must be Daisy," he said, lifting his drink. He was willing to get into the spirit, he really was.

"I don't think Daisy ever got pregnant." She turned, glancing down at her stomach as if there were anything to see there yet. She smiled, but her eyes were solemn. He'd likely caused that, mentioning Flivey—she hadn't been around when he had died, but it didn't take much to throw her off. Deal had chalked it up to changing hormones, but felt he was walking on eggs these days.

He glanced toward the main cabin where Thornton Penfield, Flivey's father, was holding court for a knot of south Florida movers and shakers, hustling backers for a Major League Baseball franchise. The city was in competition with a half dozen others around the country, including two more in Florida.

The prize was that you got to spend ninety-five million dollars for one of the two available spots, shell out another forty or fifty million for startup costs, then endure a decade or so of cellar dwelling, while payroll costs skyrocketed and television revenues plunged. It was no wonder that the baseball commissioner was insisting on "demonstrated fiscal solidity" for successful applicants.

And it was no wonder Penfield had had the teak on the yacht refinished. He was desperate for some angels.

There was a banner strung across one end of the teak-paneled room: TROPICS BASEBALL IS COMING. Penfield and Deal's father had done business together, in the grand old days. Now Flivey was dead, Deal's father was dead, and DealCo was a shambles. The truth was that he and Janice had been invited to this party for old times' sake.

She widened her eyes slightly. "I don't know how you'd get over something like that."

"You don't," Deal said. He could suddenly see Flivey as clearly as he saw Janice now. "You work yourself so hard you can't think about anything else for twenty years." He had another swallow of his drink. "When you get tired of that you try and start a baseball team."

She gave him a look. "You should talk, Deal. We haven't been out in a month."

It was bait he nearly went for, but he forced himself to calm. He shrugged, finished his drink. "It's a nice night," he said, tightly. "Let's enjoy it."

"You're right," she said, her tone just as strained. How quickly these skirmishes came, like squalls blowing in off the bay. "Baby can stand one drink," she said brightly, patting her stomach.

"What'll it be," he said.

"No." She put her hand on his arm. "I'll get it." And then she was moving across the deck toward the crowd.

Three or four drinks later, Deal found himself in the stuffy main cabin talking to a blond woman in a black sheath dress. "You're a developer?" Her hair was swept up in tousled ringlets, her pale skin almost translucent. Her lipstick was so dark her mouth seemed like a bruise.

"It depends upon who you ask." He had caught sight of Janice at the other end of the room, a dark-haired man in an Italian suit leaning over her, his back to Deal. The man was speaking earnestly at her ear. Janice toyed with a drink, nodding as if she were listening, but her eyes were on the musicians who worked earnestly at a *samba*. She was in her element, Deal had to admit. And they hadn't been out in a long time.

Christ, she was the most beautiful woman on the boat, he thought. He'd seen the other men, the old guys, the young guys, the waiters, the musicians, all of them popping a glance her way when they got a chance. And who could blame them. It wasn't just the way she looked. It was the way she *was*. For an instant, he felt like Rapunzel's keeper.

"You're good at this, aren't you?"

It was the blond again. He turned. She had an olive speared on a toothpick, was rolling it across her lower lip. She flicked her tongue out, and the olive disappeared. "With this cocktail chat, I mean."

Deal thought about maneuvering her into the galley, or one of the staterooms down the hall. Maybe that's what was going down here. They could go at it standing up, be back for canapés in fifteen minutes. He'd be doing it for spite, and it wouldn't do him a damn bit of good.

"I'm a just a friend of the family," he said to the blond, and moved away.

"John Deal," he said, as he wedged himself between Janice and the man in the suit. Janice looked up, startled. Deal had taken a deep breath. He had put on his most amiable smile. And if the guy so much as looked crosswise at him he was going to jerk him out across the deck and pitch him into the bay.

"Of course," the man said, turning to him, extending his own hand smoothly. "We have met."

Deal stopped short.

"I am Raoul Alcazar," the man was saying.

Deal stared. It was true, they had met, a couple years before, but it was hard to believe it was the same man. He'd lost twenty pounds, learned how to dress, found a good barber. If he hadn't known where he'd come from, how he'd come by his money, he might have mistaken him for a European financier.

"The Latin Builders' Association party," Deal said, finally. "When they opened the Centrust Building."

"Exactly." Alcazar beamed, as if Deal had passed some kind of quiz. Deal wasn't sure why Alcazar would want him to remember.

Deal and Janice had been among the few Anglos at that party, the others being politicians and lobbyists. Deal suspected the invitation had been a mistake, but Janice had wanted to see the Centrust corporate offices, which were rumored to give bacchanalian excess new meaning.

He'd left her by a Modigliani sculpture in a foyer while he went off for drinks, had come back to find her pinned to the wall by Alcazar, then a Hialeah city councilman with the look of a used-car salesman. When Deal arrived, Alcazar had backed off Janice and suggested there was great opportunity for builders in Hialeah public housing. Deal thanked him for the advice and took Janice out on the terrace.

Alcazar had even called the office a couple of times afterward, but Deal had never gotten back to him. Alcazar had since moved out of government and into business in a big, if shady, way. He'd been called before at least two grand juries investigating influence peddling, but nothing had come of it.

Now, here he was, in a suit John Gotti would envy, a little gray at his temples, his accent cleaned up, hitting on his wife again.

He took the man's hand, testing. Surprising strength. Deal gave some back. Alcazar nodded, gauging Deal as well.

"You're interested in baseball?" Deal said, skeptical. Involving Alcazar in a franchise would be like trying to put Pete Rose on your board of directors.

"Everyone from my country is interested in baseball," Alcazar said. "As I was telling your lovely wife, I am simply here to show my support."

Deal glanced at Janice who gave him an amused smile. *I'm* not responsible for these men, she seemed to say.

"I read about you in the papers," Deal said.

Alcazar dismissed it with a wave. "Your enemies will try anything." He shrugged, his face almost mournful for a moment. "For money."

"Anything for money," Deal nodded. "Some people are like that."

They stared at each other for a moment. Janice pretended to watch the band.

"And you, Mr. Deal," Alcazar said. Composed. A predator's face. A man who sprinkled his morning cereal with chopped razor blades. And as assured as if he'd had a look at the pathetic condition of the DealCo books. "How are things going for you?"

"Hanging in there," Deal said, without missing a beat. He raised his glass to Alcazar and smiled. He was wondering how that expensive suit was going to hold up in salt water.

"Good," Alcazar said. "I wish you the best. And now if you will excuse me . . . " He raised his own glass in a gesture of farewell.

"It has been a pleasure," he said. Janice turned and gave him a smile.

They stood together for a moment, watching Alcazar weave his way out through the crowd.

"I felt like we were on a playground," Janice said.

Deal glanced at her. "You know who that guy is?"

She shrugged. "He reminded me."

"I'll bet. Did he bring up his indictments?"

"He was telling me how interesting American women were. We're smart. We demand to be taken as individuals. He says woman from his country could learn something from us."

Deal turned. "Jesus Christ. You *believe* that? He was climbing down the front of your dress."

She laughed. "Really, Deal, relax. I saw you talking to Madonna over there in the corner."

Deal rolled his eyes, but still glanced across the room. The blond had disappeared. "You about ready?" he asked.

"In a minute," she said. "I like this group."

The trio was playing something more languid now, some jazz standard he couldn't quite place. There were couples swaying to the music on the afterdeck. "Want to dance?" he said.

She gave him a speculative look. "It's okay," she said. "I'm just listening."

He took a deep breath. It was like taking a test to which there was no correct response. "I'm going to get a drink," he said. And walked off.

"Johnny-boy!" Deal had had three drinks, in fact, and was weaving slightly as he made his way back across the crowded room. He felt himself being pulled off course, and turned to find Thornton Penfield toasting him with a full glass. "You're dry, Johnny."

Deal tried to protest, but Penfield made a gesture and a waiter darted toward them. "I want you to meet Terrence Terrell, Johnny."

Deal glanced at the fortyish man by Penfield's side. A deep tan, a flat belly, a sport coat, and a polo shirt. *This* was Gatsby, Deal found himself thinking, blearily.

"Mr. Terrell's down from Palm Beach," Penfield said. "You know Jobe Computers. This is John Deal, DealCo Construction."

Deal looked at Terrell again as they shook hands, finally registering things. No wonder the guy looked at ease. Net worth some factor of the Gross National Product, you'd have to look good.

"Commercial or residential?" Terrell asked.

"Whatever comes along," Deal said.

Terrell pursed his lips, nodded. "These are difficult times," he said. Deal wondered what Terrell's concept of difficulty was, in fact.

"That string of condos down Brickell," Penfield said, pointing out the window at the glittering city skyline. "That's DealCo work."

Terrell glanced out, then back at Deal, a glimmer of interest there now. Deal shrugged. Typical Penfield bullshit. His father *had* built the condos, and what they lost had finished off the company for all practical purposes. But let Terrell think what he wanted. Deal was going to find Janice, get them the hell out of there.

"I've been trying to convince Mr. Terrell that we're a baseball town, John. We could use him in our group."

Deal seemed to think about it. He gave Penfield a studied look. "You bring him in, I want my ten million back."

There was a stunned moment of silence, then Penfield exploded into laughter and clapped Deal on the shoulder. "That's good, Johnny." Deal took the drink the waiter brought, toasted Penfield and Terrell with it. His head was swimming with the drinks, with fatigue.

Terrell smiled. "Actually, I've been telling Mr. Penfield much the same thing. I'm not accustomed to group ownership. It's not my style."

Deal nodded. It wasn't reasonable to begrudge Terrell his fortune. At least he had done it all himself, if you could believe the stories. Maybe they'd have been buddies in another world, cutting deals over tennis.

"That's all right," Penfield said. "I told him, he buys enough shares, he can do anything he wants." Penfield laughed and put his arm around Deal again. "Good to see you, Johnny. Where's that pretty wife of yours?"

Deal glanced at the corner where he'd left Janice, but now she was gone. "More than you know . . . " the bandleader was crooning. The afterdeck was crowded with couples now and he felt an unreasoning stab of anxiety.

"I was just going to find her," Deal said. He nodded at Terrell, already on his way out of the cabin. "Nice meeting you. Buy the team, Mr. Terrell."

Penfield raised his glass. "Better keep track of that one, Johnny," Penfield was saying. "And think about that offer we had . . . " but Deal had already spotted her outside and was gone.

They were alone in the water taxi—brought over from Venice, the captain had volunteered on the way out—heading from *The Queen*'s mooring back to the hotel docks where they'd left the car. Deal had his head back over the cushions, his feet up on the seat across from them. He watched the still-blazing *Queen* recede in the distance behind them.

"Maybe we could call off morning," he said. He put his hand on her leg.

"I had a nice time," she said. She put her hand atop his. Laced their fingers together.

A hopeful sign, he thought. "We'll have to start getting out more," he said, nudging his hand higher.

"*Deal,*" she said, pushing it back.

"It's okay," he said. "The captain won't mind."

"Deal!"

"Really. The owner's a friend of mine."

And so it went until he fell asleep.

"Janice, all I said was maybe we could try to cut back for a while." He sat on the edge of the bed, trying to will his headache away.

She came to the bathroom door and took the toothbrush out of her mouth. She'd pulled off the T-shirt she'd slept in.

"There's a baby on the way," she said, mildly. "We're going to need things." She glanced around the bedroom, their furniture crowding every space, waved her arm about. "We *need* a bigger place."

Deal nodded, still staring at her. It was only her second month, but there were signs. Deal liked that, her changing that way. He found himself aroused. He remembered they'd started something last night, but he'd been so tired . . .

"I know," he said. "Things are tight. But we have to take the long view. By the time the baby's here . . . " he trailed off, suggesting a future of endless possibility.

She wiped toothpaste from the corner of her mouth, giving herself a moment. "By then," she said, "we'll be bankrupt."

He wanted to say something, but he wasn't sure what. Every argument seemed weary, even to him. Janice stuck the toothbrush back in her mouth and disappeared into the bathroom.

Deal swung his legs down from the bed and sighed. He felt exhausted, as if he'd spent the entire night running in place. He was almost weary enough to do it: Forget DealCo and all the hassle, take the supervisor's job with Kendale Homes. Security, security, security. Maybe it was the smart thing to do.

He reached for the television remote and pointed it at the tiny set that rested on their dresser. The face of a local weatherman congealed gradually and Deal pressed the volume button in time to hear ". . . back to a normal summer pattern, high in the low nineties, an eighty percent chance of thundershowers. We'll keep an eye on those developing tropical waves for you."

"Terrific," he said, flipping the channel.

He caught a brief glimpse of a reporter finishing a standup in front of a burned-out gas station, police milling about in the background. The place looked familiar but the image faded into another weatherman about to proclaim the same sad news. Deal snapped off the set and stood up.

He was pawing through his sock drawer, looking for a mate to the only white one he'd come across, when Janice came out of the bathroom in her walking gear. She had gotten involved with a group from the condo, and he was glad for that, though he suspected they encouraged her more extravagant tastes.

Her dark hair was pulled back beneath a sweat band, her breasts hidden now under a spandex top. She wore a dark leotard beneath that, and white socks crumpled in rolls at her sneaker tops. She looked like the kid he'd met fifteen years ago.

Something in his gaze must have caught her. She stopped and

sighed, then came to him. "Oh, Deal," she said. She looked at him sadly for a moment, then reached to kiss him on the cheek.

She started to pull away, but Deal held on.

"I'm late," she said.

"*Be* late," he said, nuzzling her.

"Deal," she said. But she arched her neck at the touch of his lips.

He edged them backward, toward the bed. He licked the underside of her ear. "They're waiting on me," she said, but her breath was quickening.

They toppled over onto the bed. "I'm already dressed," she said.

Deal had his hand hooked under the band of her leotard. "Not for long," he said, his own voice thick, his fingers probing.

"Oh, Deal," she said again, lifting her hips against him. And then he was lost in the heat and the musk and the dampness.

Though his eyes were closed, Deal had convinced himself that he was floating on a diving raft somewhere in the middle of a broad lake rimmed by snowcapped mountains. Where he lay, it was warm and pleasant, the planks as soft as cotton, the sun beating down on his bare body, drying him. There was a faint scent of jasmine, and of sex, and the comforting touch of Janice's shoulder at his side. Only the slightest trembling of the raft to disturb him and the sound of quiet sobbing.

Sadness, he thought. How could there be sadness in such a lovely world? And then he came awake.

Janice lay with her back toward him, her shoulders shuddering, her face pressed into a pillow. Deal pressed his eyes closed momentarily, longing for the dream to take him up again, but what he saw instead was an image of fighter planes swooping low, strafing a deserted beach. He was in the picture somewhere, a gaunt man shaking a stick at the planes, his eyes as crazed as Job's.

He opened his eyes and moved close to her, his chin tucked over her shoulder. How many times had this happened, would it happen?

"Janice," he said. He reached to move the pillow from her face. Her eyes were squeezed tight, her cheeks streaked with tears.

"Janice?" he repeated. He raised himself up and placed his hand on her shoulder. With his other hand, he began to knead the tautness at the base of her neck. Her sobbing began to subside. He moved both hands to her shoulders and pressed his thumbs into the long muscles of her back.

Gradually, he felt the tightness fading, and after a few moments she sat up, wiping at her cheeks with a corner of the tangled sheet. She took a deep breath, her hands folded in her lap.

"I'm trying to make this work," she said, staring at her hands. "I am. I am."

Deal had the odd sensation that she was talking to herself, that he was not even in the room at all, and he put his hand atop hers to reassure himself.

She glanced up at him. "I'm not going crazy, if that's what you think."

"I know," Deal said. "I know."

"Sometimes, things just get to be too much," she said.

Deal nodded. "I'm going to take care of everything, Janice. You don't have to worry."

She glanced around the room again, and Deal saw it as an accusation. They'd had to sell the house in the Shores, almost a year ago now, and though they'd tried to keep contact, they'd apparently left most of their friends behind in the move. It had gotten to be a big city, Deal thought sadly. And he'd been so busy, busting his ass trying to stay afloat, that he hadn't had time to put much of a personal life back together.

"Mr. Penfield told me he wanted to talk to you last night," Janice said, breaking into his thoughts.

Deal nodded.

She was staring at him. "Well, did he?"

Deal felt the awful weariness piling down on him again. He'd managed to drive it away for a bit, and here it was, climbing back on his shoulders, ready to ride him around until he dropped, if it could.

He sighed. "He said he had somebody else interested in the fourplex."

"And?"

"I told him the same as last time. We weren't interested."

She stared at him. "What was the offer?"

Deal shrugged. "Three sixty-two five."

She nodded. "That means you could get three seventy-five."

"Maybe."

"The land is clear. Subtract the construction loan, that leaves nearly a quarter of a million dollars." Her expression was determinedly neutral.

"Which we could piss away."

She threw up her hands. "I don't understand you. Look at how we live. We could buy a house . . . "

"We can't sell the fourplex, Janice." He was trying to keep his patience.

"You mean you *won't*."

Deal bit his lip, trying to keep his voice even. "We don't want to sell when the market's down. We have to finish the building. Then we rent it out. We'll have something to put down where it says 'assets' on the balance sheet. And a little cash coming in besides. We use that all to finance the next project. *Then* we can sell. Times get better, the property will be worth another hundred thousand, finished and generating income. We'll be on the road again."

She seemed about to snap back at him, but forced herself to calm. "Deal, you're building an apartment in a place where nobody wants to live. If it were worth anything, your father would have built on it when he was still alive. If it were a good investment, Mr. Penfield wouldn't advise you to sell it. If he can find someone to buy it, take him up on it, for God's sake."

"He means well," Deal said. "That neighborhood's coming back."

She stared at him for a moment, then shook her head in resignation. She turned and swung her legs over the side of the bed, bent to pick up her wadded clothes.

"It's not just you and me any longer, Janice. That's the whole point. I sell out now, it's all over. I'll end up working for wages the rest of my life, we'll never get anywhere. That's not what I want for my family."

She turned to him. "Let me get this straight. You'd sell the building if it *weren't* for us?"

He threw up his hands. "Selling isn't the point. Hanging on is the point. Doing what you have to do until things get better. Believing in yourself, that what you do is right . . . " He knew his voice was rising, that any moment she would turn away, that he would lose her. "Janice," he said, quietly. "It's for us. For all of us."

She stared at him in silence, taking it in. Her anger seemed to have faded. He doubted he'd convinced her. But at least she was thinking about what he'd said, and that was a victory of sorts.

After a moment, she glanced away.

"Look at this," she said, absently. She'd unfolded the leotard, was staring at a tear Deal had opened in the fabric.

"I thought it was kind of exciting," he said.

She paused, then glanced up at him, finally gave him the smile he'd been angling for. "It was," she said.

"Let's try it without the clothes," he said, reaching for her hand.

But she was up and hurrying down the hall. "Go to work, Deal." She turned and shook her head. "Just go and get the damn thing built."

Deal was moving across what had been an empty traffic lane when it happened. Some idiot barreling up from nowhere, heading for the same open spot. Deal, still feeling prickly from the argument with Janice—as if he'd bullied her into silence—never thought of backing off. He'd made his move, had been there first. He cut his wheels and settled in.

It was a black Supra, the windows smoked as dark as the paint, filling up his rearview mirror now. They were doing sixty-five, locked in by morning commuters on either side and the guy was maybe six inches off his tail.

Deal saw the Supra's headlights roll up, the lamps flash. The guy had to be crazy. There was a Sunshine bread delivery truck a few feet in front of them, Deal close enough to read the "Bring Baseball to the Tropics" sticker on its bumper.

There was a flatbed carrying a load of coconut palms to the left, a pair of old school buses painted white taking up the right. Even if he'd been inclined to let the asshole past—which he wasn't—there was no place to go.

Deal glanced up at the windows of the nearest bus. Rows and rows of white-turbaned blacks, staring implacably into the blaze of sun that was just clearing the bank towers downtown. Yahwehs, he thought. Two bus loads of Yahwehs going somewhere at seven thirty in the morning.

He didn't know much about them—they dressed like some of the Black Muslims he'd encountered in college, back in the 1960s—but they seemed interested in things material as well as spiritual. They had bought up a bunch of hot-sheet motels around Seventy-ninth and Biscayne, which they had proceeded to paint black and white, with the emphasis on white. They were renting most of the motels, using some for temples, schools, whatever. A couple of coats of paint and tropical sleaze becomes Morocco.

He glanced back at the Supra, which had inched closer to his bumper. Deal thought about slamming on his brakes—let the guy pile into him, use the insurance money to cover a paint job for The Hog, which had begun a serious fade from sitting out so much. Ever since they'd had to let the house go and move into the condo, he'd let Janice use the one underground spot for her VW.

He lifted his foot from the accelerator, tapped his brakes lightly. The Supra fell back abruptly. Think about it, friend. Deal stared into the mirror, willing his thoughts backward. The sun was a white blaze on the Supra's windshield—no way to see who might be driving. It closed in again as Deal accelerated.

One of the Yahwehs—a big guy who looked like it'd take two sheets to wrap him—glanced down at Deal, then back at the Supra. The man's gaze came back to rest on Deal. He lifted his brows as if to ask a question, then he turned back to stare at whatever his buddies had discovered.

Deal remembered a recent news story. A pimp who'd had a certain interest in one of the motels transformed by the Yahwehs had come around to discuss things. A couple of big Yahwehs showed up and the pimp landed in the emergency ward at Jackson, a fracture in each of his arms and legs. There'd been some outcry about it, but the pimp lobby at city hall wasn't very influential. Besides, the cops had been trying to clean up Seventy-ninth and Biscayne for years. If the Yahwehs could accomplish that, the city would probably let them paint the streets and the palm trees white.

Deal saw his exit sign loom up overhead, then flash past. He'd been asleep. Only a quarter mile to the exit and two more lanes to cut across. He backed off the accelerator again and heard the whine of the Supra behind him as it dropped a gear. Fuck him. Deal had subs to check on at the job site. Miss this exit, he'd have to go all the way across the river, then be stuck in the hospital traffic coming back. Turn up late and the subs would have long since declared another holiday.

It *was* tough, fighting this traffic every morning. He was used to heading the other way, against the river of cars heading downtown. For years, construction had been moving west, nibbling inexorably toward the Everglades. GDC, Kendale Homes, DealCo, munching away at the vegetable farms, reclaiming wetlands, throwing up subdivisions and office parks, metro council falling all over itself to issue permits and variances. But times changed, boom had slid into bust.

GDC under indictment. DealCo wasted away. Others vanished completely. Only Kendale hanging on, so far. The lot where Deal was building his fourplex was saved from the days when there had been a real company, when his old man had been alive, when, in his old man's words, "you didn't need an interpreter to get a chalkline snapped."

Deal had never minded working with Hispanics. After all, he'd started in as a grunt working alongside the other framers and rough carpenters, more and more of whom spoke Spanish as the stream of immigrants from Cuba and points south increased to a flood. He'd picked up enough of the language to get by, was reasonably fluent in the basic topics of conversation on the job: carpentry, food, baseball, getting laid.

No, it wasn't accommodating himself to another language that bothered him. Furthermore, he admired the industry of the immigrants, even those his old man considered "pushy." As far as Deal was concerned, they had a right. They'd been fucked over at home, wherever that was, and now they had come over here and were desperate to make it, simple as that. No, he had no problems with that. It was just that it was getting harder and harder for Deal to keep his own little part of the pie.

Right now, he was a month shy of the due date on his construction loan, with maybe six weeks of work to go and the rainy season cranking up. He needed dry weather. He needed to kick the subs into hyperdrive . . . or else he needed to do as Janice wanted and sell out.

Meanwhile, the Yahwehs had finally inched ahead. Deal glanced over his shoulder and motioned to a woman in a minivan. She waved him in. He cut his wheels, then winced at a shrieking of brakes behind him. The Supra had rammed in on his tail, nearly clipping the minivan, which had begun to fishtail wildly.

Deal hit his own brakes instinctively, but felt a surge of panic when nothing happened. Because the traffic ahead was slowing for the tollgates, The Hog actually seemed to pick up steam. He glanced down wildly, hoping to see he'd somehow hit the accelerator, but sure enough, it was the brake pedal that was slowly sinking toward the floor.

The sonsofbitches, Deal thought, even as The Hog rushed toward the back of the Yahweh bus that loomed ahead. He'd had The Hog in to the dealer three times for the brakes. First, they'd said it was shoes. Then, after he'd picked it up to find there was still no pedal, they'd said the cylinders were leaking. The last time, they'd flushed the lines and replaced the master cylinder. It had been doing fine for three days. Until now.

Two of the Yahwehs sitting in the back of the bus, flanking the emergency door, had turned and were staring in alarm as Deal closed in. It was a converted school bus, with a high ass-end, and the two women were probably going to be safe. With any luck, The Hog would slide in under the floorboards of the bus, just about windshield level. The frame girders of the bus would come through The Hog on a line with Deal's skull.

They were on the bridge approach now, climbing slightly toward the toll plaza. Deal checked the traffic to his right, found a solid wall of commuters checking for change, switching stations, applying lipstick, no one aware of his plight.

The Supra, meanwhile, had not left his tail. Just behind, at the bottom of the hill, the minivan had broadsided to a stop, blocking the two right lanes. A roofer's ancient pickup towing a wheeled tar pot slammed on its brakes and swerved to avoid the minivan. As the pickup jounced onto the shoulder, the tar pot tipped to the right and broke loose from the tow bar. The thing passed the pickup like it had been shot out of a sling, then slammed into a light stanchion.

Deal knew about breakaway poles, how they'd been designed to reduce fatalities, but he had never seen one in action. He'd always doubted the principle, in fact. How could you hit one of the massive looking things and not die?

The tar pot did die. It hit the pole and exploded, sending a wave of black over a bright new Cadillac just ahead. The pole, meantime, fell like a fighter going into the tank. It crashed down across the roofer's pickup and the minivan, showering sparks and glass across the lanes.

. Ahead of him, the rear of the bus blossomed huge. The two Yahwehs were fighting to reach the aisle. They have seen the coming of the apocalypse, Deal thought. The Supra bore down mindlessly from behind. At least, he'd take that bastard out with him.

He was staring at the big block letters EMERGENCY EXIT stenciled across the back of the bus when his hand locked on The Hog's brake lever at his side, but there had been no connection in his mind. It was all reflex as he jerked up hard on the emergency brake and felt himself begin to spin, out of control.

He saw the headlights of the Supra flash by, and felt a small surge of satisfaction—imagine the look on the bastard's face—as he braced himself for a collision. "You could have done it smoothly, Deal," he was thinking. "You might have applied gentle pressure to that emergency brake. Everything would have turned out all right."

He caught sight of the Yahwehs again, but too quickly to see how they were taking it. He saw a gull wheel past, thought he heard its scream, saw another lamp dome whiz overhead like a spaceship, the Supra again, a Cadillac with a horrifying black paint job, a flash of concrete, an abrupt *thump,* somebody groaning, then silence.

He was turned around, The Hog pointing its snout back down the bridge approach toward a knot of chaos that had closed off all the traffic behind him. The minivan looked as if a giant had karate-chopped it. The Cadillac had slid to a stop and was steaming in the sun. Someone was struggling to get the driver's door open, but the thick tar, which had lapped down over the roof, would only give so far.

The roofer's crew had stepped down from the pickup to stare nervously at their ruined tar pot and the light pole that still sputtered ominous sparks. Deal heard something and turned to stare through the open passenger window of The Hog. The Supra sat idling in the lane beside him, its exhaust pulsing like a heartbeat.

Deal stared as the heavily smoked window opposite slid down. There was no passenger. The driver, a blocky Latin, leaned his way, though his face stayed mostly in shadow. The man was wearing a dark suit with threads that glinted in the sun, a gray silk shirt, a dark red tie. When he raised his hand, Deal saw the pistol, most likely a .357. The barrel seemed immense. Deal felt his entire head slipping down the tube, his bowels watering, greasing the long slide down.

It seemed very quiet for rush hour. He could hear the tinny voices of the Haitian roofers down below, the burble of the Yahweh buses up ahead, at the tollgates. He wondered if the Yahwehs would bear witness to his death.

And for what? Because he'd broken the south Florida commandment? *Thou shall not cut a man off in traffic.*

Abruptly, the whooping of a siren broke the silence. The man in the Supra raised his eyes to his rearview mirror. A police cruiser was picking its way through the tangle of traffic behind them.

Deal saw the man's thumb move to the hammer of the pistol, saw the hammer ease back to its rest.

"You must be more careful," the man inside the Supra said, over the hum of the car's exhaust. "You don't know who's out here. You could die."

Deal heard regret in the voice. Sure, he could understand that. Try to run a guy off the road, you can't. Then you want to blow him away and here the fucking cops show up. Hell of way to start your morning.

More sirens whooped in the background. "Have a nice day," Deal said.

But the smoked window was already rising. And then the Supra was gone.

Deal limped The Hog down Calle Ocho, as SW Eighth Street had come to be called, holding a steady ten miles per hour, ignoring the chorus of horns behind him. He swung left off the main drag at the first break in the oncoming traffic. A few blocks down the avenue, which featured a series of boarded-up shops and vacant lots, he caught a glimpse of the burned-out gas station he'd seen earlier on the news.

The cops and reporters were gone, but a yellow police line still fluttered in the wind. Arson, Deal supposed. That was one way out of your troubles.

He turned back to his driving just in time to see an old man in an ancient coupe edging out from a stop sign into the path of The Hog. Deal never even considered the horn. It'd still be blaring when he crushed the old fart to a pulp. He cut his wheels to the right and down the side street, praying it wasn't a dead end. The old man drove away, unaware.

Deal finally reached the site about ten A.M., covering the last dozen feet locked in a four-wheel power slide.

Emilio, the cabinetmaker, was leaning over the hood of his pickup, reading the paper as The Hog climbed over the curb and came to a stop.

"You drinking already?" Emilio asked, walking over.

Deal relaxed his grip on the emergency brake and sat quietly in the driver's seat, getting his breathing under control.

Emilio held out the sports page he'd been reading. "So what do you think? We gonna get a baseball team?"

Deal glanced at the sports columnist's headline.

LEAGUE SEEKS DEEP-POCKETS OWNER—FINANCING QUESTIONS LINGER.

"I couldn't tell you," Deal said, getting out. "The Commissioner stopped returning my calls."

Emilio nodded. "Lot of Cubans down here. They'd like to have it."

"They should take up a collection," Deal said.

Emilio stared at him. "You got something against the idea?"

Deal stopped. Emilio was a good man, a careful cabinetmaker. His father had worked for DealCo until he died of emphysema and Emilio, whom Deal could still remember as a solemn twelve-year-old, fetching tools and sweeping up scraps around the jobs, had picked up the baton. He charged more than his sloppy, cut-rate competitors, less than the equally sloppy glitzy shops clustered around the design center. Only what was fair. He'd never hung Deal out to dry on any job. And he wasn't responsible for this day's ration of shit.

"No, I have nothing against it, Emilio," Deal said. "It's just been one of those days."

Emilio nodded. He'd had his share of those days. He tapped his paper again. "You gotta understand, they bring the game down here, the people—*our* people—they are going to go crazy. Next best thing would be to put Castro to the firing squad on opening day, know what I mean?"

Deal had some idea. He also knew the money men would be counting on Emilio's "people" to put the turnstiles into an endless spin. But that was being too cynical, wasn't it?

Emilio took a swing with his newspaper bat. He watched an imaginary ball soar out of sight. "Canseco!" Emilio said. "Bam!"

He turned back to Deal, grinning. "But what am I telling you, man? You *played* baseball."

"I participated," Deal said. "*Canseco* plays."

Emilio laughed and clapped him on the shoulder. "You're okay, Deal. They get the team down here, we gonna go to the park."

"No question about it," Deal said, feeling weary.

Satisfied, Emilio bent for a handful of rocks, began chucking them toward a post where the temporary power line was hooked up. Deal watched, envying Emilio his preoccupation. When *he* looked at the post, all he could think was, now it's time to call the power company, get the line switched over to the electrical panel in the fourplex.

How nice it'd be to worry about something like baseball, he thought, looking around. Save for Emilio, the site was deserted. The windows on the second floor gaped open, waiting for casements on back order for three weeks now. The stucco man had covered about half of the graffiti-scrawled block walls—Deal had studied some of the messages: not Spanish, not English, not anything that he could interpret. Maybe they were hieroglyphics from outer space—*Your mama, ET. Sell this property, earthling.*

"I been waiting for my helper," Emilio said, finishing with the rocks. "He's got those vanities for the bathrooms in his truck."

Deal nodded and checked his watch.

Emilio continued. "He had some parking tickets he had to see about."

Deal sighed. "That kid went anywhere near the courthouse, we'll never see him again."

Emilio shrugged and lit a cigarette. He pointed toward the unfinished building. "Somebody's been using the toilets. You ought to get the water turned on so they can flush."

Deal gave him a look. It was probably Emilio's helper using the toilets. "We're waiting on the inspector to clear the hookup to the main," he said. "You see the stucco man?" Emilio shook his head. No one had seen the stucco man since his mixing bucket seized up last Thursday. Deal had been calling his home all weekend to no avail.

"Haven't seen nobody," Emilio said. He exhaled a ribbon of blue smoke into the sultry air. The summer heat had kicked in early. Deal glanced at the open windows again, thinking glumly of the endless cycle of thunderstorms about to begin.

He sighed and turned aside. Not far from The Hog's front

wheels was a two by four jutting from a pile of rubble, sixteen-penny nails writhing up from one of its ends like a clutch of armored worms. He paused to stomp the nails down flat with his heel, then picked the chunk of wood up and backhanded it toward a Dumpster near the curb. The wood cracked against the raised lid and dropped neatly into the hopper.

"Deal to Alomar to Boggs," Emilio said, grinning. "All-Stars out of the inning."

Deal ignored him, still wondering if there was some way he might bring Janice around. He'd started a book for new parents, recently. There was a chapter called "Feathering the Nest," and Deal had the uneasy feeling that he and Janice were battling it out exactly like the book said: "Mom," circling the wagons, getting every last thing in order for the new arrival, "Dad" full of energy, ready to start new projects, take on the world.

After four chapters of "Mom" and "Dad," Deal had tossed the book in the trash. Still, the argument went on. And on. He would simply have to be patient. And persistent. She was upset right now, but it would pass. *Stay the course, Deal. Stay the course.*

He sighed, kicked at the rubble in front of him. "Well," he said finally, looking up at Emilio. "I have to go see about this car. You be around a while?"

Emilio nodded, flicking his cigarette butt into a pile of wood scrap near the curb. Deal thought of the wood igniting, sparks leaping to the unfinished fourplex. He could take the insurance money, stiff all his subcontractors, flee to the Caribbean with Janice. Or better yet, take the cash to Penfield, see if they'd cut a minority position in the baseball ownership group, one-thirty-second of one-half of a percent, something like that.

"You see the inspector," he said to Emilio, "tell him." Emilio was frowning. Deal broke off and began again. Nobody "told" the building inspector anything. "*Ask* him if he'd go ahead without me being here, okay?"

Emilio nodded, but his expression was doubtful. "Maybe he wants to see you."

Deal shook his head. "I already saw him, Emilio. He's taken care of."

Emilio shrugged. "Maybe he forgot."

Deal took a deep breath. Emilio was just trying to be helpful, reminding him to expect the worst. It was a philosophy you took for granted in the construction business.

It would be perfectly reasonable for the inspector to forget the bill he'd palmed on his last visit. Protocol held that the hundred would cover Deal through the plumbing and electrical stages, but it was always possible for the inspector to "forget." And without the inspector's approval of the various steps along the way, the project was dead. Deal himself might defy a red tag and keep on working, but his subcontractors never would. It would cost them ever after, on every job in the county.

"I'll try to get back by noon," Deal said, finally.

"Okay," Emilio said, "I'm just going for a *cafecito*." He started for his truck as Deal swung himself back into The Hog.

One little coffee, Deal thought. That meant Emilio was probably gone for the day. He eased The Hog down off the curb in reverse, then dropped into low without bothering with the brake. There was a sickening clank as the gears caught, then The Hog shuddered and began to inch forward.

"What's wrong with your car?" Emilio called.

"See you in a couple of hours," Deal answered. He waved at Emilio, tapping experimentally on the brakes as he moved off. The pedal sank smoothly to the floor.

The Hog was in actuality a 1982 Seville that had been converted to an El Camino, its rear seat and trunk removed and replaced by a shallow pickup bed. Its former owner was a man named Cal Saltz, an old friend of Deal's father who'd owned a string of used-car lots up and down U.S. 441 in Broward ("Come on down and see Crazy Cal").

Saltz had taken an interest in Thoroughbred racing and bought a horse farm on the edge of the Everglades. He had the Seville converted and used it to haul tack and feed out when he visited the place on weekends. Saltz liked gentleman farming so much that he determined to build a house on the place. He engaged an architect to draw plans based on the Ewing spread in "Dallas" and hired Deal to build it for him.

Deal was about halfway through the project when Saltz went

bankrupt, his successful car operations overwhelmed by a long streak of losers at the track. Deal got out with enough to pay off his subs, and the Seville, which Saltz, having no further use for, had thrown in.

Deal, whose own fortunes had begun to slide about the same time, had used it for his work truck ever since. It was Janice who christened it "The Hog." She favored small foreign-built cars and was fond of pointing out the surveys that showed how much of America had come to agree with her. Deal, on the other hand, would drive twenty miles to avoid buying Japanese nails for his jobs. In any event, The Hog had functioned well, until the episode with the brakes.

It was almost noon by the time Deal swung onto the lot of the dealership. To Deal, who had grown up at a time when men who drove Ford pickups would readily fist fight the owners of Chevys, Surf Motors was an anomaly, more of an empire than a dealership. The place sprawled over several blocks on both sides of Surf Boulevard just north of downtown, and a series of huge signs advised that you could buy lines from Chrysler, Ford, and GM on the premises, not to mention Saab, Maserati, and VW. Deal wondered how it was possible.

He snaked through the complex series of turns toward the proper service bays, twice warning drivers out of his way with blasts from the mighty after-market air horn Saltz had installed in The Hog.

As he approached "Customer Accommodation," an awning-covered area flanked by rows of potted Queen Anne palms, Deal spotted the service manager darting inside the bays. He gave another blast on the horn and jerked up on the emergency brake. The Hog's wheels locked again and the car went into a leftward hook, gliding over the smooth finished concrete as if it were ice. It finished up just short of the first attendant's counter, clipping one of the twenty-foot Queen Annes, which fell over with a crash.

The attendant was moving warily from behind her counter when Deal got out of his car. A woman who had been dropping off a yellow convertible stood braced in front of her car as if she'd been willing to shield it with her own body.

The service manager hurried out from the service bays. When

he saw The Hog, he stopped short. "What the *fuck*?" he said. He turned to Deal, a look of disbelief on his face.

It seemed to take him a minute to comprehend. "What's wrong with you coming in here like that?" he said, finally. He was a dark-complexioned kid in his late twenties, maybe four inches shorter than Deal's six feet. But his shoulders swelled inside the blazer they made him wear, and his neck was as thick as his blocky head. It looked as if he were deep into steroids.

Deal knew he cut no imposing figure. He carried a hundred and ninety pounds, maybe, but he was big-boned, and weight seemed to get lost on him, a trait Janice envied. "Five pounds on me and it goes right to my ass. It looks like I ate cement," she'd moan, even though Deal liked the feel of her flesh.

Deal stepped forward and took the service manager by the arm, steering him quickly toward The Hog. The guy tried to pull away, a surprised look coming over his face when he realized he wouldn't be able to, not without some serious effort. Deal hadn't been pounding a whole lot of nails lately, but years of guiding a twenty-ounce hammer, thousands of blows a day, had left him with a grip you couldn't build at Scandinavia. He could feel the muscles through the guy's coat, all right, but he wasn't even squeezing. He brought them to the driver's window and pointed in at the raised emergency lever.

"Those brakes you've been trying to fix. You haven't got it right yet," Deal said.

The guy looked up at him. "You going to let go of my arm now?"

Deal let go. "I'm sorry about the palm tree," he said. A pair of lot boys had righted the tree, only to have the pot disintegrate. The dirt had fallen away from the nearly rootless base and the two of them struggled with the thing as it swayed in the breeze off the nearby bay. "I couldn't get stopped, okay?"

The service manager gave him a look. Finally he nodded. He turned and shouted at the lot boys. "Get that fucking thing out of here."

The two lot boys looked at each other, then started dragging the tree off. The service manager waved his hand at the woman who was still braced in front of her convertible. "Sorry about the language," he said, then turned back to stare at The Hog.

"Yeah," he said finally, making it seem a big effort. "I remember this thing. You got a lot of after-market stuff on a car, you have trouble, know what I mean?"

"There's nothing after-market about the brake system," Deal said evenly.

The service manager shook his head without looking at Deal. "These body shop guys," he said, "they come over here from Coconutville, you don't know what they screw up."

"Look," Deal said. "Nobody but you has touched those brakes. Ever." Deal felt his breath going flaky, had to stop. There was a little pinging sensation at his temples.

"I nearly died out there on the freeway a few minutes ago." The kid was still eyeing The Hog, shaking his head.

Deal stepped in front of him. "I want you to fix my brakes. I already paid you something like five hundred dollars and the brakes still don't work. Do you understand me?"

The service manager glanced up at him. "You got an attitude, right?"

Deal looked around. The blond woman with the yellow convertible and the young service attendant were watching him warily. They'd already pegged him a maniac, a probable substance abuser. He wanted to deck this punk, wanted to plant him alongside the palms where you could see him anytime you came in, wave, ask "How you doin', Carlos, miss the workouts at the gym?"

He forced himself into ultracalm, then turned back to the service manager. "This is my only transportation," Deal said. "I'd like to get it fixed. You think you can help me?"

The manager studied him, looked back at the car, chewed on the inside of his cheek. Finally, he nodded. "Sure," he said. "Step right over there. Lucy'll get you written up."

"Thanks," Deal said, watching the service manager walk off.

"Not in there, you fuckheads," he was bellowing at the lot boys, who had dragged the palm tree inside one of the service bays. "Out in the fucking Dumpster."

Deal took a deep breath, smiled at the convertible lady, and went to get written up.

 Deal sat in a canvas chair under the Customer Accommodation awning, waiting for the scheduled limo service, idly flipping through the newspaper.

He glanced up at the service attendant who had been ignoring him ever since he'd been written up and the two lot boys had come to push The Hog into the service bays. The attendant was paging someone named "Homer" to the front.

Deal turned back to the newspaper. Yesterday's edition, with another story on the baseball issue, this one front page, with a picture of the preliminary applicant group, a clutch of men in business suits and baseball caps, all holding bats. One, of course, was Thornton Penfield, their host from the night before. The story identified Penfield as a minor partner in the baseball group and quoted him on various concerns:

The $130 million price tag? "We're lining up some *Fortune* 500 backers." The rainy summer weather? "We'll put a dome on our stadium, if we have to." And which stadium would that be: the city's aging bowl or a pie-in-the-sky site, to be financed by a $100 million bond issue, straddling the county line, way north in the boondocks? "We're committed to a downtown site—the bowl can be converted to baseball for less than $10 million." But, in that case, what of the parking and access problems for the outmoded stadium? "These are details that can be worked out."

Penfield sounded confident, but the writer wasn't so sure. Other cities had deeper pockets, less rain, and bigger, newer venues already built. The expansion vote was coming up soon, and it was a contest for millions of dollars to be pumped into the lucky community's economy. More like billions, when looked at in the long run. Don't count on it, south Florida, but don't give up hope. We're talking Klondike.

Klondike, Deal thought, wearily. He tossed the paper down. If it *did* work out, maybe Penfield could get him season tickets. He heard a horn tap then and glanced toward the counter. The attendant was in earnest conversation in Spanish with someone on the telephone, something about a *puta* who was messing with her boyfriend. When she noticed Deal was staring at her, she lowered her voice and turned her back on him.

The horn sounded again. A LeBaron convertible had pulled up in the driveway, but from where he was sitting Deal couldn't see anyone at the wheel. The service attendant turned to him and jabbed her pencil at the LeBaron. Deal stood up, puzzled.

Now he could see into the driver's seat of the convertible. There was a small man behind the wheel, an old couch cushion wedged under him, another propped behind his back. He glanced up at Deal. "You waiting for a ride?" Deal nodded.

"Well, get in," the man said and flung himself across the passenger seat to open the door.

"You're Homer?" Deal asked, over the convertible's rush of air. They were whisking up a ramp onto the Dolphin Expressway, headed west. The rain had held off, although there were towering thunderheads building far out over the Everglades.

"That's right," Homer said. He glanced over at Deal. "You can relax. I never lost a passenger yet."

Deal laughed. He'd been watching Homer's feet, clad in rubber boots that reached nearly to his hips, dancing over the pedals. Homer's arms and legs were tiny, child-size, his torso that of an adolescent's; yet his head was of normal size, his voice husky. The effect was disorienting.

"I can move the seat back," Homer added, waving at Deal's knees that jutted up in front of the glovebox.

"That's okay," Deal said.

"You're lucky I was on today," Homer said. "You'd have had to wait another hour for the limo."

"I appreciate it," Deal said. "I have to meet a guy."

"In Little Havana?" Homer asked. "What kind of business you in?"

"I'm a contractor," Deal said. Homer raised his chin to acknowledge the remark, then stared in silence down the expressway.

Maybe it sounded too lofty. "I'm an independent. Just a little guy trying to make a living," Deal added.

"Me too," Homer said, mildly.

It took Deal a minute to get it. He felt his cheeks flush. "I didn't mean anything," he told Homer.

Homer waved it away. "I'm a dwarf. It ain't exactly something you keep secret." He glanced at Deal, grinning. "My old man was six two and weighed two thirty when he croaked."

Deal nodded, uncertain.

"Don't worry about me," Homer said. "I'm just happy to get out of the soapsuds for a while. We'll go to Naples, if you want to."

"Little Havana is fine," Deal said. After a moment he added, "That's what you do normally, wash the cars?"

"Nothin's normal at that outfit," Homer said, his eyes on the road. "But yeah, that's generally what I do." A Porsche rushed past them in a whine, doing ninety maybe, maybe more.

"Some car," Deal said. The Porsche had already disappeared, but you could still hear the engine somewhere up ahead.

"You got enough money, you do anything you want," Homer said. They were over the river now, descending the same bridge where Deal had had his earlier adventure in driving. Across the dividers, Deal saw a crane lifting some of the debris. They'd had to close a lane for the work and the eastbound traffic was snarled.

"Look at that," Homer said. "I'll have to take the streets coming back."

Deal nodded. "I would, if I were you."

"This town's got crazy," Homer said.

"It's the big city, all right." Deal checked his watch. If he'd missed the inspector, he might be down another week.

"It's more than that," Homer said, guiding them toward their exit. He glanced in the rearview mirror, then swung onto the ramp. "What's your company's name, anyhow?"

When Deal told him, Homer turned in surprise. "DealCo," he repeated. "Who are you shittin'. That's the big time. They built the Grove Hotel, all that stuff along the bay."

"Used to be," Deal told him. "That was my old man. I'm the small time, now."

Homer turned back to his driving. They were on Twenty-seventh Avenue, now, the lanes heavy with afternoon traffic. "So your old man was John Deal, huh?" Homer thought about it before he continued. "He used to come into the Carneses' all the time."

"He wouldn't go anywhere else," Deal said. The Carnes brothers were men of his father's generation. They'd owned Surf Motors from the days when it was the only Seville dealership in south Florida. His father had always traded there, even after the Carneses had long since decamped from the show room to diversify their interests. Deal had serviced The Hog there solely out of habit.

"You're the kid that played baseball," Homer said.

Deal shook his head. Ten years, maybe, since anybody'd brought it up. Now, twice in the same day. "In high school," he said grudgingly.

"Yeah?" Homer screwed up his face, trying to remember. "I thought you got a scholarship, something like that."

Deal shrugged. "A couple years in college. That's about it."

Homer gave him a look. He was just trying to pass the time, wasn't going to press it.

Deal could imagine his old man booming around the dealership the day he got the call, telling the Carneses and anybody else within earshot about it, "Yeah, the boy has him a full ride with the Seminoles. Next stop, Yankee Stadium." And on and on. Easy for him to dream. He had never tried to hit a curve ball. Deal glanced at Homer. He wondered if they were going to talk about getting a team down here, now.

"Your old man threw some dice with the bosses now and then," Homer said. Not bad, Deal thought. Set him up with a fast ball, then the change of pace. The little man glanced over to see how Deal was taking it. "I'd hold the money. Watch the door, in case somebody got a stupid idea."

Deal nodded. He'd tried to forget about that too. He had a fair suspicion how much of DealCo had skittered away on the craps table.

"So what's your old man doing?"

"He's dead," Deal said. And probably throwing dice with the devil, he thought.

Homer stared at him, then had to swerve around a step-van clogging the middle lane. "Fuckhead," Homer grumbled. He shot a bird in the rearview mirror.

"Sorry to hear about that," he said, easing back into the center lane. "I won't ask you what happened to *your* business," he said, finally. "I been at Surf thirty years. I saw how the Carneses got screwed." He made a thoughtful hissing sound between his teeth. "Ain't the same with them gone."

Deal turned to him, surprised. "The Carneses sold out?" he asked.

Homer pulled to a stop at a light. He thought for a moment before answering. Finally he turned to Deal. "You seem like a good guy, but I don't know you. I say something, you might be having a drink someday, tell a guy, 'Hey, guess what this midget works down at Surf told me.'" The light changed and Homer hit the accelerator, leaving some of the LeBaron's tires behind them. "Let's just say the Carneses got tired of the car bidness, okay?"

"Sure," Deal said. "It's okay. I was just surprised, that's all."

"Things change," Homer said.

"I'm a little tired of change," Deal said.

Homer laughed mirthlessly. "You're in a shitload of trouble then."

Deal nodded. "I always have been."

Homer said nothing until they'd stopped at another light on down LeJeune. A slender, black-haired woman in Lycra tights and a tube top strode across the intersection in front of them, carrying a Coke from a take-out joint. Homer tapped the horn and the woman turned, a withering look on her face. When she saw Homer, the look softened. She smiled and added a little extra switch to her walk as she mounted the curb.

"That's another thing might surprise you," Homer said, as they drove off.

"What's that?" Deal asked, mildly.

"The women we get. They hear all the stories, you know. They want to find out if it's true."

"If what's true?"

Homer patted his crotch. "Nobody's ever complained, either," he said. He laughed, swung off the boulevard in a swooshing turn, pointed down the street in front of them. "That the guy you wanted to meet?"

Homer guided them to a stop in front of the unfinished four-plex. A florid-faced man in a panama hat was just getting into a beige sedan with a city seal emblazoned on the side. The man stopped when he saw Deal.

"That's him," Deal said, scrambling out. He reached into his pocket for his money clip, but Homer raised a hand to stop him.

"Forget it," he said. "You got me out of the soapsuds, remember."

"Take it anyway," Deal said, holding out a five.

"Can't do it," Homer said, pulling off. "Good luck with your guy," he added. "You hit the big time again, maybe you'll have a job for me."

Deal nodded, but Homer was already gone. He turned and hurried after the inspector.

The inspector's name was Faye. He mopped his glowing face and pointed down into the hole where the sewer and gas lines were capped off, ready to be joined to the main. "Who told you that gas line would work?" he said, his voice wheezy. His breath was rapid and shallow, as if the twenty-foot walk from his car had exhausted him.

Deal followed his gaze. "What's wrong with it?" he asked.

Faye shook his head. "That's a half-inch line. Code calls for inch. One inch galvanized from the main to the meter."

"Bullshit," Deal said. "This is a fourplex. You're talking about a high-rise."

Faye shrugged. "The original permit called for twenty units."

"I changed that," Deal said. "Months ago."

"Only paperwork I seen says twenty units." Faye was wiping the back of his neck with his soggy handkerchief.

"Well, look at the goddamn building. You can see it's a four-plex."

Faye gave him a neutral stare. "I can see, Mr. Deal. I can see just fine. You get your ass in a crack, can't float the loan for what you wanted to build, it's okay by me. But I'm a duly appointed official of this city. I got to go by the book." He thumped a thick pad in his shirt pocket. "Until I see paperwork that tells me different, you're going to need a one-inch line down there." Faye hawked, then spat into the hole. "Galvanized," he added, swiping at his chin.

Deal pondered it. He could tell Faye to take a flying fuck at the moon, which would mean the end of his hopes of meeting deadline. He could spend the next day down at City-County which might or might not do him any good. Even if he found someone cooperative, it'd be a week or more getting any paperwork out to Faye. He sighed and reached into his pocket.

Faye palmed the bill, checked to be sure the right picture was on it, and nodded back at the hole. "I'd just cut her back two, three feet, weld a joint, step her up to an inch."

"Why don't I just have you do it?" Deal asked.

Faye narrowed his porcine eyes. "I'm just tryin' to be helpful."

"Great," Deal said. "Be sure and warn me when you're going to be a pain in the ass."

Faye waved his hand airily as he walked toward his car. "Glad to see you're still in there pitchin', Deal. Be a shame to turn the whole damned construction business over to the His-pan-yoles."

Deal watched him back up over the broken curb and crunch into the scrap pile, then pull out. If there was any justice, he'd just picked up a nail in his tire. It wasn't until Faye was out of sight that Deal remembered he'd meant to ask for a ride back to the dealership.

Leon tried three pay phones on the street near the dealership before he found one that worked. The first one was lacking its handset and cord. The second one took his quarter. When he dialed the eight-hundred number for help, the recording told him to deposit fifty cents.

The third one, outside a convenience store, looked battered, but the call went through. He got the recording that wanted to know if he was at a touch-tone phone. Leon glanced at the keypad. It looked as though someone had touched it repeatedly with a pickax. You really couldn't read any of the numbers, but he pressed what had to be the "one," just like the voice wanted him to. Then he pushed the code that would get him through to Alcazar. Just one more of his boss's paranoid safety measures. A secure line. Like he was the fucking president.

While Leon waited for the connection, he shifted his feet and felt something crunching under the Balys. He glanced down. There was a regular snowdrift of broken bottle glass there, beer bottles, wine bottles, who knows what all. A flattened work glove. A mangled butter knife. By the post that held the phone, a pile of grunt that looked too big to have come from an animal.

Leon shook his head. Ten blocks south, you could see sky

scrapers, bank buildings, the big red-tiled roof of the cultural center. Up here they were shitting in the streets.

"Yes?" It was Alcazar's voice. Impatient, as usual. Like who was Leon to be interrupting the president.

"We got bad news and good news," Leon said.

"Get to the point," Alcazar said.

"Alejandro fucked up," Leon said, feeling a smile on his lips.

"What happened?" Alcazar said. Leon knew he had his jaw clenched. You could hear breath hissing through the man's teeth. Guy was going to blow out a blood vessel before long.

"Nothing happened," Leon said. "That's the point. Except for the biggest traffic jam you ever saw. Man drove away from it, not a scratch on him." Leon kicked glass over the grunt at his feet, glanced about the neighborhood. Boarded-up this, caved-in that. There was an old VW on its side down the block, all the wheels gone. Only two blocks off Biscayne, it looked like he was in Beirut. They ever got their business finished up in Little Havana, he'd mention this neighborhood to Alcazar.

". . . supposed to be a simple accident. Can't you do anything right?"

Leon tuned back to the phone, registered Alcazar's barely contained fury. "Hey," he said. "Was Alejandro fucked up, not me. He was ready to shoot the dude. Got his macho way out of whack, you know what I mean."

Leon heard a sigh on the other end. When he spoke again, Alcazar sounded weary, his voice faint, like he was ready for a nap. "Why are you calling me, Leon?"

Leon nodded to himself. Now that was better. One of these days, the man was going to reflect back, tally up all the times of who was a help and who was a hindrance, he'd realize what he had in Leon Straight.

"Well, the man's had him some car trouble," Leon said. "And you'll never guess where he went to have it fixed."

"I don't care, Leon . . . "

"Man is having his car fixed at Surf Motors," Leon said, feeling his smile growing wide. He could hear the wheels in Alcazar's head spinning all the way across town.

"Look, Janice, somebody's got to pick up The Hog by six. Otherwise, you'll have to take me down first thing in the morning."

Deal switched the receiver to his other hand. It was one of the off-brand pay phones, bolted to the block wall outside a *Supermercado*. Between the static that rattled in the cheap receiver and the rumble of a low-rider that was idling in a parking space just behind, he could barely hear.

"You have to speak up," Deal shouted.

The line was suddenly clear. "I said tomorrow is my tennis lesson. Can't you take a taxi?"

Deal closed his eyes. "I don't have any cash. I had a little emergency and . . . " He broke off as thunderous music erupted from the low-rider. Deal stared. The receiver was vibrating in his hand. He'd spent plenty on a pair of Bose floor speakers when they still had the house. The best sound wouldn't have touched what was coming through the windows of the low-rider.

"Just a minute," he shouted into the phone.

Deal left the receiver dangling, strode to the car. There was a skinny kid about eighteen leaning back in the passenger's seat, his chin barely nodding to the blare of the music, his expression dreamy. When Deal's shadow fell across his face, the kid looked up, not very interested.

"I'm trying to talk," Deal said, his words lost in the vortex of sound. Deal pointed at the telephone, then mimed holding the receiver to his ear. The kid glanced over the dash, then back at Deal. His face had taken on a pained, disbelieving look, as if he were staring at a roach crawling across his windshield. He shook his head and fell back in his seat, back to dreamland.

Deal felt something sizzle in his brain, a bright little spot snapping just behind his right eye. He lunged inside the low-rider, pinned the kid back against his seat with a forearm at his scrawny throat, snapped off the ignition with his free hand. He jerked the keys out, then spun in one fluid motion and tossed them far out into the nearby intersection.

"Hey, man," the kid squawked. Although there was plenty of traffic, it seemed very quiet. Deal felt a wash of peace come over him.

"Don't say anything," Deal told the kid. "Just go get your keys." Deal felt a throbbing in his shoulder. He could hear the echoes of a dozen coaches from his boyhood: "Never throw till you've warmed up, son. You don't want to hurt yourself."

The kid read something in Deal's eyes, nodded, and got out, hurrying toward the intersection. Deal went back to the phone.

"You still there?" he asked.

"Deal, what's going on?" Her voice was tired, faint. She'd been that way lately. Deal chalked it up to living for two people.

"Janice," he said patiently, "my brakes went out and I nearly crashed into a busload of Yahwehs on the Dolphin Expressway. Then some asshole pulls a gun on me because I cut in front of him. Then the building inspector threatens to flag me up after I already paid him off . . . "

"Someone pulled a gun on you?" she cut in, a note of alarm in her voice. "What are you talking about?"

"Just some cowboy in a suit," he said. "I spun out in his lane so he had to defend his manhood."

There was a long pause on Janice's end. "Deal, that's not funny." She sounded truly distressed, all her anger gone.

There was a long silence and Deal felt immediately guilty. Scare the shit out of your pregnant wife so she'll cave in and do you a favor. That hadn't been his intention. But still, you had to handle things. Put aside the problems that weren't problems any longer, grind on ahead. He sighed.

"Janice, forget about the guy. He was just showing off." When she didn't respond, he plowed forward. "Look, you've got to help me out. I have to wait at the fourplex for Emilio. And the plumber. And the stucco man . . . "

"Where is it?" she said.

Deal nodded. So he'd won. She hadn't said yes, but he recognized her tone. He watched the kid from the low-rider, out in the street now, dodging a concrete truck in the intersection, snatching up his keys. An enormous woman in her fifties had come out of the *Supermercado* with an overloaded shopping cart and stood by the silent low-rider, staring about impatiently.

"Where it always is," he said to Janice. "At Carnes's."

He heard her groan. "You're sure it's finished? I've got a hair appointment and then I'm supposed to go to Lee Ann's tonight, for that shower."

"It's ready. I just got off the phone with them. You just need to get down there before six, give them a check." The kid had made it back to the low-rider. There was much animated back and forth between him and his mother, but no gestures came Deal's way.

"Look, Janice, you don't have to pick me up. Just get The Hog and go on to Lee Ann's. I have a key to your car. Leave it in the lot. I'll get down there later, somehow."

"You mean you want me to *drive* that thing?" Her voice had risen dangerously.

"Janice," he said patiently, "the door locks don't work. I don't want it sitting out after they close. I've got tools in there . . . "

"Why don't you *sell* that car!"

He had his eyes closed. "It's one of those things, Janice. Can you help me out, or not?"

There was a long pause. "Okay, Deal," she said wearily. "I'll do it."

Deal knew he should have felt gratitude, but it was a difficult sensation to summon up. "Thanks," he said, finally, but the low-rider had cranked up again, and he couldn't be sure she'd heard.

 After he'd finished with Alcazar, Leon made his way back to the dealership. He stationed the big Electra in a vacant lot a half block down from the service bays and went across the street to have a few words with Mario, the service manager. It was a struggle to get the guy to focus in on the matter at hand. He knew Leon had played ball and always wanted to talk about who was really bad, about getting in shape, stuff like that. Today it was about some muscle-building powder he was buying through the mail from Mexico, supposed to make steroids look like One-A-Day vitamins.

"They got a lot of stuff you can't buy in the States, man. My friend's father, he went down there for this cancer he had?" Mario looked at Leon like he was supposed to care. "They fixed him *up*."

It could have been Rice Krispies and rat shit Mario was stirring into his carrot juice, Leon thought. Listening to him rattle on, you knew it wasn't brain food.

Leon had to promise to take him down to the Fifth Street gym, introduce him to one of the old-time trainers worked with Ali, before he could get him to pay attention. Mario brightened up when he found out whose car they were talking about. "Yeah," he said to Leon, once he'd figured it out. "Deal. The guy who thinks he's a bad dude." After that, it was easy.

*   *   *

Leon, who had missed his lunch, caught the roach wagon out in the parking lot, took the last half-dozen Jamaican meat patties, the hot ones, and a large Coke. He walked back to the Electra, tears welling in his eyes as he finished off the blazing food.

He wedged himself in behind the wheel, slid the seat back to its last notch, and drained the Coke, then went to work on the ice, trying to put out the flames in his insides. When the heat died down, he kicked off his Balys, checked his watch and settled back to wait.

It was a good choice, the Electra. Big V-eight been bored out, had a four-barrel carburetor on it. Good for heavy work, and so old and faded-out, nobody would be able to describe it in any helpful way. "I dunno, officer. It was big. And blue. Or maybe brown." Mmmm-hmmm. That was one thing about working for Alcazar: man owned a dozen dealerships, most of them with three or four brands. You need a car, you got whatever you wanted. Only trouble is, this one was so old it lacked a cassette. He was still thinking about that when he fell asleep.

He dreamed of a big coal fire, underground. Which he had started, playing with matches. His old man was there showing him where the seam had opened in the earth, right in the middle of the woods, a whole bunch of slash pines flopped over and smoldering in this big smoky hole, and when Leon looked over the steaming edge, he saw their piece-of-shit cabin had slid down there too. His mother stood on the porch with her hair up in flames, stretching her hands out and hollering for Leon to do something. Leon saw he had a bucket in his hand and, grateful for that good luck, flung what was in it toward her. Confetti showered down into the hole, each flake bursting into fiery pinpoints as the heat struck it. His mother was a whole pillar of flame now. His father kicked him in the ass so hard it snapped his head back.

Leon came awake with the jolt, sweating in the late afternoon heat, scared shitless by his dream, vaguely aware of a searing pain in his stomach. He blinked, checked his watch to see that it was almost six o'clock, then stared across the street in a panic. He relaxed when he saw the sawed-off Seville sitting there in the ready line, but tensed again when he felt a dull thud shake his own car.

He got his shoes on, jumped out of the car, shook his head to

48

clear away the cobwebs. Then stared, wondering if maybe he was still dreaming.

A guy in a long overcoat and a leather cap with ear flaps was hunched down by the rear wheel of the car, hooking a length of logging chain around the axle and into a metal plate.

"Hey," Leon said.

The guy glanced over his shoulder. One of his eyes might have been focused on Leon, the other one looked off toward Mars. His face had a flattened, scarred-over look, like somebody had decided to grind everything off and start over, then given up on the job.

He turned back to his work without a word. Leon heard something snap shut. He started forward. "What the *fuck* you doing?"

The guy stood up, turning toward him in one motion. "Boot!" he said. He dusted off his hands and pointed down at the Electra's wheel. Leon stared. Some kind of parking boot, all right. He wondered how the guy had managed to steal it. The thick chain looped around his axle and fitted into an eye-bolt welded to a heavy L-shaped metal plate. There was a combination lock holding it together, set back in a protective niche, where you couldn't bust it loose. Try to drive away, you'd shear the whole quarter panel off.

Leon grabbed the guy by the lapels of his coat. "Get it the fuck off my car," he said, lifting him off the ground. The guy rattled around inside the floppy coat. He might have weighed a hundred pounds. It was like holding a moth.

"You pay," the guy said, pointing at something. His good eye was a little wider, but he seemed more angry than afraid. Leon turned away from the guy's horrifying breath, saw a faded sign on the warehouse at the back of the lot. "ort Authority Parking—five dollars—No In and Out," he read. There'd probably been a *P* there once, but it was covered up by a realtor's sign that had been nailed overtop of it. Both signs were peeling and sun blasted. It looked like they'd been painted in another century.

Leon turned back to the guy. He couldn't believe it. A free-lance parking lot attendant. He was almost ready to laugh until he heard a motor rev up across the street, saw a cloud of exhaust smoke puff up behind the Seville.

"Get it off there," he said, shaking the guy again. "Get it the fuck off, now."

"Five dollars for parking, five dollars boot charge," the guy said. The Seville had backed out of the ready line, laid a short burst of rubber on the slick concrete.

"I'll tear your fucking head off," Leon said.

The guy saw him looking at the Seville, which was now pulling out onto Biscayne and was speeding away north. "Plus five dollars combination charge," the guy said. "My lot, my boot. Seventeen dollars."

"Mother *fuck*-er," Leon said, dumping the guy back to his feet. He found a twenty, wadded it into the guy's hand. "Do it." The guy held the bill up between the sun and his wandering eye, finally nodded. "Get in the car," he said to Leon, warily.

"Yeah, sure," Leon said. He gave the guy a last murderous glance, then got into the Electra. The Seville was a tiny dot way up the boulevard now, and by the time the guy got the boot unhooked, Leon had lost sight of it altogether.

Leon checked his rearview mirror in time to see the guy stand up and throw his hands into the air like some cowboy just tied off a bull. That meant he was finished, Leon hoped. He stomped the accelerator, his wheels chewing thin, rocky soil all the way to the curb, which he banged over, losing a hubcap on the way. He saw it rolling crazily across the boulevard in his rearview mirror, the crazy guy swooping out after it, the tails of the heavy coat lifting like wings.

Leon's only hope was that Deal was on his way back to the condo they'd tailed him from that morning. Only one way out to that part of the beach from where they were, and maybe he could catch up, but once he hit the commuter traffic, he knew that his chances of overtaking him were nil.

He fumed all the way up the boulevard, light after light, then everybody slowing down to a crawl to watch a guy up on the curb changing a tire—what the fuck went on in these people's *minds,* he wondered, that something like that could be interesting. It took him half an hour to reach the turn, out across the causeway, then a left and across a series of bridges connecting the islands, the traffic thinning as he went, but still no sign of the Seville. He was ready to give up, already rehearsing his speech for Alcazar, tell him all about the crime problems of that neighborhood around Surf Motors, when he caught sight of the Seville, moving up from the dull horizon onto the ramp of the last drawbridge between them and the guy's building.

Leon felt his spirits rise. Still a chance to make something of his day. He floored the Electra, felt the slight hesitation, then the powerful lunge as the jets kicked in. He was doing eighty when he hit the ramp, felt the heavy car sway as the tires bit into the steel gridwork of the bridge.

The Seville seemed to be dawdling, maybe the guy slowing down to have a look out over the railings at the birds swirling around, the pink sky reflecting the last of the sun, a couple of boats churning out to sea. Nice view, Leon thought. Nice way to check on out of life.

He cut his speed, timing it, drew up on the Seville's flank as they started down from the crest of the bridge. Way down the street was a car pulling out of a parking garage, but heading the other way. Everything fine.

He floored the Electra once again, cut his wheels sharply to the right. The big car jumped forward like a big jungle cat, taking down something soft and choice on the plains. It happened so quick, it was almost like it didn't happen. The Seville veered off as if sideways gravity had taken it. It climbed up the concrete abutment, cut the aluminum rails like they weren't there. The car seemed to hesitate at the top, everything stopping, a picture in Leon's mind:

The driver's window down. A big bird swooping overtop of them. Bunch of pink sky. Clank of metal from somewhere. Whitecaps out on the ocean.

And Leon, seeing who was driving, saying, "Jesus Christ, what else?"

You are out of control, Janice was telling herself, just before it happened. *Bitchy and whiny and totally out of control.* The way she'd seen her mother grinding on her father those last years. Reason had nothing to do with it.

The hum of The Hog's tires on the bridge grid had set her mind drifting. She'd been sitting with her mother at the breakfast table one morning, a view out the back windows of one hundred and sixty acres of frozen flat farmscape, a leaden Midwestern sky, the haze of her mother's cigarette smoke, the nasal twang of the radio announcer reading the glum news of grain futures. They hadn't spoken a dozen words to each other, Janice girding herself for a day at work, she'd be a happy little teller at the First National Bank of Findlay, her mother girding herself for another day.

And then the clump of her father's heavy boots down the stairs, across the living room floor, out into the kitchen. Janice turned, about to say good morning to her father.

"Oh shut up, Francis," her mother barked.

Her father stopped, stared at her mother, then went to pour his coffee, went on out without a word. Janice watched him from the window, moving stiffly toward the barn, shaking his head, his coffee trailing steam in the frigid air. A month later her parents were dead.

She shook her head, noticing some crazy driver coming up fast in the mirror behind her, somebody crazed to beat the drawbridge, afraid to spend an extra five minutes getting home. She edged The Hog farther to the right, and checked her watch.

Was that it? she wondered. Some genetic code kicking in, triggered by her pregnancy—*stomp on your man*. Dear God, she'd thought she'd left all that behind her. And now, here she was, unable to have a discussion, unable to talk at all, really. She loved Deal. She wanted this baby. And yet she was scared and angry and feeling so alone . . .

Stop it, she told herself. *You have got to break out of this.* She checked her watch, again. She could blow off the shower. Go by the market, pick up something for dinner. Surprise Deal. Maybe they'd have a bottle of wine, although she'd been drinking too much for the baby lately, hadn't she? Still, they had to talk. Deal could help her. He had always been there for her.

It was a plan. And she would follow through on it. *First step, Janice, turn around, back to the market.* She sent her window down, catching the rush of salt air. Checked the lane beside her.

And screamed.

She caught one glimpse of the big man's face as his car slammed into hers. His eyes were set ahead, his expression grim. There was a grinding shriek of metal, and a smell of burning rubber. She felt The Hog lurch sideways, toward the spindly guard rails on her right— she had told Deal once, wasn't it nice on this old bridge you could still see out, over the water, no high curb to block the view.

She jerked the steering wheel back to the left, felt something snap, felt a shudder all the way up her arms. She stared in horror. The steering wheel was turning freely in her hands.

The Hog skipped the low curb of the walkway and her head drove up hard into the padded roof. She felt something warm and wet in her mouth and realized she'd bitten her cheek or her tongue.

The Hog tore into the railings with an awful rending noise, like train wheels chewing through glass. She glanced out her window at the car that had crashed into her. The driver was still beside her, staring back now, his face registering shock, or surprise.

"Deal!" she screamed, as The Hog soared out into space. "Deal!"

And then she was in the water.

She wasn't sure how long she was under. She watched the light above her go slowly black and realized her hands were clawing to release her seat belt. The passenger cabin was full of water, slowing her movements, pressing her deeper and deeper into the seat cushions as they sank. The car pitched over in the swift current, and she felt her ears caving painfully inward.

She felt something give at her shoulder and then she was tumbling free, her face sliding along the slick inner surface of the windshield. It was pitch black now and she sent her hands scrambling frantically for the steering wheel, then the door frame.

Something soft and bulky brushed past her face, and she recoiled. Just her purse, she told herself. The pressure was tremendous now, like gravity doubling, then doubling again, pressing her down and down with the tumbling, plummeting car. She grasped the door frame with her other hand and pulled herself forward, forcing her shoulders through the open window. The car was rolling again, threatening to flip her back inside, but she levered her foot against something hard and shoved with all her might.

She felt her legs scrape over the sill and then there was a sudden sensation of weightlessness, and she knew that she was free. Free, but carried along in the grip of an incredible current.

Her lungs were beginning to ache and she kicked and clawed at the dark water, as if there might be handholds that would lead her to the surface. Bright lights had begun to ping behind her eyes. Please, she thought, please. Give me the time.

She tried to calm herself, tried to synchronize the movements of her arms and legs. *Steady, steady, you can't have gone that deep . . .*

And then she opened her eyes again and realized there was light. At first, only the merest sense of it, then a murky haze high above her, and then, mercifully, a wavering shaft of light in which she saw a hand churning through the water—her own—and finally, she burst to the surface, her lungs swelling with the sweetness of the air.

She spun onto her back, letting the current carry her, grateful for the buoyancy of the saltwater. She was too weak to do more than paddle feebly, just enough to keep her head out of the water. She stared back toward the bridge, expecting to see the structure looming over her, and felt a jolt of fear when she saw that it had nearly disappeared, a mere blip on the sun-setting horizon behind her.

She turned, choking as she went under for a moment, then came back up to see that she was being swept past the last reaches of the island where she lived, saw the few scrubby Australian palms that hung on in the park at the tip of land, then the jetties running out another hundred yards or so, and then the dark open sea where she'd be lost.

She thrashed at the water in a panic at first, then forced herself to calm. Angle with the current, don't fight against it, she told herself. She lunged up for breath, fell back, screamed inwardly at her own weakness.

You will die, and no one will know what happened, just like your parents, although your mother had probably said something vicious to your father, something that got him to take his eyes off the road and stare across the front seat at her, and puzzled, see the look of terror on her face, maybe not even time for her to scream or him to turn and see what hit them . . .

She kept her eyes shut firmly against the stinging water, fighting the panic, keeping her breathing steady, holding her feeble strokes as even as she could, although her head was spinning. *Pray you haven't cleared that jetty, girl.* In a moment she would allow herself to steal a glimpse and see . . . and then she felt her knees bang into something solid.

It was almost dark now, but she could see well enough. Well enough to grab hold of a chunk of tree limb that had lodged among the boulders of the jetty, pull herself up out of the water at last. She lay sprawled there for a moment, getting her breath, feeling the black swirling in her mind about to take over.

She could not allow that. Lie here like a piece of driftwood, waiting for the tide to come back in and claim her after all this work. She could not.

She forced herself to her hands and knees, clambered higher up the jumble of boulders. She slipped once, banging her head again, and felt another wave of blackness threaten her. She vomited into a crevice of rocks, lay gasping for a moment, then dragged herself up, onto the top of the pile.

She was safe here, surely. She could see a listing picnic table in the sand a dozen yards away. A rusting trash can. An old tire. Kids came here to park at night. Someone would come by soon enough.

She saw a jogger far down the beach. She closed her eyes a moment and when she opened them again, she realized he was coming her way. She struggled to her feet, cried out, "Here. Help. Please help." And then fell back again.

The boulder was warm at her cheek. Soft. Comforting. She wasn't sure the man had heard her, but she didn't care. She could rest here.

She was fading in and out now. She heard the pounding of footsteps getting closer. The rasp of a runner's breathing. Knew someone was standing over her and that she was saved. She smiled. She opened her eyes. And then she began to scream.

"Naw, naw, naw," Leon crooned, as he clamped his hand over the woman's mouth. "You don't want to be making all that noise. Wake up all the fishies and whatnot."

She was a fighter, all right, he had to give her that. And good looking, even in the shape she was now. He'd registered that, of course, when he saw her going over the side in the Seville, but he hadn't had a whole lot of time to think about it.

After the crash, he'd pulled the Electra on across the bridge and into some little park there by the water, trying to get it clear in his mind what he'd just done, how he was going to explain *this* one to Alcazar . . .

. . . and about the time he had figured out that it must have been Deal's old lady that he had managed to off, up she pops out of the water like a mermaid, and goes sailing out the channel.

Still a little winded, he glanced back toward the barricade where he'd had to leave the car and start running alongside her. A mile, at least. Most he'd run since the day they'd carried him out of training camp and his knee still hurting like a bitch, like it hadn't had all those years to heal.

"Ow. Shit!" he yelled, having to pull his hand away. She'd managed to get her teeth into some bit of flesh on the web of his thumb, and he had to shift hands, stifle all that screaming again. Of course there was no one around to hear her, but it never hurt to be careful. Just a couple of minutes ago, for instance, he'd been torn: he kept hoping she'd just go under again, but she somehow managed to keep herself afloat. He'd about run out of land to follow her with, had drawn out his pistol, what he referred to as his chief attitude adjuster, was about to blow her out of the water once and for all, take a chance someone way off somewhere might hear rather than let her drift out to sea, and that's when the current lost its grip and she started to make her way toward shore.

He was watching her fight her way in when it happened, when he'd had his revelation, so to speak. Maybe it was watching her fight so hard, or maybe it was just that he had the time to get his thoughts in order, let him see how this might all work out to his benefit. *And yea, the Lord sayeth, chicken shit will become chicken salad, mmmmm-hmmmmm.*

At the very least, it was lucky for him, unlucky for her, he thought, dragging her back down the rocks now to a place where he could keep his footing. She was still trying to bite, pounding at him with her fists, making grunty, angry noises deep in her throat. It wasn't until her feet went thrashing back into the water that her tune changed—her eyes going wide and wild, the sounds she was making suddenly more like screams that couldn't get out.

So maybe she figured out what was coming, he thought. Add smart to being tough and good looking. Maybe she could even read his mind, knew exactly what he had in mind. Wouldn't that be something? Kind of woman you would want, all right. Kind of woman you might do anything to have.

He took a last look around, made sure there were no fishermen, no joggers, no kids out fucking on a beach towel he hadn't noticed. No more screwups today, thank you kindly.

He turned back to her, to those wide, pleading eyes, found himself giving her a kind of sorrowful nod, some kind of apology, he supposed. Then he plunged her head under the water and held her there.

Of course, none of the subs had shown up at the fourplex, so the whole row with Janice had been wasted. Deal walked the entire seven miles to Surf Motors, found Janice's VW parked under a sign that advertised something called a "Lexus." By then, Deal was bone tired, too weary even to stop for dinner. He'd get home, shower, order in a pizza.

He fished out his keys, found the spare for the VW, unlocked the door, which opened with a creak. He'd have to put something on that. Sure, in some of his free time.

He was pawing around in the dying light, searching for the ignition switch when his gaze held on something across the street from the dealership: Homer, the little guy who'd driven him to the job, was sitting on a bus bench, his legs dangling in the air like a kid's. He was leaning back, his head lolling as if he were exhausted too. A tough life for everybody, Deal thought, and knew that he would offer Homer a ride.

Then, as he started the VW, a city bus passed southward down the boulevard. It drew up to the opposite curb, obliterating Deal's view of Homer. When the bus drew away again, Homer was gone, replaced by a tall man in a baggy overcoat, a sleeping bag under one arm, a paper sack in the other. The guy stood wavering near the curb, then began to turn in a slow circle, shaking his head as if he were trying to understand how he had come to that place.

"Good luck, pal," Deal heard himself saying. And hurried away.

He was stopped in a long line of traffic approaching the Mule Pass Bridge. It spanned an outlet from the Intracoastal out to the Atlantic, so it wasn't unusual to encounter a backup while the bridge was raised, even at this hour. He checked his watch. Still, it was taking a hell of a long time to move. Maybe the bridge was stuck open. That'd be par for today's course.

Ahead and behind, other cars were pulling out of line, circling backward. They'd wind through the streets all the way out to Surf, then go north to the Broad Causeway, come back across the Intra-coastal there, drop back down into condo canyon. That would be about twelve miles of driving to get to the very buildings that Deal could see glittering up ahead, separated from him by a few hundred yards of water and some parking lots. The thought of the extra driving made him want to weep.

He missed his CB. If he were in The Hog, he could flip the scanner on, maybe catch somebody talking about the problem with the bridge. Here, in Janice's car, he had "Trevor" introducing some bogus jazz on the evening show. Closer to elevator music than jazz, however. Plenty of horns, lush background vocals, a disco beat. Play Miles Davis, their transformers would melt, he thought. There was a tape jutting partway out of the radio and he pushed it into the player.

There was a moment of silence, then something that sounded like a great wind whooshing over the steppes. The wind calmed, was replaced with the sound of rushing water, maybe a waterfall. Then some random chimes. Deal stared at the radio.

A man's voice came on, soothing, mellow, untouched by the troubles of any world. "Inner peace," the voice intoned, as if a question were being answered, "the keys to inner peace." Deal was dumbfounded. "We recognize our essential self, our strength of being, and from that core . . . " Deal snapped the radio off and the car was silent except for the whirl of the air-conditioning. What the fuck was Janice listening to?

He snatched the tape out, searched for the dome light, remembered he was in a soft top. He twisted in his seat and held the thing up to the taillights glowing in front of him. There was a title for the tape, the script too complex for the bad light. "Aquarian Concepts" was lettered below. An address in California. He tossed the tape aside. For an instant he had the sensation he'd driven the wrong car away from the lot.

Aquarian Concepts. The strength of the inner self. Janice had grown up on a sugar beet farm south of Toledo, Ohio. She'd had two years of college before her folks died in a head-on with a trac-tor trailer rig. She'd come to Florida, worked her way up to office manager for a large realty firm, where she and Deal had met. After they married, she'd stayed on a dozen years, until Deal finally con-vinced her to quit, that things were going well enough for her to take it easy. Maybe, with the stress of the job aside, they'd have kids.

They worked hard at getting pregnant for a couple of years. Fertility charts, sperm counts, plumbing checks, the works. They'd been looking into *in vitro* when Deal's old man died, and they found out from the attorneys how fragile DealCo had become. It had been a long game of catch up ever since. And still no kids.

Deal had expected Janice might want to go back to work, but she hadn't, and even though they could use the money, he'd never suggest it. She'd gotten into her walking and tennis, the occasional class at the community college, and apparently, Aquarian Concepts.

His fault, again. He hadn't helped to give them much of a social life once he'd learned the truth about the business. Oh, they'd made an effort at keeping in contact with their old friends after they moved, but Deal was often on a job until last light, six and seven days a week, working by himself long after the subs had decamped. He'd drag himself home, ready for bed, at most a sand-wich and a beer in front of the television, not interested at all in a trek across town, a dinner with people who'd spent the afternoon on the golf course, the effort to keep up appearances: "How's busi-ness, Deal? How's your hammer hanging? Har, har, har."

The weekly dinners become monthly, then more random, and finally stopped altogether, until it had become Deal and Janice in the condo, a lot of take-out food and movies on the VCR, most of which Deal had never seen the end of. Deal knew things were strained between them, but he held fast to the only principles he knew: put your head down, work hard, make your own luck. Once business turned around, everything else would fall into place.

They'd been talking about going back to the doctors, but Janice was uncertain. The procedures left to them were expensive. And somehow strange and threatening.

And then, miraculously, the fertility charts long forgotten, the determined regimen of sex fallen off into casual encounter, Janice had become pregnant. That's the way it often happened, the doctor told them, when he confirmed it. Stop worrying about what you're doing, things change. Deal had been ecstatic.

He came home with a soccer ball and an armload of green and yellow baby items, ready for either sex. Although Janice hadn't passed her sixth week, Deal had taken to laying his head softly on her stomach, attempting telepathic communication with the baby: "Think about a good college." "Girls are just as tough as boys." "Kick if you hear me." So far, there hadn't been a return message.

Janice had been less enthusiastic. She had begun to worry about her age, her capabilities as a mother, and a great deal about money. Their new health plan was vague on certain aspects of maternity coverage. And the condo was too small, the school district lousy, it took in a bad neighborhood on the mainland . . .

It saddened Deal, but he chalked most of it up to changing hormones. And he really couldn't blame her for worrying about the money. If he'd been able to unsnarl the tangle his old man had created, they'd still have the house, their savings, the perfect bruiser of a health plan.

But Deal was a contractor, not a businessman. The joint ventures, cross-collateralizations, and contingency deals his old man had committed them to were beyond Deal, who knew how to build, and took great pleasure in it.

Deal's approach to the business tangle was simple. Like Alexander, he had lifted a great sword to the knot, and severed the connections with venture capitalists, mall developers, and the others. He'd gone back to building houses, just about the time the bottom of the market fell out. And now he was on his own, a little guy trying to make it, about where his old man had been forty years ago, he guessed. Only times had changed, and it seemed like what he was good at wasn't enough anymore.

He laughed, mirthless. Good old self-pity, he thought. Tired to the bone and getting weepy. That's what you had to fight, the wavering that would lead to self-doubt. No. He had a plan. He would finish the building, as he had told Janice, as he had told Penfield, who was only trying to help. He was not going to sell out, give up, go to work for someone else. He knew what he had to do.

He surfaced from his thoughts, his eyes gradually focusing on the glowing taillights in front of him. The traffic hadn't budged. His head was starting to throb and his neck and back were stiffening in the frigid blast from the A/C, which seemed to have no middle ground. Abruptly, he yanked the wheel of the VW to the right and pulled onto the shoulder, nosing into someone's sea grape hedge.

Out of the car, he felt better at once. The damp heat soothed the knot at the base of his neck and the cramps that had been building in his calves disappeared as he began to walk. He still felt it in his arm, from throwing the kid's keys, but it was a comfortable ache somehow, the kind he remembered after a game—plenty of action in left field, maybe he'd cut down a runner or two trying to score. Yeah, he remembered baseball. Sure. Bring it on down. He'd have a kid to take to the park, tell his war stories to.

He picked up his pace, taking a perverse pleasure in passing the stalled traffic on his left. He'd reach the bridge deck in a minute, see what was going on, while these people would just stew and wonder.

When the damn bridge finally came down again, he'd jog on across to his building, be there when Janice got home. It'd give them a chance to talk. A plan was forming gradually in his mind. Maybe, once the baby was old enough, she could ease her way into the business, bring certain of the skills they'd need to grow. She'd always been able to kick ass at Realty World. She could handle business affairs for the new DealCo.

He was feeling good by the time he reached the bridge. He saw Janice out of Aquarian Concepts, back on ground he recognized. They'd be together, he thought, a team. He was enthused . . . and then just as suddenly was glum: how far apart they must have grown for him to be thinking this way.

Something else was troubling him, too. He had reached the concrete path that flanked the bridge approach ramp, close enough to see the drawbridge wasn't up. The deck was littered with burning safety fuses, and a long string of traffic snaked off from the other side. A crew had set up a bank of portable lights that shone down into the swirling waters of the broad canal.

A generator's roar echoed along the bridge span, and Deal felt the rumble of even heavier machinery through his feet.

When he saw the silhouette of the crane against the backdrop of the distant city skyline, his first thought was that the bridge had caved in.

A tiny drum of panic had sprung up unaccountably inside him, and he hurried onto the steel deck of the drawbridge itself. "Hey," someone yelled, and Deal caught sight of a cop in a reflective jacket coming toward him.

Deal waved as if he were greeting the cop and ducked under a broad yellow ribbon that was meant to cordon off the work area. He was so close now that the glare of the unshielded lights nearly blinded him. The clatter of the generator was deafening, drowning out even the grinding of the winch, the diesel engine of the crane.

Deal reached the rail of the bridge, stopped, blinked until his eyes adjusted to the blue-white flame of light. A section of the rail at his right was gone, where something had ripped through it. The hollow aluminum girders waved crazily out above the dark water, twisted arms reaching for something they'd meant to keep. Deal gripped the rail in front of him, stared down. There were boats down there, divers, men with hard hats, cops. Civilian boats lurked in the background: whalers, a sailboat, a Donzi.

A thick cable was twisting up into the maw of the crane, spitting water and seaweed over the boats. Deal saw a shape congealing underneath the water, like an immense ray he'd once encountered off Pennekamp Reef, the whole floor of the ocean coming up to envelop him.

He heard shouts. "Look out. It's coming up. Get back."

The car broke water then, twisting, glistening in the glare of the lights, draped in tendrils of weed. "Jesus Christ," Deal cried, his insides frozen. "Oh Christ. Jesus Christ."

There was a hand on his shoulder, jerking him back. "Nobody's allowed here, buddy," the cop was saying, but Deal shook him off, turned back to the sight of The Hog, twisting in the air now, gouts of seawater cascading from its open windows, its snout.

"Janice . . . " he screamed, but it was cut off by the cop's arm about his throat, his other hand pressing his head forward, choking him. Stars danced at Deal's eyes. He stamped down hard on the cop's foot, felt something give. He flung the man off him and started toward the broken railing.

He heard footsteps on the steel deck behind him, turned, threw his hand up.

"Wait . . . " he said. Then felt something slam against his head. There was pain, but then there was also peace.

**8**

"You're sure it's your car?"

Deal was sitting on the back step of an emergency van while a technician swabbed something that stung on the back of his head. He looked up at the cop who wanted to know about his car. The cop was in his late twenties, with a thick neck, closely trimmed hair, shoulders that crowded in on his ears. He was giving Deal the same stare he'd worked up for winos he caught pissing in the bushes.

"It's my car," Deal said. Workmen were hooking The Hog to a tow truck a few feet away. The right fender was caved in where it had gone through the railing. The doors still hung open. The leather seats were oozing water and shone in the glare of the portable floodlights.

The cop nodded and jotted something down on his clipboard. "You leave your keys in the ignition, doors unlocked?" he said, still writing. "Anything like that?"

Deal tried to stand, but the technician caught him by the shoulder and pushed him back down. "I'm almost finished," the technician said.

"I'd like you to take these handcuffs off," Deal said to the cop. His arms were twisted behind his back. The cuffs dug into his wrists at the slightest movement.

The cop finished writing, glanced down at him, then over by the police line where the cop who'd hit Deal with his stick was giving a statement to another officer. The cop in front of Deal shrugged.

"You all calmed down, now?"

Deal forced himself to take a deep breath. "Yes," he said. "I'm okay."

"Good." The cop went back to writing on his clipboard.

Deal stood up, this time ignoring the technician's hand on his shoulder. He heard the technician curse and the sound of things breaking on the pavement behind him. Deal strode forward, ramming his chest against the cop's clipboard, driving him backward, off-balance.

"My wife was in that car."

The cop was still back-pedaling. He dropped his clipboard and was scrabbling for the nightstick at his belt. Deal closed in on him, kicked his legs out from under him. The cop went down hard on his back, his breath ripping from him.

There were shouts behind Deal now, the sounds of footsteps drumming over the metal grid of the drawbridge. There was the whine of a motor, and a set of headlights washed over Deal suddenly, over the fallen cop. A car slid to a stop somewhere close by. The whole bridge shuddered.

Deal heard a door open, felt a thick pair of arms encircle him, pull him away from the fallen cop.

"You're in enough trouble," the voice said. Deal caught the scent of spearmint on the man's breath. He did not resist as he was pulled away.

The man dragged Deal back to his unmarked sedan and pushed him into the backseat. He poked a finger in Deal's face. "Now sit there and keep the hell quiet."

He slammed the door and went off toward the group gathered by the cop Deal had knocked over.

The detective was in his late fifties and moved like a bag of heavy parts trying to find a way to mesh. He waved his arms a few times as he spoke to the cop, jerked his thumb toward Deal once or twice. He bent down and retrieved the clipboard, patted the cop on the shoulder. Finally, he sent the cop off with his partner, the slender one whose foot Deal had stomped. The two limped toward their cruiser.

The detective glanced inside The Hog, then made a gesture to the driver of the tow truck. As the truck ground slowly off, the detective came back to the car, got in the driver's seat and turned to stare at Deal through the heavy mesh dividing the seats.

"You're Jack Deal, right?"

Deal closed his eyes, nodded, reopened them.

The detective was shaking his head. "I'm sorry about what happened."

Deal took a breath. "Look. My wife was in that car. She could be out in that water somewhere and you got fuckheads asking me for my driver's license."

The big man nodded. "We're doing what we can. That car went into the water hours ago. We've had boats out there, divers . . . " He broke off as a police helicopter swooped down over the bridge, its searchlights washing the water into a white sheen.

The detective waved at the helicopter. The thing was hovering low above the water now, the water a white and green froth beneath the clattering blades. "You see what I mean?"

Deal turned away, seething. He wanted to slam through the mesh, tear this man to pieces with his teeth.

"Hey," the big man said, softly. "Look here a minute."

Deal found himself turning.

"You're John Deal's boy, right?"

Deal stared. Did he know this man?

"My name's Driscoll. Your dad and I have some history together."

Deal stared at him. Didn't everyone?

Driscoll turned to glance at the helicopter as it circled farther and farther out the channel toward the sea. "When the call came over, I wondered if it wasn't you." He paused. "Your dad built a bunch of these buildings out here, didn't he?"

"I don't remember you," Deal said.

Driscoll gave a mirthless laugh. "'Course you don't, son. No reason you should." His gaze had drifted off into some other place.

Deal leaned forward. "Look, Mr. Driscoll, can you do something for me?"

Driscoll came back from wherever he'd been. He was measuring Deal now. "That depends," he said.

"I'd like you to get these handcuffs off."

Driscoll looked at him as if he'd just remembered what they were doing there together. "Sure," he said. "Let me just get a key from Carlos."

He started out the door, then turned back. "Listen, I'm real sorry what happened, son. We'll find her, if she's out there, okay?"

Deal nodded. He heard the tone in Driscoll's voice. They both knew what that current was like beneath the bridge. "Sure," he said. "Thanks."

Driscoll got out of the car. Deal turned away, feeling the tears hot in his eyes.

Deal pulled into a 7-Eleven just on the other side of the bridge. A guy in dreadlocks was camped on the phone, but when Deal came to stand a foot away, he mumbled something into the receiver and slunk away.

It took Deal two calls to information, but he finally found the number he wanted, a Hallandale exchange. It rang several times before a machine picked up with a squeal. The drawl that followed seemed as familiar as yesterday to Deal: "This here's Cal Saltz and I ain't here. You can leave a message, but I'm not promising anything."

Deal would have hung up, but the beep came while he was still holding the receiver, wondering who he could try next.

"It's Jack Deal," he said, woodenly. It seemed hard to make his voice work. "Something happened and I . . . " he trailed off. What the hell was he doing, talking to a machine.

He was reaching up to cut the connection when he heard another version of Saltz's voice cutting in. "I'm here, for Christ's sake." An electronic howl had set in on Saltz's end. "Hold on. God-damn thing's supposed to turn off."

By the time the howling stopped, Saltz was coughing, great chest-rending hacks that made Deal wince. Finally, he heard the old man's voice again. "Yeah, Johnny. I'm here. What the hell do you want, anyway?"

"Something's happened to Janice," Deal heard himself saying. "I'm feeling a little strange, Cal . . . "

Saltz's voice came back, alert and firm, suddenly, the old Cal, Cal in control, with the world by the tail.

"Where are you, Johnny?"

Deal told him.

"You wait right there. Go inside and get you a beer. I'll be there in twenty minutes."

Deal nodded and hung up. A beer. He glanced inside the 7-Eleven. A woman at the self-serve counter was spreading mustard on a hot dog. Lifting it. Taking a big bite. A little boy beside her had his hand plunged into a bag of Chee•tos. There was an orangish ring around his mouth.

A beer. Sure, Deal thought. A beer.

He took one step toward the entrance and then he was down on his knees, his stomach turning inside out.

9

"It should never have happened, Cal." Deal heard his own voice echoing, as if he were a third person in the room.

"'Course it shouldn't have, Johnny." Saltz was pouring himself another drink. He came out of his little den onto the screened porch of his condo where they'd been sitting for hours.

"I told the bastards. I told them . . ." Deal broke off, glaring at Saltz.

"Those people are *responsible*," Deal said, after a moment. It wasn't the first time he'd said it. Somehow, the words seemed to give him comfort, warmed away some of the iciness that came with every thought of Janice.

"That's right," Saltz said, raising his glass of Scotch. "But you just need to take it easy right now." It was getting light enough to see the beach down below, still deserted at this hour. A bank of clouds was rolling in from the east, and the wind had picked up. It looked like rain.

"They're gonna find her," Saltz said, his gravelly voice doing its best to sound reassuring. "Hell's fire, remember when we thought you drowned that time up in Jupiter? Your old man was crazy, thinking he lost you, and you come floating in at midnight." Cal lifted his glass. "They could call any minute, tell you the same."

Deal nodded, but he wasn't buying into Cal's optimism. Sure, Deal had made it out of a tight spot, once, but he was a good swimmer. Janice needed water wings to take a bath.

"I appreciate you sitting up with me, Cal. But you don't have to bullshit me."

Saltz stared at him a moment. "A man gives up hope, Johnny . . . " he trailed off, shaking his head sadly.

A moment passed. They listened to the surf piling in. Growing louder.

Saltz swirled the ice cubes in his drink. "I used to be on top of the world, Johnny. But I was always doing a lot of stupid things, like I was ashamed to have the money, all the things that went with it. Like I had to piss it all away." He smiled, tilting his drink at Deal. "And I did it, too."

Deal looked away as Saltz continued. "Elizabeth stuck with me all the way, though. That's what kept me going. Then, when she died, I said, well, that's it, there really isn't anything left, go ahead and take the pipe, Cal."

Saltz got up, went inside, opened a desk drawer. He came back out, showing Deal a pistol. "I brought this out here one afternoon a week or so after the funeral and watched the sun go down, had myself a big Scotch, figuring that would be the time."

"So what stopped you?" Deal couldn't imagine Saltz doing himself in, but how could you really tell about anyone?

"I've often thought about that, Johnny. I was sitting there with the pistol, thinking about how a cop told me once what happened to your face if you had your mouth closed around the barrel when you pulled the trigger. Not that the end result was a whole hell of a lot different if you had it open, but the mess and all was a lot worse . . . "

Saltz shook his head, remembering. "And then I thought, Jesus Christ, I'm worried about how I'm gonna *look* after this is all over? And then the next thing, I'm watching some cruise boat heading out of port like Christmas all lit up and thinking how good the Scotch is tasting. And I thought, damned if I won't have another one."

He stared at Deal and shrugged. "So I guess you could chalk it up to whiskey, why I didn't do it. Anyway, the moment passed, or I passed it." He smiled and downed his drink. "Couple big Scotches right about dinnertime. Seems to keep me going."

Deal stared at him. "That's good, Cal. I'm glad you didn't do it."

"Whatever works," Cal said, shrugging.

Deal picked up the drink Saltz had poured him and slugged it down. He didn't feel anything, except empty. Like he was throwing the drink into a big empty drum.

"The whole world wants to cop a plea," Deal said.

"What are you talking about?" Saltz had one shoe off, was massaging his instep.

"Janice is dead, that's what I'm talking about. And it wasn't an accident."

Saltz put his shoe back on. His face looked gray with fatigue. "You need sleep, Johnny. You wake up, things'll be better. You'll be able to think."

Deal shook his head. "I'm thinking just fine." He watched a gull on the boardwalk, tearing at something stuck to the bicycle path, something run over many, many times. He could hear Saltz wheezing, breathing through his nose.

The phone rang and Saltz walked inside to get it. Deal sat woodenly, listening to the murmur of the old man's voice, refusing to let himself hope. A gust of wind blew a fine mist of rain through the screen. The sky was leaden.

It didn't surprise him when Saltz came back with the news: they'd had to call off the search because of the weather. They'd be out again, though, as soon as the front passed through. Boats. 'Copters. Divers. The works.

Deal nodded. He had picked up Cal's pistol, sat cradling it in his hands, staring out at the water.

"Be careful," Saltz said, gently. "That thing's loaded."

"Don't worry, Cal," Deal said. He extended his arm and sighted down the pistol barrel at the gull. Something hung in tendrils from the bird's beak. Deal eased the hammer back to rest. "I'm just letting the moment pass."

Leon Straight put the drink down on his boss's desk, then sat down to wait as Alcazar went on with his wheeling and dealing. Had to be something about money. Leon, who'd done some time, had seen prison dogs find all sorts of shit in the Georgia swamp, in the piney woods, track a possum across a knife blade, but nothing they could do held a candle to this man's scent for cash money.

Sooner or later, they'd get back to the matter at hand, which was his colossal fuck-up. Come on, get it over with, he thought. He had some things of his own to take care of.

The desk backed up on some big windows that looked out on the Intracoastal Waterway, and even though it was a gray day, the glare was hurting Leon's eyes. He turned and stared out the other direction at a big sweep of lawn surrounded by thick hedges. There was a golf course on the other side of the hedges, although Leon had never seen it. There was a gardener working out on the lawn, clipping a bush into a weird oblong shape. Why wouldn't you just let the damn thing grow, Leon wondered.

"We are very, very close now," his boss was saying. "An item or two, nothing more."

Leon felt the glance that came his way. What the fuck, it wasn't his fault.

"I understand, but put it out of your mind. We will meet the deadline. I assure you. Absolutely." Alcazar replaced the phone and turned to face him fully.

"Now, Leon," he said, "I believe I've explained to you about the complexity of this endeavor. How timing affects our efforts."

Leon nodded. He turned away from the gardener. Forget the words. He knew Alcazar had every dime on the line. That's what he was trying to say.

Alcazar glanced down at his desk, gathering his patience. When he looked up at Leon, he seemed almost relaxed. "Over the past eleven months, I have accomplished something that no business-man in this city could have dreamed of. Through subordination agreements, option arrangements, and outright purchase, I now control the largest, the most important block of commercial real estate in this city." He stared off, wistfully. "It's almost a shame that no one can be allowed to learn of it."

Agreement and arrangement, Leon thought. He knew about some of those, all right. Mmmmm-hmmmm. If you knew how, you could buy land for a penny on the dollar. "I was thinking, maybe I could get a job in real estate," Leon said.

Alcazar stared at him for a moment. He pursed his lips. "I'm sure you could, Leon. Someday."

Leon stared at him. Leon was not supposed to be smart enough to know his boss was fucking with him. Like he didn't notice it was Alejandro, guy with the brain of a pea, always trailing along with Alcazar. Alejandro with his haircut and his clothes, always taking the choice trips, stay downtown whenever he could and Leon all the time up to his ass with the tough stuff. That's just the way it was.

Leon using the same barber. Buying the selfsame suits from the selfsame dispenser of hot suits, and still a party of the wrong tribe. Blood thicker than water. Hmmm-hmmm. That's what he ought to say to Alcazar. But what good does it do, talking about the cross you have to bear.

"Thing I don't understand," Leon said, "is what you want to do with this bunch of property. Most of it people wouldn't want any-way."

"Someone is going to want it very, very much, Leon. Be assured of that."

Leon shook his head. "Look to me like a war zone around there."

"Well," Alcazar said. "That's something that you're going to have to acquire, Leon. A sense of vision. I've invested everything I have, and a good deal that I don't. Because I can see what will become of it. Papers will be signed, men will shake hands, and a small fortune will become a colossal one."

"I hope you're right," Leon said. "I had a small fortune once, my signing bonus. Pissed it away like a champ."

"I am right," Alcazar said, patiently. He gave Leon another look. They were through dicking around. "But, now I would like for you to explain it to me. Very carefully. Try to make me understand how it happened you could not carry out such a simple assignment. How you could kill his *wife?*"

Leon liked it, seeing Alcazar almost out of control like that. Playing like he had it all absolutely together, we got all the time in the world, and underneath, ready to lose it. Yeah, this could be some of your executive burnout percolating there. Get all stressed out and careless, give old Leon the opportunity he'd been looking for.

Leon shrugged and had a slug of his own drink. Four flavors of Gatorade mixed together. His power drink. Send you out of the blocks strong, no matter how hot it was. And it got hot as a motherfucker in this part of the country.

"Sometimes things don't work out." Leon finished the rest of his drink and stole a glance toward the bottles arrayed on the top of the bar. Almost out of the cherry flavor. Shit.

When he turned back, his employer was pointing a finger at him, jabbing it with every word. "Leon. Don't. Ever . . . ." The man stopping, getting his breathing under control.

How'd he like that finger snapped off, stuck up his ass, Leon wondered idly, and his arm too, right after it? Leon couldn't do it, though. Not just yet.

"You do *not* tell me what doesn't work," his employer said. "You are to come in here and tell me you completed the task you were sent to do. That is what you tell me."

Leon nodded, sucking on an ice cube, then cracking it between his molars. The gardener was standing back, staring at his bush, cocking his head this way and that like he was working on some goddamn work of art.

"So the bitch had an accident. Happens all the time in this city."

Alcazar pinched the bridge of his nose between his manicured fingers. "First, the incident with Reyes, now this. Your carelessness is bound to draw attention, Leon, and that is something I must not have . . . "

"That Reyes thing was Alejandro's fault. *He* was supposed to be watching him."

Alcazar stared at him in disbelief. Finally, he turned away, shaking his head. "I am surrounded by idiots," he said.

He stayed that way for a long time, like maybe he was studying the same goddamn bush the gardener was in love with.

"So what you want me to do with this Deal?" Leon asked.

Alcazar shot him a vicious look, then turned back to his bush. "Thanks to you, we must let the matter rest," he said. "Perhaps when the man has passed his grieving, he will listen to reason yet."

"Okay by me," Leon said, and ambled out. And it *was* okay. He could use some time to himself.

Deal stood at the bridge railing, staring down at the roiling green current. It was late afternoon, the light almost gone. The rain had stopped, but the sky was still leaden, more like Maine's than Florida's. A yellow police line ribbon was stretched across the gaping hole where The Hog had ripped through nearly twenty-four hours before.

The cops, the boats, the generators were all long gone. They were sorry. All very sorry. Deal counted the orange pylons set up to shield other motorists from the shattered rail. Five little cones. Nothing much to distinguish the site from another metro construction project, now.

Cal stood nearby, watching warily, as if he thought Deal might be ready to jump.

"It'll be a month before they get around to fixing this railing," Deal said, not looking at him.

Cal rolled a toothpick he was chewing into the corner of his mouth. "What's on your mind, Johnny?"

Deal shook his head. He'd been thinking about the baby. Not really a baby, of course. No bigger than a fingerling or a seahorse. Just one more organism returning to the sea, now. He would not think about it. He could not allow it. He willed his mind to trace the patterns in the swirling water below.

He had stopped in this same spot, stared down from the same railing on sunny days, coming back from a jog, or killing time on a lazy Sunday. Stare down and you might think you were looking at gentle waters swirling past the pilings. Fish from one of the abutments beneath the span, and if nothing's doing, you're getting bored and hot, you might even find yourself thinking about swimming across, trying your luck on the other side.

It would, however, be a serious mistake. The water was seventy feet deep in spots, the current impossible to imagine, unless you found yourself in it.

Deal had, once. Not here at Mule Pass, but at Boca Chica Cut, well to the north, where the tide sliced through the outer beaches to join the Intracoastal Waterway, near Jupiter.

It had been that brutal July afternoon Cal had referred to earlier. Deal and Flivey Penfield had been working on their tans atop a dune in front of Flivey's parents' beach house, drinking the Hamm's they'd bought with a phony ID at the Elbo Room, waiting for happy hour to begin at Dirty Dick's. They'd let anybody in at Dirty Dick's.

Deal stared across the channel that separated the islands into North and South Banquette. You could see the blue-and-white striped awnings of Dick's, which fronted on the marina tucked away on South Banquette, a quarter mile away.

"Let's swim across," Deal said.

Flivey propped himself up on his elbows, moved his sun visor off his face and squinted eastward at the ocean where a few die-hard surfers fooled around in the slack tide waves. "England or Africa?" he asked.

"Across the channel to Dick's," Deal said.

Flivey fell back to the sand and covered his eyes again. "You're fucking crazy. We might make the Azores," he said. "We could never make it to Dick's."

"I don't see why not," Deal said.

"The current," Flivey said, arranging himself deeper into the sand. "This isn't Stiltsville."

He was referring to the place where they'd spent the previous week, framing up a house, part of a bizarre development rising up on pilings from the shallows of Biscayne Bay, five miles out from

11

shore. It was like working on an oil rig. Bored silly, Deal had suggested swimming home one evening. Flivey paced him in their Boston Whaler for two miles before it got dark and Deal finally climbed in the boat.

Deal punched open the last of the warm beers and pulled off the thong that held the church key around his neck. He tossed it onto Flivey's stomach, who swatted the hot metal away into the sand.

"Asshole," Flivey muttered.

During the school year, Flivey and he roomed together at Florida State. Summers, they carried hod, framed walls, mixed mud on Deal's father's building sites. Flivey's father was an attorney, a genteel Southerner who'd come down to the big city to make his way. Long before the elder Penfield had become one of the city's movers and shakers, he and Deal's father had hooked up in a land deal, and they'd become fast friends, joined together at the hip by Jack Daniel's, as Deal's mother put it. Holidays since he could remember, the two families would converge at the Penfields' up the coast or at the Deals' down south in the Keys. This time, he and Flivey had come up a bit early, getting a head start on the Fourth of July weekend.

"Swim'd be good for that leg," Deal said, staring at the purple zippers that boxed Flivey's kneecap. Flivey had started the last three games at flanker their sophomore year, then finished his career when a Florida lineman put him down with a late hit along the sidelines. Deal, who rode the bench as a fourth string linebacker, despite the baseball coach's objections, had heard the knee burst from ten yards away. Deal had run to take one look at Flivey's twisted leg, then caught up with the lineman, who was trotting off toward midfield. Deal tore the Florida player's helmet off and hit him in the face with it, which started a riot. Someone hit Deal, then someone else—someone very, very big—rode him to the ground. Deal put his right arm out to break the fall. And heard the same terrible sounds as when Flivey's knee had blown.

He and Flivey got adjoining beds in the university hospital, shared the same orthopedist, heard the same bad news together. At least they'd had plenty of time to study, after that.

"You got no hair," Deal said, tracing the scars that laced his shoulder.

Flivey settled deeper in the sand. "I have brains," he said.

Deal nodded. Sometimes he envied Flivey. Nothing showy, nothing to prove. But give him twenty minutes at Dirty Dick's, just sitting on a stool looking around, he'd have half a dozen girls eager to buy him drinks.

Deal turned back and stared across the channel. It was a six-mile drive to Dick's. Three out to the highway, most likely a wait at the drawbridge across the channel, three more back down to Dick's. All of it in holiday traffic.

He gunned the rest of the beer, heard it singing in his ears. He was rocking on his heels, then was up, across the blazing ribbon of sand, clambering over the boulders that lined the channel from erosion.

There was an old black man sitting just above the water line, a spinning rod propped in the rocks at his feet. The rod tip bowed and danced but the old man seemed unconcerned. When Deal passed him, he glanced up, stared a moment, then turned away, as if nothing a white person might do could surprise him.

Deal stood watching a Chris-Craft cutting along the middle of the channel, headed out to sea. It was planing off the water, kissing the waves with whumps that he could hear clearly above the racket of the engine and the crashing of the ocean on the jetties that ran out with the channel a half mile or so from land.

Deal had a momentary image of his head popping out of a wave just as the boat was slamming down, but it didn't bother him. Anything was possible, but the odds were against it. There wasn't another boat in sight.

"Hey, man!" Deal turned and shaded his eyes. Flivey stood above him, at the top of the jumbled boulders. His angular frame was a dark shadow against a nearly white sky. "Seriously. You can't do this."

Deal grinned, waved, dove backward off his rock. As he hit the water, he saw Flivey turn and run back toward the beach.

A dozen strokes or so from the bank, Deal felt the current piling into him from his right, but it was nothing he hadn't expected. He was a strong swimmer, had more than once ridden a rip tide for the hell of it, go out a half a mile or more, paddle back in and start again. And the injury that had ended his baseball career was only strengthened by his swimming. But now, when he turned to glance over his shoulder at the shore, he felt a nudge of surprise. The shape of the old black man had already receded fifty yards up the channel from where he'd pushed off.

Good sense should have told Deal to turn around then, but he had started something. He locked himself into five minutes of stubborn crawl before he checked again.

His shoulders had begun to ache and a fire was building in his lungs. He raised his head and tossed the wet hair out of his eyes as a huge swell lifted him. He had time to catch a heart-stopping glimpse: he was nearly halfway across the channel, but he'd already been swept out even with the end of the jetty, and the shore had become a distant ribbon. Then, the wave shifted and the bottom fell out of his ride.

He tumbled beneath the surface, swallowing water, his lungs ready to burst, his mind on fire: the current was incredible, far stronger than anything he'd ever encountered. He was already a half mile out from shore and it seemed he was picking up steam. Something slimy had wrapped itself around his legs—just seaweed, he told himself—but he kicked frantically, as if it were arms pulling him down toward the dark.

He stroked hard against the turbulent water and felt himself steady, then begin to move up. The light appeared above him in a vague nimbus, then as a shimmering mirror, and then, his head broke the surface and he could finally breathe.

He struggled up the crest of a swell, gasping, and spun around toward the shore, his heart seizing momentarily as he saw how far he had come. The skeleton of the unfinished condo tower on North Banquette was a tiny Tinkertoy on the horizon, swallowed by a wall of green as quickly as it had come into view. Deal had just enough time to catch a second breath before the water fell on him and hurled him down. As he went under, he would have sworn he heard his name.

He was ready for the plunge this time, and rode down with the water's force until it finally relented and he could scissor back toward the surface with easy, measured strokes. He could ride this current, he told himself, until it faltered, and it would, even if it was a mile, or two, and so long as he did not wear himself trying to fight it, he could make his way back in.

He came up easy this time, pushing through a tangle of seaweed and lobster floats, wondering if he could feel a slackening in the swells. Then he heard it clearly, someone calling "Deal!" and his heart went heavy.

He struggled up the side of a swell and kicked hard to lift himself out of the water. Sure enough, there was Flivey, a hundred feet back, pounding the water like the awkward swimmer he was, his good buddy come to save him. Deal envisioned the long swim back, carrying Flivey all the way.

He caught his breath, then scissored up again, waving. "I'm all right, Flivey," he called. Flivey stopped swimming and began to tread water like a man jumping on hot stones.

"Over here," Deal called. He stole a glance toward shore. The light was already going, the dunes a faint sliver of white.

Flivey saw him finally and his face lit up. "You stupid bastard," he called.

"Just ride with it," Deal shouted. "We'll be fine." Flivey waved and started to paddle his way. A swell rose between them and Deal shook his head. He was tired, but if Flivey could just keep himself afloat, they could make it. He pushed himself over the swell, already rehearsing the words that would reassure his friend, then caught his breath.

Flivey was gone. Deal spun about, searching the water.

Maybe he'd misjudged the angle. But he made an entire circle, then a second, before he was sure. He sucked in air and dove, driving himself down deep until he couldn't see, until his lungs were ready to burst. He kicked wildly to the surface, gasped, dove again.

On his third pass, he thought he felt something, but it turned out to be a chunk of carpeting, gelled to the consistency of flesh by algae and the endless surge of the tide. He cast the thing loose in disgust, and popped up from the surface, screaming "Flivey! Flivey . . ." Then a swell dropped on him and he caught sight of a four-by-four ringed with a crust of barnacles plunging toward his skull.

When he came to, he was sliding along a trough in calm seas, his arm clamped over the four-by-four in a death grip. The sky was dark now, the lights he saw on the distant shore could have been any lights, anywhere. "Flivey!" he called, and felt the pain throbbing in his face.

He raised his hand gingerly to his broken cheek. His nose was a ragged flap of flesh.

"Flivey!" he called again, knowing he was alone.

Once more. "Flivey!" He closed his eyes. There would never be an answer.

When he opened his eyes again, Cal was at his side, pulling him from the railing. "Got to get you home, Johnny."

Deal glanced across the water at the building where he and Janice lived. Had lived. "Home?" he repeated. It seemed an impossible concept. He stared down once more at the water, then gave in and let Cal guide him toward the car.

12 Deal found himself in his condo, wandering through the rooms, a drink in his hand. A day later? Two days? Five? He wasn't really sure.

The television in the living room was playing, a promo for a talk show: a tearful woman holding a photograph she said was of her son. MIA in Southeast Asia for twenty years, but someone had come up with this photo last week, the picture so fuzzy it could have been anybody with a beard and hair, maybe there was a UFO in there, too.

Deal found the remote, clicked off the set. Chin up, pal. Anything's possible. Sure. Just like Flivey. They never found him, either. He took a swallow from his glass.

Sure, Deal. Flivey's voice. *Any minute now, Janice and I will both come floating in with fishies in our hair, we'll go to Dirty Dick's and celebrate.*

Deal finished his drink, noticed he had some mail in his hand. A circular with pizza coupons. A postcard that said he'd won a free hour's session with a doctor of chiropractic. An envelope with his name in pencil, a child's awkward scrawl, no return address. He found himself opening that one.

There was a card inside, a glossy picture of Surf Motors on the outside, "Congratulations on your new purchase," printed on the inside. Someone had crossed through the printing and penciled a brief message at the bottom: "I heard what happened. I'm sorry.— Homer." Good old Homer, Deal nodded, Homer guarding the door, watching his father toss the bones.

There had been other notes of sympathy. A few calls from the old crew in the Shores. A turkey someone had sent over from a deli, still on the counter, growing a greenish fur.

Deal hadn't returned any of the calls. In fact, he didn't remember speaking to anyone, except for Cal, who'd handled the few details. Amazing how simple life became when you had no family and no real friends.

From Cal he had learned there was a nominal waiting period when people disappeared. Seven years before you could settle an estate. But in this case, there were special circumstances. And there was no estate. Deal could probably get a declaration, hold a funeral service, if he wanted. "How about a wake?" Deal had said, waving a bottle at Cal. "Why don't we have an Irish wake. Or one of those fucking New Orleans jazz funerals, up and down Biscayne." On and on until even Cal had gotten tired of his act and had gone out, mumbling to himself.

Well, too fucking bad, Deal thought. He propped Homer's card on the dinette counter and looked around the place with the interest of a distant friend come to visit:

A kitchen with avocado appliances and a balcony overlooking the Intracoastal, ten floors down; a dining nook with a glass-and-wicker table, wicker chairs; the living room opening onto the same balcony.

If you sat on the couch, you missed the view of the water. All you got was a shot of the condo fifty yards away, a guy out on his balcony in his undershorts, right now, watering a bougainvillea vine. That was okay, Deal thought. Life goes on. The guy straightened, scratched his balls, and went back inside.

Deal stood up. There was a painting over the couch. A bright watercolor of a village high in the Andes. He and Janice had picked it out together at the Grove art fair one year after he'd finished a series of luxury duplexes on the water. The artist was Peruvian, a likable guy who spent six months in South America painting, six months doing the art fairs in the United States. He painted places "only you cannot drive to." He hiked far up into the mountains, used the local stream water to mix his paints. *"Muy autentico,"* he had said, sweeping his arm over his work. Authentic enough for Deal and Janice, anyway.

They carted the painting home, invented a Peruvian dish to cook, got drunk on Chilean wine. Janice in a T-shirt, leaning over the couch, her back to him, marking a spot for the painting to hang. Deal coming up behind her, reaching under the shirt, marking a better spot. Janice backing into him. It had taken hours to hang the painting.

Deal rolled off the couch, his chest on fire. They'd spent a year or two after that planning a trip to Peru. Something they'd never got around to doing.

He went into the bedroom. Stopped. All the drawers were out of Janice's dresser. A series of boxes, some full, a couple still trailing arms and legs of clothing. He'd dumped the clothes, sealed most of the boxes, but had to stop when he pushed down on a mound of blouses and her scent rushed up over him like a cold ghost.

That sent him to the kitchen for a drink. Which was now nearly gone. He gunned the rest, put the glass in the windowsill, walked out and down the hall, glanced in the other bedroom, which had been his office until recently. He'd started packing it up the day Janice came home from the doctor.

"I'm pregnant, Deal."

Smiling, but still worried. She'd been reading the books, how the odds tip once you pass thirty-five. Standing there in a cotton print dress, a tropical swirl of fronds and blossoms, her tan bringing out the freckles, her hair bleached from the sun. She could have been twenty-five.

Deal out of his mind happy, of course.

"Good grief, Deal. It's too early to tell if it's a boy or a girl."

"Everything's fine. We're both fine." Her laugh. One of the great let-it-all-go laughs. He found champagne. "Yes, you can do that. You won't hurt the baby. Oh, yes. Do that. And that . . . "

Deal stood in the doorway of the second bedroom, staring at the carpet where they'd ended up. Twinges of pain at his elbows, his knees.

He shook his head to clear the memory. Stared at all the things still there in the room, waiting. Three gallons of frost green latex, one of sunburst yellow, for the trim, still stacked in the corner. Two prints leaning against the wall, one a Leroy Neiman of a tennis player, an overhead in a shower of paint, the other a reproduction of Degas's tiny dancer. "Hey," Deal said, the day he brought it all home, "we're going androgynous. I don't even *want* to know the sex."

Deal turned from the room, his gut aching. How in God's name did people *handle* these things? He moved off down the hallway toward the kitchen. He'd *had* to move them into a condo, hadn't he. If they were still in the house, he would just set a match to it, walk away. Maybe he'd just walk away anyhow. Yes, he thought, he could always do that. In the kitchen, he found the gin.

"I'd like to see Thornton Penfield, please." Deal spoke into the steel-clad intercom in the receptionist's booth.

The woman stared out from behind an inch of glass, appraising him. Her booth was a sealed island in a vast marble-clad lobby. A rent-a-cop lounged against a wall in a corner. He was probably wired into the booth, too.

"I'm Jack Deal," he added, in his calmest voice.

The woman jotted something down on a pad and picked up a phone. Deal watched her lips move. He couldn't hear her voice, but he saw what she was saying: "Some cowboy wants to see Mr. Penfield."

He'd taken a course in lip-reading one summer when he was twelve. It was offered as a service to the deaf, their family members, and volunteers. That was in the days before signing had become the mode of choice. Deal had no connections with anyone who was deaf—he'd simply read a spy thriller where the hero foiled a Russian plot by being able to read lips.

Deal badgered his parents until they found the course and permitted him to sign up. It had become a talent chiefly of use during sporting events when the cameras closed in on coaches disputing calls with referees. Deal had learned that you could scream "You ignorant cocksucker" into the ear of a referee not two feet away and not be thrown out of a game.

The secretary twiddled with her pen, waiting for a response on the other end of the line. Deal glanced down at his clothes. A plaid cotton shirt, jeans, woven belt, lizard boots worn soft and straining at the outersoles. His standard on-the-job attire. He'd thrown on the clothes out of habit.

The secretary wore a blouse with about three yards of paisley printed silk and a black wool skirt that curved over her knees. She had her legs crossed under the tight fabric and dangled an Italian pump off her printed stockinged toes. Her hair was cut mannishly—there were diamond studs in her ears and a matching stickpin in the flouncy tie of her blouse. Deal could make his condo payment for two months on what this woman was wearing.

Finally, someone must have spoken on the other end. The receptionist lifted her hooded eyes to Deal. "You can go up. The forty-third floor. Take the far elevator." Her voice crackled from some unseen speaker as she jabbed her pen in the direction of the rent-a-cop.

"Thanks," Deal said. He stood there until she looked up at him. "I'm actually a Seminole Indian."

She was still gaping at him as he walked off.

Thornton Penfield's office looked out over Biscayne Bay, offering a panorama all the way from Williams Island on the north to Key Biscayne on the south. It was so clear on this afternoon that Deal could make out the tiny dot of Soldier Key several miles beyond that. Tiny bright flags that were actually sail boats dotted the sweep of water in between.

Deal had been here rarely since his father had died. Once for the postmortem of DealCo, a few months later when his mother died, wasted away without Deal's father to fret over. He was aware that Penfield, who'd been Senator Layton's campaign manager, who'd chaired the state racing commission, who now was point man for the baseball group, had far bigger fish to fry, and it always made him feel uncomfortable, as if he were trading on his father's friendship. Today, however, he'd made an exception. This was different.

Penfield stood at one of the floor-to-ceiling windows staring down at the Metro Seaport, shaking his silver-maned head sadly. "It's a terrible tragedy, Johnny. Just terrible." He raised his eyes to look out over the glittering horizon. "That ocean out there looks beautiful, doesn't it? But it's not. It's not beautiful at all."

Deal cleared his throat. Penfield was lost in his own memory, inviting Deal to come along. But he didn't want to rehash things. Couldn't rehash things. It was important to nourish the numb feeling he'd been cultivating.

Deal picked up a framed photo from the table beside him: Penfield wearing a ball cap beneath a banner, "Think Tropics Baseball." He was hoisting a glass of champagne with a bunch of other men in three-piece suits. Deal wondered if they added up to a hundred and thirty million.

Penfield saw what he was looking at. "Bunch of foolish old men, aren't we?"

Deal shook his head. "I wouldn't say that."

Penfield stared at him. "If Flivey'd had good sense, he'd have stayed off that football field, played baseball instead," he said.

Deal felt uncomfortable. "I don't know. It all comes to the same thing, Mr. Penfield. They're just games."

"Not baseball." Penfield shook his head. "I'm referring to the history, to the purity of it. The simplicity. No clock. No X's and O's. Two foul lines. A fence. Nine men out there where you can see them, everything they're doing."

He gestured out the window as if there were a diamond laid out before them, floating in the air. "You know this for yourself, John. All the calls are simple. You hit or you don't hit. No yellow flags or whistles. It's fair or it's foul." He turned to Deal, solemn. "It's what we need more of down here in the tropics. We've got too much of the glitzy and showy, too many things that grow in the dark and send out their shoots and get all tangled up. Roll a log over, you don't know what you're going to find cooking up beneath it."

Deal stared at him, wondering what was going on. Penfield had always been a politician, but he surely didn't need Deal's vote. "I expect there's some money in it, too," he said.

Penfield regarded him a moment, his enthusiasm dampened. "Yes." He seemed almost apologetic. "That's one of the inducements we present to potential investors. You hear about the average salary approaching a million dollars, that television revenues will be cut in half the next time around." He waved his hand in dismissal. "But the point is, even the most dismal franchise appreciates. Look at that pathetic Oakland club. In 1979, they drew about four thousand fans a game. They had a total of seventy-five season ticket holders. *Seventy-five!*"

Penfield's voice had risen at the indignity of it. He seemed to sense he was getting carried away and took a moment to calm down. "The man who makes Levi pants bought that club a dozen years ago, Johnny. And he paid about thirteen million dollars for it. People thought he'd lost his mind." Penfield glanced at him. "Today you couldn't buy that team for a hundred and twenty-five million." He nodded sagely, as if Deal were a prospect.

"No matter what anyone tells you, a professional sports franchise is a mortal lock as an investment, John. Not to mention what it would do for the local economy as a whole. Urban revitalization, inducement of outside investment, ancillary development near the ball park . . ." he shook his head. "Hundreds and hundreds of millions of dollars, John."

Deal shrugged. "Then you shouldn't have any trouble raising the cash."

Penfield gave a mirthless laugh. "You might not think so. But like they say, it takes money to make money. In this case, about a hundred and fifty million, with everything taken into account. In demonstrable, liquid assets. No leveraged buy-outs for the commissioner, I'm afraid." He raised his hands helplessly. "And there are other obstacles. The makeup of the ownership group has to be just right. We had a fellow with a string of hotels in the Bahamas wanting to come on board, but they *gamble* at those places so we couldn't use him."

He shook his head sorrowfully. "They worry about your stadium, your weather, what kind of hot dog mustard you plan to use, just every damned thing. You read the papers."

Deal nodded. "I've got every confidence in you, Mr. Penfield."

"I wish I could be so sure," he said, staring back out the big windows at his imaginary diamond. "It'd be a wonderful thing for our community. A healing thing. Hispanics, Anglos, blacks . . ." he trailed off, envisioning some happy world buying itself a Coke at the ball park, Deal supposed. If he'd been uncertain about this visit in the first place, he was now ready to slip out without a word, leave Penfield to his dreaming.

Deal stared back down at the picture, the collection of men in their ball caps and suits, their arms thrown around one another in a paroxysm of smiles and bonhomie and well-being. No, he thought. He had begun this. He would see it through.

He put the photo down. "I want to go after them," he said, quietly.

Penfield turned from the windows. "Go after whom, Johnny?" His voice was distracted, as if he'd never thought there might be some real purpose to their meeting.

Deal tried to find the man's eyes, but Penfield was a shadow against the bright backdrop of ocean. "Surf Motors."

Penfield's head was shaking again, this time in puzzlement. "What are you talking about?"

Deal fought against a sudden wave of uncertainty. It had seemed so clear in his mind, but now he would have to explain the logic of it to someone else.

He felt his resolve slipping and glared up at Penfield. "I took my car in the day of the accident. Janice picked it up for me. It was the fourth goddamn time they were supposed to fix the goddamn brakes." Angry was better. It warmed him.

Penfield thought about it for a moment. He came around his massive desk and sat down in one of the green leather wing chairs beside Deal, reached out for Deal's shoulder.

"I'll be glad to help any way I can, John." Penfield squeezed his arm. "But you know this isn't going to bring her back."

Deal watched a steel cable materialize outside the window nearest him. The thing slithered straight down, matched by another a dozen feet to his right. Then a man's head rose over the sill, followed by his shoulders, his hips. A window washer, or a painter— Deal couldn't tell which—rising up on a motorized scaffold. The man stared sightlessly in through the smoked glass and glided swiftly out of sight. *Hey, Deal,* Flivey called from somewhere. *Tell him we're already back. Tell him you talk to us every day.*

Deal turned to Penfield. "I'm aware of that," he said evenly.

Penfield raised his hands in a conciliatory gesture. "I'm sorry," he said.

"I know you're busy, and I don't have a lot of money . . . "

"Don't be silly, John." Penfield shook his head. "I just want you to be certain of your feelings. These things can be very difficult to prove." He paused, his expression pained, searching for the right words. "If it *is* a question of money . . . "

Deal fought down his anger. Penfield was only being an attorney. What was he supposed to think? "Look, Mr. Penfield. The bastards were supposed to fix my car. Four times. They didn't do what they were supposed to do, and Janice is dead because of it."

Deal broke off, forcing himself to calm. "I bullied her into picking up the car, so in a way, it's my fault. I accept that. But I've made this decision. Those people over at Surf, they don't give a crap what happened. For them, today is just another day, the citizens coming in buying their cars, leaving their cars to get fixed, and the guys who run the place are shoveling the money into the bank and doing whatever else they like to do. Maybe they're even decent guys, with families and all that, they like to go to the ball park . . . "

Deal felt himself choking up. He had to turn away from Penfield for a moment, chew on the inside of his lip, draw blood, before he could go on. "You're right. There's nothing I can do to bring Janice or the baby back. But this is something I can make happen. I can force these people to admit what they did was wrong. I can make them account for it."

Deal paused and took a deep breath. He folded his hands in his lap. He looked at Penfield. "The alternative is I'm going to become irrational."

Penfield started to laugh, but when he saw the expression on Deal's face, it turned into a kind of strangled moan. Penfield cleared his throat and began again. "We can try. The trend is away from the larger awards, but circumstances such as these might influence a jury . . . "

Deal was about to get up, storm out of the office. Leave the old bastard to his white-lined fair-and-foul bullshit. He would never be able to explain it the way he intended.

"Mr. Penfield," he said, keeping his voice as steady as he could. "It's not the money."

Penfield gave him a hooded glance, then stood and went to his credenza to pour a glass of water.

Deal stared at him, searching for words.

Last winter, on his way downtown, he'd been driving past one of the shallow lakes near the airport expressway. Some loony on a pontoon boat way out in the water. The guy had furled the sails so he could run up a banner: "I ACCUSE. US ATTORNEY LEHTINEN, A RACIST THIEF." Ten-foot letters that backed up rush hour traffic for miles. It turned out the loony was a parolee, a white-collar drug dealer named Diaz who'd been a developer in a former life. He'd had his house, his cars, his planes confiscated after his conviction. All things Diaz claimed he'd earned in his straight life. Shortly afterward, his wife had left him. His kids wouldn't speak to him. So the guy got hold of this boat and painted a sign.

The cops tried to roust him, but he was far enough out in the water to avoid any applicable law. Every morning, every evening, out there snarling traffic, pissing everybody off, the papers hounding the U.S. attorney's office—"Just why did you take the poor guy's house," etc.—until a winter squall whipped across the shallow water and flipped the pontoon upside down on top of its owner. The guy lived, but he'd been underwater a long time before they fished him out. He was still on feeding tubes at Jackson.

Penfield finished his water and sat down behind his desk. Deal met his gaze. His best rational gaze. Deal heard his own voice, even, logical. The closest thing to warm in his veins since the accident.

"I want to nail the bastards, make them admit what they did." His voice was rising, but he couldn't help it. "I have to do something, Mr. Penfield. I have to *do* something."

Deal felt his fingertips digging deeply into the soft leather arms of the chair. He took another deep breath and waited for Penfield's reaction.

Penfield sank back in his chair. He made a sound in his throat that might have started out as a laugh. He stared up at the ceiling, drumming his fingers against the silk tie on his chest. Deal noticed the pattern: dozens and dozens of tiny yellow men each holding a golf club aloft, about to strike.

Finally, Penfield raised his hands in surrender. "I'll do what I can. I don't want you to expect too much, but I'll do what I can."

"Good," Deal said. "That makes me feel very good."

Penfield studied him carefully. "You haven't changed much, John . . . " He paused. "Flivey was always calling you 'the bulldog.'" Penfield's eyes clouded over momentarily. "He thought the world of you."

"I thought the world of him, Mr. Penfield." Deal stood and put his hand on Penfield's shoulder. "I appreciate your doing this for me."

Penfield reached up and took his hand. "You did everything you could that day, John. You nearly killed yourself trying to save him."

Deal met his gaze for a moment, then turned away.

Penfield squeezed his hand. "I told your father how much it meant to me. I told him many times, John. I don't know that I ever told you."

Deal nodded, but he did not trust himself to meet the man's gaze. "You didn't have to, Mr. Penfield."

They were quiet then, Penfield staring out his big windows into the past, Deal at his side.

There was a big print hung on the wall behind Penfield's desk, an aerial photo of a bank of spoil islands surrounded by miles of wide scarlet shrouds drifting lazily in the water. Christo. A major piece of environmental art that had caused a shit storm of controversy in the city council chambers and elsewhere. Flivey had scoffed at the enterprise—why would you want to spend all that time and money on something that would just get taken down the next week, he wondered. It didn't do Deal any good trying to stand up for the notion.

Deal glanced out the window. Up there past Williams Island you could see those same spoil islands, shroudless now, unless you wanted to count the tons of trash that would be bobbing along their tide lines. Maybe Flivey had been right, after all. What the hell good *was* the grand gesture?

But let it come to something, Deal prayed. Let it come to something.

They stared out over the water, mourning together.

Leon Straight tooled his BMW down Fitzgerald-Bush Boulevard, past the Opa-Locka City Hall, shaking his head at the building, which had been constructed during the 1930s to resemble some kind of camel-jockey palace. Turrets and spires and domes all over the place, over it and a bunch of other buildings in the downtown, making it look like Lawrence of the fucking A-rabs, lost in the middle of Florida.

There'd even been a lot of fuss in the papers recently, museum people wanting the county to put up money, refurbish all the shit. Leon couldn't believe what white people were capable of sometimes. They should pray all this would fall down and blow away, save everybody some face.

He turned off the main street, went down a block past a gas station, a boarded up bakery, and a machine shop, pulled into a vacant lot where a grocery store used to be. The store had been a riot target, had still been smoldering embers when Leon first came here, flunked out of college for the last possible time, and desperate for help.

On the other side of the lot was an antiquey two-story house with a brass LAW OFFICES sign on the porch, lots of gingerbread trim and stained-glass windows, as out of place as the city hall was in what had become a black man's suburb, essentially. Kind of house more common to a yuppie white folks' neighborhood in Georgia, Leon thought, which is probably why Wylie Odoms bought it and why Leon had felt reassured the day he first laid eyes on it. Another serious lapse in judgment.

Leon glanced around. Only other car in the lot was a glossy black Jag with a personalized plate: GETBACK. Leon shook his head. Wylie's idea of class.

Leon took the back way in, although he knew the girl was gone. He'd called just a minute ago, told her she'd have to get right down to the post office, sign for an important package for Mr. Odoms. Leon had been in the lobby of the post office at the time.

He knew she'd be on her way. Leon had seen Wylie open more than one package of money that had come in the mail. Yeah, the line at the post office had looked about an hour and a half long to him. If the brothers in Opa-Locka had any suck, they'd have a branch office here and there, cut down on the traffic. Meantime, too bad for them. And for Odoms's girl.

"Wylie," Leon said, by way of greeting. He was standing in the doorway of his ex-agent's office. He'd already slipped out front, made sure the door was locked, taped a closed sign to the window.

Odoms glanced up from some papers he was reading, startled. When he saw who it was, his natural frown dissolved and was replaced with his bullshit smile. "Well, goddamn, look what fell to earth."

Leon nodded, came on in the office. What used to be the dining room, maybe. Big desk, some file cabinets. Bunch of sporting goods cluttering up the place: basketballs, footballs, baseball caps, boxing gloves, you name it, all of it signed with somebody's name: Dr. J, Mean Joe Greene, Magic, Iron Mike T.

Leon suspected Wylie had signed all the names himself. "First Round" Odoms, was how he introduced himself to Leon, way back when, "crown prince of sports agents." Leon had been impressed at the time. Now he knew better. Odoms had never had an actual client go higher than free agent.

"Mr. *Le*-on Sta-*raight*," Odoms said, rising to shake his hand. Saying it like Leon was walking across the ring in Caesar's Palace, ready to slap skin with Don King or somebody, watch a championship fight.

It looked like Wylie had tried to copy Brother King's hairstyle, in fact, but the color was wrong and he wasn't using the right brand of hair spray or something. Where it should have looked like smoke was rising up out of his brain, Wylie's 'do more resembled some kinky garden of snakes fallen over to one side, never going to get up again.

"How you been, Wylie?" Leon shook the man's flabby hand. Saw the gold watch, took in the spilling gut, the flashy suit. Wylie hadn't been denying himself, that was plain to see.

"Moving and grooving, Leon." Wylie straightening his tie. "Any better I'd have to be two people." A black tie with some planets and comets and whatnot swooshing through space. "What brings you up this way? You slip your boss man's leash?"

Leon ignored him. He could afford to ignore him.

"I need some legal advice," Leon said, settling himself in one of the leather chairs across from Wylie's desk.

"None finer available," Wylie said, smiling, sitting on the edge of his desk. He was toying with a pinkie ring, had a diamond in it the size of a pea.

Leon thought about what Wylie had said, his pitiful estimation of himself, but decided to let it pass. "I was wondering about how the law reads in Florida," he said. "Say if a married person dies, who's in charge of the property that's left."

Wylie studied him for a moment, trying to read what this was about. "Well now, that depends."

"On?"

"On whether or not there's a will, for one thing."

Leon nodded, reached in his pocket for the papers there, things he'd borrowed from Alcazar's files. He found what he was looking for, handed it to Odoms. Odoms scanned it quickly.

"Tenancy by the entireties," he nodded, looking up at Leon.

"Say what?"

"It's a standard way for spouses to hold property. It means if one of these people dies, the whole of their common property passes on to the surviving spouse." Odoms glanced at the document again. "Who's John Deal, anyway?"

"Nobody," Leon said. "This just an example."

Odoms stared at him. "Where'd you get this, Leon? You into B&E now? Lawyer's offices?" His fucked-up grin, thinking he was funny.

Leon took the papers back from Wylie. "So, let's say two people like this were to own a company. Then one dies, the other one wants to sell it."

Wylie shrugged. "There shouldn't be a problem."

"Even if the company owns property?"

Wylie gave him another of his mind-reader looks. "What are you getting at, Leon?"

"You know, going through all that bank shit when you have to sell a house. Waiting forever till the thing's done."

Wylie rolled his eyes. "Closing on the property, you mean. No, you don't have to go through all that. The property stays with the corporation, if that's what it is."

Leon nodded, handed Wylie another paper. Odoms scanned it, glanced up at Leon. "DealCo? I heard of that."

"Just tell me, Wylie, is it set up the way you say?"

Wylie looked through the papers again, pursing his lips, nodding, looking backward, then forward, sucking on his teeth. Looking like a guy trying to pretend he could read, Leon thought. Finally, Wylie handed him the papers. "It's a corporation all right. With two stockholders, the guy and his wife. That's it."

"So if one of them is dead, the one who lives can sell. Sign the documents and all that shit."

Wylie nodded. "And all that shit."

"No waiting around to read the will, getting the lawyers involved?"

Wylie chuckled, shaking his head. "No, Leon. You've been watching too much TV."

Leon tented his big fingers under his chin. Tone of Wylie's voice like Leon was two degrees above brain dead. Guy fucking with him, but let him have his fun. "You're certain of all this, Wylie?"

Wylie seemed insulted at the question. "Any first-year law clerk knows this stuff." He stood, pulled down a thick book from one of the shelves behind his desk, thumbed through it. "Florida Statutes, Chapter 689. 'Blah, blah, blah.'" Wylie tossed the heavy book on the desk. Leon judged it to weigh quite a bit by the stir of air it sent up, ruffling the other papers, sending Wylie's coffee cup into a rattle.

Leon stared at him. "I was just bein' sure," he said. "I seem to remember some other things you were sure of, once upon a time."

Wylie stared at him, wary. "Such as?"

"Such as my contract, for instance. The one that was an iron-clad motherfucker, what you called it. You know, the one the Dolphin lawyers went to work on after I tore up my knee?"

Wylie waved it away. "We could have sued those bastards."

Leon nodded. "We did."

Wylie stopped. Leon watched him remembering. How they got worked over downtown, reporters laughing, it'd have to be embarrassing, even for Wylie. Even the judge was calling him names.

Finally Wylie shrugged. "Hey, they agreed to pay the hospital bills, didn't they?"

Leon stared at him until Wylie dropped his gaze. Finally, he let his breath out.

"Never mind, Wylie. Wasn't what I came to talk about." He tossed the last of the papers he'd brought down on the cluttered desk. A copy he'd made of what Reyes had signed. "I wanted you to have a look at these, too."

Wylie gave him a suspicious look, then unfolded the papers. He scanned them briefly then looked back at Leon. "These are standard corporate stock certificates. So what?"

"I just want to be absolutely certain," Leon said. "Say I had some blank ones just like that. Say I fill in the blanks for some other outfit, DealCo, whatever, the person signs on the dotted line, then I own what it says?"

Wylie shrugged. "Assuming anybody'd want to sign under those terms."

"Assume they would."

Wylie threw up his arms. "It'd have to be notorized. Some consideration—that's money—change hands. Then you'd own the goddamn thing."

"Simple as that?"

Wylie gave him another of his what's-this-really-about looks. "You'd have a valid contract, if that's what you mean."

"I'd be in control of the property involved? No having to close, no title company, no bank, none of that."

"I already told you, Leon." Wylie getting impatient, his manners starting to fray. Leon checked his watch.

"But," Wiley was smiling now, his oily smile this time, the one that came from his heart, "you'd probably want someone like myself around to help out, Leon. Just to be sure."

Wylie turned back to the contracts, was scanning the descriptions, when Leon reached over and snatched them away, folded them back in his coat. "I'll keep that in mind, Wylie." He remembered something then, the other thing he'd meant to ask.

"How about Doc Hammer," Leon said. "You ever see him around?" Hammer was short for Jameroski, a washed-up old Pole, ex-fight doctor, a steroid and painkiller connection for Wylie's needy clientele.

"The junkie?" Wylie laughed. "They finally pulled his license so he went straight to the source. Runs a pharmacy over on the beach now."

Leon nodded, making a mental note. Wylie pointed at the papers in Leon's pocket. "I could be of some real help to you, Leon. There's the matter of that outstanding debt for services I'm still carrying. This might be a way to clear it up."

Leon nodded. He checked his watch again. Assume the line at the post office was moving quickly, then what?

He reached across the desk, caught Wylie by his planet whooshing tie before he could move, jerked him across the desk. Good silk like it was, had a hell of a lot of strength in it.

He pinned Wylie back over his desk with his good knee, pulled that thin tie knot so tight it disappeared under the flaps of flesh at Wylie's chin. Wylie got his hands on that heavy law book, banged it over Leon's head once or twice, but Leon hardly felt it. On the third pass, the book fell out of his hands and fell to the floor, a bunch of its pages tearing loose.

"Yeah, we clearing that matter up," Leon said. Wylie's eyes glittered, but if he'd had a change of heart, Leon would never hear about it. He put all his effort into tightening Wylie's out-of-this-world tie.

When he was sure Wylie was out there riding one of those comet tails, Leon tidied up, then drug Wylie out to his secretary's desk. He used the man's pudgy fingers to type out a suicide note, not worrying about spelling, for he'd had the opportunity to read a couple of Wylie's handwritten letters, back in the old days.

Then he stood on the desk to hang him by his tie from the ceiling fan there. The fan blades tilted up all cockeyed from the added weight, and a couple years of dust drifted down to powder Wylie's fucked-up hair-do, the shoulders of his expensive suit, but the bracket held fast. One thing about an old house like that, they used solid hardware, Leon thought.

He gave the dangling Wylie a last glance, then left by the front way, leaving the door unlocked. "Cleared up every last bit of it up," he said as he got in his BMW and drove away.

On the way down the boulevard, he spotted Wylie's secretary headed the opposite direction, a pissed-off expression on her pretty face. He was sorry for what he'd put her through, but at least he'd left her a present. That'd perk her up when she got back to the office.

Deal left Janice's car under the canopy of the Shores Country Club and strode up the broad front steps, pointing at the car when the valet came trotting up for his keys. Not yet noon and already crowding ninety, Deal thought, as he registered the blast of icy air from inside.

Down the broad hallway with the carpet that swirled with what Deal had always referred to as the chicken feather motif, then left off the hallway into the men's grill, where there was only Henry, squaring away his glassware, getting ready for the lunch crowd.

Deal's father had been a charter member of the club and his privileges had been passed on to Deal, who remained dueless in perpetuity. The privilege didn't mean much to Deal, who seldom went there, except for the occasional lunch with a client. But Janice liked it, especially the tennis and golf. He didn't know what had brought him here today. He'd been driving aimlessly, found himself on the oak-lined boulevard that led to the place, then turning in the drive, as if he had some intention.

Henry glanced up, surprised as Deal took a seat at the bar.

"I was sure sorry to hear, Mr. Deal." Henry put a napkin down in front of him. "Sure sorry."

"Thanks, Henry," Deal said. "Gin and tonic. A double, in a tall glass."

Henry nodded, made the drink, centered it on the napkin. Deal finished half on the first swallow, drained the rest before he put the glass down. Deal stared out the tall windows of the bar. Long green fairways bordered by live oaks and rangy melaleuca trees. People in golf carts, zigzagging along, hopping out to swing, jumping back aboard, having fun.

His father's game. And then Janice's game. She'd started taking lessons after she'd left her job, played a Wednesday-morning league here, up until last year, when things had gotten a little tight. She complained about her handicap, but Deal liked to watch her swing: butt out, her tongue at the corner of her lips, she let fly like nobody's business. He liked her sweaty, her color high in her cheeks, her breasts flushed and heaving. Maybe that's why he was here, that memory.

Deal sucked on the ice in his drink. He'd brought home a tiny set of golf clubs, not long ago. He would call Hermione, the woman who cleaned for Janice on Saturdays. Hermione could deal with the boxes, the little golf clubs, all those things.

Deal cracked an ice cube between his teeth and glanced up. Henry was staring at him doubtfully. "Another one, Mr. Deal?"

Deal thought a moment, then shook his head. "No. That's fine. I think I'll play golf this afternoon."

Henry nodded, his eyes averted. Although Deal's father had been a fixture on the course, Deal had never held a club. Deal signed the check and slid it over to Henry. Henry gave him his mournful bloodhound's smile. Who knew what the man was thinking.

In the pro shop he charged a pair of pants printed with the same sort of golfers he'd seen on Penfield's tie, some spiked shoes, a visor and polo shirt, and a set of Ping clubs to his account. "Are these the best you have?" Deal asked the young man in the shop. "Glenn," his name tag read. "Assistant Pro."

Glenn looked as though he'd never spent a sleepless night. He checked the price tag on the set of clubs. "The best we have in stock, anyway," Glenn said. "We'll throw in the bag."

Deal nodded. "I think I'll spend a few minutes on the driving range," he said, and added a bucket of practice balls to his ticket. His words sounded strange in his own ears. Deal had the sensation he was being dragged somewhere by an annoying relative passing through town.

Deal changed in the locker room, hung his clothes in the locker that bore his father's name on a brass plate. There was still an ashtray full of tees on the top shelf. Deal took a handful on the way out. He glanced at himself in a mirror near the doorway. He wondered who was wearing the funny pants.

Deal had the practice range to himself. Given the heat, he wasn't surprised. His bag and clubs had been propped against a wire stand, the balls, each one glistening from the wash and striped in red, had been spilled out on a patch of grass that seemed to be thriving in the onset of the monsoon season.

Deal selected a wood, its sleek black head reflecting his visored image and the arms of the huge live oaks overhead. He teed a ball up, gripped the club, and assumed a position he'd picked up from watching his father. "Never play a game you have to practice," was his father's comment on the driving range.

Deal drew back and swung. He gave it everything. There was a sharp crack as the ball arced high out over the range. The ball landed somewhere past the 200-yard marker and bounded on, past 225. Deal watched it roll, finally stop. Two hundred and forty yards, give or take. The first time he'd ever swung. He looked at the club. Replaced it in the bag. Tossed his visor on the grass.

He took off the shoes and left them beside the clubs, peeled off the bright red shirt, stepped out of the funny pants.

He walked back toward the locker room in his briefs and socks, past a stunned foursome of onlookers, went inside to the showers. He turned on the water fully hot, at full force. *Yo, Deal. Fan-fucking-tastic shot.*

He stood in the stream of water for what seemed like hours. Said good-bye to Flivey. And to Janice. And wept.

16

The next morning, Deal found himself back on the job, his hammer rocketing nails as if of its own accord.

The sound must have worked a charm. Emilio showed up at noon, with his helper. On their heels, a driver from Nachon Lumber arrived with the windows. The following day, Deal arrived to find the tile man already at work.

Deal got on the subs in earnest. The casements went in, Emilio hung the cabinets, and the tile man set a personal speed record. The electrician hooked up the inside panels and hauled away the construction drop. The lights hummed and the toilets were singing. He had the painters scheduled for the first of the week and had placed an order for sod and shrubbery the following Friday. Now all he had to worry about was renting the place.

He'd spoken to a couple of realtors who were gloomy about occupancy rates, the uncertain demographics of the area, the phases of the moon. Well, there were other realtors, he reminded himself. There had to be someone who could rent his units.

He was standing at the curb in front of the place, inspecting the wooden lintels he'd just hung above the entryways.

It was three hundred dollars' worth of material that the architect hadn't included, but once they were painted white against the peach backdrop Deal had chosen, the lintels would add a Caribbean touch. Throw in a few palms, he'd have the most attractive facade in the neighborhood, if it cut any ice.

He heard a horn behind him and turned to see Cal Saltz pull up in an unfamiliar low-slung sedan.

"What do you think?" Cal said. He levered himself up from the car and pointed. "Ain't it something?"

Deal looked inside. A lot of leather and wood. Old-fashioned seats, without headrests. He turned back to Cal.

"What is it?"

"I can get a hell of a deal on this one, Johnny. Goddamn car is worth twenty thousand dollars, guy'll unload it for five." He paused, shaking his head. "This is an *automobile.*"

"Yeah, but what kind is it?"

Cal shrugged. "Ribalta or Rivolta, I forget how you say it. Some kind of Italian. Got a Chrysler V-eight and power train, though. And it's sure pretty, iddin't it?"

Deal nodded. "What if somebody kicks a rock through your windshield? You'll have to write the Pope to get it replaced."

Cal nodded glumly, then looked up at the fourplex. "Who knocked out *your* window?"

Deal followed his gaze. He'd missed the hole in one of the upstairs casements. But he wasn't surprised. Another reason to get the place sold.

Cal glanced at him. "I heard what happened at the country club, Johnny."

Deal nodded. He had no way of explaining what he'd done.

"Henry picked up your things, put 'em in your dad's locker," Cal said. "Must have looked like a golfer up and vaporized." He tried a laugh and Deal nodded along, trying to imagine Henry standing at the window of the grill, watching it happen. Poor Henry.

They stood quietly for a while. Finally, Cal kicked one of the Rivolta's tires. "Well, I just thought I'd look in on you. You sure you're doing all right?"

"I'm fine, Cal." Deal put his hand on the old man's shoulder. "And I'm sorry about the other day. About the funeral and all. I'm not ready for something like that, you understand? There's no family, no real friends. I don't see the point."

Cal nodded, patted Deal's hand. "You don't have to apologize to me, Johnny. Wasn't any of my business in the first place."

"I'm just getting adjusted, Cal. That's all." Deal turned and gave him a smile. "Just bear with me."

"Whenever you need me, Johnny," Cal said.

He worried the toe of his boot in the dirt for a bit, then brightened. "You want to take this here Revolting for a spin with me? I'll put a hundred-dollar bill on the dashboard there. If you can reach up and get it when we take off, it's yours."

Deal laughed. "You got a hundred?"

Cal snorted. "Always got a hundred. Day I don't, they can bury me."

Deal nodded. "Maybe another time, Cal. I got a lot to do here."

"That's okay, I'll drive you."

Deal hesitated. He was probably as lonely as Deal felt. "I'm sorry, Cal. I'll catch up with you though."

"Suit yourself," Cal said. He paused. "You sure you're all right?"

Deal nodded. "I'm fine. I took a few days off. Now, I'm fine."

Cal didn't seem convinced. He got back in the car and started the engine, gunned it enough to send a cloud of dust down the street behind them. "You better start sleeping here," he called. "They'll carry the goddamn place away, you're not careful."

Deal waved, watching Cal whisk away. It *did* seem like an enjoyable car. Maybe he could broker his fourplex for a bunch of used cars. He and Cal could find a vacant lot, set up shop in a double-wide.

He bent and picked up a nail from the curbside, tossed it into the trash. The used-car business? Maybe he was losing it, after all.

Leon Straight watched the weird car go past him from behind a newspaper he held up in front of his face. This day Leon was using some piece-of-shit Chevrolet with the side windows smoked dark as you could get, but still it paid to be careful. He'd spent plenty of time in the neighborhood already, could still get a whiff of that burned-up gas station down the street.

He watched the sedan disappear in his rearview mirror, trying to figure out what kind of car it was, anyway. Strange car, strange guy driving it. The same guy who had been talking to Deal by the curb. Boots, big broad brimmed hat like he was some kind of cowboy got jerked out of his life in the Wild West, dropped down here in the tropics. Leon got the license number. He'd let Alejandro find out who the guy was. Paperwork. Kind of thing Alejandro was good for.

A couple trucks piling up to the curb down the street in front of this Deal's place, now. A bunch of skinny black guys jumping out, firing up a tar pot, shinnying their ladders up the sides of the place. Dumb-as-squat brothers from the islands, blistering their black asses for nothing on a roofing crew. Leon shook his head in disgust. The black losers worked on roofing crews, the white ones on the tree-trim outfits. What was it about heights that drew in the lame brains, he wondered. Some kind of natural selection process, he'd figure it out. Meantime, it looked as if the building was getting built.

Leon shook his head. This Deal guy wasn't so smart either. Still building his building, put Leon in the mind of that wind-up bunny rabbit in the television commercial. Boom, boom, boom on his drum, no matter what. Well, they'd see about that. Leon would let Alcazar know what was going on here, maybe Leon could make some adjustments, tear him a new battery hole.

He stretched, checked his watch. He had a man to see, but it was a little early yet. He could stop by that crap-ass market up on the corner, see if they had any Gatorade, although he doubted it. They'd have guava juice, mango juice, every kind of dog-shitting-peach-pit juice you might think of, but he'd ask for Gatorade and they'd look at him like he'd dropped down from some other planet and shake their heads, No, no, no, señor, no Gatorade in *here*. Especially, not for any black señor like you. No secret to Leon what the Cubans thought of blacks, especially American blacks. Some Cubano might have been an astrophysicist down home, up here he finds himself selling papaya juice and Kotex. Have to take it out on somebody. It made Leon tired just thinking about it.

There was an old woman walking down the street toward the Chevy now, holding onto the leash of some scroungy dog, dog looking like it had been put together out of spare parts down at the pound. Dog was sniffing everything in its path, the woman moseying along behind it like that's all she had to do in life, and it probably was. What a fucking neighborhood, Leon thought.

The dog nosed along through the grass by the curb, came up to the Chevy. Woman right behind it. Eighty maybe, maybe more. She looked through the windshield, looked at Leon, wrinkled her nose like she saw something she didn't like. Leon holding the paper low enough so he could stare back at her. The dog hiking his leg now, pissing all over the Chevy's front bumper. Steam curling up in the air. The old lady giving him a look, like fuck your *Negro* ass, and moving along with her dog, down the street to her piece of shit house.

Leon waited until the roofers were gone, Deal was gone, everybody was gone, he was late to see the man he had to see, until he was soaked through with sweat sitting in the heat in a closed up car waiting for everyone to leave. He read the paper through and through, knew the temperature in Caracas yesterday, how much Burdines wanted for three kinds of VCR.

Finally, he got to fold up his paper, step out into the evening sun, stretch, feel 100 percent better right away. It might have been ninety out there in the street, but who knows what it had gotten to inside that car. Ready now. Something he shouldn't be doing, but had to be done anyway.

He walked down the buckled sidewalk past a couple of vacant lots, past a boarded-up house, up the sidewalk of the old lady's place. Door was locked, of course, but hard as he turned the knob, everything gave way, and not much in the way of noise, either.

He eased inside. Some kind of disgusting cooking smell making his stomach want to turn over. Something she'd brought over in a jar from Cuba about 1960, he supposed. Having to do a little dance step backward as the dog charged down the terrazzo hallway, its nails clattering, the thing making a snarling dive at him. No warning barks, just straight-ahead vicious, you had to give old spare parts that much.

Leon caught him, tucked its body under his arm, clamped its jaws shut with his massive hand. Moved quiet and quick down the hallway, he had places to go.

Nobody in the living room except for the Virgin Mary and her off in a terminal plaster statue nod overtop of some dead candles and a spray of plastic flowers all tucked away in a corner of the room where a sane person would have put a television set. Scared him for a second though, the statue was so big.

Nobody in the dining room either, a gloomy place with a dark wood table and six dark wood chairs and some painting on the wall so dark you couldn't tell what was in it. The dog wriggling around in his grip, but its heart not really in it. Some live things have the sense to know when it's worth making a fuss, when it isn't, Leon thought.

And into the kitchen where whatever it was cooking. Or festering, was more like it. Something inside an old white stove, huge and rounded off, remind you of a Studebaker. And some refrigerator like they didn't make any more of, either. But still no old lady.

Leon went to the sink, glanced out the window at the scraggly backyard and saw her, hanging up some of her undies on a clothesline. Industrial-strength undies. The kind that would keep you safe from attack.

Mmmm-hmmm, lady, you be safe, all right. He knew now what he was going to do. Another inspiration, you could call it.

Leon turned back to the stove. Opened the oven door. Grabbed him a towel off the sink counter, pulled out the racks, bringing along something in an oven dish that broke all over the floor, and didn't that stink to high heaven. Plenty of room in there now, though. And whoo-ee, hot, until he closed the door again.

He was all the way back to the car before he heard the old lady start to scream. Scream to wake the dead. Good old Spare Parts, he thought. Good dog. *Hot* dog. Piss up *that* rope, lady.

 A couple of days after Cal dropped by, Deal got a call from Penfield's office. The assistant would tell him nothing over the phone. He had to get down there, the sooner the better.

There was a new receptionist this time, a woman in her thirties with red hair and a spray of freckles across her face. She'd folded back a gate in the Plexiglas so you could actually talk to her. The rent-a-cop was outside the building trying to roust a *churrasco* vendor who was grilling his little shish kebabs right there in the middle of the financial district.

"That's a shame, don't you think?" The receptionist spoke to Deal, but she was watching the action outside.

Deal turned just as a big swirl of charcoal smoke whipped up from the grill. The rent-a-cop staggered back, flapping his hands against the smoke. The *churrasco* vendor handed one of the beef sticks to a man in a three-piece suit and palmed a bill.

Deal looked back at the receptionist. "I'm betting on the little guy," he said.

She smiled up at him. Green eyes, bright, even teeth. "Me too," she said.

There was a pause. For a moment, Deal had forgotten why he was there. "I'm Jack Deal," he said, feeling the weight sink on him again. He'd been keeping it going, but sometimes he felt as if he were walking on one of the outer planets, where a cupful of him would weigh a ton. Fix your eye on a distant point, he reminded himself. Keep walking.

"Can I help you?" Her gaze was a little puzzled now. Was he some weirdo off the street, some pocket pool artist, some mooch?

"I'm here to see Thornton Penfield," he said.

"Of course," she said. She sat down and punched a number into the phone. "What was your name again?"

"Deal," he said. "Jack Deal."

She nodded and spoke into the receiver. Deal made a quick check of his clothing. He'd traded the checked shirt for a white oxford button-down, the jeans for a pair of chinos, the boots for a pair of Top-Siders. Added a sport coat. He'd been ready for the former receptionist: "Some yuppie wants to see Mr. Penfield."

This one, with her red hair and honest eyes, listened to the phone, nodding, glancing up at Deal, then making a note.

Finally, she hung up. Her expression had changed. Now her eyes seemed heavy, her smile faded. "You can go up now. The top floor . . . "

"Elevator's right down there," Deal said, finishing for her.

"That's right," she said.

Deal turned to go.

"Oh, Mr. Deal."

Deal stopped.

"I . . . I just wanted to say how sorry I was."

Deal looked more closely at her. "Do I know you?" he asked.

"No," she said. "I don't think so. I'm Barbara Cooper. Mr. Penfield's secretary told me what happened . . . " she trailed off.

Deal nodded. "You weren't here the last time I came in, Barbara."

"No. I mean, I guess not. I was out sick a couple days." She glanced over his shoulder and Deal turned.

The *churrasco* vendor had edged his cart out from under the granite overhang of the building onto the sidewalk proper. The vendor pointed at a line on the concrete and said something to the rent-a-cop. The first part was rapid Spanish, but Deal caught something about "public property."

The rent-a-cop shook his head, then started back inside. The vendor wasn't quite finished. "Fuck you," Deal read, in perfect English.

The rent-a-cop either didn't hear it or decided to ignore it. He came through the revolving door, wiping soot from his face with a handkerchief. He glared at Deal and the receptionist on his way toward the rest rooms.

She looked at Deal, her face flushed. "I read about what happened. It took me a minute to realize who you were and I just . . . " she trailed off. "Anyway, I'm really very sorry," she said.

Deal nodded. "Thanks," he said. He gave a little wave and turned for the elevators.

"Good luck," he heard her say from over his shoulder.

Penfield sat behind his desk, appraising Deal with an expression Deal figured he'd had to use on thousands of clients in the same position over the years.

"They're offering us a very reasonable settlement, John. More than I expected, under the circumstances."

"What exactly *are* the circumstances, Mr. Penfield?"

Penfield untented his fingers. "I sent Fred Lang, one of our investigators, over to the police impound yard with a mechanic. There was a great deal of damage done to the car's undercarriage when it went through that railing. The brake lines were ripped, and the front right wheel was nearly shorn from the axle. According to the mechanic, there's no way to determine whether the brakes were functioning at the time of the accident. The bridge tender didn't see anything. We simply don't have much of a case."

Deal reached into the pocket of his jacket and leaned across Penfield's desk to drop some papers there. "I found every damned receipt. Four times they 'fixed' the brakes in less than a month."

Penfield barely glanced at the receipts. "Listen to me, John. Our man writes a nationally syndicated column on automobile mechanics. He's testified as an expert witness for us in any number of accident cases. If he says there's no way to ascertain if the brakes were functioning, if we don't have eyewitness testimony as to a situation that might have called for the brakes, then we don't have a prayer."

Deal waved his hand between them. "You show the jury these

receipts. Put me on the stand. People can put two and two together."

Penfield sighed. "We don't want to go to court on this, John."

Deal stared hard at him. "We don't?" he said.

Penfield dropped his gaze. "I'm sorry. I meant to say, let's remember your own stated aims. We're after an acknowledgment of liability . . . "

"I said I wanted to nail them. Make it public. If we settle out of court, under these conditions . . . " Deal broke off, snatching the document that Penfield had handed him earlier.

"This offer is a good faith gesture of compassion and in no way acknowledges nor may be held to indicate any culpability of Surf Motors, Inc., its owners, agents, or employees, in the aforesaid matter."

Deal broke off. He wadded the paper in his fist and tossed it across the room. Penfield watched with his unflappable attorney's expression. Deal could bury a machete in his mother's breast, he thought, and Penfield would nod sagely, saying "Now that you've got that out of your system, John . . . "

"Look, Mr. Penfield, they wouldn't offer me money unless they knew they were in deep shit. Let's just turn the screws down. Let's take them to court."

Penfield stood up, shaking his head. He walked to one of the big windows and looked out. "A young woman came to see me a few years back, a widow, in fact, with three small children. Her husband had died of a blood disorder. He was a hemophiliac and had taken a number of injections of a clotting agent from a lot subsequently recalled by the drug company that manufactured it.

"The recall was a matter of record, as were the lot numbers of the drugs issued to him by a local hospital pharmacy. The recall also detailed precisely what might occur should anyone actually inject this contaminated product, and in fact, the husband developed the symptoms in short order. His was a textbook case. Despite everyone's efforts, the young man died, but not until after he had exhausted his insurance and every penny to his family's name."

Penfield turned to Deal. "Now let me ask you, does that sound like an open-and-shut, roast-them-over-the-coals, bleed-the-deep-pockets-sons-of-bitches-until-they're-dry kind of a case to you?"

Deal nodded.

"Well, that's what it sounded like to me, too. I was already working on my summation before the woman got out of my office that first day."

Penfield struck a pose: "The very elixir that had given this young man a normal life turned upon him and ripped that life away, not only from him, but those who loved and depended upon him."

Penfield laughed mirthlessly. "Well, I'm an old war horse and I should have known better.

"In the end, the company argued that fully fifty percent of the nation's hemophiliacs had come to test positive for this same disorder and that furthermore, all had been injecting similar clotting agents manufactured by any number of companies for years. Given the lengthy incubation period of the disease, which a number of experts contended was as long as a decade, there was no way to determine just when any individual might have become infected."

Penfield walked to his window and looked down. A battleship had docked at the port. Sailors in white uniforms milled about the decks.

"Other experts testified that the defendant company had in fact performed a great public service by instituting theretofore unheard of quality controls, alerting the public to the potential dangers, thereby forcing the entire industry to clean up its act, not to mention having voluntarily placed its sales program for a very profitable product under a cloud."

"Yeah, so it was harder than you expected," Deal said. "I'm sure you got out with enough."

"We didn't get a dime, John. The jury bought their argument, recall, widow and children be damned." Penfield shook his head. "The company dropped its claim for court costs, on the condition the widow forgo any further action."

"Jesus Christ," Deal said.

Penfield shrugged. "She was lucky. She could have ended up owning *them* more than two million dollars."

Deal stood and walked to the windows himself. Far down below he could make out the yellow umbrella of the *churrasco* vendor. A little plume of smoke rose from the grill and a dark knot of customers appeared to have gathered about the stand. Chalk one up for the little guy, Deal thought.

On the other hand, the poor shit was out there in the open, now. Somebody could lean out a window and drop a brick straight down, it'd be like a laser bomb tearing through that yellow umbrella. Stay there long enough, somebody would drop it, all right. Drop a fucking piano on him.

Deal nudged Penfield. "Call them up, Mr. Penfield."

Penfield glanced at him, something like hope in the old man's eyes.

"Tell them I don't want their money." Deal said. "Will you do that for me?" Penfield stared at him sorrowfully. Deal clapped the older man on the shoulder and went to see about his job.

Deal swung off Eighth Street down Twenty-ninth, past the combination bodega-hardware-coffee stand on the corner. There was always a line for coffee there, mostly workmen, but never any of his subcontractors, at least not when he came looking.

This time, he didn't bother to check. He was driving on automatic pilot, a sense of foreboding growing inside him. He passed the gutted service station where the yellow police ribbon had long since been shredded. A guy with a knitted watch cap jammed atop of a wild frizz of hair was coming away from one of the wrecked cars out front, something clutched under his arm. He lurched toward the street as if the ground were tilting in front of him and gave Deal a crazed glare as he drove by. Welcome to the neighborhood.

Deal made a turn, trying to reassure himself. Three blocks east, a couple more south. Somebody ought to get the burned-out station bulldozed. He'd put that on his list.

It was gnawing on him, Penfield's urgings to go along with the attorneys for Surf. He'd thought the issue had been settled. Still, he supposed, Penfield was just trying to get things over with quickly, cut his losses. But if the man didn't understand now, Deal thought, he never would.

Deal shook his head . . . and as he did, he registered the city trucks parked in front of the fourplex.

He stomped the accelerator of Janice's VW, not that it had much effect. He had to listen to the high-pitched whine of the automatic transmission all the way down the block—sounding like they were blasting into the stratosphere and the speedometer hovering around forty—his eyes fixed on the arm of the backhoe that was tearing into the dirt above his sewer connection.

Two city trucks, one out in the street, a flatbed that had apparently carried the backhoe, the other a pickup from water and sewer, two guys in green shirts and ball caps inside, working on lunch. The pickup was pulled up over the curb, deep tracks gouging the fresh sod he'd laid there the day before. The backhoe had sheared a couple of limbs off a gumbo limbo he'd planted. There was a mound of soil and coral rock spilling onto the sidewalk, growing larger with every scoop of the machine. Deal tried to visualize what the lantana bushes he'd placed there must look like.

He was striding toward the growling backhoe, waving off the driver, but the machine merely backed away for a new charge. That's when Deal saw Faye. The inspector was standing on the other side of the hole, a Coke held to his lips, his throat bobbing like a goose's as he guzzled the drink. He tossed the empty can into the lowering bucket of the backhoe and was mopping at his face with his scrungy handkerchief when he caught sight of Deal advancing upon him.

"Just hold your horses, Deal," Faye said, his florid face deepening another notch.

Deal ducked under the descending arm of the backhoe without breaking stride. It couldn't have missed him by much.

"Jesus Christ!" He heard the angry voice above the roar of the engines, a rending shriek of metal as the operator slammed the heavy arm into an emergency stop.

"We'll just go inside a minute," Deal said to Faye, taking the inspector's arm. Faye's toes clipped across the tops of the clods of dirt as Deal propelled him along. He gave a panicked glance at Deal, who smiled and relaxed his grip a bit. Deal turned to give the same smile to the backhoe operator. The guys in the pickup truck weren't paying attention. They'd seen Faye disappear with any number of distressed contractors.

Deal had to let go of Faye to fish the fourplex keys out of his pocket. "So," he said, keeping the smile. He nodded at the back-hoe, which had swung back into motion. "What's going on?"

Faye glanced at him warily. Deal swung the door open. A gust of paint smell rolled out over them. Deal showed Faye the way in. Faye shook his head, walked inside.

"You got an illegal connection out there," Faye said, as the door slammed. Deal crowded in on his heels. "A serious code viol—"

Faye's breath left him in a whoosh as Deal drove him into the foyer wall. Outside, the backhoe was grinding on.

Deal had one arm across Faye's throat, his hand tucked into the crook of his other, his free hand levered at the back of the fat man's head. He jerked backward and Faye gasped again. There was a smear of sweat on the freshly painted drywall where Faye's face had been.

"I paid you off twice, Faye. What are you doing, fucking around with me?" Faye gave him some strangled sounds. Deal eased up. A sweet-rotten smell emanated from the man. Cheesy stuff percolating beneath the dewlaps and folds of his flesh, Deal thought. Places the sun had never shone.

"I received a citizen complaint," Faye croaked. "You best let me go. You're already in deep shit."

Deal slammed him back against the drywall. Faye groaned. Deal had framed the studs on sixteen-inch centers even though he could have gotten by with twenty-four. That made the walls stronger, firmer to the touch. A new argument for sturdy construction, Deal thought, jerking Faye back again.

"Listen to me, Faye. I'm under a lot of stress. I really don't give a shit what you're going to look like when I'm finished with you. I'll tell them you tried to shake me down and I snapped. I have a very good lawyer. And mostly I don't give a damn. Are you starting to get the picture?"

Faye managed to nod.

"Good," Deal said. "Now tell me what you're doing out there."

"It ain't me," Faye wheezed. "For Christ's sake, it ain't me."

Deal heard the seeds of panic in the man's voice. A deeper, more pungent odor had arisen from him.

Deal leaned him into the wall again. "Who, then? What's so important about my gas-line hookup?"

Tears were leaking from Faye's eyes now. "I get orders, god-damnit. I have to do what they tell me. The boss calls me in, wants to know if everything is hunky-dory on your job. I said sure, every-thing's jake. But that ain't the right answer, okay? So I have to find something."

His eyes rolled back, trying to find Deal. "I'm just doing a job. You want to know who, you ought to ask yourself, Deal. Who *you* been fucking with?" He turned his face away. "So go on, do what-ever. That's all I got to tell you."

Deal pushed him away. Faye stumbled, caught himself against the wall. He turned, glowering at Deal, as he tucked at his shirttail. Faye measured the distance between himself and Deal, compared it with the distance to the front door. Outside, the backhoe's roar had kicked up a notch. The glass in the foyer sidelights had begun to rattle.

"The last guy put his hands on me went out of business, Deal. He's squeezing lemonade down in front of the courthouse, now."

Deal wasn't paying attention. He was trying to understand. Faye could be lying about his orders, trying to save his own ass, but Deal doubted it. If Faye had wanted more money, he'd just find something new, something easy to flag. He'd never go to the trou-ble of digging up the gas line.

There was a wrenching sound outside, a shriek of metal on metal that cut through the machine's engines. Maybe the guy would shear the gas line, they'd all go up in a fireball.

"You made a big mistake," Faye said, hitching at his belt. He had his lower lip puffed out. It was an inviting target, Deal thought, but it wasn't worth it.

"Your mother made the big mistake," Deal said. "Go tell her about it."

He shouldered Faye aside and walked out, into the growling.

**19**

He left the VW in front of the building, two wheels up on the curb. The *churrasco* vendor was gone, but there were two moon-face Indian women camped out on the steps to the plaza surrounded by buckets full of carnations and roses. The rent-a-cop was coming out to meet Deal as he pushed through the doors.

"I'm with the window cleaners," Deal said, before the cop could open his mouth. "Keep an eye on it, will you?" He nodded at the VW. The cop glared at him, then stepped farther out from the building. By the time Deal reached the reception desk, the cop was out there on the sidewalk, staring up, searching for scaffolding.

It was the same receptionist, the pleasant one. Barbara, he thought, surprised to remember her name.

She looked up from a paperback book tucked under the edge of her phone console. "Oh," she said, a smile coming to replace her surprise. "Mr. Deal."

"I'm here to see Mr. Penfield, Barbara. Can you buzz me through?"

"Sure. I just have to call . . . "

Deal waved, already on his way toward the elevators. He vaulted the gate, caught one of the doors just as it was closing. He got a look at the rent-a-cop running after him. The guy tried to jump the gates, using the same maneuver as Deal, but he was carrying extra weight around the middle. His hand slid on the polished rail and he caught the tip of his shiny black shoe going over. His hat flew off and there was a panicked look on his face. The elevator doors slid closed just as the cop's chin bounced off the parquet.

Penfield met him in the outer office. The old man looked grave, tight little lines radiating from the corners of his mouth. The door to his office sat ajar and Deal could see part of some client in there waiting: a pair of crossed legs, silk suit pants, dark socks, some Italian leather shoes, no wear on the sole that faced him. He caught a glimpse of the man's profile before Penfield blocked his way, but he really wasn't paying attention.

"John . . . " Penfield put out a soothing hand.

Penfield's secretary gave Deal a wary glance, her hand close to the telephone.

"I know you're busy," Deal said. "I can wait." Deal was listening to the words coming out of his mouth. Sure, he could wait. About a minute. Maybe a minute and a half. "Somebody's putting the squeeze on me," he said. "I'm about to go out of business."

Penfield nodded, as if he knew all about it. "Just calm down, John. I'm involved with a matter just now . . . "

Deal glanced inside the office, a vague concern beginning to register. That suit. That profile he'd glimpsed. Someone he'd seen before. The chair where the client had been sitting was empty now.

A big guy had appeared at the door of Penfield's office, not the client in the silk suit. This guy was wearing tan slacks and a sport coat straining at the shoulder seams. He was black, and wore one of the stand-up hairstyles, shaped like a bucket of sand upended at the beach. The guy had to hunch his shoulders to clear the door frame. He stared across the deep green carpet at Deal as if he were measuring a quarterback with a slow release.

"The fuck *you* doing here," the big man said.

Deal shook his head. "Do I know you?" he said.

Penfield gave the big man a sharp glance. "I'll take care of this." The big guy didn't seem convinced, kept his eyes on Deal.

"Look, John," Penfield said. "I'm really very busy." He forced a smile. "Give my secretary a number where I can reach you, I assure you we'll talk yet today."

He patted Deal on the shoulder and turned quickly back for his office. The big guy waited for him to pass, keeping his eyes on Deal.

Penfield paused at the doorway. "And John . . . you caused quite a ruckus down in the lobby. Try to be a little more careful going out." He gave Deal a fatherly nod and disappeared, the big man drawing the doors closed behind them.

The secretary looked up at Deal, her pen ready. "What was the number?" Her eyes were bright with hostility.

Deal thought a moment. "Who's in there?"

"I'm not permitted to discuss Mr. Penfield's clients."

"I don't want to discuss them. I just want to know who he's talking to."

Her jaw tightened. Deal saw her fingers twitching, ready to stab a panic button somewhere. He imagined the big guy crashing through the double doors, King Kong with a rocket up his ass.

"Yeah, well, forget the number," he said. "I'll get back to him."

When the elevator light clicked down to *L* Deal took a deep breath. By the time the doors opened again, he had forced himself into something like calm.

The lobby was anything but calm, however. There was a Fire Rescue van parked on the curb behind Deal's VW, its flashers whirling. Two paramedics in jump suits were inside, tending to the rent-a-cop, who was propped up against the marble wall in a corner. One of the paramedics was tidying up, while the other finished with a butterfly bandage on the rent-a-cop's chin. A Metro patrolman stood to one side, writing on a clipboard.

Deal had to walk past them, over a splash of blood on the marble floor, to get to the gate. The rent-a-cop's eyes met Deal's as he walked by, but he didn't say anything. The real cop glanced up at Deal, then went back to his writing.

Deal heard the gate click shut behind him. Deal forced himself to walk slowly across the gleaming floor. The receptionist's booth was empty. When he got outside, Deal saw why.

There was a second patrolman standing around back of Janice's car, his ticket pad out. Barbara was standing in front of him, gesturing at the building. The cop was shaking his head. When Deal approached, Barbara smiled.

"I was just telling him you'd be right out, Mr. Deal." The way she said his name made Deal sound like someone important.

"This your vehicle?" the cop said.

"That's right, officer."

"This lady says you're doing some work here?"

Deal glanced at Barbara who stared back deadpan. "Yeah, that's right," he said.

"Where's your permit?" the cop said, pointing at the windshield of the VW. He meant one of the cardboard tags they issued at City-County. You could double-park a freight train with the tag. If you had the suck to get one.

Deal stared at the dash. A gum wrapper, a dried up ring from a coffee cup, the plastic case that had been on Janice's "cosmic concepts" tape, curled up like a slug from the sun. Deal feigned a double take.

"Son of a *bitch!*" he said. "Somebody took it?" He turned to stare at Barbara, who shrugged her shoulders.

"I'm sorry, Mr. Deal."

Deal turned back to the cop, shaking his head in disbelief. "Jesus Christ. Somebody *stole* it. You know what it takes to get one of those things?"

The cop nodded, softening. "You gotta keep it locked up, Mr. Deal. Anything isn't nailed down . . . " he trailed off as his partner came out of the building, his clipboard under his arm.

"Everything under control?" the cop with the clipboard said.

"Yeah," his partner said. "Unless you want to file a report, Mr. Deal."

"No, the hell with it," Deal said. "My own fault."

The cop waved and followed after his partner. The paramedics came outside and got in their van without a word.

Deal stood with Barbara, watching the two vehicles pull away. "I appreciate it," he said, finally.

"It was the least I could do," she said. "I've been waiting for a year for that jerk to get his." She gestured toward the lobby.

Deal looked inside. He couldn't see the rent-a-cop anywhere. "I guess he'll be okay."

"We can always hope not," she said.

Deal studied her a moment. "There's a little mean streak under all that nice, isn't there."

She smiled. "Nobody ever sees it, though."

Deal nodded. "I wonder if I could ask you something."

"Ask." She had gray eyes. A stare that wouldn't waver.

"Somebody went up to see Penfield, just before I came in. Somebody important, a big guy with him."

"So you saw Leon," she said. She turned to him. "Leon Straight . . . you know, he played for the Dolphins one year."

Deal nodded. Leon Straight. A high-school phenomenon from rural Georgia who couldn't even cut it in junior college. A couple seasons with the World Football League, a half year with the Fish during the strike, one blown-out knee, one career in the dumper. "So who's Leon's boss, now?"

Barbara gave him a look, puzzled. She looked away from Deal, across the broad boulevard toward the park where a couple of maintenance men were propping up a sagging palm tree with two-by-fours. At ground level you couldn't see the water that was less than a block away, but you could smell the seaweed on the breeze. "It's no real secret, I guess. He works for Raoul Alcazar."

"Alcazar?" Deal glanced up the sheer facade of the skyscraper despite himself. No wonder the warning bells were going off.

She was silent.

"That's Raoul Alcazar up there?"

Barbara nodded, uncomfortable. Across the street, a man in a tattered T-shirt had stopped his shopping cart and was shouting instructions at the workers, who were still struggling with the palm tree.

Deal shook his head. "What's he doing with Penfield? Trying to buy into baseball?"

She shrugged. "He's a client."

Deal stared as she continued. "Another firm handles his litigation. Mr. Penfield does his corporate work."

Deal laughed, still not believing it. "Mr. Above Reproach and the Great Corrupter?" he glanced in at her lobby station. "How do you know all this?"

Barbara glanced away. "Sometimes I work upstairs, I type

things . . . " She hesitated, giving him a look he couldn't quite interpret. "I really should get back, you know."

"Yeah, sure," he said, still trying to figure it. Thornton Penfield
and Raoul Alcazar.

Barbara seemed to have drifted off somewhere. He reached out,
touched her shoulder. "Look, thanks again for helping me out."

She nodded, a pained expression on her face. Deal had the feeling she'd left something unsaid.

"Is there something wrong?" he asked.

Across the street, one of the maintenance men had attached
one end of a rope to the neck of the sagging palm, then looped it
over the limb of a nearby poinciana tree. He'd tied off the rope to
the bumper of his dump truck and was slowly backing up, levering
the palm off the ground. His partner was standing by with the
wooden brace, ready to slide it in place when the palm rose high
enough.

"That's right. Looking real good!" the man with the shopping
cart called to the workers. Deal noticed the man wore no shoes.

"I thought that's why you were here," she said.

Deal shook his head. "I'm not following you."

"I thought Mr. Penfield was getting the two of you together."

Deal was baffled. "Alcazar and me? Why would you think
that?"

She turned to him abruptly. "Look, it's public record, all right. I
mean you'd have to find out, sooner or later."

"Barbara . . . " he began.

"He owns Surf Motors," she blurted. "Raoul Alcazar owns Surf
Motors."

There was a loud snapping noise from the direction of the park.
The truck driver had apparently pulled back too far. The head of
the palm had sheared off the base and now dangled upside down
over the poinciana limb. It looked like someone had decided to
lynch a palm tree.

Deal stared at her, not certain he had heard correctly. He felt a
high-pitched whine start up somewhere in his head, like a huge
wind gathering, ready to sweep away everything in its path.

"I didn't *think* you knew that," she said, watching him. "I'm
sorry."

"Thanks, Barbara," Deal heard himself saying.

"Sure," she said. She put her hand on his arm. "Are you okay?"

Deal felt his head nodding. He thought of those mechanical dogs people put in their rear windows. He glanced up at her.

"Why did you tell me this?"

She gave him a look. "I don't know. I'm getting tired of working for attorneys, I guess." She took a breath. "I shouldn't have said anything . . . but you'd have found out sooner or later, right?"

Deal was nodding again. "Right." He forced a smile for her. "Sure I would've."

She nodded herself, a bit uncertainly, then turned and hurried inside the building.

He stopped at the *mercado* up the street from his fourplex. He could see the pile of dirt and coral mounded on the sidewalk from a block away. The city trucks were long gone. He went inside the hardware and bought a scoop shovel with a square blade and a pair of leather gloves.

There was a stop order stapled to the door of the fourplex, which Deal ripped down and wadded into a ball. It was the first thing he tossed into the gaping hole surrounding his gas and sewer connections. Then he put on the gloves, got his new shovel out of the car and started in on the pile of dirt and rock.

It took him three hours, but by last light, he was tamping the last of the dirt back into place. The tile men had left a hose attached to the outside faucet and he used that to nourish the smashed plants by the sidewalk. His arms and legs were rubbery with fatigue.

He wobbled back to the car, drove back up the street to the *mercado* and bought a six-pack, Jamaican Red Stripe in squatty little bottles with the label painted on.

"Good beer," the clerk said, snapping a sack open. He was an affable Cuban man in his sixties, an unlit cigar in the corner of his mouth.

Deal nodded, bleary with exhaustion. He and Janice had discovered the brand on a weekend cruise, years ago. The ship had lost power ten miles out of Montego harbor. A million old farts clamored at the buffet tables, the casinos, bitching about the broken air-conditioning, the food, the stingy slots. He and Janice stayed in the cabin rubbing themselves raw on the tangled sheets, calling room service again and again for ice and beer. The labels were foil then, and slid off easily in the icy buckets of water. They'd made them up into little medals and pasted them on each other, various parts of their anatomies, *for meritorious service, for valor, for courage and bravery beyond the call of duty . . .*

He glanced up at the clerk. "Yeah," he said. "It's good beer."

The clerk nodded and handed him the sack.

Deal pocketed his change and stepped out into the humid evening. He stopped short when he saw Driscoll there, leaning back against his city-issue sedan. He'd pulled into the curb behind the VW.

"Hey, Deal," Driscoll said. He unfolded his arms, pushed himself away from his car.

"Lieutenant," Deal nodded, wary. "What brings you down this way?"

Driscoll shrugged. "Nothing much. Just passing by my old haunts." He glanced around. "I was a beat cop in this neighborhood, back when. You should have seen it in the 1960s, when it was boom town, all the Cubans rolling in. This was the promised land."

"It's still okay," Deal said. His shoulders ached. He wanted to get back to the fourplex, drink his beer, loll in his stew of sadness, outrage, self-pity.

"You must think so," Driscoll said, glancing down the block toward the fourplex.

"Is that it? You want to invest in my project?"

Driscoll laughed, a short bark that sounded like gears grinding up glass. He put his big arm around Deal's shoulder. "Naw, son, I just came by to see how you were doing, that's all. I told you, your dad and I had some history . . . "

"You didn't say what it was," Deal cut in.

"Naw, you're right, I didn't."

Deal stared at him.

"Whyn't we drink one of those beers," Driscoll said, pointing at the sack.

Deal put the sack down on the hood of Driscoll's car, fished out a beer. Driscoll flipped the cap off with his thumb, caught it with his other hand.

Driscoll took a long swallow, then turned back. "Hell, son, he run him a dice game, you ought to know that. Him, the Carneses, buncha guys owned some restaurants. Floated around town for years. You can't keep a thing like that a secret."

"So they paid you not to bust them?" Deal asked.

Driscoll laughed again. It turned into a cough that made him pull out his handkerchief before he was finished. "This was different times, you understand. I'd say it was more like a public service, me keepin' the real crooks away from a friendly game, know what I mean?"

"You should have busted him," Deal said. "Before he pissed everything away."

Driscoll gave him a sympathetic look. "Maybe so, son." He drained the beer, held it up to the light to check the label.

"Anyways, you want to keep your cool, that's all I wanted to tell you."

Deal tried to read the man's expression. "Did somebody send you down here?"

Driscoll tossed the empty bottle into a carton of trash at the curb. He thought for a moment, then fixed Deal with a stare. "Why would somebody send me down here? I keep my ear to the ground, that's all. Somebody creates a ruckus in the banking center, I'm likely to hear about it. I know you been having a tough time. That's all it is."

Deal returned his gaze, trying to find something there, some trace of guile, some hidden message. It was like staring into the eyes of a Buddha wearing clothes from Sears.

"Is there something you want to tell me about?" Driscoll asked.

Deal thought about it for a moment. "I've been having a little trouble with the inspector on this building," he said, finally.

Driscoll glanced down the street. "That so?" he said, sounding surprised. He turned back to Deal. "You want me to look into it?"

"I thought maybe that's why you were here."

"Hey, I told you . . . " Driscoll began, bristling.

Deal held up his hands in surrender. "It's okay," Deal said. "I appreciate it, Driscoll. I'm doing fine."

Driscoll watched him for a moment. "Good," he said, at last. "You keep yourself out of trouble." He gave Deal a last pat on the shoulder and started away. "That's good beer," he added. Then he got in his car and drove off.

Deal tried to open one of the Red Stripes on the brief drive back to the fourplex, mimicking Driscoll's easy motion with the bottle cap, but it felt like he was going to rip all the flesh off his thumb. He had to wait until he'd parked, then lever the top off using the door latch.

He sat for a moment, wondering about Driscoll. If he had been carrying a message, he'd failed. Deal didn't have a clue what it was or who it might be from. Maybe it was just honest concern, like he said. In any case, Deal was too tired to think about it any longer.

He finished the beer and turned to the back seat to fish out a sleeping bag and nylon duffel he'd packed at the condo on his way back from Penfield's. He lugged the stuff up to the front door, dug out his key, and walked inside, into the smell of paint and new carpet. Moving in, he thought, and then shook his head. More like *digging in*.

He finished another of the beers sitting on the bar top of the kitchenette, watching it get dark outside, considering his options. Actually, there wasn't much to consider. His attorney in bed with the very people he was after. And those "people" had turned out to be Raoul Alcazar, the biggest slimewad in the county. Deal shook his head. He could go back downtown to confront Penfield, but he didn't see what good it would do. Who knows how much Penfield was pocketing from Alcazar. The attorney wasn't about to jeopardize an account like that. But why hadn't he just admitted it to Deal in the first place. Was he ashamed? Did he think Deal would eventually come to his senses, back off the suit?

In any case, he didn't see what talking to Penfield would accomplish. Given his present state of mind, there was always the possibility he'd end up throwing the old bastard out one of his windows, which would only complicate things.

He could hire another lawyer, but it seemed useless. Who could he be sure of, going up against Alcazar, whose influence at City-County was storied. He could maybe get some kid fresh out of law school, eager to make a reputation by going down, guns blazing, but that seemed like a waste of money, of which there was a relatively short supply.

He could give up, of course. Go groveling to Penfield and to see if *he* could get city hall off Deal's back so he could finish the fourplex and unload it before he went belly up. Whether or not Driscoll had any knowledge of it, Deal was certain that Faye was just doing what he'd been told.

Sure, groveling would be the logical approach. Forget the goddamn brakes and the fixers and movers and shakers you couldn't beat and his wife and his child who never was, and move it the fuck on down the road.

"No," Deal said, out loud, although he said it softly. "That's not the logical thing. How could that be the logical thing?" His words echoed about the empty rooms.

A two-story house across the street was catching the last pink glow on its upper reaches, a color the sun pumped out of the Everglades most every night about this time. Deal, exhausted, found himself nodding off, thinking of the gators just waking up out there, stirring around in their mud holes, ready to paddle out and find a nice duck nodding off in the reeds or maybe somebody's Pekingese run away from home and come down to the pond for a little lap of water. If you're tough, you take what you want. If you're weak, you get taken.

He blinked, rubbed his eyes, stared groggily at the stubbed out plumbing where the stove and refrigerator would be installed, assuming that it would in fact be installed. Too bad the refrigerator wasn't here right now, so he could store what was left of the beer in the freezer while he went in and took a shower.

There being no refrigerator, however, he did the next best thing and popped another beer, took that down the hall with him, leaving his options to percolate for a while.

He did his very best not to think at all while he stood under the steaming water, the beer singing in his veins now, although it did occur to him that whoever moved into the place was going to appreciate the good water pressure and the fact that the hot water seemed to last a long time. He also congratulated himself on springing the extra $82.50 per unit for the shower doors he'd installed. Be a shitload of water all over the floor without those doors, mmmm-hmmm, because he'd brought no shower curtain. He finally turned off the water and got out. Opened another beer.

He *had* remembered to pack a towel, a thick one, a Janice towel to be sure. Before they were married, he'd favored thin white towels on extended loan from motels he had visited. But Janice had been right about a thick towel, he had to admit. He rubbed himself down, luxuriating in the fading ache of his thighs and triceps. Then the glow went away when he realized who he'd been thinking about.

He had another slug of beer, then began to hum, a nice, heavy sound that filled up the inside of his head and left no room for thinking. He broke off momentarily to finish the beer. Then the hum became a kind of growl and finally segued into a rendition of "Louie, Louie," a song which Flivey Penfield favored when they were college roommates. No ache thinking of Flivey. A good sign.

Deal moved into the bedroom that adjoined the steaming bath, adding a little body English to the music. Just as good as stereo. Better than stereo, in fact. Groping in his bag for his briefs, one leg, *hump,* other leg, *whump, where you gonna go now . . . pull up yo pants, whoa-o-oh, now . . . but what was that strange popping noise . . . ?*

And then he froze. *. . . fuck shit piss, back against the wall. . . .* A huge man, across the room from him—Leon Straight, no doubt about that—he must have been leaning in the doorway of the bedroom all the time, idly cracking his knuckles, waiting for Deal to notice, waiting for him now to get his pants pulled up.

"I knocked," the big man said, "but I guess you didn't hear me, on account of the shower." He nudged his massive shadow away from the door frame. It was too dark to see his lips move, but who else could have spoken? Deal felt the smooth wall behind him, getting himself steady, getting his balance. He thought of that huge ray lifting off the ocean floor when he was snorkeling. About the size of Leon's shadow. The same threatening grace.

"That's right. I didn't hear you." Deal felt his throat creaking. Had he left the door unlocked? He couldn't remember.

"The boss asked me to come pick you up."

"Alcazar?"

"That's right."

"What if I got something to do, I can't come right now."

Leon's head swiveled about the barren room. "Like you were getting ready to throw a party or something?"

"Whatever," Deal said. His irritation was growing, the adrenaline shock beginning to leach away.

"Okay by me," Leon said. He turned, his shadowy mass headed for the door.

"Wait a second," Deal said. Leon stopped. "What's this about, Leon?" There was a pause. "That is your name, isn't it?"

"Doesn't matter my name, Mr. Deal. I don't know what it's about. Maybe he wants to build something. That's what you do, isn't it, *build?*" He said it the way you'd humor an idiot.

Deal thought about things a moment. It was an option he hadn't considered, except for the stray thought of waylaying Alcazar, tying him and Penfield back to back and dropping them both out the window of Penfield's office.

But why not? Why not go to the source?

"You mind if I get dressed?" Deal said.

"Take your time," Leon said, and ambled off, down the hallway.

Leon ushered Deal into the back of a soft gray limo parked at the curb outside, snapped on the television, showed him the bar, the tape player. "There's fuck tapes, new movies, whatever you want." He pointed out the stereo, the CD, the button for the sun roof, then got in front and pulled out.

A City-County cruiser was parked down the block. Neither cop so much as glanced at the limo as they passed. They might as well have been a ghost car, Deal thought. How could you ignore a stretch limo in *this* neighborhood? And then the answer occurred to him. They damn well knew to ignore it.

It took them about thirty minutes to reach their destination, a sprawling auto-sales complex laid out on some acreage newly skinned from a melaleuca forest at the north end of the county.

They spiraled down off the turnpike on a brand new ramp that would one day serve a gojillion commuters. Right now the only lights in the area came from a series of television transmission towers strung out in the distance, and closer in, the dealership, lit up like downtown Vegas.

The place was actually a series of glassed-in pavilions, each featuring a different make of car, set up around some artificial terraces and lagoons they'd dug from the coral plain. The ponds all had fountains and rock waterfalls and the same kind of landscaping you'd expect at Walt Disney World.

Broad swathes of lawn connected the various pavilions, sparkling in the sprinkler irrigation that was pulsing just now. Take out the buildings, you could play golf here, Deal thought. An enormous American flag fluttered at the entryway, a road that seemed as broad as the freeway interchange they'd just left.

Leon took them down the road toward the large central building, a conglomeration of fieldstone and smoked glass that hugged the ground and featured several different foreign makes discreetly lit behind the windows. Leon found a break in the curb that Deal hadn't seen, and piloted the limo along a narrow strip of blacktop, straight for the huge glass windows.

The big slabs of glass slid back as they approached and Leon took them right up a hidden ramp into the showroom itself. Deal sat there while Leon said something into a car phone, then got out and came to open his door. The television inside the limo was still playing, an old black-and-white flick with Rod Steiger in some outrageous makeup and a marcelled hairdo ogling a pretty girl in a mortician's workroom. The picture was wavering, now that they were inside. Deal hadn't bothered to turn up the sound.

Leon jabbed his sizable thumb toward the rear of the building. "Mr. Alcazar'll be with you in a minute. You can wait out here."

Deal nodded and got out. The place was quiet, only the soft rush of air-conditioning in the background. There was the same smell of paint and new carpet as the fourplex, but he doubted there'd been any flak from the building codes office on this project.

Leon stood by the limo with his arms folded, watching Deal like some palace guard. He'd been watching too many tough-guy movies, Deal thought.

He strolled over to a wedge-shaped yellow car, a Lotus, glanced at the sticker on the window. Eighty-nine thousand. Flivey had owned a Lotus once. He saved up two thousand dollars from the construction job one summer, bought the car, ten years old, from a guy in Fort Lauderdale. He drove it a week before it refused to start and spent another two thousand on the electrical system before he sold it in disgust for fifteen hundred.

Deal felt someone's eyes on him and straightened up, surprised to see a middle-aged man in shirt sleeves staring at him from an open-air desk near a window. The guy had been running some figures on a calculator, it looked like. There was a ledger sheet spread out on the desk beside him. The guy got up, wiping his hands on his pants, coming after Deal as if he were a customer.

"I'm just waiting for Mr. Alcazar," Deal said.

The guy cut a glance at Leon, who was inspecting a thread on one of his coat buttons.

"Sure," the salesman said, uncertain. "Look around, you have any questions, I'll be glad to help."

Deal nodded.

"We have a lot of interesting cars here."

Deal nodded again. The inveterate salesman, he thought. Once his button's pushed, the whole tape's got to cycle.

The guy pointed at a pair of black Ferraris angled nose to nose near the front. "The one on the right is a Ferrari Daytona, the real thing. The other one's a copy. A McBirney kit over a 1969 Corvette chassis. That's what Sonny Crockett drove when the 'Vice' series started."

"Is that right?" Deal said. Not that it mattered to him, but he still couldn't see the difference.

"We're asking sixty for the McBirney. The Ferrari's at two-fifteen. That's a steal."

Deal stared at him.

The guy shrugged. "Black's not a mover. Lot of folks go into a Ferrari for the investment. You'd want red in that case, like the F-forty there."

The guy pointed at a fiery red machine sitting on a pedestal in the center of the showroom. It had a vague resemblance to the black Ferrari, but, with a huge spoiler hulking over the rear deck, it looked more like a race car than anything you'd see on the street.

"Eight hundred thousand dollars' worth of automobile," the guy said. "A special edition. Top-end of two hundred two miles per hour. You need a special license to drive it."

"A license to print money?" Deal said.

The guy hesitated, then laughed. "That's good," he said. "A license to print money. I like that."

Leon glanced up from his grooming. "Give it a rest, Morton. The guy's not in the market."

Morton gave him a look, but his tape had clearly wound down. "Here's my card," he said to Deal. "Call me any time."

Deal stared at him. Maybe the guy really did wind up with a key. The guy still had the card extended when a door opened in a distant corner of the big showroom and Alcazar strode out, flanked by two Latinos, one slender, the other stocky, with a designer's haircut and a suit nearly as well draped as his boss's.

Leon stepped away from the limo, toward Deal. Morton saw who was coming and pocketed his card. He was scurrying back to his desk when Leon called after him.

"It can wait till tomorrow, Morton. Go on home."

Morton never broke stride. He made a smooth cut to the right, snatched up his suit coat from a chair and disappeared outside.

The trio advanced across the thick carpet. "Mr. Deal," Alcazar said, extending his hand. "I am glad you could come."

Deal stared at his outstretched hand, then at the man's face, Alcazar's gaze about even with his own. He hadn't paid much attention that night aboard Penfield's yacht but now he noticed a shading of gray at the temples, like himself. And a similar set of sun lines at the eyes, although not from working outside. Composed. Intelligent. More so than you'd like to give him credit for. He'd have a Latin jury eating out of his hand.

"My attorney . . . " he paused, flashing the briefest of smiles, ". . . Mr. Penfield told me you turned down our offer."

A car rumbled away outside—Morton in a smoking Chevrolet, its vinyl roof poofed up in the wind. "That's not what I'm interested in, Mr. Alcazar," Deal said.

Alcazar went on as if he hadn't heard. "I'm very sorry about your loss, Mr. Deal. Very sorry. Your wife was a lovely woman." He paused, his tone shifting slightly. "It is a tragic matter and I wanted you to know that I respect your feelings. I wanted to say this to you personally." Alcazar stopped and stared at him, as if he'd said something momentous. Deal looked around at the three oafs who wore practiced expressions of disinterest in their employer's affairs.

Alcazar continued. "If a cash settlement offends you, perhaps there is something else I might do. I speculate in real estate, for instance. Possibly your current project is something I'd be interested in."

His current project? What, had Penfield told him everything? Shown him the balance statements, come up with the right figures, the right buttons to push. Poor old Deal, he's in a bad way, let's get this over with, get him out of his misery . . .

Deal felt himself swelling with rage, but he contained himself. He shrugged. "Come see me when I'm finished."

"The status is not important," Alcazar said magnanimously. "I am merely trying to help."

Deal stared at him, ready to explode. This scum bag, extending his charity to Deal?

"I appreciate the thoughts, Mr. Alcazar," Deal said. "But can I tell you something?"

Leon glanced up, on the alert. Alcazar waved him off, then nodded at Deal. Deal glanced around the lobby, at all the shining cars. Porsches, Jaguars, the malevolent-looking Ferraris. Every paint job glowing as if with inner life.

Deal cleared his throat. Why did he feel intimidated by a bunch of cars? He shook off the feeling, reached down deep. He'd try to make his point, one last time.

"Used to be, Mr. Alcazar, every kid in school learned that old story about George Washington, he cuts down the cherry tree and then he comes and tells his dad, he did it, he's sorry, but he has to own up for what he did." Deal paused. "Maybe you never heard that story."

"Something like it," Alcazar shrugged. Leon stared at Deal with something between astonishment and disgust.

Deal continued. "I don't have to tell you how things have changed these last few years, Mr. Alcazar. Not that anybody really did what George was supposed to have done, of course, at least not after you got old enough to understand that owning up got you a good ass-whipping. But we, all of us over here, we *pretended* to believe in the story, you know what I mean?"

A hint of a smile had come to Alcazar's face. He was either amused, or was convinced Deal was mad as a hatter.

Deal nodded, took a few steps toward a Porsche Targa. Glossy black on the outside, buttery gray upholstery on the inside. Deal kicked one of the tires and Leon glowered. Deal turned back to Alcazar.

"But lately, I try to think about that old story, instead I see this little kid in a Richard Nixon mask, he chops the tree down and when his father comes out to see what's going on, the kid plants the hatchet right in his old man's forehead."

Leon smirked. It was apparently something he could identify with.

There was a silence in the room so deep you could hear the rush of the fountains outside. Deal pondered the madness of it, standing in the middle of an autos-of-the-gods dealership, lecturing Raoul Alcazar about owning up. For a moment, he had the sensation that this was all some terrible dream, that he might wake up, back in his condo, Janice turning restlessly in her sleep, asking if Deal might rub her back.

Instead, it was Alcazar who spoke. "Every country has its myths," he said. "I grew up hearing about the streets of America, how they were paved with gold." He waved his hand about the showroom, gave Deal his thin smile. "And I have found it to be true."

Deal glanced around, nodding, feeling Alcazar measuring him, hearing the man's voice sliding into a patronizing, we're-all-friends-here tone.

"I think you have been under a great deal of strain, Mr. Deal. Mr. Penfield tells me you are a decent man. I am a decent man—"

Deal turned back, interrupting. "You asked what I want, Alcazar. And I've just decided." He glanced at Leon who barely concealed a sneer. "I'd like you to buy some time on television, take out a couple of pages in the *Herald*," he said. "I want you to explain what happened and why your people were at fault. That if everyone had done what he was supposed to, my wife would still be alive." He took a breath.

"Just admit you were wrong, Mr. Alcazar. Stand up. Maybe it'll help turn the tide. But most important, it's going to make me feel better. You can forget about George Washington—I just used that to make my point."

A phone was ringing somewhere. The smile had disappeared from Alcazar's face, his gaze stony now. He drew a breath that seemed to tax him. "Mr. Deal, am I to take you seriously?"

"What do you think this is about, Alcazar? Lawsuits? Money? Bringing my wife back?"

Deal paused. "What I'd really like to do is beat the living shit out of you." Leon started forward, but this time Deal waved him off. "But now that I've spent fifteen minutes in your presence, I figure this would hurt you a hell of a lot worse."

Alcazar shook his head in disbelief. "In my country, it is a particular sin to harm a madman. But you are testing me . . . "

He broke off. The phone had stopped ringing and the stocky thug, the one with the good suit, had come to whisper in Alcazar's ear. Alcazar's eyes flickered, came back to Deal.

"Excuse me," he said and followed the thug into a glassed-in office. After a few moments on the phone Alcazar covered the mouthpiece. He glanced out at Deal, then said something to the thug with a dismissive gesture.

The thug looked through the glass at Deal, shrugged, and came outside. Alcazar had returned to his phone conversation.

"Mr. Alcazar wants you to have something," the thug said, his voice echoing as he approached Deal. Deal had the odd feeling that he had heard the voice before somewhere. Then he forgot that, wondering what Alcazar might be offering. A pair of broken arms? Cement overshoes? An ice pick in the ear? There wasn't a soul who knew he was here. He could join the primeval sludge of the Everglades. Disappear without a trace. Like Janice.

"Mr. Alcazar says take any car you want." Alejandro waved his arm about the showroom. Leon's eyes had narrowed in disgust.

Stunned, Deal followed his gesture. Alcazar was still engrossed in his conversation. Deal looked back at the thug.

"He wants to give me a car?"

"Except for the red Ferrari up there," the thug said. "It's sold," he added. Deal didn't think he said it very convincingly.

Leon spoke up. "Man wants to do right by you. He didn't ask me. If he did, I'd tell him to kick your crazy ass. Kick your ass so bad you could tell George Washington about it."

"It's what Mr. Alcazar wants," Alejandro repeated.

Alcazar was leaning back in his desk chair so that Deal could see the top of his head, where the hair was thinning. Deal turned back to Alejandro. "Like, he'd give me the Lotus, here?"

Alejandro stared back at Deal, widened his eyes enough to mean yes. It looked like he'd had his face sanded, but you could still make out the blue craters of acne scars in the bright lights of the showroom.

"So I could drive around in a little yellow car, forget anything ever happened?"

Alejandro shrugged.

"You can jam it up your ass, you want to," Leon said.

"Mr. Alcazar wants us to give him the keys, Leon," Alejandro said.

Leon glanced at Alejandro, then toward Alcazar's office, as if he were about to seek confirmation. Finally, he grunted, then moved off to a wall cabinet, shaking his head. He spun the combination dial, opened the door to a bank of keys, took a moment finding the right ones. He brought the keys and tossed them at Alejandro. Alejandro caught them at his chest and after a moment of simmering at Leon, turned to hand them to Deal.

Deal took the keys, hefted them. He stared through the thick glass walls of the room where Alcazar was speaking vehemently but soundlessly into the phone, facing the showroom now. Deal watched, idly reading what the man was saying. . . . *Doing exactly as we agreed,* Alcazar said, his expression angry, as he listened to whomever was on the other end. Abruptly Alcazar broke in. *Fuck your baseball,* Deal read, or thought he did. Maybe he had missed something, or maybe it was some kind of idiomatic curse. Alcazar glanced up, saw Deal staring at him, then turned away.

There was a heavy rumbling noise behind him and Deal turned to see the skinny thug pressing a button at a control panel, the big glass doors that had slid shut behind the limo rolling open again.

Deal glanced at the Lotus, remembering what Morton had told him. He calculated the figures. Nearly quadruple what they'd offered him through Penfield. This was an *automobile,* as Cal Saltz would say.

"So that's it, I just drive right out?"

"We'll send you the paperwork," Alejandro said.

Leon glared at Deal, his pupils down to pinpoints. Deal looked at the car. Maybe there was a bomb beneath the driver's seat, Deal thought, but then discounted it. Nobody looked ready to run.

Deal nodded. They wanted to give him a car.

The strange hum he'd felt earlier that evening had returned, filling his ears, crowding out thought. It was his blood whistling down his veins, maybe, or his brain shorting out. So the streets were paved with gold. Little boys with hatchets ran wild.

Deal glanced at Alcazar, who had his back to them, waving his hand as he spoke into the telephone. Janice was dead. Deal was a madman. Raoul Alcazar was the prince of reason. A car. The universe inside out. Where a moment before, there had been blood running in his veins, Deal felt them now carrying nothing but a hot, angry wind.

Deal smiled at Alejandro. Or thought he had. The look on Alejandro's face seemed unsure. Deal, on the other hand, had never felt more certain.

He opened the door to the Lotus, folded himself down inside, gripped the thick leather wheel. It took him a moment to find the ignition, another to get the seat back where he wanted it. He was aware that he was still smiling at Alejandro, through the windshield now. The wind inside him had risen to a scream. He saw walls of caverns pulsing with a volcanic light of their own.

Deal turned the key over, gunned the engine to life. The rumble was muted, but Deal could feel something immensely powerful coursing the frame of the car, some inexorable machine strength that came up through the soft leather and the wheel and leapt to join the maelstrom inside him. He found himself grinning as he gripped the wheel. *Fuck your baseball.*

The skinny thug stood nearby, motioning him to back out of the showroom. Leon looked as though he were considering throwing his considerable body in the way, but he simply turned aside.

Deal felt the heat inside him fanned to a white, cleansing force. So searing, he felt calm. He had surely ascended to some other plane. Beatific, he found himself thinking. Beatific. Still repeating this one-word mantra, he engaged the clutch and backed his Lotus slowly out.

*   *   *

As the heavy glass doors slid closed, Alcazar put down the phone and emerged from the inner office. He glanced at Alejandro, who reassured him with a nod. The second thug was turning off the lights in the showroom. Leon was locking up the key bank, still snorting his disapproval.

The roar of the Lotus's engines reverberated through the heavy glass as the car wound down the blacktop lane toward the freeway entrance. The brake lights flashed on as the car stopped at the juncture of the dealership property and the access road.

"Don't know why we fuck with this guy," Leon grumbled.

"Let him enjoy his car," Alcazar said. "When the time is right, we . . . " Then he stopped.

Something seemed wrong. The Lotus was turning around, the headlights aimed at the building, flashing from bright to dim, back to bright again.

Leon started around the front of the limo, his hand going inside his coat. There was a tremendous engine roar outside, and a squalling of rubber that sent twin tendrils of blue smoke up into the bright sodium lights near the entrance to the complex. The headlights of the Lotus were fixed on Raoul Alcazar, or so it seemed. And they were growing very, very large.

The Lotus leapt up like some mechanized animal when it hit the ramp at the curb, and again when it clipped the ramp just outside the huge windows. When it roared through the thick plate-glass slabs, the driver's door was flapping wildly open. It banged shut at impact, but flew open again as the car screamed on inside.

Alejandro had already bailed out over the hood of the limo. His partner dived through the doorway of the sales office. Leon was back-pedaling, a pistol waving in his upraised hand, but back-pedaling was one of the moves the several operations on his knee had curtailed. Still, he might have made it clear, if it hadn't been for the door of the Lotus, which whipped into his good leg with a crack that was instantly lost in the chaos. He sent two shots into the ceiling as he went down.

The Lotus slammed into the limo, and glanced away, like a small-caliber bullet careening off the skin of a tank. It chewed its way up the hood of the Porsche, flattening the windshield, its right front tire dipping into the driver's compartment and hanging up for an instant on the exposed bar of the Targa top.

That sent the Lotus catapulting end over end, ripping off the engine cover of the Porsche and slinging it high into the ceiling. The heavy sheet of metal tore out the main feeder for the sprinkler system and sliced the maze of ceiling wiring in a shower of sparks.

The Lotus dropped its hind quarters onto the rear of a Jaguar sedan, and snapped its front end into a kiss with the red Ferrari. The three cars slid against the "Miami Vice" imitation, squashing it against a section of outside wall. Shards of black Fiberglas snapped about the showroom like huge angry insects.

Finally, it was quiet, except for the gush of water from the broken pipes overhead and the ominous crackle of a mounting electrical fire. There was also the soft keening of Leon, who lay holding his second ruined leg, rocking back and forth, alternately cursing and groaning.

Alcazar pulled himself up in the backseat of the limo, peering out the lowered window at the wreckage. The television in the limo was still playing silently. The image was still black and white, now an enormous fat woman flat on her back, pinned to her kitchen floor by a refrigerator that had tumbled over. The woman was unfazed. She gnawed at the leg of a cooked turkey she'd been trying to pull out of the refrigerator, while Rod Steiger in his crazy makeup wrung his hands and looked on.

"Kill the sonofabitch," someone said, as a fire alarm began to sound. There were murmurs, groans, even shouts of agreement. All of which were drowned in the roar of the first gas tank's explosion.

20 Deal was a mile or so from the dealership by the time he saw the glow in the sky. He'd heard a few muffled explosions earlier.

No mistaking what it was. He heard sirens far in the distance, but doubted there'd be much left of the place by the time the trucks arrived. One of the hazards of building on the fringes of civilization— you had to wait for all the city services to catch up with you.

He bent and massaged his aching knee. He'd banged it a good one rolling out of the Lotus, but as long as he kept moving, he'd be all right. Only trouble was, he wasn't sure which way to move. He'd decided against using the highway, intending to cut cross-country to the television towers, then work his way to civilization on the levee roads. Now, he'd come to a broad canal flanked by feathery Australian pines that ran off in either direction as far as he could see. A chorus of bullfrogs pulsed rhythmically in the darkness.

It was probably the C-112, the broad flood-control channel that had always blocked development in this part of the county, at least until the turnpike extension had gone through. Deal should have remembered it was there—he'd heard his old man bitch about it often enough.

144

He could see the warning lights of the towers through the trees, no more than a mile away. There had to be a lock or service crossing somewhere nearby. But should he turn right or left? He listened to the sirens grow. The wrong choice could send him straight back the way he'd come, which did not seem like a good idea.

"I wouldn't swim it, I was you."

The voice rose from somewhere in the darkness, startling Deal, nearly sending him off the bank. He grabbed a limb for balance.

"Gator hole just across the way. Seen him poke his snout up just about dark. Big sucker." The same voice.

A flashlight snapped on a few yards down the bank, the beam cutting across the water to the opposite shore. Deal made out the man's image in the backwash of the light. His skin was ebony, his hair and shortish beard glowing white in the reflected light. He had a bamboo pole crooked in one arm, was sitting on an overturned plastic bucket. When he turned to Deal his eyes were glittering silver disks. It took Deal a moment to realize—just the light reflecting from the glasses that he wore.

Deal had a sudden flash—the old black man watching him dive into the current, headed for Dirty Dick's, all those years ago—but it couldn't be possible. This man didn't look a day older. It was just that Deal had placed himself plop in the middle of another stupid action, that's all. On the shore of shit's creek and no paddle in sight.

"You scared the hell out of me," Deal said, finally.

"You didn't do a bad job on *me,*" the old man said. "I usually have this spot all to myself."

"Yeah," Deal said, glancing back at the glow in the sky. "Well, I broke down on the turnpike, a couple miles back. I couldn't get anybody to stop, so I thought I'd just cut across here to call for a ride."

"Mmmmm-hmmmm," the man said, glancing up into the sky over Deal's shoulder. Then he turned back to the water, waving the flashlight beam, indicating that Deal should look too. Deal followed the light out across the water, saw two points of red reflecting back at them from the darkness. That would be the alligator, all right.

"Just head on down that way a piece," the old man said, using the flashlight for a pointer. "There's a gas main goes across. That's how I do it," the old man said.

"Thanks," Deal said.

The old man snapped off the light. He'd never bothered to illuminate Deal's face with it. There was the glow in the sky behind them, occasional bursts of sheet lightning far off to the south. Just enough light to make out the old man's silhouette, steady as a statue's.

"You're welcome," the man said. "Hope you find your way home."

Me too, Deal thought, heading off. *Me too.*

"You *walked* all the way here?" Saltz asked. He had Deal's leg propped on a footstool in the little den of his condominium. Deal was in Saltz's television-watching chair, trying to see what Saltz was seeing in his swollen knee.

"I got a cab from Pembroke Pines," Deal said, trying to flex his leg.

"Sit still," Saltz said. He probed the swollen tissue and Deal went rigid, his breath hissing in through his clenched teeth.

"We ought to wrap this," Saltz said, standing up. He stared down at Deal, shaking his head. "Then tomorrow, we'll get you to a doctor, see about a brain transplant."

Deal looked away. "It was just instinct," he said.

"Well, I didn't suppose you *thought* about it," Saltz said. "Jesus Christ, why didn't you just drive that goddamn car into a brick wall and be done with it."

Deal turned back to face him. "If he'd done anything else, Cal. If he'd said 'go fuck yourself,' if he'd had his assholes rough me up, if he'd said 'I'm very sorry, please go home now,' I think I could have handled it. But the sonofabitch wanted to give me a car . . . "

"Yeah, and I wish you'd have given it to me if that's what you were going to do with it." Saltz snorted and moved toward the door. "You wasted one hell of an *automobile,* Johnny."

"That's true," Deal said, resigned.

"Well, I'm going to the drugstore," Saltz said. He sounded as tired as Deal felt.

"The hell with that," Deal said. "I don't need anything."

Saltz stopped to stare at him. "Maybe *you* don't," he said, pointing at the empty quart of Wild Turkey on the side table. "I know the guy runs the late shift. He'll open up the liquor shop, slip me a bottle of whiskey."

Deal sighed and waved him out.

"I'll pick up one of those knee bandages they make for the ball players while I'm at it," Saltz added. "I'll get one with Michael Jordan on the box."

He was still talking when the door closed.

Deal stared at the closed door for a while, then reached for the drink Saltz had poured him while he'd told the story. Enough of the ice had melted finally so that Deal could sip the whiskey. The pain in his knee had seemed to abate now that Saltz had stopped poking around. A couple of aspirin, another drink or two, a good night's sleep, he'd be ready.

But ready for what? Call Penfield and beg for a deal, I'll say I'm sorry if you will first? Fat chance. And the funny thing was, he didn't even feel sorry. He didn't feel justified, necessarily, but he sure as hell didn't feel bad about what he'd done. How would George Washington handle this one?

He reached out for the television clicker, snapped on the set. The host was interviewing a man from Omaha, the second richest man in America. What was he doing living out there, the host wanted to know. "All you need's about one good idea a year," the man said. "Omaha's good for that." The host laughed and they cut away to a commercial.

Deal was about to change the channel when the Channel 10 news brief came on. First it was Ann Bishop, ramrod straight in her anchorperson's chair, ". . . on a fast-breaking story in north Dade," then a cutaway to a young, impeccably dressed Cuban woman in front of the entrance to Alcazar's new dealership.

You could hear the big flag snapping over her head as the young reporter spoke breathlessly into the microphone. Deal was struck by the way her lipstick glistened in the light, by the soft drape of her beige linen suit. This one was destined for the networks, he thought.

". . . where firefighters have just about wrapped it up, Ann.

"We're told that Raoul Alcazar was in the building when it burst into flames, but that he and some of his employees escaped without serious injury. Officials are telling us that it was an electrical fire, but they're keeping everyone away from the building while the investigation continues."

There was some commotion off-camera, and the reporter glanced over her shoulder, then began to edge away, directing her cameraman with little gestures of the mike. She smiled and spoke as she edged along. "We're just getting out of the way here, Ann."

An EMS van bumped down over the curb, followed by a fire chief's sedan. Neither seemed in a hurry—no flashers, no sirens. "We don't have any firm estimate of damage yet, but the building looks like a total loss, and we understand there were several luxury imported cars in there."

The camera shifted to a long shot of the main showroom, which was still smoldering. A pair of firemen were halfheartedly guiding a stream of water about. Another fireman poked cautiously at the edge of a smoldering car with a long pole.

"She means *automobiles,* Ann," Deal said, taking another swallow of his drink.

The image cut back to the reporter. "They were all set for a grand opening on Saturday, but that seems out of the question, now." Her voice was cheery, her smile wide. Deal wondered what the expression on Raoul Alcazar's face was. "Back to you, Ann," the reporter chirped.

"What a shame," Ann said, shaking her head, her lips pursed in disapproval.

Deal hit the power button, and Ann became a white point of light that faded into nothing. He dropped the clicker back on the table, finished the drink, and closed his eyes. He would just rest a moment before Saltz came back to berate him further. He fell asleep like a baby.

In his dream, he was back at the canal, stymied, pacing back and forth, wondering where the old black man had gone. Ann Bishop sped down the levee road on the opposite bank in a yellow Lotus. Little Homer, wearing nothing but a jockstrap and a big pair of rubber car washing boots, stood up in the passenger's seat, gripping the top of the windshield for balance and whooping like a cowboy.

They saw Deal and waved, someone shoved Deal from behind and he was in the frigid water, which was salty, and also heaving with waves when it should have been piss warm. But still, he panicked, for he knew what was under the surface, that monstrous creature with eyes glowing bright enough to turn the water red and even redder, the jaws of the thing widening, bearing down on him . . .

When the phone rang, and he came awake, clawing at the air, gasping as if he were about to drown. He looked about the empty apartment, getting his breathing under control, checking his watch, still groggy. He'd been asleep a couple of hours. The phone rang again, and this time Deal registered it.

Saltz at the drugstore, he supposed, to tell him they'd only had Larry Bird on the knee brace box, and to say he'd stopped at Flanagan's for a couple of pops.

Deal picked up. "Yeah, Cal?"

And knew right away it wasn't Cal. There was a roar of static over the line, a faint background chatter between two men in Spanish, *"sun fist, sun fist"* he heard, in what sounded like pidgin English. "Hello," Deal said, a trickle of fear springing up in his gut. Alcazar tracking him here? Already?

"Deal?" The voice hardly audible above the two Spanish speakers who seemed to be arguing about something, now.

Deal went numb. He wasn't sure if he was still holding the receiver, if he was still in Cal's chair. He could have been drifting in ether somewhere.

"Deal?" she repeated. The tone unmistakable. Not just fear, but outright desperation. Except it couldn't be.

"Janice?" he said, knowing it was impossible. He was still asleep, drifted off in front of Cal's television. This dream brought to you courtesy of all the fine folks down at Wild Turkey.

"Deal, you're *there*. Thank God you're there."

Deal sat up straight in his chair, swung his bad leg down from the stool. He felt a surge of pain and knew he was not dreaming.

". . . told me about what happened tonight. You're in terrible danger . . . " her voice, rushed, frantic.

"Janice, Jesus Christ. This is you, isn't it? Jesus Christ. Are you all right? Where are you, for Christ's sake?"

"Deal, listen to me. I'm not sure how much time I have, and this damned phone . . . "

There was a burst of static that obliterated her words for a moment, then she was back.

"... where I am or not."

Deal thought he heard a burst of *salsa* music in the background, but it might have come from the other conversation which nattered along, weaving in and out of the static.

"I couldn't hear all of that, Janice."

"... *going to need a heading on the channel, do you read me?*" It was another voice, this one crystal clear, male, a hint of a British accent, overpowering everything else on the line.

"Fuck! Shit!" Deal pounded the receiver against his palm, then held it close. The static was back. His heart was surging, great waves of pressure pressing against his chest, then receding, and building again. His breath was coming in gasps. "Janice?" he called. Alive. She was alive.

"Can you hear me, Deal?"

"I can hear you, Janice. You're cutting in and out." He took a breath, his mind racing. "Where are you? What is it, Janice? What's happening?"

He stood, testing his knee. It was sore, but it supported him.

"I'm all right, Deal. I got out of the car and there was this man . . . " She broke off as another crash of static overtook the line.

He jumped in the instant the line cleared. "Janice, look, just tell me where you are. I'll get there. I'll handle it, whatever it is."

"That's just it," she said, her voice ready to break. "I don't *know* where I am. I woke up and I was in this room, a bedroom. The windows are boarded up, but I know we're on the water. Right on the water . . . "

"... *problems with that bloody generator.*" It was the clear male voice again, wiping everything else away.

Deal pounded the phone again in a panic. He clapped the receiver to his ear again. "... *if they have parts in Kingston, roger.*"

Then, "I'm afraid, Deal . . . ," and she was gone.

"Janice," he called. "Janice?" The line was filled with crackling now, his brain roaring a static all its own. Abruptly, the connection broke altogether. After a few clicks, Deal heard the dial tone. He stared at the receiver, stunned.

"Janice?" he repeated, his voice barely a whisper.

Deal stared at the receiver, then across the room, at his reflection in the mirrored tile behind the tiny bar. He looked like a stranger, a wild man in torn slacks, his hair in disarray, his eyes bloodshot. A junkie who'd broken in, about to ransack the apartment.

The phone was talking to him now: "If you'd like to make a call, please hang up and dial the number. If you'd like to make a call . . . " Deal came out of his trance. He broke the connection, dialed the operator.

"Southern Bell, Miss Apple speaking."

"I just got a call, long distance, I think. Is there any way I can find out where it came from?"

There was a pause. "I'm sorry, sir, did you say you had *placed* a call?"

"Jesus Christ, *no* . . . " Deal stopped, forced himself to lower his voice. Patience, patience. "I said I *got* a call. Long distance. I thought maybe there'd be some way to check where it came from."

"I'm sorry, sir. There's no way I can help you. If you had *placed* the call, then . . . " Deal slammed the receiver down.

He heard someone at the door then, the knob rattling, somebody putting a shoulder to the wood. Deal raised the phone, instinctively. So this was it. He saw his likeness in the bar mirror, a wild-eyed man with a phone for a club, waiting for Leon Straight and the Cuban Bushwhacker Twins.

The door flew open, then, and Cal Saltz followed it in, off balance, still clinging to the knob, a bottle of Wild Turkey in one hand, a drugstore package tucked under his arm. "Fix the goddamn door, Cal," the old man was muttering to himself.

He broke off when he saw Deal. "Hey, Johnny," he grinned. "I just stopped in at Flanagan's . . . " He fought to bring his glittering eyes into focus.

"Sonofabitch wouldn't sell me a bottle at the drugstore." He shook his head sadly.

Deal realized he was still holding the telephone aloft. He turned and replaced the receiver in the cradle, suddenly very, very tired.

"Hey, what's with you?" Cal was saying. Deal gripped the counter, watched in the mirror as the old man cocked his shaggy head. Deal felt the high-pitched whine starting up inside him again. It made it hard to hear. He couldn't be sure what Saltz said next. He thought it was pretty funny, though. He thought Cal said: "You look like you seen a goddamn ghost."

"You about to fuck up everything, sweet cheeks," Leon said. The woman was sprawled across the bed where he'd tossed her, glowering at him. He'd turned his newly injured leg, hurrying after her, and he had to wait a moment for the pain to subside.

"Big mouth like you have, I should have held you under a couple minutes longer." And would have, if he hadn't figured out how to use her.

He turned to inspect the strange handset he'd ripped out of the phone set on the floor. It was a big, boxy looking contraption, looked like something out of an old John Wayne war movie. "This a ship to shore outfit?" he asked. "Maybe it's an antique. Ought to get it fixed up, make it worth something."

She still hadn't spoken. Her cheeks were red, like maybe he'd slapped her, but he knew it was just her being pissed off at him. In any case, she *was* a fox.

"You call the police?" he asked.

She hesitated. "They're on their way."

"Hmmm-hmmm," Leon said. "On the way to where?" He'd been listening outside the door for a moment, puzzled when he heard her voice, thinking maybe someone was in the room with her, better figure it out before he went barging in.

"I don't *know* where I am," Leon said, mocking her. "We on

the *ocean* someplace. Maybe *Puerto Rico.*" He shook his head. "Shee-it!"

"What do you want from me?" color high in her cheeks, all right. Making her look excited.

"When the time is right, sweet cheeks," Leon said. "When the time is right." Though he would *like* to explain it to somebody, proud as he was of his plan. Going to show *Seen-your* Alcazar a move or two that had nothing to do with football or how tough you were. No, Leon was operating on brain power, here. Wait for the right moment, and *wham* . . . take the man's head off with a brain power forearm, that's right.

He bent to pick up the phone set then, hefted it, then glanced at her as he let it drop to the floor. There was a crashing of glass from deep inside the thing and Leon laughed.

"Bunch of funky old tubes and shit in there," he said, sadly. He tapped a pouch that was strapped to his belt, where the stubby antenna of a cellular phone protruded. "We get ready to call your old man, we'll do it the right way." He gave her a last smile and then walked out.

**22**

Raoul Alcazar took the drink that Leon had brought him, then leaned back in the big leather recliner, tensing his muscles against the undulations beneath him. He had a sip of his drink, forcing himself to give in to the powerful rollers meant to soothe. "The Stress Eater," was what the sales clerk at Men's Toys on Worth Avenue in Palm Beach had called it. The chair had cost something over five thousand dollars. If you could afford such a chair, how much stress could you have, Alcazar had wondered aloud. The clerk found that ever so amusing.

Alcazar touched the tender spot on his forehead as he watched Leon hobble back toward the bar in a far corner of the room. It had been a very long time since Alcazar had found himself in physical danger, and he had not enjoyed the sensation. But there was something positive in the evening's experience: He had come to think of himself as invulnerable, he realized. And clearly that was a very grave mistake. His family had fled to this country with nothing. His father died of tuberculosis in a public hospital, his mother had been a hotel maid. He had grown up on the streets and he had never once felt secure. But acquire a bit of money and see what happens. You surround yourself with bodyguards, security devices, attorneys, and before you know it . . .

Well, Alcazar thought, he owed that much to Deal. Although Leon owed Deal even more.

The big man still hadn't made it back to his stool at the bar. He was wearing some atrocious-looking athletic shorts, his good knee swathed in yards and yards of elastic bandaging. The other knee sported a maze of scar tissue from myriad operations, the old incisions glazed and glistening like slug tracks. Leon's normally surly expression had turned murderous.

"Go on to bed," Alcazar called after him.

Leon turned and glowered. Finally, he nodded and limped on out of the room.

Alcazar waited until Leon was gone, then lifted his glass to his guest, who sat in the shadows across from him. "Enjoy," Alcazar said.

Alcazar saw Penfield's glass rise in the glow reflected from a vapor lamp outside, near the entrance to his private dock. There was a sound from deep in Penfield's throat. After a moment, the glass came down. "What is it?" he asked.

"A fermentation of the cactus plant," Alcazar said. "Though to call it mescal or tequila would be misleading."

Alcazar swirled the liquor in his glass. "The distillery has been in the hands of the same family for over two hundred years. This is young, however. No more than a century."

"Very smooth," Penfield said.

From outside came the faint throbbing of diesel engines. There was a view out the glassed-in room, across the broad swathe of lawn, then to a hundred yards or so of bay water glittering in the moon. Out there was the vague shadow of a pleasure craft moving up the Intracoastal, its running lights gleaming.

"I purchased the facilities, but I left the operations in the hands of the family," Alcazar said.

"Probably wise," Penfield said.

"I didn't want to interfere with tradition," Alcazar said. "The patriarch had reservations for that very reason. His family came from Spain, after all."

"He got over it, I guess."

"He passed away," Alcazar said, nodding. He put his drink down and leaned forward in his seat abruptly.

"I will tell you something, Mr. Penfield. I am an impatient person by nature. And this has tested my patience to its limits. I have tried to be reasonable, at your urging, but we could have handled this far more simply. Do you understand me?" Alcazar felt a throbbing at his forehead.

"It's clear," Penfield said. He cleared his throat. "I know Deal's been a problem."

"I'd call that an understatement."

"I thought perhaps his wife's death would distract him, he'd let the damn place go."

"As I did," Alcazar said.

"But maybe there's another way . . . "

"Precisely my point," Alcazar said, leaning forward. Penfield held up his hands. "Let's just give it a few more days. There's a great deal at stake here. A great deal of money for both of us. A few more days, Raoul, that's all we're talking about." Alcazar heard a note of pleading in the voice. It did not please him.

"I think you have allowed your emotions to cloud your thinking," he said.

"My thinking is fine," Penfield said gruffly. "We're both going to come out of this just fine." Penfield finished his drink.

"I hope so," Alcazar said. He had not missed the tremor in the old man's hand. He raised his glass in salute. "I sincerely hope that you are right."

He sat back as Penfield left, holding the cold glass to his forehead. He heard the soft ping of the alarm as Alejandro ushered Penfield out, the muted sound of Penfield's car winding away.

In a moment, Alejandro was at the door of the study.

"Is there anything else?" Alejandro said.

Alcazar thought a moment. His own poor judgment had led him into this tangle. He had only himself to blame. He had been timid and now he would have to be bold. He glanced up at Alejandro. "We are certain of Mr. Deal's whereabouts, then?"

Alejandro nodded. "He arrived at his friend's by taxi. The old man, the one with the strange automobile. If anyone leaves, we will know it."

Alcazar held his fingers thoughtfully to his lips. He thought about Penfield's weakness, about human weakness in general. Yes, a new plan would have to take effect, but he was not distressed. In fact, he had been thinking of this since the moment he rose from the wrecked and sodden floor of his new showroom.

He cleared his mind of every sentiment, then, and reminded himself of how it would work. It was a risk, but given the crazed machinations he had already agreed to, it was nothing. So many compromises he had agreed to just for the sake of others' emotional attachments. And if what he had in mind worked out, the return would be so great. He glanced up at Alejandro, his decision made.

"Go wake up Leon," Alcazar said. He gave the puzzled Alejandro a razored smile. "We must resolve *this* deal on our own."

"You sure about this, Johnny?" Cal gave him a cautious look. The old man sat in a chair across from Deal, a diet soda in his hand. The Wild Turkey sat untouched on the counter behind him.

"It was Janice, for Christ's sake," Deal said. "You think I wouldn't know?"

" 'Course you'd know." Cal looked aside, uncertain. "It's just . . . "

"She's alive," Deal said, his mind racing. "She's alive."

Deal felt Cal's eyes on him. Assessing, probing, wondering if he were crazy. He felt a sudden jolt. What if he *were* crazy?

And then he remembered Janice's voice: *Deal!* Calling his name.

Deal shook his head. He had heard it. No dream. No delusion.

He glanced up at Cal, bringing his breathing steady.

"She never said *anything* about where she was?"

"Just that it was by the water." Deal shook his head, still trying to make sense of things. "It was a terrible connection. I heard some other people talking in the background . . . "

"You mean in the room with her?"

"No, like crossed lines. Some guys arguing in Spanish. Then some guy talking about a channel and a generator." Deal looked at

158

Cal. "He had a British accent." He thought a minute. "Maybe Janice was calling from the islands. Maybe somebody took her to the islands, that'd make sense." There was a tiny flame of urgency starting up inside him.

Cal looked at him. "Sense to who? If she was in the islands, how would she have heard about what happened tonight?"

Deal fell back in his chair. He felt exhausted, but his mind was still racing. Something nagging at him, something he couldn't put his finger on . . . and then he had it. How *had* she heard about what happened?

Deal sat up. "Cal, nobody mentioned my name in that story. Alcazar must have seen to that." He broke off. The little flames were a fire inside him now. "What's that tell you?" He turned on Cal.

"That the sonofabitch has his own plans for you, Johnny. You got to get someplace where you'll be safe."

Deal shook his head. "Somebody's got her, Cal. Somebody who knows what I did tonight."

Cal reached out his big hand to Deal's knee, a sorrowful expression on his face. "That's a stretch, Johnny."

Deal's face hardened. "Yeah? Then you explain it, Cal."

Cal withdrew his hand, stung. His gaze wandered to the carpet where a big palmetto bug lumbered over the thick shag. Cal absently lifted his foot and cracked the bug under his heel. "Goddamn things," he said. Finally, he looked up at Deal.

"Johnny, if you tell me Janice called you, then Janice damn well called you. I ain't gonna argue with you about that. But who in the hell would want to kidnap your wife?"

Deal shook his head.

"You never got a note, a call, nothing. How do you explain that?"

"I can't, Cal."

Cal ignored him, waving his Coke at the television. "What I do know is, you got your ass in a big-time sling. You ought to wish Alcazar hung your name off his sign for those television people, put the cops all over you . . . cuz that's a kind of trouble you could get a good lawyer and walk away from. Now . . . " Cal's face had turned beet red and for a moment, Deal thought he was having a stroke.

The old man took a breath then, and went on, in a slightly calmer tone.

"First things first, Johnny. I held onto that fish camp out in the Everglades. There's food there, the skiff, everything you need for a few days until we can make some arrangements. I got a buddy down in Curaçao I'll get hold of. He can take care of you a while, get you into South America if we have to. I'll be here to look after things . . . "

"Cal," he said, "I'm not running off somewhere. I'm going to find Janice."

It was Cal's turn to stare. "You leave that to the police, son. You call them up and tell them about this phone call and then you get the hell out of Dodge or there won't be any *you* for Janice to come home to."

Deal shook his head. A big breath now, fanning the flames. He would find her. He would find her if he had to walk across water to do it.

"If I call the cops, they'll just think I'm crazy, like you do," he said.

Deal saw the hurt spring up in Cal's eyes and he had to turn away. It wasn't Cal's fault. Anybody might think the same. Unless they'd heard her voice. Excuse me, officer, I think my wife's been kidnapped. We all thought she drove her car off a bridge but somehow she didn't die, and by the way I'm the guy who blew up Alcazar's showroom, that's how I know . . .

Deal stood then, and walked out onto the little porch. It had cooled off a bit, though you could still eat the air with a spoon.

He gripped the railing, leaning back momentarily to stretch the taut muscles in his back. The exhaustion he'd felt for the last endless days was gone, replaced by a wild anxiety, a jittery energy aching to be given some place to go.

Far out to sea were a series of dimly lit freighters, drifting, killing time until morning when they could head into port. So maybe Janice had been swept out to sea by the current, where she was picked up by a banana boat bound for Haiti with a cargo of stolen bicycles. The captain is not about to call in the Coast Guard, so he steams on to Port-au-Prince and stashes her until he can figure out what to do. Meantime, Janice sees a television broadcast bounced off the satellite into Port-au-Prince, figures out Deal's in big trouble, escapes, makes her way to a phone and . . .

. . . *and my ass is a short-wave radio,* Deal thought, as Cal joined him on the porch.

"Hey, Johnny . . . " Cal began, but Deal cut him off.

"It's okay, Cal. I'd think I was crazy too. Besides, what are they supposed to do? Put a wall up around the islands? I'm not even sure that's where she was calling from."

"Maybe the phone company could do something."

"I already tried that."

"Well, shit," Cal said, shaking his big head. He gazed out across the water and nodded. "Sun's going to come up pretty soon. Things always look better in the morning."

Deal followed his gaze. Sure enough, there was the barest hint of pink at the horizon where the sun was getting ready. The "sun fist," he found himself thinking. The two guys in the background of Janice's conversation, jabbering about the "sun fist." What the hell was that in Spanish, anyway? Sun fist? Pidgin English for Sunfish? Two guys talking about a little sailboat?

Deal tossed the idle thoughts aside, turned and looked inside the apartment. Cal had wandered back in to the bar where he stood, his shoulders slumped, hefting the bottle of Wild Turkey, checking it against the Coke he held in his other hand, weighing things.

Deal was about to go back inside and give Cal some help on the Wild Turkey, when he stopped short. Sun fist. Sunfist. *Sunfest.* He felt a little jolt. Maybe that was it. Maybe that was what they were talking about. Sunfest.

Deal went inside the apartment, took the bottle out of Cal's hands. "Where's your paper, Cal?"

Cal looked at him, puzzled, then pointed to a stack in the corner. Deal went over, pawed through the pile until he came to a Weekender, the entertainment supplement for the *Herald.* It took him a minute, but there it was in the music section, a double-page layout: SUNFEST TO ROCK MONTEGO BAY, plenty of pictures from last year's reggae festival in Jamaica, a hundred thousand or more from all over the world, and the story predicting twice as many visitors this time around. Seven days of party, mon. Irie. Ganja city. No problem. Starting tomorrow night.

Deal looked up from the paper and met Cal's questioning gaze. He held up the story.

"That's what the two guys I heard in the background were talking about. And the other woman, with the British accent. Jamaica. Maybe she's in Jamaica, Cal."

Cal rolled it over in his mind. "Yeah," he admitted, "it could be. Or she was calling from Pismo Beach and the lines got crossed up."

Deal felt the excitement go out of him as quickly as it had come. Of course, it was crazy. And even if she were on some island in the Caribbean, what could he do about it? Conduct a house-to-house search? He sighed, feeling very tired. "You're right, Cal. But what am I supposed to do, for Christ's sake? Somebody took Janice somewhere. *Somebody* knows where she is. The same somebody told her what happened tonight."

Deal had an image of himself, waving his newspaper under the nose of some Jamaican desk sergeant. They'd lock *him* up. His head had begun to ache. Maybe Penfield had some connections in the islands. Maybe Penfield . . .

. . . and then he stopped, unwilling to consider the possibility that had suddenly occurred to him, but unable to let it go. *Fuck your baseball,* Alcazar had said.

"I need to borrow your car, Cal."

Cal looked at him dourly. "What's on your mind, Johnny? You gonna drive over to Montego Bay?"

"Forget Jamaica, Cal. I need to see Thornton Penfield."

Cal raised a shaggy eyebrow, but shrugged acquiescence. "All right. I'll go with you."

Deal glanced at him: a man in his sixties, veins crisscrossing his florid face, his breathing raspy, ready to walk in front of a truck if he asked. If what he'd suspected were true, that's about what he'd done, Deal thought. Propped him up in front of a thundering, free-wheeling semi. Cal and anybody else crazy enough to get in the way.

"It's okay, Cal," he said. "You've done enough."

"I haven't done anything," Cal said.

"Really," Deal said. "I have to handle this one myself."

Deal saw the hurt look in Cal's eyes and reached to clap him on the shoulder. "I'll call you."

Finally Cal nodded. "I'll be here, Deal."

"I know you will, Cal."

He embraced the old man, felt the answering squeeze. For a moment, he wanted to give it all up. Call Driscoll, hope for the best.

"I know you will," he repeated. And then it was time to go.

Deal spent most of the thirty minutes it took him to get from Hollywood to Miami Beach nurturing the memory of Janice's voice, the one clear beacon amid a welter of confusing thoughts. He didn't want to believe Penfield could have anything to do with Janice's disappearance. Couldn't believe it. But he would find out.

It was still dark, and he stayed on A1A all the way south, avoiding any freeway traffic, letting the thump of the tires on the old pavement fill his mind, savoring the ride of the powerful car, the empty streets, the traffic lights that for once stayed in sync, the look of old Florida in the storefronts of one oceanfront hamlet after another.

In a few hours there would be more than you could want of orange juice, beach towels, T-shirts, and suntan oil for sale, as it had been since God made Florida, he thought. Most of the places hadn't seen the need for renovation, save for the occasional crudely printed sign reading *Bienvenidos!* or *Parlez-Vous Français?* tacked above the awnings or wedged in the windows between the inflatable alligators and killer whale floats. The signs had been added over the past few years to comfort the waves of South American and French Canadian tourists who'd replaced the American tourists here. Different accents, but business as usual once the sun came up. Right now, everything was shut tight, and Deal was taking an odd comfort in the quiet.

A shower had swept in from the Atlantic, leaving the streets gleaming in the vapor lights that switched from orange to blue once he hit Dania. He found himself speeding then, hurrying past the stretch of antiques shops there, a place Janice had loved to browse, although Deal had always favored sturdy and comfortable over frail and delicate. He saw a lamp stand holding up a huge Boston fern spotlighted in one shop window and felt a sudden jab in his gut, remembering talking her out of a similar piece the last time they'd come to window shop. It had been a year or more ago, but he could still remember the look of disappointment in her face.

"For Christ's sake," Deal said aloud. He switched off the air-conditioning and sent the window of the Rivolta down, willing his attention to the hiss of his tires through the rain, catching some spray from the streets as he leaned his face out into the breeze. Most couples their age were supposed to splurge once in a while, wasn't that so? And here he was, back to square one, trying to par-lay his last little building into a decent life and somebody trying to screw even that up.

He tightened his grip on the thick wood steering wheel, squeez-ing the anger out, forcing himself to calm. He was south of Dania now, moving along a broad dark stretch where the shops fell away. The highway was being widened here, and the streetlights were still waiting to be hooked up. Gulfstream Park, where Cal's horseman dreams had come to ruin, lay across the highway on Deal's left. Deal could see a few lights far off in the stairwells and maintenance sheds, although the horses and trainers were long gone, not to return until October, when with luck, the weather would begin to break. Yes, Deal thought. Things would be better by then. The weather and everything else.

There was a guard on duty at the entrance to Sunrise Island, a Vene-tian-styled bridge that arched over the narrow cut separating the mil-lion-dollar homes on the island from the rest of Miami Beach. The guard was a guy in green fatigues and a visored cap who'd come out of his little shack to lean on the rail of the bridge and stare down at the flat gray water like something might be ready to rise up there.

The guy turned when he heard Deal's footsteps whacking on the pavement, his hand moving automatically to the holster at his belt. He wore thick glasses that glittered in the gray, predawn light. Deal imagined his effective range with the pistol to be about a foot and a half. Still there was that foot and a half.

"Morning," Deal said, holding his jogger's pace.

He'd parked the car a couple of blocks back, on a side street just off Alton Road and stripped down to a pair of Cal's baggy swim trunks and T-shirt.

The cop moved his hand off his holster and grunted as Deal ran past him and up the incline of the bridge. Try to drive past the guy and there were probably land mines in the pavement that would blow you sky high, Deal thought, chugging over the crest of the bridge. But put on some running gear, Charles Manson and Squeaky could jog past, no problem, go out and hack up all the millionaires they wanted.

Deal was headed for the second island, which had never seemed much of a drive before. And it probably wasn't much of a drive, he thought, his lungs beginning to burn. He had slowed to a geezer's pace by the time he crossed the little bridge—no guard on this one, of course—that took him out onto the familiar winding boulevard, but he kept his legs pumping. Everything would be easier if he got there before the sun came up.

His toes were practically dragging the asphalt now. Past the sprawling colonial that housed (or had, the last time Deal had been here) the president's nephew, then beyond that, on the landlocked side of the street, the former Beach mayor's stone-and-glass compound (the mayor had to resign after a prostitute's diary had come to light).

Finally, past the still-unfinished mansion of a Kuwaiti prince. The place was sealed off behind a six-foot fence with a padlock and a couple of judgment liens stapled to the gate. Deal had seen aerial shots on local television: tennis courts, two pools, three major buildings, a pool house, nothing that had a finished roof. A local bank had been into it for three million when the Gulf War broke out and the prince disappeared.

Deal staggered over the curb and beneath the limbs of the enormous banyan tree taking up most of the vacant lot between the prince's compound and the place he was headed. He held himself up by one of the tendrils that dropped from a limb, getting his breath back, taking a close look at the house before him.

A green and white antebellum mansion, it looked like something plucked off of St. Charles Street and dropped down a thousand miles away on the verge of the Intracoastal Waterway. The Intracoastal was dead calm this morning, like the waters of some bayou, and only the fact that it was gumbo limbo and banyan instead of live oak lining the circular driveway gave away the fact Deal wasn't in New Orleans.

From where he stood, he could see the rear corner of the house as well as the front. The driveway was empty and there was no sign of activity inside. He had a moment of uncertainty. He could have called ahead, pretended a wrong number had anyone answered, but that might have sounded an alert. He'd just have to trust his luck.

Deal found the strength to give up his hold on the tree and was edging toward the rear of the place when he saw a light come on in the kitchen. He eased back into the shadows of the enormous tree. Napoleon's army had once camped under the base of a huge banyan, he found himself thinking. Now how had their battle gone?

After a moment, there was the sound of a door latch working and then wood shuddering open. A black cat darted across the lawn toward the pool overlooking the Intracoastal. Somebody letting the cat out. Deal was about to step forward when the kitchen door swung open again and a thin black woman in a white dress and shoes emerged onto the back steps.

She stood there a moment, arranging a string bag on her arm, then getting her purse settled, then squinting at a piece of paper she held up in the dim light. Finally, she stuck the paper in her purse and walked across a strip of lawn and disappeared behind the garage that stood between Deal and the house. There was the sound of a garage door grinding open, then a car starting. After a moment, Deal saw a station wagon jounce down from the driveway onto the broad boulevard and pull away, retracing his route in.

Fine, Deal thought. By the time she got back from Publix, he would be long gone.

He came out from under the limbs of the banyan, glancing about the grounds to be sure no eager gardener was already at work, but there was only the cat moving about, now bending at the edge of the pool to lap up a drink. He took the knob of the kitchen door, ready to punch out one of the windowpanes with his elbow, then stopped. He smiled as the knob turned easily in his hand. That's what happens when you have a moat and a guard shack, he thought.

He slipped inside, hesitating at a strange whining sound. Some high-tech alarm? His heart was thundering. Then the smell of percolating coffee hit him. Just the last sigh of a Braun machine on the counter across from him, getting things ready for the master's breakfast when she got back.

Deal allowed himself a nervous smile, then started across the kitchen. The place had been renovated, of course, beech planks laid over the top of the Cuban tiled floor, a bank of appliances that looked like they could handle the dinner rush at Chef Allen's replacing the old stuff Deal remembered from his childhood—and there, a greenhouse window filled with herbs where the dining nook had once looked out . . .

Deal was nearly into the dining room, the ghost of some long ago breakfast glimmering in his mind, when he saw the man coming toward him. Deal ducked back into the kitchen, his eyes scanning the white Formica, the glittering steel surfaces, for anyplace to hide. Now there were steps across the dining room floor, which still uttered their familiar creaks and groans . . .

Deal edged into a nook that partitioned the enormous freezer and refrigerator from the rest of the kitchen, knowing it wasn't good enough, all the guy had to do was look his way and . . . And then what?

Oh hi, I'm the exterminator. There's something wrong with your ice maker . . .

The guy came out into the kitchen then, an older black man who might have been the twin brother of the woman he'd seen drive off in the station wagon. The guy was talking to himself as he shuffled along, shaking his head. He went straight to the door that Deal hoped still led to the pantry, a place he'd often chosen as a hiding place. The old man opened it and disappeared inside.

Deal was across the kitchen in seconds, closing the door behind the black man, slipping home the old-fashioned bolt. He was through the dining room and headed for the stairwell before he heard the first muffled thumps. By the time he was halfway up the stairs, you couldn't even hear the old guy's shouts.

 Cal Saltz had fallen asleep in his chair, the bottle of Wild Turkey cradled between his legs, the seal still untouched. He was dreaming, his lips curled into a smile as Fighting City Hall, one of his more notable losers in real life, moved out from the rail and closed the gap on Alydar. The two horses fought it out down the final stretch but any fool could see Fighting City Hall was destined. Billy Shoes on Alydar, Johnny Deal on City Hall, Shoes looking panicked, Deal merely grim. This one was for the little guy.

Though the race seemed to be the Florida Stakes, Saltz noticed that the venue had been moved. Jagged mountains lined the horizon to the south. There was a pitch-and-putt golf course set up in the infield of the track. A mustached man moved down the aisle near Saltz offering Tecate and Bohemia beer from his shoulder tray.

So they were running the Florida Stakes at the Juarez race track. Who gave a shit? Fighting City Hall was pulling ahead. Shoes was up, laying on the whip, but Alydar was fading. The fans rose, screaming, sensing the upset of the century, and even the golfers in the infield turned to stare as the horses pounded toward the pole, great clods of earth flying in their wake as if from cannon shot.

"Oh Sweet Jesus," Saltz murmured, clutching at his chest. Fighting City Hall's nose crossed the finish line, and his eye froze the moment, a photo finish, and for once things had gone his way. "Oh my God," Saltz said. Then his eyes flickered open as the bottle of Wild Turkey, drawn by some inexplicable force, slipped upward from between his legs.

"Ain't your God, white folks."

Indeed it wasn't, Cal thought, staring up into the big man's face. As big a man as he'd ever seen. Smiling and holding his bottle of whiskey. Like no kind of a god he'd ever seen.

"Jesus Christ!" Penfield had been on his way out of his bathroom, toweling his mane of white hair when he looked up and saw Deal standing there, leaning against a chest of drawers.

He staggered backward, swallowing a couple of times before he could get his breath back. "What the hell are you doing, Johnny?"

"I need some help, Mr. Penfield."

Penfield glanced around the room, trying to appear calm. Where was the thorazine brigade when he needed them?

"You had yourself quite a night, I hear." Penfield's hands were trembling as he tried to get his towel wrapped about his middle. Not much flesh there, Deal noted. Not bad for a rich old goat.

"Who told you about it?" Deal said, his voice level.

Penfield's eyes flashed wide momentarily. Deal had caught him. The old war horse making a mistake like that. Deal shook his head, not waiting for Penfield to come up with something.

"What's Alcazar have in mind, now, Mr. Penfield? Skybox for the Dolphin games? Trip to Paris? I'm curious to know what he thinks I want."

Penfield shook his head. "I don't know what you're talking about, John."

"Did he ask you about the car thing? Ask you my favorite color? Or was yellow just a guess."

There was a dim thud from downstairs, probably the old man he'd locked up throwing his hundred and thirty pounds into the pantry door frame. Deal thought about it a moment. If the guy killed himself trying to get out, would that mean a murder charge?

"I think you'd better tell me what you want, John." Penfield was trying to summon some of his courtroom manner, but it was hard, with his hair awry, one hand holding up his towel.

"Janice called me last night," Deal said. He saw something in Penfield's eyes. Surprise? Fear? The certainty that Deal had lost his mind?

"Janice?" Penfield shook his head. "That's not possible."

"She's alive," Deal said. "She called to tell me I was in big trouble."

Penfield snorted. "Well, that's not exactly news, is it? But if you think Janice is alive, you're in worse shape than I thought."

Deal turned away. There were more thumps from downstairs, but they were losing their authority. A big plaque had been mounted above the chest of drawers where he'd been waiting. He'd had plenty of time to inspect it while Penfield finished his shower: "To Thornton J. Penfield, A Friend to Tropics Baseball," in appreciation from the Chamber of Commerce. Cradled on hooks at the bottom of the plaque was a dinged-up bat inscribed with several signatures.

Deal took the bat down from the hooks and had a closer look: Henry Aaron. Roberto Clemente. Willie Mays. He glanced up at Penfield, who was watching him warily.

"Fuck your baseball," Deal said. Penfield glanced sharply at him.

"The sonofabitch is trying to buy me off with a car, and you guys are wheeling and dealing baseball."

Penfield shook his head. "John, I think you've been under a great deal of stress . . . "

"So you went to bed with Raoul Alcazar, just to get a baseball team." Deal shook his head, sadly.

"Even if that were so, I don't know that *just* is the correct term," Penfield said. "Anything that might bring baseball down here . . . "

"All that bullshit about the nature of the game, the community welfare, I should have figured it out the day I saw the bastard in your office. You guys were desperate for cash. Anybody's cash."

"You probably can't conceive of what it would mean to this community . . . "

"I can conceive of what it would put in your pocket," Deal said, patting the bat absently in his hand. What kind of salary might Mickey Mantle command these days? he wondered. How might it have gone if Deal had been able to hit the curve ball? He'd be retired now, but maybe he'd still be in the game, hitting fungoes to the kids coming up, drawing a nice pension, signing bats for kids whose fathers told them about John Deal, who'd stick his head in front of a pitch if that's what it took . . .

"Money's the last thing I'm interested in, John."

Deal glanced up at him. "Sure. What I can't figure out is how you expect to get it past the commissioner. I mean Pete Rose can't even wear a baseball cap anymore and you're going to put Raoul Alcazar on the board of directors?"

Penfield flushed all the way down to his towel line. "You're way out of line there, John. Raoul Alcazar has never been convicted of any crime. His legal difficulties are behind him. He's come to see me about making some positive contributions to the community, that's all."

Deal nodded. "That's what I figured. You *can't* be up front about it." He thought for a moment. "How does it work, then? He forks over a hundred million or so, you channel it into the baseball group through some dummy corporations. How's that sound?"

Penfield shook his head sorrowfully as Deal continued. "Then you go to work on Alcazar's public image, is that it? Four or five years from now, he's throwing out the first pitch?"

"I don't know what's got into you, John." Penfield's gaze was the picture of compassion. "You were always headstrong, but this is insane . . ."

"I'm right on the money, Mr. Penfield." Deal took a step toward him, flipping the bat around so that he could tap Penfield on the chest with the handle. "The funny thing is, I don't give a goddamn if you make Raoul Alcazar the starting pitcher."

Something seemed to give inside Penfield. His shoulders sagged and a faraway look came into his eyes momentarily. "Then let's get this over with, John. What do you want from me?" There was a renewed flurry of thumps from the pantry, but they died away quickly.

"Somebody has Janice," Deal said. "I don't know why. I don't know where. But it occurs to me that maybe you do."

Penfield shook his head sadly. "John, you're out of your mind."

"That is another possibility," Deal said. "I considered it, Mr.

Penfield. But I came to the conclusion it wasn't true." He tapped Penfield's chest with the end of the bat again. Penfield backed away, but he was blocked by a floral printed chaise longue.

"She said she knew about what happened last night at Alcazar's. How would she know that?"

"Good Lord, Johnny, I don't know."

Deal poked him again and the old man went down in a heap on the chaise.

"She found out what happened and then she called me. Who told her?"

Penfield gaped up at him. Deal patted the bat softly in his palm.

"Maybe Alcazar, but he was awfully busy, last I saw of him." Deal shrugged, looking around the room. "So maybe it was somebody tied up with Alcazar." Deal poked him in the chest with the end of the bat again.

"I'd like you to tell me where Janice is, Mr. Penfield."

Penfield stared up at him, his eyes watery. Fear? Pain? "John, for heaven's sakes, I don't know what you're talking about. If Janice is alive, I'll do anything I can to help find her . . ."

"Another possibility," Deal said. "I thought about that too, all the way down here. But you've been lying to me all along about Alcazar. How can I trust you now?"

As Deal took another step forward, a car motor sounded in the driveway below. Keeping an eye on Penfield, he edged to the window and parted the curtains. The maid's station wagon was pulling up between the garage and the back entrance. She couldn't have bought as much as a loaf of bread in this amount of time. Had she forgotten something?

The passenger door opened first, and Alejandro, the blocky Latin with the bad complexion, stepped out, one of his pals from the dealership coming out the opposite side after him. Deal dropped the curtain and stepped back.

Penfield stared at him, his mouth quivering silently. "Just pray you're not lying to me," Deal said. A door banged open below. Then he tossed the bat aside and ran.

In moments, he was out of Penfield's bedroom and down the broad corridor that split the upper level of the house, thanking Penfield for the heavy carpeting that muffled his footsteps. He heard the pantry door wrench open down below, then shouts, and then he was through the last door on the left that had been Mrs. Penfield's sewing room and catchall in the days of his and Flivey's youth.

The attraction of the room for Deal and Flivey had been the porch that opened off the room. Cantilevered off the back of the house and over the docking area, it made for a fine diving platform into the broad waterway, if you didn't mind the possibility of falling a foot or so short onto the coral pilings that lined the shore below. He'd never minded it when he was fifteen, but today it seemed the house had retracted or the coral had bulged out from the porch. Had he really made the jump so many times? He heard more shouts inside the house as he kicked his sneakers off.

He backed up against the siding, felt the drip from the misting rain seeping through his shirt. He could see the tops of the hotels on the beach from here, a mile or so away. The Rivolta was parked under a canopy of trees somewhere in between. He felt the thumps of footsteps inside, then pushed himself off: three steps, a breath-taking rush of air, a glimpse of a Donzi throbbing down the middle of the channel thirty yards out, a blur of white jagged rock as his head tucked down, and then the soothing chill of the water as he knifed in and dove down.

**26** "Mo-ther-*fuck*-er," Leon Straight said, wrenching his hand away from the pillow he'd been bearing down on. The sonofabitch had bitten him, right through the feathers and ticking, hard enough to draw blood. Leon was shaking his hand, trying to keep the guy pinned with his weight, but the old sonofabitch was a fighter. This had already taken more time than he'd counted on. Things he had to do, just to keep on Alcazar's good side. Something he had to do, for the time being. But it was all going to work out to Leon's advantage, and that was some consolation. Call it realtor's work.

The old guy rolled aside and struggled off the couch, Leon going after him as quickly as his still-aching knee would allow.

The guy turned and swung at him with the bottle of Wild Turkey Leon had taken from him earlier. Leon ducked, and the bottle glanced off his shoulder, then went flying into the wall where it shattered, sending the stink of liquor all over the apartment. Too bad. Leon had had plans for the bottle, but that was all right. Given the look of the guy's face, there'd be more hooch around.

There was a pistol across the room on a cabinet top, which was probably what the guy was headed for. Leon would just as soon he didn't get hold of it and so ignored the protest in his knee as he brought the old guy down from behind. Before the guy could get up, Leon grabbed him by the belt, then hammered his fist into his kidney. This time the guy went down for good. While he was still stunned from the blow, Leon scrambled on up his back and got one arm levered across his throat, the other behind his head. Struggle all you want, motha, he thought, as he increased the pressure steadily. He could have popped the guy's neck easily, but that wouldn't look right.

When the guy was finally quiet, Leon got up and dragged him over to the couch, dumped him down on top of the soaked cushions, the shards of glass from the bottle. Couple of cuts, what would it matter. Leon shrugged.

Leon walked stiffly over to the cabinet, took a latex glove—that would be Alejandro's idea, he'd have to give the sonofabitch that much—out of his pocket and put it on. He picked up the jack handle he'd brought up to the apartment, the one he'd taken from Deal's piece-of-shit VW. He stared at the gun that was lying there, the same gun Leon had seen Deal playing with out on the patio. Probably had his prints all over it.

Always little things you didn't expect, some good—like Leon spotting this guy and his silly-assed car the other day. Then some not so good, like Deal taking off, before they were ready.

Still, he thought, hefting the jack, it was always best to stick with your game plan close as you could. Inside one of the cabinets, he found a bottle of 151-proof rum. Nearly full, just what the doctor ordered. He left the gun where it was, poured the rum over the rug and furniture, and then, when he was finished with that, took the rest of his business to the couch.

**27**

"He's gone," Alejandro said. He dabbed at a scratch on his face with a handkerchief, checking for blood. "Someone ought to cut the weeds around here."

Penfield was pulling on a pair of suit pants. He'd donned a white shirt, but it was still unbuttoned, the sleeves loose at his wrist. The second thug stood by the doorway, his arms folded.

Penfield shot Alejandro an angry glance. "Well, the sonofabitch was here. He threatened to kill me, for Christ's sake." He pointed at the bat Deal had tossed aside.

Alejandro followed Penfield's jabbing finger. He bent down and examined the baseball bat that had rolled underneath the corner of the bed. He glanced up at Penfield. "With this bat, he threatened you?"

Penfield's face flushed as he straightened, snapping the button at his waistband. "You're goddamn right with that bat—" he began, then broke off, his gaze fixed on Alejandro, who was wrapping a handkerchief carefully about his hand, picking up the bat, walking quickly his way.

"What the hell . . . " Penfield managed to get out.

Alejandro took a last step forward and swung backhanded, bringing his weight along with the blow. "It is not me, doing this," he was saying. Penfield tried to turn, but there wasn't a chance. The last thing he saw was a blur of wood, the trademark growing huge, then something warm, even searing, at his temple.

". . . is Mr. Deal killing you." The bat shattered down its length and a splash of blood flew to the ceiling. "The man betrayed, go on a rampage."

Penfield tumbled backward over the chaise longue, his hands clawing at the miniblinds on a nearby window, bringing them down on him as he fell. Alejandro leaned over the chaise, waiting. The blinds rattled for a few moments, then went quiet. Alejandro bent to grasp Penfield's wrist. He waited for a moment, then finally stood and nodded to his companion.

"Home run?" the companion said.

Alejandro smiled. "Beesbol been berry, berry good to me," he said.

"*Que?*" his partner said, puzzled.

"Just an American joke," Alejandro said, tossing the ruined bat to the floor. "Let's go."

**28**

Homer Tibbets wheeled the big Lexus over the speed bump separating the preparation area from the ready line at about fifty, amazed at how well the sedan took it. The faster he hit the speed bumps, in fact, the less noticeable was the nudge under him. How in the hell had they done it? Next time, he'd try to get up to sixty.

He imagined himself starring in some television commercial, the car hurtling over a series of speed bumps, driven by no one apparently, then screeching to a halt, the door flying open and, *ta-da,* Homer steps out, wearing a tux or a cutaway: "Hey, it wasn't always like that, folks."

. . . and then a jump cut to a Caddy or a Lincoln pounding over the same speed bumps and Homer's head flying up above the door sill again and again and again. He'd get it stopped, then stagger out of the car, loony as Bugs Bunny from all the bouncing, and the Lexus logo would come on—Christ, it'd *have* to sell cars. Well, maybe not nationwide, but at least down here. No, he corrected himself, *especially* down here.

Jesus, he thought, whisking the Lexus precisely into the front line, a foot and a half clearance on either side. The things your mind does, just trying to get you through the day.

He glanced up over the wheel as a guy who'd been pushing a

shopping cart along the sidewalk shied out into the street at his approach. By the time Homer got out, the guy was bending over, picking up some aluminum cans that had spilled into the gutter. He glared at Homer, muttering something.

"Sorry, pardner," Homer said, noticing that the man wore a tennis shoe on one foot, a rundown wing-tip on the other. One side of his face was fine, but the other half looked like somebody'd stomped it with track spikes, then filled the craters with roofing tar.

Homer shrugged, trying to be nice. Most of these guys were harmless, but a real cuckoo could always wait until it got dark, flutter down off his roost with the pigeons, come back, and fuck up one of the cars while the security cop was around back jacking off in his golf cart.

And *this* guy had definite possibilities: He was still muttering as Homer locked the Lexus and trudged around the shuttered parts-and-service bays to the wash-'n'-wax canopy. He heard a distant rumble of thunder and glanced up to see a dark bank of thunderheads gathering in the south.

Great. The front'd whip up a stiff wind on its way in, cover every car on the line with sand and powdery dust, then the rain'd come in, streak everything to hell. Tomorrow he could come in and start all over again. He shrugged. He could handle it. He got paid by the hour, which, he noticed by the blinking clock on top of the bank tower down the block, was well past six in the P.M. Time to call it a day.

He rounded the back corner of the service bays and stopped short when he saw the strange car parked in front of his canopy. Homer was immediately indignant. One of the used-car salesmen trying to fuck him around, bringing some piece of shit back for detail work without clearing it first. Well, fuck that, he thought, leaning against the fender of the car to shuck his waders. No yellow ticket under the windshield wiper, no washee from Homer. Not unless you were around to slip some green his way.

What the hell kind of car was it, anyway? he wondered. He glanced back at the thing as he moved to toss the boots inside the storage shed where he kept his things. He'd taken it for some European version of a U.S. sedan, but that was wrong. The car sat too low, its lines were a bit too sleek, and wasn't that leather upholstery on the front buckets? He turned to pitch the boots in the shed and gasped as a hand clamped his T-shirt and jerked him roughly inside.

"Homer?" A voice came out of the darkness. Homer aimed a kick toward the voice but the guy had him pinned against the back wall of the shed, at arm's length. Homer ran a quick inventory of his debts and transgressions, but nothing serious registered. He'd laid some pipe a couple days ago, an older woman he met in the lounge of the Cadillac Hotel downtown, but she'd claimed to be divorced.

"Naw, I ain't Homer," he said, pawing a couple of soft right crosses into the darkness. "I'm just a regular guy got caught in the wash, shrunk up a few sizes."

"It's Deal, Homer," the guy said.

Deal? Homer thought.

"I didn't mean to scare you. I just have to be careful, coming around here."

Then it registered. Homer relaxed, going limp in the guy's hands. He laughed, a wry, barking sound. "No, man, you don't have to be careful. You have to be out of your fucking mind."

They drove down Biscayne the mile or so to Homer's place, Deal slouched down in the backseat, Homer barely visible behind the wheel of the Rivolta.

"Maybe you can find something on the radio," Deal said, his mind still whirling from what Homer had told him.

"You don't believe me?" Homer said.

Deal didn't answer. Homer shrugged and began punching the buttons on the Blaupunkt until he found a bulletin that bore out what he'd already told Deal about Penfield, "victim of a vicious attack in his palatial home." Deal hadn't been listening to the radio. He'd spent the entire day hunched down in the Rivolta, waiting for Alcazar to show up before he decided to try Homer.

"Police have not yet established a motive for the killing," the report continued. "But Miami builder Jack Deal is being sought for questioning. Police would not explain their interest in Deal, said to be distraught since the death of his wife in an auto accident just a few weeks ago."

"Jesus Christ!" Deal said, as the broadcast cut away to a commercial. He thought of Alejandro and his pal, moving grimly toward Penfield's house. Could he have been wrong about Penfield?

"I told you," Homer called from the front seat. "Hey, maybe there's a reward. I could just swing over to Metro Dade, drop you off at the suspect window."

"You could do that, Homer," Deal said, his voice flat.

"Nah. Vicious killer like you might escape, track me down. I'd never live to enjoy the money."

They pulled up at a stop light and Homer hiked himself over the seat to smile down at Deal. "Even if you did nail the old fart, I still owe you one for what you did to Alcazar. I'd give anything to have seen it. Besides, how would you find your old lady if you were in the slammer."

Deal stared up at him. "Thanks, Homer." Homer waved it off. "And I didn't kill Penfield."

"Don't worry about it," Homer said, dropping back out of sight. "I ain't the one you have to convince."

The commercial on the radio had ended and the lady rock jock was back, schmoozing with the newscaster. "So what effect will Thornton Penfield's death have on our chances for a Major League franchise, Gene?"

"Right, let's get to the important shit," Homer said.

"Be quiet," Deal said. He was trying to sort it all out, but his mind spun in circles.

"Nobody's quite sure, Irene," said the newscaster. "But sources close to the local committee tell me the application is complete and in the hands of the commissioner's advisory board. It *shouldn't* affect anything."

"Well, that's *some* good news, Gene," the disk jockey said.

"That DJ's got community spirit," Homer said, snapping off the radio. "Also a nice rack. I see her around the dealership now and then. She drives a Lexus, the station leases it. She's married, but her husband's a real schmuck. Guy runs the station's probably banging her."

Homer broke off, wrestling the Rivolta around a cab waiting to make a left against traffic. Deal heard horns blare behind them.

"You're going to get us pulled over," Deal called from the back seat.

"Stop worrying," Homer said. "You think a Miami cop gives a shit about traffic violations? Get real."

Deal felt another lurch as they swung back into the left lane. More horns behind them.

"Highway patrol pulled me over on the expressway one time, though. What he tells me is, the car was 'moving erratically.' Besides, it was dark and he couldn't see anybody behind the wheel. He thought maybe the driver had a heart attack or something."

Homer hit the brakes suddenly and Deal had to brace himself. Homer levered himself up on the seat with his elbow and looked back at Deal, his face going pink with the exertion.

"So anyway he puts his flashlight in my face to see if I'm plowed, you know, and this guy, who is clearly no Sherlock Holmes, finally notices there's a broad in there with me, got her head in my lap, right?"

They pulled away from the light with a squeal of tires, and Deal slid back against the seat. "Christ, Homer. Why don't we just call the station house, turn me in?"

"Tricky clutch, that's all," Homer said. "Lot of horses up front. What would you guess they put under the hood?"

"I don't know, Homer. It's not my car."

"Great. Do a guy, steal a car, that's a hell of a day. Too bad the banks are already closed, you could go for the hat trick."

"It's not funny, Homer," Deal said. The car made a hard right, then bumped over something and it was suddenly dark inside the Rivolta.

"Covered parking," Homer said. "One of the attractive features of life at the Shabby Arms."

They squealed up a couple of ramps and finally pulled to a stop. Homer levered himself up on the seat again and glanced around outside. "It's okay," he said, finally.

Deal followed after him into the stairwell, which stank of urine and other, unidentifiable odors. "Only four flights up," Homer assured him, moving into a kind of gallop that Deal had trouble keeping up with. His knee was still a little tender, but he suspected he'd have trouble staying even with Homer even if it weren't.

At the door marked Six, with *Seis* scrawled under it in magic marker, Homer motioned Deal to wait, then poked his head out into the corridor.

Abruptly Homer stopped. "Christ, officer, don't shoot!" he cried, throwing up his hands. "He's right in here."

Deal stood frozen. Homer turned to him with a manic smile on his face.

"Just kidding," he said. He pushed the door open on an empty hallway.

"Hilarious," Deal said, his heart pounding.

He followed Homer down a hallway that was even stuffier than the stairwell. There were graffiti scrawled along the walls, as mystifying as cave paintings, a carpet that had once been a green shag, an odor of mildew adding to the ripe musk of the air. Breathe this a few hours a day, maybe you'd turn out like Homer, Deal thought.

At the end of the hallway, Homer worked two keys, then let them into his place. Deal felt air-conditioning rush over him and took his first deep breath since he'd left the Rivolta. He followed Homer in, stepped aside as the door swung shut.

More surprises. A tidy efficiency, dishes stacked neatly at a drainboard, a couple of sling chairs, a futon bed beneath a pair of windows that gave a view north and east over Biscayne and out to the bay where the running lights of boats were beginning to glow in the dusk.

Deal became aware of a pink light pulsing on the rear wall of the apartment. He turned to Homer who pointed out one of the windows.

"Coppertone Girl's right outside," he said. "We're right about bare-ass level on the big sign. Wanna look?" Homer went to throw the window up.

"I want to use the phone, Homer."

Homer turned, clearly disappointed. He pulled the window closed, brought Deal a phone from a concrete block that sat as a table beside the futon.

Deal punched in Cal's number, and waited. After the fourth ring, a man's voice answered. Familiar, but not quite right.

"Cal?" Deal said, uncertain.

"This isn't Cal," the voice said. "Who's this?"

Deal took a breath. "I must have dialed the wrong number."

"You got the right number," the voice cut in. "This is Vernon Driscoll, Metro Dade Police. Who am I talking to?"

Deal felt an unreasoning dread sweep over him. "It's Deal," he said. His voiced seemed almost a whisper. "John Deal," he repeated. "What's wrong?"

"Where are you, Deal?" Driscoll's voice had lost the kindly undertone Deal remembered from the night before. Had it only been last night? It seemed like a century ago.

Deal felt as if a huge wave were rolling toward him, its crest about to come crashing down. The light was nearly gone outside. The ocean was slate gray all the way out to an even darker horizon. Deal watched the pink glow from the Coppertone girl paint and unpaint the windowsill in front of him.

"Where's Cal?" he said, dread filling him. "What's happened to Cal?" Homer had punched on a tiny black-and-white television he kept on his dinette table, was flipping around the dial. When he registered Deal's tone, he turned to stare. Driscoll's voice was muffled now, as if he had covered the receiver, was shouting to someone at the other end of the line. Could they trace this call somehow?

Abruptly, Driscoll came back. "Somebody beat him to death, Deal. Then, just to be sure, they set him on fire."

Deal felt himself go numb. "Jesus Christ."

"It's real pretty up here, Deal." Driscoll's voice was angry now. Accusing. "I'd like to talk to you about some things, okay? Including a tip from a concerned citizen who says you're the one who tore up Surf Motors last night. Why don't we set up a place to meet."

Deal steadied himself against the windowsill. Homer shot him a worried look, hurried over with one of the chairs from the dinette. "Cal? Is he all right?"

"Just tell me where you are," Driscoll was saying. "I'll send somebody for you."

Deal sagged into the chair. "I can't do that right now," he said. They had come to Cal's looking for him. That's what it was. "Process of elimination," as Cal had said. Some irony. Poor Cal. And all because of Deal, as surely as if he'd shoved him out in front of that big, runaway truck.

"Suppose you tell me why not?" Driscoll's voice brought him back.

He could meet with Driscoll, explain it all. Tell him who killed Penfield, who killed Cal. Sure. And while they were dragging him to his cell he could tell him where the Easter Bunny lived too. He stared across the room vacantly. Homer was in the kitchenette, rooting through the refrigerator for something.

"My wife's alive," Deal heard himself saying. His voice sounded hollow in his ears. Driscoll didn't respond. "She's alive. She called me."

"Your *wife* called you?" Deal heard the disbelief in his voice.

"I'm going to go now," Deal said, woodenly.

"Look, Deal, you been under a lot of stress. Make it easy on yourself, okay? All you gotta do—"

Deal dropped the phone back in its cradle and sat staring blankly at the television set where Don Noe was pointing excitedly at a vortex of red and yellow computer paint obliterating the Caribbean.

"It looks like a bad one, Don," the anchorperson said as the scene cut away.

"It's still a tropical depression," Don said. "But we'll be keeping an eye on it. We could be looking at the first hurricane of the season." He seemed enthused.

Homer was back by the phone, handing Deal a beer he'd retrieved from the refrigerator.

"Of course, bad summer weather is one of baseball's concerns with our area," the anchorman said. "Here with a report on what's coming out of the owners' convention is Frank Forte—"

Homer snapped the set off and Frank sizzled away. The room was dark now, except for the glow from the sign outside. Half of Homer stood pink for a moment, then went dark. Then went pink again.

"We talking about the Cal I know?"

Deal nodded slowly. "That was a cop answered his phone. Somebody killed him, Homer."

Homer shook his head and went to the refrigerator for another beer. "Goddamn," he said, taking a long pull from the bottle.

"The same people who killed him were coming after me, Homer."

"Yeah? How do you know that? Maybe it was just some garden-variety crack head broke in . . . "

"Homer . . ." Deal said. "You know who it was. Who ordered it, anyway."

Homer stared at him for a moment. "Alcazar," he nodded, finally. He took another slug of his beer, thinking about things. "The cop thinks you did it, right?"

"I might as well have," Deal said. He put the beer on the windowsill and rubbed his face in his hands. He couldn't remember ever feeling so tired. "First he killed Penfield, now Cal."

"Wait a minute," Homer said. "So you piss Alcazar off, fuck up a million dollars' worth of his cars, fuck with his ego. That'd be his style, to off you, for it. And Cal happened to get in the way, his goons wouldn't worry about that, either. But where's Penfield figure into it?"

Deal glanced up at him. "Alcazar had gotten involved with the baseball thing somehow. Penfield needed money, Alcazar wanted to make some . . ." Deal trailed off, trying to think it through.

"But why would he kill Penfield, then?" Homer shook his head.

"I don't know." Deal stared at him. "If he wanted to buy a baseball team, Alcazar would need Penfield as a front man." Deal threw up his hands. "It just doesn't make sense. But I have this funny feeling, like I gave Alcazar the excuse for all of this."

Homer thought it over.

"So you spent last night with Cal and then you went to see Penfield this morning. I'm the only other guy you spent any time with the last twenty-four hours, what do you think that makes my chances?"

Deal looked up at him. "I wouldn't write you an insurance policy, Homer."

Homer laughed. "Sense of humor. Maybe there's hope for you yet."

Deal took a breath. It seemed to take a long time to get his lungs inflated. He stood up, finally, and went to stare out the window. "I have to find Alcazar, Homer. If I'm going to find Janice, I've got to find Alcazar first."

Homer stared at him, incredulous. "You think he's got her *too*?"

Deal stared at him. "Where does he live, Homer?"

After a moment, Homer's gaze wilted. He shrugged. "I ain't exactly on his guest list."

"You never drove him home, delivered a car?"

"Naw, he's got a thing, thinks somebody's gonna blow him up. Leon does all that shit, or one of those Cuban muscleheads."

"For Christ's sake," Deal said, turning back to the window.

"All I know, it's out on one of the islands there."

Deal stared out toward the east. Separating the beach—that mile-wide strip of hotels and apartment houses—from the mainland, lay the waters of the bay, dotted here and there with man-made islands that showed up as ragged shadows now that the light was gone. Most of them—like Sunrise, where Penfield's house was—were connected to the beach or one of the causeways by bridges. A few you had to be ferried to. That would suit Alcazar and his paranoia, Deal thought. Maybe he and Homer could rent a boat, go island hopping. Sure.

He turned his gaze back toward the city, wincing at the glare pulsing from the Coppertone girl. A few blocks away was the bank tower where Penfield had kept his offices, all lit up itself in gold and green floodlights.

Come back from the dead, old man. Tell me what you know, he thought. Tell me where my wife might be . . . and then, as he stared at those blank glass walls, something occurred to him.

He turned to Homer. "You got a phone book?"

Homer gave him a look. "How do you think I get comfortable at dinner?"

Deal glanced over at the other chair by the dinette. Sure enough, two thick phone books arranged like the couch cushions in the cars Homer drove, building up the seat and chair back. Deal went to the table, grabbed one of the books.

"He ain't listed," Homer said, as Deal flipped the book open, traced a finger down the long list of Coopers. A Betty, a Benjamin, no Barbara. Two initial *B*'s, one in Hialeah, one without an address. He tried the one in Hialeah first, just to be sure, hung up when he got a message machine speaking Spanish.

He dialed the second number and she answered on the second ring. "Barbara?" Deal asked.

"This is Barbara," her voice strange, wary, on weirdo-guard.

"It's Deal," he said. "John Deal."

"Oh," she said, her surprise there, but muted.

"I get you up or something?"

"I'm up," she said, her voice gathering strength. "Way up." She laughed, a strange, sad laugh. "You heard about Mr. Penfield, I guess. They sent us home early this afternoon. . . ."

"I heard," Deal said. "They think I might have been involved."

"Is that right?" she said, sounding dazed. "Did you?" she asked, after a moment.

"No," Deal said.

"I didn't think so," she said, her words slurring.

"Listen, Barbara, I think I know who did it . . . "

She broke in. "I've just been sitting here having a glass of wine . . . well, more than a glass of wine, really, trying to make sense of things, you know. I mean, it's really a pretty scary world . . . " Her voice trailed off and Deal wondered if she might be about to hang up.

"Barbara, are you all right?"

Her voice was abruptly bright—too bright. "So you probably called for something, right? I mean, if you heard about what happened. So why *are* you calling?"

Deal stared at the receiver for a moment. What on earth had happened to the calm, together lady who'd backed down a Miami cop, bailed him out of a jam? He had the feeling that if he so much as mentioned Alcazar's name, he'd lose her. "Look, Barbara, I need your help."

"*My* help?" She broke off for a moment, laughing. "You *must* be desperate." He could hear the sound of ice falling into a glass. "Shit."

"Barbara, I'd rather not talk over the phone . . . "

"Well, you're welcome to come over," she said. "We'll have a drink to dear, departed Mr. Penfield."

"Great," he said. "That'd be great. Just tell me how to get there."

He repeated the directions out loud, motioning for Homer to pay attention. When he hung up, he held out his hand to the little man.

"Give me the keys."

Homer stared at his hand, thought a moment. He looked up at Deal, shaking his head. "I'll drive," he said. "I'm the designated driver."

"Stop fucking around, Homer. I'm going to find Alcazar. You don't want to be in the middle."

"You told her ten minutes," Homer said, and was out the door before Deal could stop him.

It was actually closer to twenty minutes before they were pulling up in front of a high-rise off Brickell. Sheets of rain had swept in off the bay, slowing even Homer's driving. Street lamps up and down the boulevard were dark and the wind had begun to shred the canvas canopy that shielded the front door. A matronly lady in an evening gown was holding onto her permed hair, tottering toward the entrance while the parking attendant drove off in her Town Car.

Deal knew the neighborhood well. His father had built one of the towers next door. It was a dozen years or so ago, when developers were in a contest to see who could cram the most accouterments into huge condos aimed at the South American market. Construction costs were running about two hundred dollars a square foot, sales prices twice that. Things had long since cooled off in South America, but this was still pricey territory.

"Just leave it," Deal told Homer, clambering out of the backseat. "Take the keys."

When he got out of the car, the air surprised him. At least ten degrees cooler, and the spray whipped under the canopy by the wind made it seem twice that. He thought of the mountains. Fly fishing. Him in a pair of leaky waders, struggling against some heavy current in the middle of a stream, Janice watching from the rocks on shore, chewing on one knuckle in concern. A trip from another life.

They'd spent that evening on the balcony of a hotel room, watching an evening storm rumble down a New Mexico mountainside a few hundred yards away. Gray mist erasing the pines in a placid smoke, the rush of cool air, the first chilling drops that hit them, sent them diving under the covers of the big, Inn-of-the-Mountain-Gods bed . . .

"We goin' in or what?" It was Homer looking up at him, wiping droplets of water off his chin.

"Yeah," Deal said, as a bolt of lightning blew everything white, the crack of thunder instantaneous, deafening. "We're going in."

There was an ironwork sculpture in a flagstone and waterfall garden, cast-bronze doors for the entryway, a chandelier they could have used in Versailles just inside. The matronly lady had disappeared. A guy at a desk in the lobby wearing a suit and tie gave Homer a squinty look, but buzzed them through an inner gate after he called upstairs.

"We're going to the top," Homer said, watching the steady blips on the elevator's control panel. Deal nodded, feeling his ears popping as they rose.

"How do you know she didn't call the cops?"

Deal glanced at him. "I don't."

"Then why are we doing this?"

"Because I'm fresh out of choices, Homer."

Homer nodded grudgingly.

The elevator opened onto a marble foyer with a smaller version of the chandelier downstairs, all of it surrounded by mirrors that bounced the light and crystal back and forth in a way meant to hurt your eyes, but in a subtle way. There was a set of doors opposite the elevator, but they were looking for "A."

Homer stood in the foyer, his eyes about level with an odd-shaped marble table bearing a vase of cut flowers. "Reminds me of my place," Homer said.

Deal glanced down a long hallway on his right. There was a door open at the end, a square of light falling out into the dim corridor.

The sound of breaking glass echoed down the hallway toward them. Deal moved toward the open door, Homer on his heels, his gait rolling like a tiny sailor's.

"What's this lady do?" Homer called after him.

"She's a clerk-typist," Deal said. "Isn't that what it looks like?" He felt his jaw tightening as he spoke.

When he got to the doorway, Barbara was on her knees in the marbled entryway of her condo, trying to pick up shards of glass in her bare hands. She was wearing a long robe, silk, a dark maroon, the kind of thing you paid a couple hundred dollars for, would make you comfortable just thinking about putting it on. He wondered what it was to feel comfortable. She glanced up at Deal, one slender leg sticking out, the front of her robe gaping open. She met Deal's gaze, then gathered her robe as Homer joined him.

"Damn," she said, staring down at her fingers. A bright thread of blood trickled to her wrist. She stood, weaving, licking the blood away.

"You scared me." She was smiling now, but her eyes were hooded and glassy. Her gaze went back on Homer, uncertain.

"This is Homer," Deal said. "He's a friend of mine."

"Well," she said. "Come on in."

She moved unsteadily down the hallway, her shoulder pushing a painting askew—it showed a man poised in middive over a swimming pool, the back of a pristine suburban home—everything so perfect you knew it was impossible to breathe there, Deal thought.

They followed her into a vast living room, black marble floors, white Natuzzi sofas and chairs, a bar that seemed to have grown out of the dark stone and mirrors of the place like live crystal.

"Sheee-ee," Homer whispered. His gaze held on a bank of windows overlooking the city to the west.

Lightning was spidering the horizon out by the Everglades and an evil-looking bank of clouds smothered everything to the south. A pair of EMS vehicles blinked the wet ribbon of I-95, sirens lost at this distance.

"What can I get you?" Barbara was at the bar, dropping ice into some glasses.

Homer turned, interested.

"Nothing," Deal said. "We're kind of pressed for time."

"Right," Barbara said, eyeballing the vodka she was pouring into her glass. She swished the liquid around, had a taste. She stared over at Deal, working for a moment to get him into focus. "You needed some help." Humoring him.

There was a door cut out of the mirrored wall behind her. A bedroom. Carpeted, but more of the black and white. Drawers pulled out of the dresser. A couple of bags on the bed, trailing clothes.

"Mr. Penfield was into black and white, huh?" Deal ran his hand over a sofa back. End of a hard day, you could sink into something like this, have a beer, forget about whether your subs were going to show up in the morning.

When he looked back at her, she'd put her glass down, some of the blear gone from her face. There was color in her cheeks now.

Anger? Embarrassment? Homer edged backward, his shitstorm antennae starting to quiver.

Finally, she looked away, shrugging. "He bought it this way. From the previous owners." She allowed herself a smile. "If *he'd* had it decorated, it'd look like the goddamn Hunt Club in here."

Deal came to the bar, sat on a white leather stool, watched her staring out the windows for a moment. Finally, she turned back to him, her smile still there, but sad now. "Pretty pathetic, huh?"

Deal shrugged. "It's a nice place." He looked at her, watching the mist burning away. "You deserve it."

She laughed again. "I doubt my mother would agree with you on that one."

"So," he nodded at the bedroom door. "You're going somewhere."

She followed his gaze toward the half-packed bags. "Yeah," her voice resigned. After a moment she turned back to him. "It's not like I'm paying the rent for this."

Deal nodded. She gave him a weak smile. "He was nice enough, even after Maria came along." She broke off, taking a swallow of her drink. "You met Maria, right? Maria with all the hair and teeth?"

"The one downstairs. The week you were off," Deal said.

"That was her," she nodded, finishing her drink. "Five years, Thornton and I were together. His wife had been sick a long time, you know. And then she died . . . and then, just when I thought we could finally be together, Maria came in. Like some hurricane."

She smiled and swept her hand about them. "But I got to keep the place." She glanced at Deal. "Until now."

Deal nodded. "Is that why you told me about Penfield and Alcazar that day?"

She shrugged. "Maybe. Like I said, I'm fed up with lawyers."

"Could I have a beer or something?" Homer called from his place near the hall.

"Barbara," Deal began, "I need to find Raoul Alcazar."

She stared at him.

"It's important," he said. "He's got a place out in the islands, right? It's not like I can go around asking a bunch of people right now and I figured you might know where he lived."

She shrugged. "Thornton knew. He went out there a few times." She glanced at Deal. "I guess that doesn't help you right now, does it?"

Deal stared at her. "Maybe it's on the Rolodex, or some of those papers you were talking about, down at the office."

"You want me to go down there?" She looked at him, incredulous.

"Like, *now?*"

Deal shrugged.

"I don't know if I'm up to that," she said, reaching for her glass.

Deal put his hand atop hers. "Janice is alive."

Her eyes widened. "Wait a minute . . . "

"She called me," he said. "Somebody has her. She didn't get a chance to tell me where she was. But I think Alcazar might know."

"You think Alcazar kidnapped your wife?" Barbara shook her head, dazed.

"I've got to find him," Deal said. "Will you get the address for me?"

She took a breath, her eyes somewhere else for a moment. "I told Thornton," she said, softly. "I told him not to trust that bastard." She turned to Deal. "But Thornton was desperate for the money. That's what they all love, more than anything, you know?"

Deal stared at her, waiting.

Finally, she dropped her gaze, wiping at her eyes. "Give me a minute, okay?"

He nodded. She pulled her robe tightly around her once again and disappeared into the bedroom.

29 "Doc Hammer," Leon said, his voice booming out of the darkness.

"*Got*-damn," the old man gasped.

Leon had been waiting the better part of an hour for the old bastard to lock up, duck into the scrungy back room of his pharmacy for a fix. The syringe flew out of Hammer's hand, skittered out of sight.

Leon flipped on the lights and the old man lunged for the syringe, which was lying in the middle of a linoleumed aisleway. Leon grabbed him by his flapping white coat and pulled him back. He kicked the syringe out of sight, underneath a rack of shelves piled with pill bottles and dusty merchandise.

"Damn, Doc," he said. "Here's your old friend Leon, come calling, you don't even say hello, kiss my ass, nothing?"

Hammer stared mournfully toward the spot where the syringe had disappeared, then glanced back at Leon through his thick glasses. His bleary eyes came gradually into focus.

"Yeah, Leon," he said finally, trying to pull from his grasp. "Christ. You scare shit out of me."

The doctor tried a laugh, wanting to see how that would go.

"That why you're shaking, Doc?" Leon smiled at him. A few more minutes, the guy would be a puddle on the floor.

"Bad neighborhood here, you know? Got-damn bastards broke in last month, steal every-ting."

"Mmmm-hmmm," Leon said. "They get your stash, too?"

Hammer stared at him, offended. Christ, he'd caught the dumb bastard shooting up, he still wanted to pretend. Leon let him go.

"So, there's something I can do for you, some strength medicine, huh?" The doc was jittering around, anxious to get rid of him, would do anything he asked.

"No, Doc. Not that."

"Something else? Pills? You got pains in your leg again?"

Leon smiled, shaking his head. He still had pains, but he'd learned to listen to them. Better that than what had happened. Get an injury, tell your agent, First Round Odoms, who says he'll handle it. Meantime, play with pain, son. Once we get you through training camp, we can renegotiate, cut a better deal. But if you have to sit down, we're lost. So, go see Doc Hammer, he'll fix you up. Get good and numb so you can keep going, fuck everything up, once and for all.

"Too bad about your leg, you know." The old fart trying his sympathy routine. "One hell of a ball player, you were."

A fucking quack, ruined Leon's career, and what was there to do about it? Sue Doc Hammer? Would have been like suing a turnip.

Leon pointed to one of Hammer's reference books he had lying open on the counter. Had taken him a while, using a flashlight and all, but he finally figured out how to read the damn thing. He tapped an entry with his big finger.

Hammer glanced at the page. "Ergotomine?" he said, turning to Leon. "You have some lady in trouble? Don't fuck around with this, Leon. Take her to doctor."

"These pills do what it says there?" Leon asked. He had hold of the doctor's arm again.

Hammer writhed in his grip. "Yah. Sure. If it isn't very late. They work."

"Good," Leon said. "Then that's what I want."

He gave Hammer a shove toward his pill shelves and waited for him to try to fill a bottle. After watching the sonofabitch spill half the tablets on the floor, Leon swept him aside, turned the container over, dumped a handful in his pocket.

"Thanks, Doc." He turned back to Hammer, something else in his hand now. "And just to show you what a good guy I am, I brought you a present."

He held up another syringe, look like something you'd use on a horse, gave Hammer his finest grin.

"That's okay, Leon." Hammer was backing away. "You don't owe me nothing."

"That's not how I see it," Leon said, moving in on him. He had the skinny old fart slung over the counter in an instant, his arm—all those needle tracks up and down it—laid out straight, the big syringe poised, needle puckering the skin now.

"Best load of your fucking life, Doc," Leon said. "Send your ass to Polack heaven."

"Leon . . . " his eyes watery now. "Please . . . "

"There's guys on the team now, make a half million a year, Doc. So fat they can't see shoe leather. So slow they run backward. Too dumb to make a half a person. What do you think of that?"

The doctor stared up at him, shaking his head from side to side in fright.

"I said, what do you think about that?" Leon jabbed with the needle, brought up a bright dot of blood.

"Not right . . . " the doctor croaked.

"Say what, Doc?" Jabbing him again.

"Not fair," the old man gasped. "You were good. A got-damn shame."

"You ain't got it yet, Doc." Leon leaning hard on top of him now, could feel the man struggling to breathe. Heart thumping to beat the band. "We're talking about your part in the story, what *you* did. Big dumb nigger with a bad knee, Doc Hammer gives him a shot, says, 'Put some heat on it, Leon. Run it out.'" Leon leaned in harder. "You remember that, Doc? You got enough brain cells ain't too juiced to think?"

"Sorry . . . " His voice a bare whisper now.

"What?" Leon eased up a bit. "You're not talking too good."

"I'm said, I'm sorry . . . " There were tears leaking out of the old man's eyes now.

Leon paused, stared down at the pitiful bastard. Finally, he shook his head. "Well, you sure to hell ought to be," he said.

He lifted the needle, brought it in front of Hammer's weepy eyes, suddenly pressed the plunger. Hammer squeezed his eyes shut, tried to turn away as the liquid streamed against his forehead, ran down his cheeks.

"Just tap water, Doc," Leon said, straightening up, dusting himself off. He tossed the empty syringe aside.

Hammer stared up at him, his mouth popping open and closed like some fish wiggling on the counter to clean.

"But keep it in mind," Leon said, moving toward the back. "Anybody ever come around, asking questions, just remember." He was at the door now. "Hot load come along anytime." He nodded before he went out. "Fucking *drugs* can kill you."

 As Deal expected, the cops had sealed Penfield's offices. Homer parked the Rivolta in one of the Bayfront Park turnouts, catercorner from the bank plaza, and they sat watching as Barbara, wearing a hooded raincoat and her go-to-work clothes now, picked her way through the puddles on the broad boulevard. She ran up the steps, and spoke to the cop at the door. After a little hand waving and pointing upstairs, the cop shrugged and let her go inside.

"Suppose she tells somebody you're out here," Homer said.

"She won't," Deal said.

"What if she does?"

"I have the best getaway driver in the state."

"That'd make me an accessory," Homer said.

"What are you now?"

Homer considered that as a metro cruiser swung around the corner and passed them, hustling north, leaving rooster tails in its wake. The thunder and lightning had abated, but the rain was still pouring, whipped into sheets now and then by the wind.

Deal raised his head as the cruiser disappeared. Homer glanced at him over the back of the seat.

"Your old man always did right by me, Deal. The bones were good to him, he'd give me a nice tip for watching the door. He didn't do so well, he took care of me anyway. Him and the Carneses too. No midget jokes, no Homer get me a drink, Homer get that. Those were different times. I already told you how things changed down there."

Homer turned back to the wheel. "So don't ask me what I am, okay? Tonight, I'm doing you a favor. Maybe you'll find your old lady, maybe you'll take the cocksucker out." He shrugged. "And if it don't happen that way, tomorrow, I'll get up, go in to work, wash some fucking cars."

Deal leaned back in the seat, trying to ease the stiffness in his back. "I appreciate it, Homer," he said finally.

Homer grunted. The rain drummed harder on the roof. Deal heard the radio volume go up, a new Bonnie Raitt song, which seemed perfect for the situation.

Deal wormed his way into another position, and lay staring up at the headliner, trying to put it all together, but it just wouldn't come. Alcazar and Penfield's little business deal, that made sense. And Cal, poor goddamn Cal had just been in the middle, Deal's fault. They'd killed him, then made it look like Deal had done it. Maybe they figured it would get him picked up and out of the way. But why would Alcazar kill Penfield too? One frame was plenty. What on earth had he done to deserve all this trouble? And where did Janice come in? What if he was wrong? What if Alcazar didn't have her? What if Deal had dreamed it all up . . .

And then a radio announcer's voice had gradually wormed its way into his consciousness: ". . . here in Atlanta, where the announcement of Terrence Terrell's participation in the south Florida ownership group seems to have swung *everyone* around. Baseball will be coming to south Florida, folks, and you can take that one to the bank."

"Who gives a shit," Homer said. "What we need's casino gambling, OTB—"

"Quiet," Deal said, coming up from the backseat.

It was Terrell's voice then, as full of smooth confidence as Deal remembered from the party on Penfield's yacht, ". . . just pleased to have the means to play a part in this effort. But I want to emphasize that making money has nothing to do with it. I consider baseball an inalienable American right and I'm proud to help bring it to south Florida."

"My aching ass," Homer groaned.

"Shut up," Deal said, his mind spinning, as the announcer came back on.

". . . Terrell, whose genius with computer systems built the largest privately held company in *that* industry, lends both the business savvy and the financial clout that the other owners have been looking for in an expansion package. From the depths of despair to the highest of highs, that's the kind of ride south Florida fans have had this day, and Terrell had this to say about the passing of Thornton Penfield . . . "

Deal fell back in his seat as Terrell intoned his sorrow at Penfield's demise. Deal felt his spirits sinking. If Terrell *was* the major player the baseball group had been praying for, then what in the world was going on between Alcazar and Penfield? Maybe all of Deal's speculations were off base. Maybe he was wasting time even now . . .

"Here she comes," Homer said, as another gust of wind rocked the car. Barbara was hurrying across the empty street, her head bent against the driving rain. As she ran around the front of the Rivolta, Homer leaned across to throw open the door for her.

She fell inside, breathing heavily, water streaming down her face. "They weren't going to let me in," she said, still gasping from her run. "I told them I left my birth control pills upstairs."

Homer blushed, and turned to stare out the window. Barbara reached over the backseat to Deal. "Here," she said, handing him a card from a Rolodex. "It's a place out on Vanderbilt Key."

"More rich people," Homer muttered.

Deal stared at the card, still distracted by what he'd heard on the news. But what choice did he have? He forced himself to concentrate on the card he held. A place he knew, all right.

Originally the family estate of the Vanderbilts, who didn't fancy neighbors when they wintered in Florida, the place had been sold off by the heirs and its acreage divided into a few slightly less ostentatious compounds. You got there by helicopter, seaplane, or boat. The owners maintained a ferry for themselves and their guests, but Deal doubted he and Homer could qualify.

"Where's everybody want to go?" Homer said, starting the Rivolta.

"You can take me home, I guess." It was Barbara, sounding tired.

"We're going to need a boat," Deal said.

Homer turned to stare at him. "Are you nuts? Look at it out there."

"It's okay, Homer, you don't have to go," Deal said.

Homer glared at him. "I never said that. I just said, look at the weather. You gonna ask a guy, 'Rent me your ship, I'd like to go down at sea'?"

A peal of thunder punctuated Homer's words, but it was distant. Deal avoided his gaze. "It's blowing over."

Homer threw up his hands and sat back in his seat, disgusted. Deal glanced up at the sky. At least there was no lightning. It'd have to clear, sooner or later, didn't it?

"Penfield has a boat." It was Barbara's voice, surprising them. They both turned to stare at her.

"*The Mandalay Queen?* That's not what I had in mind," Deal said.

She shook her head. "This is something no one knows about. It's a kind of a Gary Hart fishing charter. He keeps it down at Traynor's."

"This is a serious boat?" Homer said, doubtful.

She shrugged. "It's big enough. Cabins fore and aft. Nice galley. A cozy little stateroom in the middle."

Deal stared at her, trying to picture it: Barbara in a sundress mixing up margaritas at the teak bar, Penfield and another guy in their yacht caps talking baseball.

She stared back at him, tossed her wet hair back. "I liked the boat. It was clean and clear out there, all the stink blows away, you know?"

Deal raised his eyebrows. "Maybe. My old man had an Aquasport. An open fisherman. He liked to drag me along deep-sea fishing. Maybe I wasn't old enough to appreciate it."

"Maybe," she said.

"Let me get this straight," Homer said. "We just go down to Traynor's, overpower the dock master, and steal this yacht, right?"

Barbara shook her head. "You take me with you," she said.

"I don't think so," Deal said.

"They know me down there. I'll get you past the gate, then you're on your own."

Deal thought about it. The rain had eased to a drizzle on the windshield. He could see the ragged outline of a cloud, backlit by the moon. Barbara smoothed her hair back, still watching him. She might have been someone's secretary, caught in the rain, ready for a ride home. He found himself nodding.

It was a long shot, but finding Janice was the important thing. If Alcazar could lead him to his wife, that's all that mattered. He'd worry about the whys and wherefores later.

"Okay," he said, motioning to Homer. "Let's go to Traynor's. Let's get ourselves a boat."

Never mind that it was a stormy Tuesday night, an occasional downpour still sweeping in off the bay. The parking lot outside the popular Grove hangout was packed. There was a real restaurant and bar inside, but all the action was on the huge terrace outside. There was a reggae band blasting under a chickee hut, plastic sheeting unfurled around the sides to protect the musicians and their equipment. The dance floor was under the roof that slanted out from the main building and most of the crowd had simply left the open-air tables to jam in under the eaves, drink their Red Stripes, their Meyers and Coke, their Rumrunners.

The place had been remodeled, rebuilt, given a coat of pink-and-aqua stucco, but it had maintained its laid-back atmosphere over the years. After Lindy Traynor sold out, off to federal prison on tax evasion charges, the new owners hung a bunch of ferns off the porch rafters, brought in a series of bands with horns and girl singers who wore spandex. Before that, Deal had always liked to stop for a beer at Traynor's, if he was ever in the neighborhood, unwind after a day of wrangling with the subs. He was gratified to see reggae was back, at least.

They'd had to park way out near the street. As they passed the walkway to the terrace, the off-duty cop looked the three of them over, then turned back to his bored, tough-guy chat with the young woman who was collecting the covers.

They continued on along the sidewalk that skirted the back of the bandstand, weaving through thick hibiscus hedges to the water's edge. Deal sensed something and glanced at the bandstand, at a rift in the thick plastic sheeting where a big Jamaican in a flowered shirt stood guzzling a beer. Their eyes locked momentarily and the guy nodded slightly, as if they knew each other. A stage hand? A body guard? One of the musicians? There was no way to tell. Deal nodded back and moved on after Barbara.

The dock master's shed sat at the end of the path, blocking the way onto the floating docks. There was a chain-link fence with a gate, a little window where you rang a bell and hoped someone let you through.

Barbara tapped on the window and an old guy wearing a T-shirt that read IRIE in big black letters peered out. After a moment the window slid up.

"Hi, Miz Cooper," the guy said. He glanced at Deal briefly, then came back to her. "Kind of a rough night, iddn't it?"

She nodded. "We just want to look at the boat, Harry." She nodded at Deal. "I've got a friend from up north. He's never been to Florida before."

"That right?" Harry said, punching a button that unsnapped the gate with a buzz. "Well, be careful he don't fall in."

Barbara smiled and turned to take Deal's arm. "We'll be careful, Harry."

The old guy turned away with a wave, headed back toward the little television he had set up on the desk inside. Homer moved through the gate along with them. The old guy had never even seen him.

"*Miss Daisy?*" Homer said, turning to Barbara. "That's what he called it?"

"He called it 'The boat,' " she said.

They were standing at the end of the slip, braced against the rolling caused by the incoming swells, watching as Deal clambered aboard. It was dark out here, and quiet, except for the clanking of halyards against the masts of the sailboats docked nearby. Although the rain had eased off to a mist, the sky had closed up again. Deal worried the storm hadn't truly blown over. Still, he was committed. What else could he do? By morning he could find himself in a small room downtown with Driscoll, listening to the evidence they'd stacked up against him, running his finger down a list of public defenders. Or maybe they'd have him in a padded cell, certain he was taking phone calls via the fillings in his teeth . . .

He found a set of steps stowed along the starboard rails and folded them down for Homer, who climbed up, followed by Barbara.

"What are you doing?" he said, as she stepped over the rail.

She looked at him neutrally. "You want the key, don't you?"

He nodded and stepped aside, steadying himself against the rolling of the boat, watching as she made her way to the hatchway, ran her fingers under a teak overhang. She turned to Deal, surprised, then tried the overhang on the other side of the passageway.

"Shit," she said. "It's always here."

Deal glanced up at the bridge, which sat a few steps above them, the wheel open, but protected by a canopy. No key in the ignition, that much was certain.

"Maybe Jimmy Swaggart borrowed it, forgot to put the key back," Homer said.

"Funny," Barbara said. She bent to check the deck at her feet.

Deal turned to Homer. "Did they ever show you how to hot wire a car down at Surf?"

Homer gave him a look. "*They* never did." He shrugged. "It got to be sort of a lost art after all the locking steering columns came out. What you do these days, you want to boost a car, is you get hold of a flat-bed tow truck, winch the damn thing on board, drive away."

"There's no steering lock on this thing," Deal said, nodding at the wheel.

Homer glanced up. "Sure isn't."

"So can you start it, or not?"

"I can *start* it," Homer said. "Who's going to *drive* it?"

"Don't worry," Deal said.

Homer shook his head. "I *knew* we were going to steal a boat." He started up the steps to the bridge. "I just goddamn *knew* this was going to happen."

The rain had picked up again by the time Deal had gotten the twin diesels idling smoothly. Inside of fifteen minutes, Homer not only had jumped the ignition wires but had also picked the hatchway lock leading down below. He poked his head up and tossed a poncho at Deal, who stood at the wheel, ready to back from the slip.

He turned to Barbara, who had already cast off the stern line and stood on the dock, ready to undo the bow line from the big cleat there. Deal glanced over his shoulder. The rollers were still coming in. And there wasn't much space between him and the boats moored across the way.

He imagined shooting backward into the gleaming Hatteras just opposite, or cutting too sharply from the slip, gouge into the dock, rend the hull just about waterline. They could go full fathom five, right in the slip. And maybe he'd just stay down with it. Be like that rock star who drowned under his own boat in the marina somewhere in California, could have come up, but just didn't want to.

He remembered those Sundays coming in from fishing, his father making him practice docking the Aquasport over and over again, back in, cut the power, try to slip it up against the boards, "like kissing a girl," his dad saying, the guy who ran the marina watching, leaning over a railing, chewing on his cigar and shaking his head, obviously thinking, *What a sorry piece of shit,* no matter how Deal managed. He'd wanted to tie the guy's dick to the prop of the Aquasport, run him around the bay a few times. All of that maneuvering difficult enough, and that had been in calm weather.

He forced himself to stop thinking. It was just stalling, putting off the moment.

"Okay," he called to Barbara. "Cast off."

She nodded, undid the line and slung it aboard. Deal gave her a wave, dropped the boat into reverse and hurried to add some throttle before he stalled out. Suddenly, he felt a lurch at the bow.

"Jesus Christ," he said. What now? What had he done? He turned to see Barbara heaving herself over the front rail, wanted to do something about it, but *Miss Daisy* was whisking backward, a nice swing out of the slip, but a little too quick, really, and he hurried to throttle back, then drop into forward before he circled around into the pilings that separated *Miss Daisy* from the neighboring berth.

The boat shuddered, but the engines held, and suddenly they

were moving forward, out into the channel, rain spattering his face. Barbara pulled herself back along the line that ran the foredeck, then joined him in the cockpit.

"That was really pretty good," she said. "I didn't think you knew what you were doing."

Deal shook his head. The boat was forging through the waves, already edging past the lights of some houseboats anchored in the free water at the edge of the marina waters. He'd forgotten how fast things happened out here, his eyes searching for the first marker buoy. Miss the channel, they'd be hard aground in a second. If you had a pair of stilts and knew where to step, you could walk a couple miles offshore down here, never get wet. Get *Miss Daisy* stuck in the muck here, they wouldn't drown, but Deal could fold his tent, do nothing but wait for the Coast Guard to pick him up, drop him off at the slammer.

He glanced over at Barbara. "What are you doing here?"

She shrugged. "I was standing up there and remembered, I can't drive a stick shift."

Meaning the Rivolta. He'd had Homer give her the keys. "You could have taken a cab," he said, still searching the surging waters ahead. Where was the goddamn channel buoy?

"I left my purse home," she said.

"You don't need my trouble," he said.

"That's nice," she said. "But let's call it my trouble too, okay? My chance to help even the score. Thornton Penfield wasn't any saint, but he sure didn't deserve what Alcazar gave him."

Deal stared at her, nodding. He wondered if she were right, whether Penfield deserved such loyalty. Whether he did or not, you'd love to have someone like Barbara on your side, he thought. He glanced back over the bow, searching for something to say, when suddenly his stomach clenched. He leaned hard into the wheel straining to swing *Miss Daisy* away from a blocky houseboat that was moored just off the buoy, hiding the goddamn light, not ten feet away from them . . .

"Holy shit," Homer cried, going over backward down the hatchway. Barbara bounced off the rails securing the deck hood, then back against Deal. Her feet flew out from under her and she landed in a tangle at his feet.

Deal struggled to keep upright, keep the wheel in his hands, could they maybe just plow right through the goddamn thing?

. . . and then, their bow was whisking by the houseboat, barely clearing it, but crashing into a wooden dinghy tied off at its side. The dinghy disappeared into the foaming water with a crunch, the houseboat rocking wildly in their wake. He heard a dog barking from somewhere and imagined the people inside the houseboat, bouncing across the decks, still lost in their dreams, wondering where the bus had come from.

Already *Miss Daisy* was thirty feet away, chopping the waves, Deal still with a death's grip on the wheel, trying to get his breath back.

Barbara dragged herself up, clutching his pant leg. "I guess I spoke too soon," she said, grabbing at him again as they crested a bigger wave.

Homer clambered out of the hatchway, checking a busted lip. "What *was* that?"

"Cheap bastards moored up without running lights," he said. He stuck out his hand, helped Barbara to her feet. Probably sneaked in after dark, trying to save a few bucks dockage, and they'd nearly sunk him. Well, they'd have fun getting ashore without their dinghy.

He saw the ragged fringe of the mangrove island that sheltered the marina coming up on their starboard side, and nosed *Miss Daisy* around a bit, dead into the wind and the heaving waves. He'd made it this far, he thought. There was some small satisfaction in that. He nodded, feeling the spray cool on his face as they headed out into open water.

 "I'm Mr. Terrell's assistant," the man in the vested suit was saying. "Maybe if you explained what it was about, Mr. Al-*kiz*-er, then I could help you."

Alcazar shook his head patiently. He wondered if this person knew how to pronounce his name properly, if he were actually trying to insult him. Alcazar motioned for Alejandro to take a seat at the small conference table that stood between them and this fool wearing an ill-fitting suit.

They were in the anteroom of a suite near the ballroom where a celebration was in progress, no formal announcement yet, but everyone in Atlanta for the commissioner's meeting agreed. Tomorrow, when the agenda moved to the matter of the expansion vote, the Tropics were a lock to get the franchise.

Three years of lobbying, wheedling, cajoling, junketing—even some attempts at outright bribery—on the part of a dozen U.S. cities were about to come to an end. Two municipalities had erected budget-crushing stadiums to house the team—"If you build it, they will come," went the literature of one city's effort—and those two faced the specter of servicing one hundred million dollars or more of debt with flea markets and rock concerts, tractor pulls and evangelical convocations, where they'd hoped to have the crack of bats, the slap of horsehide into gloves. Pity the poor losers, Alcazar thought. He could afford to.

Alcazar's view was out a bank of windows overlooking the hotel's lavish inner court. There was a waterfall cascading several stories into an acre of planted rain forest where walkways wound, linking up the bars and restaurants tucked away here and there among the foliage. Huge banners carrying the logos of the various American and National League teams had been hung off standards about the balconies. On the far side of the vast court-yard, escalators zigzagged up from through the trees, linking the hotel to an exclusive shopping mall. He imagined the owners and executives down below, swilling martinis, toasting the banners that hung above them, while their wives swarmed the larded shops.

Earlier, killing time, Alcazar had strolled through the shopping area—which made Worth Avenue look a bit down at the heels to his way of thinking. There was a certain flair in this city—he'd give them that—and for a moment, he entertained the notion of moving his base into new territory, though he just as quickly dismissed it. Too many clownish southerners to test him with their egregious smiles. "Why shoor, Mr. *Az*-kizzer, we'd be glad to do bidness with you, if'n we *can* . . . " Why put up with it?

He could hear the muffled drone of music through the walls behind him. He wondered briefly what kind of orchestra had been engaged. Had it been *his* celebration, it would be something vibrant, something that exuded heat. The Sound Machine, perhaps, Gloria Estafan there to kick sparks from the stage, melt the speakers, let these moon-faced burghers from the North know what they were in for in the tropics.

Of course, it wasn't his celebration, but Terrence Terrell's, and Penfield's cohorts who'd finally convinced Terrell to buy their baseball team for them. That clutch of good old boys had probably exhumed someone from the dead to play at their celebration, someone remembering sweet strains of something from college, but nothing too exuberant, let's show our friends from the North that we're just like they are, every penny we own ground from some poor man's sweat when you got right down to it, but we're going to pretend like we picked it off these trees that grow about us . . . well, never mind, Alcazar thought. Never mind that his money hadn't been good enough, that he hadn't had a prayer of participating in the ownership group. There was a future, and there were always unexpected developments to come. And meantime, he would still benefit, and benefit greatly.

The man in the suit did not seem happy that Alejandro had sat down without being asked. "Tell Mr. Terrell I won't keep him," Alcazar said.

"I'm afraid this isn't the time . . . "

"Just explain that it's about the Republic Holding Group," Alcazar said. "I think he'll want to see me."

The man considered it. Alcazar watched the gears turning. Throw the greasers out, or go pester his boss who was probably holding court with half the net worth of America, his hand down the back of some scooped out cocktail gown nearby.

"It is important," Alcazar assured the man.

The man fingered a thread that had unraveled at one of his buttonholes, then sighed. "Just a minute," he said, and disappeared through a doorway.

Alejandro glanced up at him, his cratered jaw swinging back and forth. "These people do not know how to act."

Alcazar nodded. "That is true, Alejandro. But it is important to walk among them now and again. To remind yourself with whom you must contend."

Alejandro nodded, grudgingly. He clearly had ideas about how to contend with such cretins.

The door opened then, and the man with the unfortunate suit was back, followed by Terrell, whom Alcazar recognized from the many photographs he'd seen: America's techno whiz, the answer to the Japanese threat, young, handsome, dynamic, ballyhooed as if the hopes of the very nation were pinned to his star.

Foolish, jingoistic stuff, Alcazar thought. He envied the man only the Palm Beach estate he'd purchased, the same venerable property that had once belonged to a railroad titan and which Alcazar, despite his wealth, had no hope of acquiring. He gave an inner shrug. So that made two things. No baseball team. No Palm Beach mansion. Perhaps it would not always be so. Meanwhile, he would do the next best thing: profit.

"Mr. *Al*cazar?" Terrell said, smiling affably.

Alcazar nodded. No veiled insult there. Terrell wore a lime

green pair of slacks—linen—a white cotton shirt with a soft collar unbuttoned at the neck, a navy blue blazer. Deck shoes, no socks. Not Alcazar's style, but bounds above his minion's taste. Perhaps he would be able to talk with this man after all.

"Claude here tells me you're with Republic Holding?" Terrell's gaze curious, wondering what might have sent some holding company's underling scurrying all the way up to Atlanta at such a time.

Alcazar nodded again. "I *am* Republic Holding, Mr. Terrell."

Terrell's expression went blank for a moment. The signals in his brain scrambling for an instant, then rearranging themselves, synapses clanging, reopening—let's try that again—channeling, processing: Yes, yes, we copy, we understand.

No more affable team owner, his gaze was suddenly hard. He turned to his assistant. "Go on back to the party, Claude."

Claude hesitated.

"It's okay," Terrell said, flashing the we're-just-folks smile. "You see what Mrs. Spidel wants to drink. I was right in the middle of that."

Claude gave Alcazar another distrustful look, then slunk back out of the room.

When the door closed, Terrell turned, shaking his head. "What's your first name, Mr. Alcazar?"

"I am who you think I am," Alcazar said.

Terrell nodded, taking it in. "That goddamn Penfield," he said. "He assured me he and a bunch of his country club buddies controlled that property."

Alcazar smiled. Terrell was quick, that much was apparent. "I assume he showed you the documents to prove it."

"Of course he did," Terrell said.

"Then, so far as anyone else is concerned," Alcazar said, "that is the truth of the matter."

"Son of a *bitch*," Terrell said, turning to gaze out the window, turning it over in his mind. "He stood to make plenty on this franchise. Why was he worried about some pissant land deal?"

Alcazar shrugged. "One gets older, one gets impatient to see the returns on an investment. Your baseball team will take years to turn a profit. This 'pissant land deal,' as you call it, stands to return eight million dollars on an investment of less than three."

Terrell stared at him skeptically. Alcazar shrugged. "It is a simple concept, Mr. Terrell. Buy low, sell high."

Terrell swung about to face Alcazar. "Earning your money is one thing. But to cut some sneaking deal with a . . . " Terrell was searching for the right insult, but Alcazar brushed it aside.

"We all have our skeletons, Mr. Terrell." Alcazar pointed at the briefcase in front of Alejandro. "For instance, my associate has with him some very interesting photographs taken aboard a certain pleasure craft Mr. Penfield owned."

Terrell's tanned face turned a shade darker. He was married, of course. The recent story in *Newsweek* made much of his "solid family values."

"If you think you can walk in here and threaten to blackmail me . . . " Terrell began.

"I have no such intention," Alcazar said. "I was simply making a point."

There was a lull in the music then, and Terrell took a breath, getting himself under control. "I've got some people to attend to, Mr. Alcazar. Suppose you tell me what you want."

Alcazar gave him a bland look. "Nothing, Mr. Terrell. Nothing you haven't agreed to already, that is. I just wanted to introduce myself, and ascertain that nothing would hold up the closing."

Terrell thought a moment. "Last I spoke to Penfield, there were still some title problems outstanding, the whole parcel hadn't been cleared."

"We are prepared," Alcazar said.

Terrell tried out his businessman's gaze. "We don't have to go with the city-center site, you know. We can go back up north of the county line, talk to the people in Broward, save a hell of a lot in taxes, have all the parking, road access we need." Terrell smiled. "That'd leave you with a whole bunch of worthless property, would fuck you and the Republic horse you rode in here on, wouldn't it?"

Alcazar sighed. "Mr. Terrell, you and I both know there isn't time for that. There are three other cities ready to walk away with your precious baseball franchise. Your participation has tipped the scales one way. But if you were to walk into those hearings tomorrow without a firm site commitment . . . " Alcazar broke off, letting the implication hang.

"You can't be sure of that," Terrell said, smiling. "They know I'll iron out anything that comes up. Pave it over with cash."

"You could take that chance," Alcazar said. "Or you could leave things as they are. You will simply conclude the arrangement to purchase the necessary land outlying the city's stadium for road access, stadium expansion and ancillary development, said lands and properties to be conveyed by the Republic Holding Group, and everyone will be happy. You'll save money in the long run, and the civic good will be served." Alcazar nodded. "There will be a base-ball team in our city."

Terrell was quiet then, ignoring Alcazar's irony, chewing thoughtfully on the inside of his cheek. Alcazar recognized the pose from a cover of *Time*. He turned and nodded to Alejandro, who unsnapped the briefcase, withdrew a document and slid it across the table toward Terrell.

Terrell glanced down at it, then stared back at Alcazar. "That doesn't mean a thing unless the titles are clear," he said.

"We are prepared," Alcazar repeated.

The door swung open and Claude peered in. "Mrs. Spidel said you promised her a dance," he said to Terrell.

"I'll be right there, Claude," Terrell said. And then bent down to sign.

"I told you, I was out," Leon Straight said into the phone, his eyes following a dancing fork of lightning that leapfrogged across the horizon. "I had some business." Thunder had nearly drowned out the voice on the other end of the line. He was sitting at the bar, looking out the big windows at the back of Alcazar's house, his sore leg propped on a stool across from him.

Alcazar raising hell with him on the other end. Leon sat up, punched a button, put Alcazar on the speaker phone. He added a little of the orange to his Gatorade mix.

". . . extremely important, Leon. Everything is in place. Every-thing is on the line." His voice sounded a little nervous to Leon.

There was another bolt of lightning and a crash of thunder. Leon sipped his drink. Too much orange, now.

". . . depending on you." Alcazar paused. "What's all that noise?"

"Looks like a storm blowing in, Mr. A." Kinda nice, he thought, sitting in here watching it blow.

"Now listen to me, Leon. It is all arranged. If the police apprehend Deal, our friends in the department know what to do. He will resist, there will be an unfortunate accident, everything will go on as planned."

Yeah, Leon thought, but we ain't gonna get that far.

"And if you should get your hands on him in the meantime . . . " Leon took a breath. He didn't like the thought of going out in this weather, but if he was going to make his own thing happen, now was the time. "You can stop worrying about Deal," he said. Some spidery lightning now, way up high.

"What did you say, Leon?"

"I said you could stop worrying about Deal. I've got something worked out."

"*Leon . . .* " Alcazar's voice, big-time agitated, so loud it was making the speaker box rattle. Leon reached over, punched the button again, picked up the receiver.

"Mmmm-hmmm," Leon nodding, waiting for the man to calm down. "Ain't nothing we can talk about on the phone, Mr. A. But don't worry. You get yourself back down here from Hot-Lanta, I'll explain it all to you."

Leon smiled, hanging up the phone in the middle of Alcazar yelling. He settled back in his chair, enjoying the thought of Alcazar shitting his britches.

Alcazar and Alejandro up there in a fancy hotel, eating the kind of food you couldn't even spell, fat chance Leon ever get a trip like that. No, he got the dirty work. "Stick around the home front, boy. We'll bring you back some scraps from the table." Well, all that was about to change.

More thunder, then, shaking those big panes in the doors, like to break them. He caught a glimpse of running lights out in the Intracoastal, but then they were gone. Dumb bastard probably sunk.

Leon finally heaved himself up off the stool. Last thing in the world he wanted to do was go out on a night like this. But that was the business world for you. You had to adapt.

He stared down at his knees, his offending knees. Body like his.

Speed like he had. And the mean. Nobody'd dealt with mean like his. That was what they meant when they talked about "desire." What they meant was "how *mean* is the boy?" Which in Leon's case was plenty.

But all of that didn't mean shit when your knees went, did it? Then you could take your mean ass on off the property, go back to Georgia, sit on the porch and watch tourist cars go by on the way to Florida, look at the white folks looking out at you—"Oooh my, George, lookit that big nigger boy over there!"

Or else find a place to put your talents to work. The pay not as good, but not bad either. The work, when it came, interesting, you'd have to say that, for these Cubans had some interesting slants on the concept of mean, too bad they didn't have the size for serious ball.

He watched more lightning streak against the sky, waiting for the crack of thunder sure to follow. Except there wasn't any trainer and nobody else give a shit about your sore knee, he thought. Leon shook his head again, then went to get his gear.

They'd nearly circled the island before they found the place, Homer finally recognizing the gazebo in the backyard from a photograph in Alcazar's office, spotting it all lit up in a burst of lightning just to the west. Deal had cut the running lights while they were still out in the channel, bringing *Miss Daisy* in on a line toward a neighbor's dock. He didn't relish the thought of trying to dock in this weather, but what was he supposed to do? The neighbor's house where they were headed looked deserted, a couple pair of davits swinging empty in the stiff wind, no lights at the boathouse, no signs of life inland, the owners probably in Vermont or Vail, toughing out the summer. Nobody there to watch Deal struggle in, at least.

A hundred yards to port was the broad sweep of Alcazar's lawn that ran down to the dock where a Donzi was tied off on spring-loaded davits that arched and bobbed over the boat like big fishing rods struck by monster fish.

There were lights on in the back of the house, but he couldn't see anyone inside. He slid the engines into reverse, keeping a light hand on the throttle, then turned to Homer, who was dancing up on the balls of his feet, trying to get a look at the place over the rails.

"Hold the wheel a minute," he said to Homer, then reached for a pair of binoculars Barbara had brought up from below decks. She was back at the stern now, clutching the rails, dry-heaving over the side. She'd gotten sick ten minutes out of Traynor's.

"What am I supposed to do?" Homer called, struggling with the wheel, which threatened to whirl him off his feet.

"Just hold it steady." Quite an invasion force he had assembled, Deal thought, raising the glasses.

The way the boat was heaving, it was hard to see, but he thought he caught a glimpse of movement inside. He reached out with one hand to help Homer steady the wheel, then braced himself against the wheel housing and ground the eyepieces down hard.

This time he caught it: Leon Straight, impossible to mistake him, wearing a yellow slicker, walking through a big wood-paneled room past a bank of floor to ceiling windows, carrying something . . . a briefcase?

The boat tipped up on a swell and Deal's view disappeared. When they came down again, the room was empty, the lights in the house were out.

"Shit," Deal said. He scanned the dark swathe of lawn with the glasses, but it was useless. Hadrian's army could be marching down to the shore, he wouldn't be able to tell.

"What's the matter?" It was Barbara, pulling herself back toward the bridge, her voice weak, exhausted.

"Leon . . . " he said, shaking his head. If the guy were to hear their motors . . . "Shit!" Deal said again. He couldn't cut the motors or they'd be flung broadside onto shore.

He nudged Homer aside, threw the engines into forward, his hand ready at the throttle. Nothing but a low hum from the engines at near-idle speed. If they creep along, could get far enough downwind, they wouldn't be heard above the rush of the storm and the waves. If he could round the jut of land at the far end of the neighbor's property, get them out of the wind, not run aground . . .

But the wind was forcing them steadily closer to the seawall: fifty feet now, then forty, the wheel useless, they were nearly broadside to the waves now, twenty-five . . . he could see the looming shape of the davits on the neighbor's dock, like deserted cranes canted nearly overtop of the bow of *Miss Daisy* . . . here we go, he thought, down the jaws . . .

. . . then suddenly they steadied, as if a giant hand had reached out from the shore to stave them off from disaster. Deal stared out at the dark waters, stunned for a moment . . . then realized. The backwash of the waves coming off the seawall had caught them. The very force that had been driving them in had passed them by, struck home, and rebounded. In a few seconds they were easing softly up to the neighbor's dock . . . "like kissing a girl," he found himself thinking.

Homer leapt ashore, trailing the forward line in one hand. He tied it off quickly, then caught the aft line that Barbara tossed him.

"Give us some slack," Deal called. "Or we'll pound to pieces."

Homer nodded, spun out a loop of rope before he secured it. Deal watched him lean out to pull Barbara ashore, then made his own leap to the dock, timing it with the upthrust of a wave that brought the decks nearly to the top of the pilings. Slack or no slack, he thought, *Miss Daisy* would be driven relentlessly into the dock. They'd be lucky to find anything left of this boat if it were tied up long.

He hurried across the slippery planks of the dock and onto shore, up through the screen of shrubbery that shielded Alcazar's house from view. He heard Barbara and Homer crashing through the tangle behind him. He was about to turn to quiet them when another sheet of lightning lit the sky, and he froze.

He'd only seen it for an instant through the brush, but the image burned steadily, madly, in his mind: huge Leon in a yellow slicker out there in the middle of Alcazar's lawn not fifty feet away, bent over something, wrestling with it, some thrashing *creature* . . .

Deal warned the others to be still, then edged closer, guided by Leon's grunts and curses. When he was as close as he dared, he pushed aside a holly bough in time to see Leon, illumined by the glow of the house lights now, lunge backward with a cry of satisfaction.

"Mother-*fucker*," the big man cried, then spun like a hammer thrower to fling whatever he was holding from his grasp. Deal ducked down, hearing a crash of glass above the storm. He felt Homer come up beside him, then they both peered out through the brush to see it:

Leon was striding away down the lawn in his slicker, leaving the scene of battle. One of the big picture windows in the house had shattered, and something that looked like an animal, a horse, a giant bird, leaned crazily through the sharded opening. A floor lamp had toppled over inside, its shade gone, its bulb still burning. You could see a tangle of roots beneath the thing that hung in the window now, see that it was no creature at all, but something green and leafy, a carefully manicured shrub of some kind.

"Jesus Christ, he killed a *tree?*" Homer said. "What's the matter with him?"

There was a great roar from the direction of Alcazar's docks, the mighty engines of the Donzi tied off there cranking up like Hell clearing its throat. Deal stared at the house, then back toward the docks, frozen. Maybe Janice was inside there, maybe Leon had lost it, was running off, all Deal would have to do was walk in through that shattered window, find her, sweep her up in his arms like some hero in the comics . . . but on the other hand, how could it be so simple? He heard the growl of the Donzi's engines even out, ready to fly . . .

. . . and then, he was crashing back through the underbrush toward *Miss Daisy,* Homer at his back, past a glimpse of Barbara's rain-streaked, puzzled face as he tore past her.

In moments they were all back aboard. Deal had rammed the throttle full, at the same time swinging her nose around into the waves. Homer and Barbara hung on desperately to the rails, banging into one another, into Deal, who leaned hard against the wheel.

He didn't look back, but felt the backwash of their wake as it piled into the seawall, was compressed, then squeezed back out and against their stern. It gave them a welcome boost against the driving wind. They couldn't have missed the wall by more than a yard.

Miss Daisy's engines were roaring now, but the Donzi's noise was far greater, carrying to them above their own racket and the noise of the storm.

"That's Leon?" Barbara called.

Deal nodded, watching the Donzi pull away from the docks.

"How come we're going after him?" Homer cried. "We got the goddamn place to ourselves."

Deal shook his head, pressing the throttle down full. He could only hope that Leon would have enough sense to keep the Donzi reined in, given the weather.

"We could go in there, take that chance," Deal said. "But think about it," he said. "You'd need a pretty good reason to take a boat ride on a night like this, even as stupid as Leon is."

Deal hoped he was right. It was only instinct, but he could always come back here, if he was wrong. He glanced at his companions. Barbara's face was a pale oval in the glow from the instrument panel. He knew she'd do anything to get off the pitching boat, and yet she was holding quiet.

Homer nodded grudgingly. He glanced over the rail at the Donzi, maybe a hundred yards ahead of them now, turning south, back toward the open waters they'd just crossed. Sheet lightning lit up the clouds above, but the rain had eased off, the wind slackening a bit.

"Okay," Homer said, finally. "Leon's stupid. What's that make us?"

"Accessories," Deal said, and turned back to the wheel.

 "We going over to Bimini?" It was Homer, glancing back at the receding lights of the city. Already they'd lost sight of a big chunk of skyline; even the huge bank towers were obliterated by a squall that had swung in behind them.

The Donzi had opened up the distance between them once they were out past the channel markers, but Leon was being cautious, apparently. The Donzi could easily double *Miss Daisy*'s speed, but so far he'd respected the conditions, no Don Johnson stuff, clipping off the seven-foot swells. And the weather was keeping all the other pleasure craft in, making it easy enough to keep track of him, even at a quarter mile or more. So far so good, Deal thought, wiping his dripping face on his sleeve.

"I don't think we're going to Bimini," he said to Homer. He had an idea where Leon might be headed, now, but he'd hold off saying anything.

Barbara clung grimly to the rail just aft, her heaves gone for the moment. She'd tried going below, lying down, but that only made things worse. Deal felt for her, wished he could do something. He wasn't thrilled to have her along, God knows. There was always the possibility Leon would swing the Donzi around, come back on them for a little chat cum torpedo practice, lob whatever he might have on hand their way.

He was also worried about Homer. Stolid Homer, who stood at the rail, rain dripping off his chin, doing his best to track the Donzi with the binoculars. He had no part in this, despite his sentimental feelings for Deal's old man. They'd gone well beyond the fun-and-games stage. Wherever Leon was headed, Deal knew there was going to be deep shit when they all piled in.

For Deal, it didn't matter. Choice was no longer an operable concept. But now he was dragging two decent people into his mess. Of course, he could bail out now, take everybody home, start over tomorrow . . .

"Forget it," Barbara said, weary, pushing herself away from the rail and back inside the shelter of the bridge.

"Forget what?" Deal said.

"If it were my husband we were looking for—forget I don't have one—you think I'd call time out, take you in?" She shook her head. "I saw the way you were looking at us," she continued. "This is one of those things you have to do, Deal. You save feeling guilty for another time."

Homer looked up at him. "All we're doin's following a guy." He waved the binoculars toward the distant lights of the Donzi. "Although I'd like to know where."

Deal felt some relief, but not much. "We'll find out where he's going, that's all," he said, glancing at Barbara. "We're going to stay out of trouble."

He nodded at Homer for emphasis, praying he'd been telling the truth, then turned back to scan the dark waters ahead. The Donzi was slowing now and Deal cut *Miss Daisy*'s engines back. He checked what he could see of the distant skyline over his shoulder. He hadn't been out here since he was a kid, when he and Flivey were part of that framing crew, but he had a fair memory of how the lights on shore got to looking around dark, when they'd pack it up, head home in the Penfield's Boston Whaler. It seemed they'd come out about the right distance.

They drifted for a few moments, his eyes turned back to the darkness and finally, he touched Homer's shoulder. He was pointing now at a series of vague lumpish silhouettes that had risen up on the skyline. They might have been mistaken for tiny oil drilling platforms, or pumping rigs, but there were no lights, no surging pumps, no stink of waste gas. More like abandoned rigs, or ghost rigs, or a kind of seaborne Stonehenge.

"Stiltsville," Deal said. Where he and Flivey had spent their last days. It would be the perfect place, you wanted to hide somebody.

"Stiltsville?" Barbara repeated.

"Fucking-A," Homer said. "I forgot all about that."

Deal nodded. Stiltsville was easy enough to forget about. It had been a dream in the first place, a crackpot dream faded into a mirage you caught a glimpse of on your way out from Traynor's to the distant reefs to dive, or using the straightest shot to the Gulf Stream and hoping you'd brought the right bait for once, you might glance over, squint, turn to ask somebody on board, "What the fuck is *that?*"

What it actually was was a series of houses built in the 1960s on pilings five miles out into Biscayne Bay, at a spot where the water might not reach your chin. The concept sounded great in those revolutionary times: no taxes, no law, no order. A great view, boat to work, fish out your bedroom window if you wanted.

And there'd been a couple dozen visionaries, or complete idiots, depending on your frame of reference, who were willing to try it. The place Deal and Flivey had worked on belonged to a flamboyant defense attorney and pal of Flivey's father who found the notion appealing. There were a dozen or so houses already completed, some of them a couple thousand square feet, all the comforts of home in place, another dozen in various stages of construction at that time, the heyday of Stiltsville. Flivey and Deal were looking forward to a placid summer, framing one house after another, swim when you got hot, drink a six-pack every evening watching the sun go down, boat home, and go to bed, get up and start all over again. That hadn't been so much to ask for, had it? And look what Flivey had gotten instead.

Deal had never been back to Stiltsville. And the summer after Flivey died, the state and federal environmental agencies got their act together long enough to swoop down on Stiltsville, slapping the project with every kind of stop order known to man. There were several legitimate environmental concerns: sewage runoff, reef infringement, and the like. But Deal suspected that the chief opposition had come from those who feared the anarchy of it all. Those good old boys in Tallahassee were not about to let the kind of bullshit that had sprung up on a bunch of hippie communes out west take root in Florida. And never mind it'd take at least fifty thousand hippie dollars to build one of the places, either. Stiltsville was out of business. What was finished got to stay. What was unfinished got to rot in the sun and the salt. He never found out what happened to the house he and Flivey had worked on.

Most residents gave up, packed it in. Some diehards made the modifications the new zoning regulations required, and actually moved in. But over the years, the novelty of a long boat ride for a box of Cheerios or a movie wore off, taking care of the permanent residents. And even the weekenders got increasingly disheartened, coming out to see what kind of shit vandals, or the summer storms, might have dumped on their living room rugs.

So now, though some of the places still stood intact, most had long since tumbled down, or were condemned, and it was rare you ever saw anyone around the places, except for the occasional fisherman tied off in the shadows, casting his rigged shrimp out toward the pilings for the unwary snapper.

What you surely wouldn't expect, Deal thought, was a big, glossy Donzi he'd tied up under one of the houses, not at this time of night, heaving in a storm swell rolling in off the Atlantic. Still, there it was.

Deal gave the throttle a nudge. He was swinging *Miss Daisy* southeastward, a quarter mile or so out from the shallows where the houses stood, his own running lights switched off. If Leon were to hear them over the waves, he might mistake them for a fisherman hurrying home from the storm. Maybe.

Deal held the binoculars to his eyes, scanning the silhouette of the house where the Donzi was moored. For all he knew, it was the house he and Flivey had built. It would make sense if it were. Say Penfield had picked it up from his pal, kept it for his little private parties, that'd square with the other things he had learned.

Sheet lightning on the horizon backlit the place briefly, once, twice, but still he couldn't see anything, not the faintest hint of light about the windows. No sign of movement. Nothing.

"What are you waiting for?" Homer said, nodding at the house. "Take us in there. We can handle the bastard."

Deal glanced down. Homer had jimmied open a locker, found a

flare gun, some extra flares that looked like monster shotgun shells. He'd also come up with a fishing gaff with a wicked point, which he brandished in the air between them.

Deal leaned backward. "Put that thing down before you stab one of us, Homer."

"Two of us, one of him," Homer said.

"You don't know who's in that place," Deal said. "Go in there with your spear, Leon and his buddies'll make a shish kebab out of you."

Deal was stalling, trying to figure out what he *could* do. He'd be surprised if many of Alcazar's men were in that house. How many guys could you convince to sit around, wait for a typhoon to blow them to kingdom come. No, not many people inside. But he thought he knew who one of them might be, and he prayed he was right. The only question was what to do now.

He could wait, see who came out. Maybe Leon was simply doing his jailer's duty, delivering the groceries, checking things out. Sure, he thought, and maybe he was going to dust and clean the windows too. A jagged bolt of lightning cut the sky just to the south and thunder rolled over the waves toward them. As he'd told Homer, you'd need a good reason to come all this way on a night like this.

"I'm going to count on you, Homer," Deal said, abruptly.

" 'Course you can," Homer said, clutching his spear. His expression was uncertain.

Deal continued. "I want you to keep the boat nosed into the waves, just like we are, hold the throttle steady. The wind and the current will hold you just about in the same spot, same as walking a treadmill."

Barbara shoved away from the railing, pulling strands of hair off her pale cheeks. "What are you talking about, Deal?"

He was ducking out of his poncho, kicking off his shoes. "You keep watch through the binoculars," he told her. "You see me get inside the house, give me ten minutes. If I'm not out, head for shore, call for help."

She stared at him incredulously, then pointed out into the darkness. "You're going to swim? In *that*?"

Deal was stepping out of his slacks. He glanced out at the

swells, thought a moment. "I've been in worse," he said. "The current'll help me out." He pointed toward the dark shape of the
house.

"You want to kill yourself, why don't you just fall on this,"
Homer said, holding up the gaff.

"You going to take this wheel or not?"

Homer nodded grudgingly. He laid the gaff aside, took hold of
the throttle, which revved momentarily then fell back as he
adjusted his grip. With the other hand he grabbed the wheel. Deal
patted his shoulder, but Homer wouldn't look at him.

He pulled off his shirt, surprised at the chill that hit him. Just
the wind and the rain, but still surprising for Florida in July. He
held the binoculars out to Barbara, who shook her head, looking
him over, him in his skivvies, trying to keep his knees from knock-
ing.

"Seems like a hell of a waste," she said. "Why don't we all head
in, get the cops on this."

"Ten minutes, okay?" He stared at her until her eyes met his.
"Okay," she said finally.

He moved quickly back the deck then, climbed up on the tran-
som, wavered, caught his balance. He sensed the water heaving
beneath him . . . and then he was off, rising effortlessly with the
toss of the boat, weightless for a moment, and then into the sur-
prisingly warm grasp of the water.

"You can sit there, stare at it all you want, it ain't gonna go away." It
was Leon, standing by the stove in the tiny kitchen of the house, his
hand on a pot of water he'd put up.

Janice glanced up from the papers he'd spread out on the
Formica table, looked around the interior of the place. It was the
first time he'd let her out of the bedroom since he'd brought her
here. Typical tract home interior, furniture from the 1960s, rental
decor, a wretched seascape above a moldering couch. All the windows were boarded over.

She could hear the storm raging outside now, the water raging,
shaking the foundations of the house. It had to be a place directly
on the water, but somewhere all by itself. She'd heard some distant
boat traffic, had screamed herself hoarse several times, to no avail.

She tried to think where she could be, but it was difficult to concentrate. She was weak, from hunger, from exhaustion, from fear. But she would die before she'd wilt in front of this creature.

"What happens if I don't sign? You're going to put my hand in hot water?"

Leon gave her a neutral look, jiggled the pot handle, as if that might make it heat faster. He reached in his pocket, dumped a handful of white tablets into the water. "No," he said. "Be a shame to mess up something as pretty as you." He peered into the pan, jiggled it again, then turned to point at her. "How about you hand me that spoon over there."

There was a teaspoon poking out of a cup on the table beside her, an old butter knife lying alongside it. She wondered briefly if she might use the knife as a weapon, then discounted it. Leon looked like the kind of person you could run over with a truck, and you'd only hurt the truck.

"Give me the spoon, sweet cheeks."

She saw the look in his eyes. Not hurt her? It was true, he'd done nothing to her yet, but she had no illusions about that. If the thought struck him, he'd have her for breakfast.

"That's better," Leon said as she handed him the spoon. He examined it, wiped something off on his sleeve, then stirred what was in the pot.

She could smell something bitter, almost coppery. He pointed at Janice again. "Let's see the cup."

She hesitated a moment, then handed him the cup. Leon didn't bother to see what might have dried up in there, what might have fallen in and died trying to get out. He dunked the mug into the pan, scooped up some of the liquid, then turned swiftly and caught her by the hair. He jerked her head back, and she felt her eyes water with the pain. He held the steaming cup under her nose. The bitter smell was overpowering, choking her.

"This ain't warm milk. This here's some pills will have your insides clutching up like you took an alum douche." He shook her by the hair in case she hadn't heard. "You have any hopes of carrying that baby inside you, you sign these mother-fucking papers."

She felt a stab of fear deep inside her. How could he know that? "What makes you think I'm pregnant?" She managed to get it out despite the fiery pain, her scalp on fire as he tightened his grip.

Leon shook her again. "I work for people whose business it *is* to know. Gonna sell or buy from folks, you have to know all the buttons to push. But it don't matter how, you sign or I'll pour this stuff down you like you was a Christmas goose."

Finally he let her go. She wiped the tears from her eyes, trying to control the trembling that seemed to come from her very core. She stared at the cup. She didn't doubt it was what he said it was.

She shook her head, dazed. Who *was* this man? Who *were* these people he worked for? If you could call them people at all. A few days ago she'd been on her way home, her biggest problem how to explain to Deal why she had been so bitchy lately, trying to decide how she could let him know that she'd stand behind him no matter what. Now, here she was, in some unknown place, at the mercy of a monster who wanted to kill her and her unborn child, unless she sold him her husband's company. As if she could even do that.

Leon stuck his finger in the cup, testing it. "Just about ready to drink," he said.

She closed her eyes, shuddering. She thought of the look of triumph on the doctor's face when he finally had been able to give her the news. She thought of Deal and his goofy smile when she told him. She thought of all those toys he'd bought. Of all the things they had planned, that they'd be a family at last.

She let out her breath and opened her eyes. She stared at Leon, willing every ounce of hatred she'd ever felt into her gaze. "This won't do you any good, without my husband's signature," she said.

He stared back at her, unfazed. "You want to drink this shit, or sign?" he said.

She gave him a last, vicious glance, then snatched up the pen and scrawled her name.

Leon nodded his approval, then picked up the contract from the table. "That man's as good as dead," he said. "And once he is dead, your signature's the only one that counts."

He folded the papers away. "If he don't manage to die somewhere else real soon, then I'll let him know where to find his pretty little wife." He tapped the phone that was still belted to his side. "Let him know if I have to take out an ad in the newspapers."

He smiled, waving the contract in front of Janice. "Kind of guy he is, he'll put himself up in my face. And once he does, we'll tidy up what has to be."

"You're crazy," she said softly.

"Naw," Leon said. "I'm in real estate. Now let's get you back in that bedroom, tuck you away safe."

Deal had tried to keep his dive shallow but the pitch of the boat had tossed him forward at the last instant. He felt the tickle of eel grass along his gut as he kicked his way back toward the surface. About ten feet deep here, he guessed, breaking atop a swell. He glanced back over his shoulder at *Miss Daisy*. The boat heaved and rolled, but seemed to be holding steady. He turned from the rancid smell of diesel exhaust and began a steady crawl toward a group of abandoned pilings a hundred yards ahead.

There might have been a house atop these supports once, but now the columns jutted out of the water empty, like the pillars of some lost civilization. Their caps were splintered, tendrils of reinforcement steel silhouetted against the vague glow from the city's lights. Deal felt something slither past his hand and froze in midstroke, instinctively jerking back, his head dipping in a swell, sucking in a half-pint of seawater.

Fucking-a, he thought. Grab a handful of seaweed and fall to pieces. Some commando. For a moment he imagined Flivey, sitting atop one of the ruined pilings, shaking his head—*"When are you going to get it, Deal? No heroes in this life."* But he shook off the vision, regaining the rhythm of his strokes. The swells threw him in and out of the water, but the current was pushing him steadily toward the ruined pilings. The burble of *Miss Daisy*'s engines was gone now, lost in the wind and the rush of the tide. Another five minutes and he was whooshing on an upswell, past the first of the barnacle-encrusted pilings, surprised at how fast he was moving. He was nearly past the second stanchion before he had a chance to swing himself into position, make a lunge for a ladder bolted there. His fingers closed around one of the crudded-up rungs and his shoulder wrenched with the force of the water. Maybe he'd under-estimated the speed of the current. Or, more likely, the wind had picked up in the few minutes he'd been in the water. The swells seemed nearly twice the size now.

He pulled himself up a step on the ladder, testing its strength. Twenty five years of salt spray, you couldn't trust anything to hold. He got his toes curled around an algae coated rung and stared across the last hundred yards of open water to where the Donzi was moored. He struggled to calm his ragged breath.

"You sure you're up to this, my man?" Flivey's voice crowding into his brain. Flivey a ghostly imp just a few rungs up the ladder now, giving the groaning metal a shake every time a swell came past. Deal closed his eyes, forcing himself to think. Leon in there, that's one, and with luck, one more of Alcazar's men on duty. And Janice.

That's the way it was, he told himself. She was there. She *had* to be there. Never mind that there were no phone lines from Stiltsville. They'd have a cellular out there. She'd gotten her hands on it, made her call while the guy was pissing off the front porch. Out here on the edge of the service area, that'd account for the crossed connections. That's what had happened.

"And what if she is in there." It was Flivey again. *"Gonna get yourself a team of dolphins, tail walk 'em up the steps, flipper Leon into submission?"*

"Something like that," Deal muttered.

He opened his eyes again, then froze: there was a splash of light atop the pilings over there, somebody standing in a doorway, some-body too big to be anybody but Leon. Leon taking his time, staring out over the water, then glancing back inside, a last look, making sure everything was set . . .

Deal strained forward, away from the pillar, trying to get a better look . . . and the rung in his hand snapped, tossing him into the surging water. He went all the way down to the bottom, one hand plunging through the eel grass into the gelatinous muck, his other crunching onto a knot of spines—a fucking sea urchin, he realized, as the pain shot up his arm. He shook the thing off, fought away from the bottom, clawing his way back to the surface, was gasping for a breath . . .

Then a wave slammed him forward into another of the ruined columns. He felt his eyes roll inward, his face tearing against the razor-edged barnacles. He spun away, carried into the open water, hearing Flivey's laughter over the roar of the waves.

He was on his back in the tub-warm water, sinking slowly, almost sleepily, down, the water pouring up his nostrils, faintly burning, but with all the other pain signals, not so bad. No. Not so bad. Just another minute or so, slide on down the tubes and into the muck, the prehistoric dark, his head reeling, Flivey motioning him forward, *"Come on man, you get to sit around, drink beer, nothing but imports, we got a five-hundred-channel TV dish, get to sit on Jack's lap for the Laker games . . . "*

No, he thought, fighting against the darkness, struggling to home in on the keen signals of pain that were still pulsing. He fought toward the pain, savoring it, fighting for anything that would keep him conscious . . .

. . . thought of Janice, that picture of her in her dumpy socks and sweatband, that sad look in her eyes, *"Oh, Deal,"* and the growing tightness in her belly, about a fingerling's size now, a little bigger, little kicks, turning and twisting in a salty, amniotic sea . . .

. . . and then Deal felt his own legs responding, scissoring beneath him, his arms leaden but doing their best, until finally he was turned over, rising, breaking the surface of the water again, gasping great gulps of air.

He opened his eyes to find himself atop a swell, no more than a hundred feet from the house, the huge engines of the Donzi roaring into life, a few extra revs and then a lower rumble as the props cut in and the boat pulled away from its moorings, Leon racing the growing fury of the storm back toward Miami.

The lights on shore were gone altogether now, obliterated behind a bigger squall that had swept up the bay. A bolt of lightning split the sky ahead of the Donzi, illuminating a square mile of ocean in a breathtaking instant of light, the darkness snapping back with a terrific blast of thunder. In a moment it was gone, leaving only the roar of the big racing boat.

Deal treaded water for a moment, bringing a hand to a ragged tear on his cheek. There was a swelling there, running up to his temple, but it wasn't anything so bad, nothing he wouldn't survive for another fifty feet of swimming, anyway. A little blood for barracuda spoor, maybe, but they'd be out in the deep, riding out the storm, or so he hoped.

He waited for a wave of dizziness to pass, then began to swim, ignoring the pain in his hand—a couple of sea urchin spines broken off there, no big thing. More worrisome was the current, which wanted to pull him away from the house toward the channel the Donzi had taken, but he could fight it. He *would* fight it.

This time, when the swells took him under the shadow of the pilings, he was ready. He flipped himself around, back-paddling, fending off the first piling with his feet, far enough under the water line to miss the really crusty shit, then a graceful twirl in the momentary eddy of a back swell, and suddenly, he was belly-flopped over the floating wooden dock where the Donzi had been only moments before.

He steadied himself for a moment, his cheek resting against the slick wet grain of the wood, his legs dangling in the water. Finally, he heaved himself up. Any barracuda down there, sorry, they'd have to wait. He drew his rubbery legs beneath him, resting a moment, listening to the receding drone of the Donzi. With his teeth he tried worrying at the stub of one of the sea-urchin spines, then gave up. Take care of that another time.

He got gingerly to his feet, braced against the rolling of the waves. There was a step up to a fixed landing, just above the dock, and he felt another wave of dizziness as he accustomed himself to the lack of motion beneath his feet. The pilings blocked the rush of the wind and the platform shielded him from the sheets of rain that had covered the bay. At the end of the landing was a flight of wood stairs that led up to the platform above. He could see a slightly brighter square of sky where the stairs emerged. He grasped the railing, felt the crisp edges on the planks. Everything freshly built.

He was halfway up the stairway when he heard the sound of boat engines. He stopped. It was just a scrap of sound, quickly swallowed again by the storm. He waited, and it came again, unmistakable.

"Sonofabitch!" he hissed, hurrying on up the stairs. By the time he stuck his head out above the deck, the sound was clear. He glanced out to sea. Sure enough, there was the *Miss Daisy*, visible through a break in the curtain of rain, cresting the waves, Homer barreling toward the platform to the goddamn rescue.

Deal scanned the top of the platform hurriedly. It was larger than he had anticipated, with room for another house the size of the one that had been finished off. The owners had probably closed in what they could when the zoning gurus appeared, he thought.

"That's right, Deal," Flivey in his ear, again. *"Maybe you can get hold of the property. Make it a duplex. Just knock, leave your card with the guy inside . . . "*

There was a stack of lumber out there, a sheet of plywood shuddering in the wind, ready to take wing any moment, but nothing big enough to hide behind. Behind him, the house itself, dark windows, the vague outline of a door.

Whoever was in there would hear the *Miss Daisy* any second now . . . *"Where to, Deal? Wanna borrow my wings?"*

Deal glanced back down the stairs, waves crashing over the dock now, lifting it, slamming it back down, like it was about to wash away . . .

He scrambled on out of the stairwell, moved to the house, pressed himself against the weathered paneling, waited, rain pelting his face. He shuddered in the chill, forced himself to concentrate.

No sounds of alarm in there. No sounds of anything in there. He fought a pang of doubt. *Miss Daisy*'s engines were a steady grind mixed with the storm now, rising to a momentary howl when the props heaved out of the water and spun madly in the air.

Another fucking catastrophe express, Deal thought, his stomach sinking. Homer had about as much chance of docking the boat in these conditions as Deal would have of landing the space shuttle. He felt the same sense of helplessness as when he read of planes going down, buses going over the side of cliffs, subway trains roaring full-bore into commuter-clogged stations, conductor puffing contentedly on his crack pipe, *"Yeah, folks, everything going to be all right . . . "*

He turned and began to hammer the door beside him with his fist. Let someone be in there, let it work . . . though he had no idea what *it* was, really . . .

. . . until the door was swung open and a guy in a watch cap stuck his head out like the goddamn geek Deal had been praying for, some kind of knife in his hand.

Deal was on him in an instant, taking him down, rolling, his hands on the knife—*a butter knife???* Which he tore from the guy's grasp, hurling it out into the storm. All the while he prayed he'd been right and there was only this one, this one whose scrawny neck he was going to snap like a stick . . .

He twisted over onto his back, his arm around the guy's throat . . .

But this is too easy, his mind was telling him. The flesh too soft, the neck a thin stalk about to snap. Not enough strength there . . .

. . . *Something not right, Deal!* And finally he registered the voice of the person he held in a death's grip atop him. The gasps, the choked desperate whispers . . . "Stop," she was saying. "Please . . . stop," and Deal did.

Rolled her off of him. Held her by the shoulders. Stared down at her face in the dim light that spilled from the open doorway. "Janice?" He could hardly draw his breath. His heart was racketing. "Dear God," yes, it was. Janice.

 She was still panicked, trying to pull from his grip, choking, kicking against the rain-slick planks of the platform. When he called her name again, she hesitated. He shook her, called her once again.

Finally, she seemed to focus on him. He felt her go limp in his grasp.

"Deal?" Her face pale, drawn. And she seemed so very thin. But it was her. Janice. Alive.

He drew her into his arms. Held her as tightly as he dared. "Oh my God," she was saying. "Oh, Deal."

He glanced through the open doorway into the dimly lit interior of the house. No movement, no sign of life. Still . . .

"Is there anyone else?" He pulled back from her. "Anyone inside there?"

She shook her head. "I thought it was Leon, coming back. I had this knife. I used it to pry the lock on the bedroom . . . "

He shook his head, uncomprehending. "It's okay, Janice. Calm down . . . "

There *were* the sounds of engines, loud again, cutting in and out of the chaos around them. But it wasn't Leon, Deal thought with dismay.

He glanced out into the darkness, trying to shield his face from the rain that swept over them in sheets. Lightning exploded atop them, and then again, peals of thunder nearly instantaneous, over-lapping into a constant roar.

He began to pull Janice toward the doorway when he heard the engines again. The roar was practically on top of them now, a new pitch in *Miss Daisy*'s whine, the big diesels straining as they dropped into reverse.

"Deal!" Janice shouted, pointing into the darkness over his shoulder.

Deal turned in time to see *Miss Daisy:* huge, lit in the glow of continual lightning, hurtling out of the mists of rain like a ship from a nightmare. The boat was being borne high on a mighty wave straight for the platform.

Deal drove Janice ahead of him, through the door, covering her body with his. The crash came, a terrible grinding and a great shud-der in the pilings beneath them. There was an explosion and a ball of flame that blew up into the sky at the far end of the platform and just as suddenly was gone.

Everything was quiet for a moment, as though the explosion had blown the storm back, as though Deal and Janice were being contested over by these enormous forces. Even the sky had light-ened, the first light of dawn struggling up.

Just as abruptly, the wind and the rain swept back upon them, more intense than ever. The sheet of plywood that had been flap-ping atop the scrap pile finally tore loose. It flipped over twice, then gained steam, leveling off like some lethal Frisbee. Deal ducked down, covering Janice as the thing slammed into the door-way and careened off into the water.

He steadied himself, then got to his knees and shoved Janice on inside. He stood and started away. She glanced up at him in panic. "What are you doing?"

"Stay here," he told her, straining to get the door shut against the wind. He forced himself back out into the storm. A boat cush-ion cartwheeled across the deck, and a chunk of stainless railing from *Miss Daisy* clattered onto the roof of the house. Deal shielded himself with his arms and lurched toward the stairwell where smoke billowed up from below.

He descended the stairwell by feel, holding his breath against the smoke, but by the time he reached the landing by the docking area, it was over, the smoke gone, the flames vanished, only sea spray in his face, the slightest hint of diesel fuel in his nostrils and that whipped away quickly by the wind. At the far edge of the structure, a dark scorch mark up the side of one piling, otherwise glowing gray in the gathering light. A barnacle encrusted timber and a few bits of flotsam surged about the pilings. But no sign of the boat, no Barbara, no Homer, not the slightest indication of tragedy. For the ocean, *Miss Daisy* had been a mere hors d'oeuvre. And now it getting ready for the meal. *"What boat, Deal?"* Flivey's voice again. *"No stinking boat around here, man."* Laughter. The familiar dismissive laughter Deal heard when they'd argued over Cristo wanting to drape the islands, when Deal got the news about his arm, when Deal said they could swim the channel to Dirty Dick's . . . *Hell, yes, Deal, you can do any goddamn thing you want to, but who's going to pay the bill?* His own stupidity, Deal thought. He'd cost Flivey his life. And Penfield. And Cal. Now Barbara and Homer. And there wasn't a good goddamn reason for any of those people to be dead, was there?

"Forget about it, Deal. Old news. The fun's just beginning. That house up there. Just wait. It'll be like Dorothy's place, lifting off from Kansas. Better than the space shuttle. You're off to Oz, my good friend. I'll keep a seat warm for you." Ha ha ha . . .

Deal felt woozy, as if he might topple over the railing any second. He stared down at a sodden chunk of something tossed from the boat. It was bumping against the dock, another cushion, a pillow or something coughed up from the busted insides of *Miss Daisy* . . . but wait, not a cushion, not a chunk of debris. Those were arms, a dark mass of hair fanned out in the water. *Barbara. A dead man's float,* he was thinking.

He pushed from the railing, scrambling onto the heaving deck on all fours, clutching at the back of her raincoat that had billowed up a pocket of air above her shoulder blades. Only that had kept her afloat.

He dangled out over the water, cupping her chin up with one hand, struggling for leverage with the other. He scanned the waters nearby, praying for just one more miracle, that somehow Homer too would appear, but there was nothing but the surge of the waves against the pilings.

Deal scrambled backward on his hands and knees, dragging Barbara after him. He got her up onto the landing and checked to see if she were breathing. Nothing. He pressed his fingers to her wrist. A fluttering there, he thought, but it could have been his own pulse pounding. He heard something and glanced up to find that Janice had followed him down the stairs. She clutched the railing like the wind might rip her off into the storm any second.

He bent over Barbara, cupping his hand beneath her neck. He'd had CPR, a class Janice had talked him into taking with her. But that had been years ago. He tried desperately to remember . . . what was first, something about an air passage? He sucked in a breath, put his mouth over hers.

"Her nose," Janice called. "You have to hold her nose."

He nodded, frantic to follow Janice's instructions now, three breaths, then pressing down on her chest, not too hard, you can break ribs, puncture a lung, sure, he remembered that, breathing again, pressing down, the water burbling out, breathing, pumping . . .

He was gasping for breath himself now, lightheaded, wondering how long he'd be good for when Janice pushed him aside, took over his rhythm. Deal watched helplessly, and then, just as it seemed time for him to start in again, he heard a cough, saw Barbara's chest begin to heave.

"She's alive," Janice raised up, shouting. "She's breathing."

Deal nodded, too exhausted to speak. The waves were crashing over the landing now, the sky growing dark, as if they'd been tossed onto some strange planet where daylight lasted a quarter hour and night was always and nothing but storms.

Barbara's breathing was beginning to even out now. Her eyes flickered, then closed again. He gave one last forlorn glance across the water, still hoping to see Homer clutching to some chunk of wood, some tree limb, somehow riding the current their way, but of course, there was nothing.

"Let's get her upstairs," he said to Janice, finally. And together they staggered up.

"I found some tea." It was Janice coming toward him, a cup cradled in her hands, coming back toward the couch where they had put

Barbara. Janice glanced back at the stove, where a pot of water still simmered, shuddering as if she were recalling a nightmare.

Deal was on his knees beside Barbara, dabbing gently at her wet face and hair with a towel. She was still unconscious, with a bruise on her cheek, a cut high on her forehead where another lump was rising. Janice put the cup on the coffee table beside him, knelt down. "Who is she, Deal?"

He heard a ripping sound on the roof above them. The shingles? The roofing felt? How long till the whole thing lifted off, tossed them into Flivey land?

Deal gave her a look. "Just someone who wanted to help."

Barbara moaned, mumbling something in her sleep. Deal touched her arm gingerly and she winced, groaning again. He glanced at Janice. "Broken, I think. She needs a doctor."

Janice nodded, then looked away.

Outside, the storm was still raging. Something heavy thudded against the siding, bounced again, then was gone. One of the planks from the lumber pile? Or just the sky falling?

Deal studied Janice in profile. There was a kerosene lantern hanging above a dinette table and the soft light softened her features. How precious she was, he thought.

Meanwhile, the storm seemed to relent. The wind died away, and the rain stopped abruptly, as if a switch had been thrown. Except for the surging of the waves beneath them, it was oddly quiet. Janice turned back to meet his gaze. She reached out and gently touched his cheek.

"What's going on, Deal?" She was fighting to keep her voice level. "Why are these things happening?"

Good questions, Deal thought. He wished he had good answers. He blotted at Barbara's wet hair mechanically with the towel.

"Where's the phone you called me with?" he asked.

She shook her head. "It was an old ship-to-shore radio. It took me forever to figure it out . . . " she trailed off. "But he smashed it." She stood and walked to the counter, began fixing herself a cup of tea. She glanced at him nervously.

Deal sighed. He wanted to wrap Janice in his arms, take her home, forget anything ever happened.

"It's all about the land, Janice." She shook her head, puzzled. "The land the fourplex sits on," he continued. "It has to be. Alcazar wanted it, and Penfield was trying to help him get it."

She shook her head in disbelief. "That's not possible."

"Believe me, Janice, it's possible. It has something to do with the baseball effort. There are millions at stake there. I'm just not sure how my little fourplex fits in."

He could hear the pinging of the steaming pan on the stove, hear the shallow rasp of Barbara's breathing from the couch. "How long before he comes back, Deal? What are we going to do?"

He heard the fear in her voice and felt a stab of guilt. He couldn't shake the feeling that he was responsible for this, for the whole crazy mess. Maybe if he'd sold the goddamn building . . . but he broke off.

He didn't know anything for sure. He would find out, of course, once he got them somewhere safe. But the worst thing he didn't know was how he was going to get them off of this goddamn platform before Leon showed up again. That was what he had to worry about. And keeping Janice calm while he figured it out.

Sure. Be brave and calm and hope the sky doesn't fall. He stood. He would go to his wife and reassure her. That was something he *could* accomplish.

And then, the door shattered open, flying inward on its hinges, and what had been bad became even worse.

36 "Well, lookee here," Leon Straight said, as the door rocketed off the inside wall.

The vibration sent a barometer framed in a tiny ship's wheel crashing to the floor. Its glass face flew off and rolled across the kitchen tile to Janice's feet.

"Havin' a party and nobody invite Leon." He stood in the open doorway, framed by an improbable gray light. He was holding something in his hand, something pointed at Deal.

The waves were still thunderous against the pilings beneath them, the whole structure groaning with the ocean's force. One monster wave, that's all it would take, Deal thought. The picture of the ruined pilings he'd swum past was clear in his mind. But the rain had stopped, the clouds thinned to reveal an eerily bright sky above.

Leon had to cock his broad shoulders to move through the doorway. He kicked the door shut behind him, but a hinge had given. The door banged off the frame and shuddered open again.

It was some kind of high-tech pistol in his hand, gray metal—maybe even plastic. It had strange, squared-off lines, something that must have been its magazine dangling in front of the trigger guard. A designer pistol, Deal thought. Jazz up death, bring it into the 1990s.

Deal stared at the muzzle, remembering the last time it had happened, out there on the Dolphin Expressway, the pinwheeling Hog, the tinny voices of the Haitian roofers, the big Yahweh staring down at him: "There's a white man, his number's come up." Deal had been scared that day, thinking it was just some macho crazy he'd pissed off. He felt some of the same fear now, but it was tempered with his rage.

"Don't get any ideas," Leon said, waving the pistol. Droplets of water glistened on his cheeks, dripped from his chin.

"This here's gas powered, computer *con*-trolled. Guy up in Hialeah makes 'em, used to work for the airlines." He wiped his face on his sleeve. "Waterproof, x-ray proof, fit in your briefcase and leave room for your laptop word processor. Also blow you a dozen new assholes 'fore you take a step." Leon grinned. "I hate to use a gun, though."

"What did you use on Cal, Leon?"

Leon laughed. "You beat his head in with your very own Volkswagen tire iron, white folks. Went crazy and did it."

As he spoke, his eyes swept the room, took in the unconscious Barbara, widened with an unspoken question for Janice.

Janice looked away. She was pale, holding on to the kitchen counter with one hand, the front of her sweatshirt clutched in the other.

"Are you okay?" Deal asked her. She managed a nod.

"She's fine. I been taking real good care of her." Leon swept his gaze about the room. "But *you* . . . " He broke off, glancing down at his bad knee. "Man try to do right by you, you go and fuck things up. Mmmmm-hmmmm . . . "

Leon turned to Janice, waving at Deal with his weapon. "This here is a dangerous killer. Do in his onliest friend, then bludgeon Mr. Penfield with his own autograph baseball bat. Good thing I came back."

Janice shook her head. "My husband didn't kill anyone. What are you doing here, Leon? You have what you came for."

He made a show of surprise. "Why sweet cheeks, I'm racing the storm on home. Then I see this explosion, I think, somebody having a weenie roast out at the ranch. I might as well go on back and warm up by the fire, try this boat shit later on."

He turned back to Deal. "This is sure a piece of luck. Everybody trying to find you. The po-lice. Mr. Alcazar. Even old Leon, just dying to get you and me together."

"Why do we want to get together, Leon?"

Leon chuckled. "Cause Leon outfoxed the fox, that's why. I'm sitting in the hen house, holding what Alcazar wants. Mmmm-hmmm."

Deal glanced at Janice's ashen face. He sensed the same madness in Leon's voice. Time. They needed time.

"Alcazar wants my land, right, Leon? That's what this is all about."

Leon laughed. "Used to be your land. Your old lady sold it to *me.*"

"He made me sign some papers, Deal." She winced, as if something were hurting her inside. "He threatened to hurt the baby . . . "

"It's all right, Janice. It doesn't matter." Deal stared at Leon, rage welling up in him. But he had to be calm. Had to think. Just keep him talking. As long as we're alive, there's a chance.

"It's baseball, isn't it, Leon? That's what it's all about."

Leon gave him a wary look.

"But where does Alcazar come in? If anyone found out he had money in the team, the commissioner would yank the franchise out of here in a second."

"Sure they would, white folks." Leon shook his head as if Deal were feebleminded. "But Alcazar don't care about baseball. He cares about *money*. He wants to sell all this land he bought up so they can build their stadium in the downtown. He owns all of that piece of shit land they need down there." Leon laughed. "Except your piece of shit.

"You had the last piece of property standing between him and a twenty-million-dollar deal, Mr. *Deal.*" Leon tapped something in his coat pocket. "Which belongs to me, now," he shrugged.

Deal stared, the last pieces coming together. So that's where Penfield came in, setting up all the transactions, keeping Alcazar's name out of it, a big pot of money for them both when the American pastime came to town.

"Let me guess, Leon. In the middle of all this, Alcazar got a bright idea, how he could get me out of the way and keep everything for himself."

"More or less," Leon shrugged. "First, you show up on old Cal's doorstep, scare him to death about how you flip out and destroy all Mr. Alcazar's automobiles, then when Cal try to reason with you—

'turn yourself in, son'—you go and kill him. Next thing, you go and do your beloved attorney Penfield cause he dropped your case."

Deal nodded. "And I'll bet any minute now, I'm going to commit suicide, tie everything up neat as a Shakespeare play."

Leon snorted. "Play for who?"

Deal turned to Janice, who stared back at him grimly. It had taken a while, but he could excuse himself for being slow, under the circumstances. It wasn't exactly like reading building plans. "Leon's just trying to cut himself in."

She shook her head, uncertain.

"They'd have killed me already, but Alcazar got a better idea. He decided to get Penfield out of the way so he wouldn't have to share any of the profits on the land deal. He might have been satisfied with half the pot if I'd gone ahead and sold out earlier.

"But once I flipped out, kamikazied his dealership, I gave him the chance. They killed Cal, who might have corroborated my story, then they killed Penfield and made it look like I did it all." Deal kept his eyes on Janice. "How am I doing, Leon?"

"Not bad, white folks."

"It didn't matter who found me first. If it had been the cops, they'd have had their murderer, a psycho deranged by grief, his fingerprints all over everything. Maybe some of Alcazar's pals in the department would see that I hang myself in a cell. If it's Leon, he'd make it look like I killed myself, too. Either way, everything's taken care of. With me out of the way, you *could* sell the company—and everything goes with it."

Janice turned to Leon in disbelief. Leon shrugged. "Just as well I come on back here, sweet cheeks. Way it is these days, your old man might have got himself a lawyer, ended up in prison." The big man shook his head sorrowfully. "I *been* in prison. Scrawny guy like him, he'd end up with no teeth and an asshole you could roll a piano through."

Janice turned away, her face ashen. Leon continued. "Hey, don't feel bad. Just like your old man says, somebody or another would have taken him out. Only thing is, I get my cut this way." He smiled. "I been *learning* the real estate business."

"What happens now, Leon?" Deal had his eyes on the pistol, wondering if he might make a leap for it. They were about out of things to talk about.

Leon glanced at him. "Why, we going to conclude our dealings, Mr. Deal." He grinned and tapped the phone at his belt. "Mr. Alcazar on his way to his house from the airport by helio-copter, this very moment. Wants to meet me, he's so anxious to see what I got to sell him. Now that I got you to show him, man can come right out here, see it's true he's got no choice but to negotiate with me."

Barbara moaned softly and Deal glanced down at her, then back at Leon. "This woman needs a doctor, Leon."

Leon stared down at her for a moment, thinking about it. "No," he said finally. "She don't."

Leon held the pistol on Deal, his gaze unwavering, and unsnapped the pouch at his side. He withdrew a tiny black phone with a stubby antenna. He took it and punched a couple of buttons.

"You blow up your own boat, white folks?" Leon had the phone tucked under his chin, waiting for his connection. "I saw part of it floatin' around out there." He shook his head. "You can't drive worth a shit."

Deal edged forward but Leon raised the pistol toward his chest. "Careful, now."

Deal stopped. Leon heard something in the phone and pulled it away from his ear with a sigh. "Some bitch givin' me the time and the temperature, you believe that?"

He dialed again, jammed the phone back under his chin. Barbara moaned once more, stirring slightly on the couch.

"Yo, Alejandro," Leon was saying into the phone. "You on the way or no?"

Deal felt a growing dread.

Leon was still talking into the phone. "Yeah, it's okay. Tell Alcazar we're at the Stiltsville place. Her old man showed up. That's right. He's right in front of me." He paused, his eyes going from Janice to Deal, back again. "Sure," he said finally, "everything's just fine."

Deal was shaking his head, his stare vacant. Lost. Everything lost.

A distant hum of engines cut the silence of the room. Leon cocked his head at the sky.

"Yeah, man going to give us a ride home," Leon said to Janice. Her eyes, filled with tears now, had not left Deal's.

"*Some* of us getting a ride," Leon was saying. He tossed the phone onto the couch at Barbara's feet and turned to level the pistol at Janice. "Most of us won't be needing no ride . . . "

"That's the last part of it, Janice," Deal said. "You're already dead, I'm about to be. You were swept out to sea. I killed myself in grief."

Leon glanced at him, chuckling, then flicked something on the stock of the pistol. Deal started forward.

Leon turned to meet Deal's charge, a weary expression on his face, *more hero shit to deal with*. He raised the pistol, was about to fire, when Janice reached behind her, flung the pot of boiling tea into his face.

Leon screamed, clawing at his eyes. Steam curled out between his fingers.

Deal hit the big man hard, driving him back against the door frame. Leon was blindly trying to level the pistol, but Deal grabbed his arm, slamming his wrist against one of the sidelights. The glass panel exploded in a shower of fragments.

"Gonna fuck you up, white folks," Leon wheezed. "Gonna fuck you up bad." A strip of skin had bubbled up from his cheek. As Deal watched, it slid away, leaving a bright pink scar from the corner of his mouth to his ear, a permanent, terrible grin.

Deal gripped Leon's arm, levering himself against the big man's bulk. All those years pounding nails, lugging concrete blocks, unloading eighty-pound bags of Sakrete by the dozen. Priding himself that there wasn't one man in ten who kept himself as well. And what did it matter, because now he was up against the one guy in a hundred, or a thousand, more like it.

Any second now, he was going to lose his grip, go over backward . . . and then he felt a sudden lurch.

Leon was staggering forward, in from the doorway, his eyes wide, the skin about them blistered and still steaming, his gaze unfocused. And Janice was screaming. And screaming.

Leon pitched on forward, as if the floor were erupting beneath his feet. "Uhhhha . . . " the big man mumbled, a pink froth at his lips. He tottered sideways, fighting to keep his balance. There was a brief *brrrrrppp* as his finger tightened on the pistol waving in his hand. Janice sagged into one of the dinette chairs, both hands wrapped tightly about her stomach.

Deal gaped at the scene before him. Something had burst from Leon's chest, something covered red and dripping, something with the long curved jaw of a gar or an eel, a creature from a horror film that had ripped out with a life of its own.

"Whuuuuaaa . . . " Leon groaned again, taking little mincing steps now, his eyes glazing. There was a terrible sucking sound coming from inside his chest.

Deal ducked as the big man swung wildly at him. Leon careened on past, against the far wall of the living room. The shaft of *Miss Daisy*'s fishing gaff trailed behind him, one end buried in his back, centered in a widening stain of blood.

And clinging to the gaff was Homer, drawn and exhausted, seawater still dripping from his sodden life vest, his face battered and bleeding. He held desperately on to the bucking end of the spear as if he were riding some monster hobby horse.

"His gun," Homer croaked. "Get his fucking gun." He clung to the shaft of the spear, clawing at his belt where he'd stuck the flare pistol.

Leon swung wildly behind him, clubbing Homer's face with the strange pistol. Homer tumbled loose from the spear and crashed into the legs of the dinette. The kerosene lantern went over with a sound of breaking glass.

Leon wavered in the middle of the living room floor, his eyes struggling to focus on this steel flower that had sprung up from his chest. He touched the dripping metal carefully, then held his fingertips in front of his face, studying his own blood with an infant's fascination.

Deal scrambled on his hands and knees toward the flare pistol, waiting for the searing pain that would rip into him any moment, bullets from a goddamn gun that didn't even *sound* like a gun. Or maybe Leon would jerk the spear out of himself like John Wayne would shrug off a redskin's arrow, impale Deal on it. Or . . .

. . . he got his hands on the flare pistol, made sure there was one of the giant shells in the chamber and rolled over onto his back, the weapon upraised. But Leon had disappeared. The hum of engines outside had become a roar. Helicopter blades popping, Deal realized. Practically on top of them, now.

Deal made it to the doorway to see the helicopter setting down on the platform near what was left of the lumber pile, Leon tacking across the deck toward it like something from a nightmare. The wash from the props was even worse than the winds of the storm. Loose shingles ripped from the roof and debris from the scrap pile clattered against the siding.

Deal turned away as a blast of sand stung him. When he looked again, Alejandro had jumped down from the helicopter. He stood by the scrap pile, trying to brace himself against the wash of the helicopter blades. He had a pistol in his hand, but stared uncertainly as Leon staggered toward him. Alcazar clung to the doorway of the helicopter, shouting, gesturing frantically in Deal's direction.

Alejandro glanced at his boss, his long hair flaring in the wash of the props. The hand with the gun wavered, swung from Leon, to Deal . . .

. . . the same hand, and pistol, and suit coat . . .

. . . *the freeway shooter, the man in the Supra.* Deal had never seen the man's face, couldn't see it well even now, but he knew they had come full circle.

"You must be more careful . . . You don't know who's out here. You could die."

Alejandro turned back, ready for business now, ready for Deal, ready to finish the job at last, no cops to drive up to the rescue . . .

Alejandro fired, but it was wasted, the bullet ripping into an empty door frame. Deal had dropped to his stomach, his elbows banging the sodden deck. He propped himself up, struggling to bring the flare pistol in line. His thumbs slipped off the rain-slicked hammer, fumbled, then caught, finally cocking it.

Alejandro fired again. Deal felt a stunning blow at his temple, the sharp sting of splintered wood at his face, the trickle of something wet in his eyes.

He squeezed the trigger of the flare pistol, praying, praying, praying . . . then the shell exploded, ripping a fiery trail toward Alejandro. There was a dull thud, then a scream, and Alejandro went over backward, clawing at the flare that had burst in his stomach.

He spun in frantic circles on the wet decking, spewing phosphorous smoke and bright flame like some human pinwheel rocket, his cries rising above the growing whine of the helicopter. Alcazar saw it all from the doorway of the 'copter, his face gone ashen. He turned, clinging to the door frame, and shouted at the pilot, who was working wildly at the controls.

Alejandro arched his back in one last spasm of pain, then went over the side of the platform as Deal pulled himself up. His legs felt like lead, his vision alternately clear, then blurry.

The helicopter's engines raised another notch, and the machine lifted off the deck, slowly at first, a few inches, a foot, then two, then six . . . *so long, Alcazar,* Deal thought, *so long . . .*

. . . and then Leon crossed the plane of Deal's vision, launching himself into one last, gargantuan leap, the desperate, career making lunge for a quarterback he never got to make on the football field. But this one was good. Better than good. Not just a sack. Way beyond that. Every defensive lineman's dream. A cataclysm.

Leon's fingers clawed, clawed, and closed over one of the helicopter's skid rails. The craft lurched and dipped to its right, and Alcazar came out of the doorway backward, his arms and legs windmilling as he slammed onto the platform.

Leon clung to the listing helicopter's rail with one hand, pulling himself inexorably over the lip of the cabin with the other. The pilot slid across the seats and kicked wildly at him, one hand still on the controls. The engines were screaming, the machine struggling skyward.

Alcazar lay stunned for a moment on the deck below, then rolled onto his hands and knees, groggy. He looked up, his head lolling, as Deal started toward him.

"You damn near pulled it off," Deal said, praying his legs would hold him. "Almost paved those streets with gold."

Alcazar edged away, but his silk pants snagged on a splinter of planking that jutted from the deck.

"I'm not going to use a hatchet, Alcazar. I'm going to do it with my hands." Deal felt his head reeling. It was like one of those awful dreams where you know what you have to do, but the car has no wheels, the gun you've got has a sagging barrel that curves its way back at you. But he would reach Alcazar if he had to pull himself across the platform with his teeth. With his eyelids.

For it had all come to this. All the effort he'd put forward, just a little guy trying to get along, look what it had got him. And yet, he wasn't going to give up now. There wasn't an atom inside of him that was going to give up now.

Alcazar was clawing at the fabric of his snagged trousers in a panic. But then he stopped. And smiled back up at Deal.

Deal wavered, watching this dream go wrong once again. Watched Alcazar's hand as it reached out for Leon's bizarre pistol, which had fallen to the platform a foot away. Deal staggered back toward the doorway, knowing it was over.

Alcazar tugged at his pant leg. Then stood, inspecting the strange mechanism of the weapon. In a moment, he would turn and level it at Deal and end this forever.

Deal was groggy, his head pounding, and the blood was leaking into his eyes. He felt the weight of the flare gun heavy in his hand. A little heavier than regulation. Not round. No stitching. Dark gray and all out of shape.

Like maybe it was a baseball that had rolled under a big, rotting log and lay there for years and years and years. Got so soggy and rotten and pressed out of shape it was good for only one thing. One last toss. One last fastball, and please, let it be over the plate.

Deal stepped forward and threw, gave it everything he had. Felt something tear inside his arm. Ignored the ripping pain there. Had a flash of some impossible baseball dream like the times he was a kid and thought, let me do something special, let me just once do what nobody else could do . . .

He watched Alcazar throw up his hands to shield himself. Watched the flare gun crack against Alcazar's upraised arm. Watched Alcazar's finger tighten upon the trigger in reflex, and the gun begin to fire.

There was a shrieking from the helicopter's engines, which wavered just above the roofline of the house, the pilot slumping over his controls, the bubbled windshield blown to fragments by Alcazar's wild firing. And then, the roaring machine, with Leon still clinging to the skid, threw itself down on them.

Deal dove back inside the shelter of the house, slamming into Homer, who had managed to pull himself up in the doorway. As they untangled themselves, the big rotor blade dug into the platform with a scream and a shower of sparks, chewing through planking and concrete until it hit something it could never cut.

A long section of tempered blade glanced upward, shearing from its mounts. Alcazar was running desperately for the stairwell when the hurtling chunk of helicopter blade sliced into him, at just about the level of his hand-stitched alligator belt. There was an agonized rending of metal as momentum carried the rest of the craft over the side and into the water. And then, for the first time in what seemed like days, there was silence.

"I'd have called that pitch of yours high," Homer said as Deal dragged himself to the doorway. " 'Course what counts is, the asshole went for it."

Deal stared out across the platform. No Alejandro, no Leon, no helicopter. Only a pair of disembodied legs clad in expensive, blood-soaked silk trousers, tottering by the stairwell. The legs wavered impossibly in midstride, something out of a sick cartoon, or a nightmare, and then the awful vision toppled down the steps, out of sight.

Deal felt his stomach lurch. A smell of kerosene, of burning wood, had crept into his nostrils and an alarm was ringing somewhere, somewhere down a distant corridor. He saw it again, in memory, Leon spraying gunshots wildly about the room, the lantern going over with a crash . . .

Deal struggled to his feet, and stood wavering. Yes, there it was, the pine paneling of the kitchen a mass of flames already, smoke boiling off the ceiling and massing toward him. Homer was dragging himself from the tangle of chairs where he had fallen.

"Barbara!" he shouted at Homer, pointing, and the little man groped his way toward the unconscious form on the couch.

Deal turned, still groggy, the smoke choking him. He blinked away blood and sweat and smoke, searching for Janice, the smoke thick now, impenetrable. He couldn't see her. But she was here. She had to be here. Then the smoke whisked away in a draft of pure heat and he stopped.

She was still in the dinette chair. Her head was flung back, her lips parted slightly. A bright red stitching ran across her body where Leon's shots had hit her, staining her sweatshirt from navel to neck.

There was a soft popping noise as the plastic tabletop bubbled, then burst into flames.

He staggered to the chair, took her by the shoulders. Her eyes fluttered open, then closed again. "Deal," she whispered, and he thought she was trying to smile. "Don't you ever give up?"

He pulled her to him. "Never," he said.

"So sorry," he heard her say.

He found himself on the floor then, beneath the flames, dragging them both toward the door. The decking seemed to be buckling under him. He felt himself going down into a vast darkness.

"So sorry," she repeated. Her breath was shallow at his ear. He was wet with her blood.

He found the door frame with his hand. Felt the heat in the wood. Searing him if it were flame itself.

"Oh, Deal," she said.

"It's all right," he told her. "It's all right."

He was so very, very tired. But he would take them out of this. He felt her sigh and go quiet against him. So unfair. He had gotten them into this. And he would get them out.

He made one last surge toward the cool air outside. Then everything was black.

37 Deal heard the helicopter blades descending on him and came up from the darkness, his arms flailing.

Someone pushed him back down. "It's all right, son." A familiar voice. "Rest easy."

Deal struggled. Rain was pelting his face again. The sky dark, darker than ever. Blinding sheets of lightning. Thunder blasting. The storm on them again. And Driscoll's moonlike face hovering over him, holding him quiet on the soggy deck.

Flames still danced at the far side of the platform. The house still burning.

"Janice," he called, fighting to sit up.

"You got her out," Driscoll said, soothing him. "You did. You and the midget."

Homer's face had appeared over Driscoll's shoulder, nodding, peering anxiously down at Deal. "She's on a chopper, Deal. Headed for the hospital."

Deal fell back, his head reeling. "A dwarf," Deal said, the faces beginning to swim above him. "He's a dwarf."

He sagged back on the deck. Deal wanted to believe it was over. That Janice was safe. That everyone was safe, so that he could rest. He wanted so badly to rest.

. . . his eyes rolled back and drifted in the darkness, fighting to see . . .

... and then he saw it, near the hatchway that led down the steps to the water. Something huge and lumbering, rising up there. A big man. The very biggest he'd ever seen. Gouts of sea water and blood pouring from his wounds, the spear gripped in one hand, something writhing in the other.

Something terrible. Deal couldn't believe what he was seeing. He drove himself backward, toward the edge of the platform as Leon advanced. It wasn't a hand at all, but some terrible eellike creature that had grown there, taking the place of Leon's hand. Its jaws snapped hundreds of yellow teeth as it advanced on him, soon, soon, soon . . .

... and then Deal sat up in the hospital bed, his heart thundering, his gown soaked, the nightmare still replaying itself in his head.

He glanced about the dimly lit room. An IV frame and some tubing in his way, but someone asleep in a chair, someone who stirred and murmured "Deal?"

He was still shaking as he sank back into the pillows. He was lightheaded, pinwheels exploding behind his eyes. Already fading out. But that dream. He didn't want that dream again. He tried to force his eyes open, but it was so very hard. He thought he saw Barbara leaning over him, one arm in a cast, one hand moving toward him.

"They're going to make it." Barbara's voice, coming from somewhere far away. "They're going to make it."

He thought he felt her hand on his forehead. He felt a twinge of something like peace and went to sleep again.

Epilogue: Joe Robbie Stadium, The Following Spring

Deal had arrived at the park early, partly to avoid the traffic, mostly because everything took longer these days, all the things he had to carry. But he wasn't complaining. And besides, it reminded him. He'd always been the first one at practice, usually one of the last to leave. It was the best time. He'd have the place to himself, the smell of the fresh-cut grass, the clay still wet and sticking to his spikes as he jogged, went through his stretching routines, enjoying the silence and the sense that all the field were his.

Not like that today, of course. At least a thousand fans had beaten him to JRS, even at this hour. They were basking in the late spring sunshine, watching the teams running through their practice routines on the field below. It was only an exhibition game, a pre-view of the real thing that was still months away, the Orioles and the Indians at that, but it was baseball. Baseball at last.

The field that had never been anything but a football grid before this glittered in the sun, the base paths fresh, the chalklines stretched out toward infinity, and Deal thought he could make out the smell of grass clippings as he found the right seats well down the first base line. This was how Saturdays were meant to be, he mused, as he set-tled in, arranging everything, amazed at his own ease, then lulled by the crack of batters in the practice cage. Ground balls chewing through the red clay of the infield. Liners drilled to left, to center, to right. Lazy flies that soared toward the fences, and in more than a few cases, into the stands where ushers raced children for the balls. He checked his watch. In ten minutes, the timer he'd installed back at the fourplex should kick on, and his yard work for the day would be done.

He had added flower boxes beneath the windows on the front of the fourplex, had even run a drip watering system up to a set on the second story. If everything worked out, that little switch would flip, and all those geraniums would get watered at once. Plenty of red geraniums against the gray-and-white facade. He'd always liked the medicine-like smell of geraniums. In the fall, when it got cool again, he'd lay in some marigolds along the walkway. Another astringent smell he liked.

A player in the batting cage swung late and launched a foul ball that arced into the stands, over Deal's head. He stood up, shielding the seat beside him, watched the ball crack down safely, a couple rows above them. He didn't have the slightest urge to go after the ball. It was fine the way it was. Sitting. Watching. Trying not to think.

He'd grabbed his mail on the way out of the fourplex, stuffed it in his back pocket, along with the sports pages, and now he leaned forward and pulled it out:

A Val-Pak of coupons for the *farmacia*, the *ferreteria*, and the *supermercado* up the street from his place. Deal's Spanish had been getting better and better.

Also a property tax notice from the county assessor, stamped in red: "IMPORTANT, THIS IS NOT A BILL."

And a little notecard with a return address in Boca Raton, his address in a feminine hand. That one he opened.

She was doing fine. A nice apartment, not much of a view, doing hostess work at a seafood place on the Intracoastal. Homer had called her. He was a lot boy at a place not so far away, in Jupiter. Had Deal heard? The people were laid-back, the food was good, life was good. She hoped his was, too. Thanks again, Barbara.

He put the note back in its envelope, stuck it away in a pocket of his jeans.

"Why didn't you go after that?"

Deal turned to see Driscoll making his way slowly down a set of steps behind him, balancing a big box of food and drinks in his meaty hands. Every step sent another splash of beer onto the steps at his feet.

Deal got up to help him, but Driscoll insisted on doing it himself, sloshing beer onto his pant leg as he settled down in the aisle seat. "I saw that ball go right over your head," Driscoll said. "I was hoping I'd see some of the old Deal in action."

Deal shrugged, smiling. "It's a nice day," he said. "Thanks for the tickets."

Driscoll shrugged, glancing nervously at the bundle in the seat beside him. "They're freebies." He took the wrapping off a hot dog and offered it to Deal, who shook his head. Driscoll took half of it with a bite, studied Deal while he chewed.

"I wasn't sure if you'd come," he said, finally. "I stopped by your place, see if you wanted a ride."

"Wouldn't have missed it," Deal said.

"Me neither," Driscoll nodded. He turned back to the field, still chewing. "Guess what they got me for retirement."

"Retirement?" Deal glanced at him. "I didn't know you were that old."

"Next month," Driscoll said. "Thirty years and it seems like sixty. And the last dozen or so . . . " he broke off, shaking his head. "I'm kind of happy to go out with a case didn't have to go to trial, though." He gave Deal a look.

Deal nodded. Neither one of them spoke for a while. Finally, Driscoll broke the silence. "You going to guess, or not, what they got me."

Deal turned to him, thought for a moment. "Season tickets. For the Tropics."

Driscoll laughed. "You should have been the detective," he said.

Deal smiled.

" 'Course they won't be called the Tropics since Mr. Ter-*rell* doesn't like the sound of it," Driscoll said.

"And you'll have to drive all the way up here to see the games," Deal said.

Driscoll gave him a look. "That's better than what would have happened, if it hadn't been for you. If Penfield and Alcazar had their way." Driscoll leaned forward, concerned. "That's something good happened from all this, son."

Deal glanced at the seat beside him. "Something more important than that," he said.

His gaze drifted off into the distance. It seemed so long ago, most days. And still, other days, he'd wake up and wonder where the hell he was.

"You doing okay, Deal?"

Deal came back, gave Driscoll a smile. "Doing fine," he said. "I spent a while convincing myself it wasn't my fault, everything that happened . . . " he trailed off.

"You really believe that?" Driscoll said. "Total assholes kidnap your old lady, put the squeeze on you that way . . . "

Deal stared at him. "I try not to work as hard these days," Deal said. "Let's just leave it at that."

There was a brief wail from the seat beside him and Deal turned to see that his daughter had awakened at last. She blinked up at him, squinting her tiny eyes against the light, then launched into a full-throated screech.

Driscoll watched Deal gather her up in his arms, maneuver a bottle into her grasping mouth. In moments, she had settled down to serious lunch.

"I gotta hand it to you," Driscoll said, shaking his head. "Raise a kid at your age, you're a better man than me."

Deal laughed then, a good strong laugh. He'd been having more and more of those lately.

He glanced out over the playing field, savoring the precious weight in his arms.

"I get plenty of help, Driscoll."

He nodded toward the field below. At the lovely woman who was making her way up the steep steps toward them. Janice was still moving with a limp, but as she'd told the doctors, she would beat that too. She was smiling, holding a baseball aloft, was shaking it in triumph.

"I don't even know the kid's name who signed it," she called. Driscoll stood up as she approached, sloshing more beer down the front of himself. She gave the detective a peck on the cheek, then leaned in to give Deal a bigger kiss.

"It was one of the Indians. I told him it was for the first lady Major Leaguer," she said, her eyes gleaming. "How does that sound?"

"Play ball," someone shouted, down on the field.

"That sounds fine, Janice," he said, embracing her with one arm, holding their daughter between them with the other. These days, everything sounded fine.